The Ste

'Now then, comrades, Party Secretary Comrade Stalin has ordered that the first priority of our operation is to cut the Germans off from those supplies. It is therefore imperative, comrades, that we know *now* if it is only the Rumanians who bar the way for us on our drive to Kalach, or if there is something more.' He looked from one face to the other. 'It will be the task of the 333rd Punishment Battalion to find that out.'

Chuikov rose to his feet and the three gulag rats did the same.

'You will be supplied with German uniforms,' Chuikov said. 'You will cross the Don tomorrow night. It has all been arranged.'

Numbly, the three rats allowed themselves to be led outside by the elegant aide. It was only when he'd left them that Vulf cried, 'But in the name of all that's holy, do you know what the Germans will do if they catch us in their uniforms?'

'Yes,' said Katukov in a voice drained of emotion. 'They'll shoot us.'

Also in Arrow by K. N. Kostov

THE GULAG RATS
BAPTISM OF BLOOD
BLOOD ON THE BALTIC

THE STEPPE WOLVES

K. N. Kostov

Arrow Books

Arrow Books Limited
3 Fitzroy Square, London W1P 6JD

An imprint of the Hutchinson Publishing Group

London Melbourne Sydney Auckland
Wellington Johannesburg and agencies
throughout the world

First published 1981

Set in Linoterm Times
by Book Economy Services, Cuckfield, Sussex

Made and printed in Great Britain
by The Anchor Press Ltd
Tiptree, Essex

ISBN 0 09 926700 4

Of all man's miseries, the bitterest is this: to know so much and to have control over nothing.

Herodotus

A Prelude

The sniper crouched in the snow-filled shell-crater and watched the scene, his telescopic rifle at the ready. Behind the crater, Stalingrad burned.

There was something very strange about the bigger 'stick', as the sniper always called the victims: sticks to be cracked – by one steel slug through the brain. He was obviously badly hurt, the sniper could see that well enough. Both he and another stick had survived the crash, injured either by the flak shell which had struck their little Fiesler Storch on the other side of the River Volga or by the impact of the plane smashing into the tight grove of snow-heavy firs. But their terribly slow movements as they staggered about the smoking wreckage of the high-winged courier plane indicated that they were in a bad way.

The sniper chuckled noiselessly. Hardly worth wasting a couple of slugs on the fascist pigs! Still, a sniper had to record ten 'kills' per day if he wanted to be entitled to the 'special hazardous duty' ration and, above all, the precious 100 grammes of vodka, the only thing which made life bearable in the hell of Stalingrad.

The Fritz with the leather helmet, obviously the pilot, began laborously to unwind a long roll of toilet paper, one end dipped in the wrecked plane's petrol tank. He carried his burden as if it were tremendously heavy, while the bigger of the two watched, one hand on the pistol at his side, the other trying, in vain, to staunch the bright scarlet blood which jetted from a gash in his neck. For a few moments, the sniper's thin face under the heavy fur cap wrinkled in a frown. What was the Fritz up to?

The pilot staggered to a stop and began to fumble with a cigarette lighter with cracked frozen fingers. Of course. He was trying to set fire to his plane!

The sniper stared intently through the circle of calibrated glass so that the cross-wires bisected the pilot's head. It would be as easy as falling off a log. The stationary pilot made a perfect target. '*Yer bohi*,'* the sniper whispered, uttering the motto of all the Red Army's snipers at the moment of the kill, for then, the sniper himself was God.

The paper ignited. The pilot dropped it carefully into the snow and stood there, swaying slightly, as the purple flame ran swiftly along the roll of paper towards the open petrol tank.

The sniper closed one eye. Grip hard on the stock, tuck butt firmly into shoulder, tight and firm. *First pressure*. . . . The pilot was outlined a clear, stark black in the circle of gleaming glass. . . . *Second pressure*. . . . Breathing slow and relaxed, the sniper whispered, 'Now, fascist – the words died abruptly on the sniper's lips.

One hundred metres away, the bigger of the two sticks had pulled out his pistol. Calmly, very deliberately, he placed the muzzle at the base of the unsuspecting pilot's skull. In the same moment that the plane exploded in a great rending crash, instantly engulfed in greedy yellow flames, he pulled his trigger.

The back of the pilot's head disintegrated. Thick flurries of blood sprayed the killer, covering the front of his elegant staff-officer's uniform. Instinctively the sniper, shocked by this strange, cold-blooded assassination, squeezed the trigger. The butt kicked back hard. Suddenly the winter air stank of burnt cordite. To the front, the officer, struck in the back, clawed the air as if he were trying to escape by climbing the rungs of an

* Revenge is in the hands of God

invisible ladder. But that wasn't to be. Abruptly he gave a thin, eerie scream, which sent an icy shiver the length of the sniper's back. Next instant, he plunged face-forward on to the body of the man he had just murdered so cold-bloodedly, dead himself. Then there was silence. . . .

'Comrade general,' the aide said cautiously. 'Comrade general, have you a moment for one of the snipers?'

General Chuikov looked up from his paper-littered desk, a scowl on his bejowled, seamed face, and thrust back the lock of tousled, black hair from his forehead. 'In three devils' names, why should I have time for a damned sniper, eh?'

The aide licked his lips nervously. The commander of the Stalingrad defence forces was a difficult man to get along with. His staff feared him more than the Fritzes. This wouldn't be the first or the last time that he had flung an aide out of the window into the debris-littered street. 'It seems that the sniper has some information of importance, general,' he said and swallowed hard.

'*Boshe moi!*' Chuikov cursed and lit a long cigarette with a bandaged hand that covered the weeping eczema which afflicted him, the result of months of nervous strain. 'Bring him in.'

The aide opened his mouth momentarily. 'Yes, comrade general,' he said and went out, leaving Chuikov puffing gloomily at his cigarette, hardly aware of the thunder of the *katuska* rocket guns outside and the stomach-churning howl of the Fritz electric mortars answering them from the other side of the Volga.

'The sniper, comrade general,' the aide announced and indicated the slight figure standing to his rear, muffled in thick, wadded jacket and heavy fur-felt boots, with a spoon stuck down the side of the right one.

'Well?' Chuikov asked grumpily, eyeing the sniper who looked like the rest of his kind, save that this one had an almost boyish cast of features – probably hadn't even started shaving yet. 'What tremendous, world-shaking news have you for me, comrade?'

His cynicism was wasted on the sniper, whose wooden expression did not change. 'This, comrade general.' The sniper placed what looked like a map, stained red with blood, on Chuikov's desk and stepped back smartly.

Gingerly, as if afraid to get his fingers soiled, Chuikov picked up the map and unfolded it with some difficulty; the blood had become as thick as jam between the sheets. He pulled a face.

Expressionlessly, the sniper and the aide waited for Chuikov's reaction.

With a roar, Chuikov smashed his good hand down on the desk. 'By the black virgin of Kazan!' he exclaimed with delight. 'It's a general staff map of the Fritz positions!'

He beamed at the sniper, who now beamed back at him. 'Tell me, little brother,' he said eagerly, 'tell me the details of how you found this map. We must be quite sure that it is not a Fritz plant. They have pulled that sort of trick before.'

Hastily the sniper explained how one Fritz had shot the other before succumbing himself, and how, even in his death throes, the German staff officer had clutched the map to his bleeding body in a vain attempt to blot out the tell-tale red and blue crayon marks with his own blood.

Chuikov's eyes narrowed when the sniper was finished. 'It all rings true,' he said slowly. 'Obviously the big Fritz didn't want the pilot to fall into our hands. He thought he might sing like a canary once our – er – specialists – ' he gave the sniper the benefit of his gold-toothed smile – 'started to work upon him. It was better to have him dead. Then he would have destroyed the map and probably shot himself. Yes, it all fits into place very nicely. . . . You have done a fine job, comrade.' He turned to the attentive aide. 'Pepper vodka and glasses, the big ones,' he snapped.

Hurriedly, the aide went to the cabinet where the general kept his own special brand of vodka. He produced two water glasses and the bottle. The general took them from his hand and poured the glasses full to the brim. 'Sit down, comrade,' he said, in high good humour now. 'Take off your cap and make yourself comfortable. Today you've had the best bag in your whole shooting career.'

Confused, a little red-faced at being asked to sit in the presence of a general, the sniper took a chair and pulled off his fur cap. Blonde curls cascaded down, released now from the constraints of the cap.

Now it was Chuikov's turn to be confused. 'What . . . what's your name, comrade?' he stuttered.

'Chernova, Tania,' the sniper answered in a small voice, eyeing the glasses greedily.

'But you're a woman . . . *a female woman!*' Chuikov stuttered. Then he recovered himself and handed her the water glass full of vodka with a great flourish, once more in control of himself. 'Well, I must say, Chernova, Tania, this is a day of surprises! For you, for me, and now, with this,' he touched the blood-stained map, 'the Fritzes.' He raised his glass in toast. '*Nastrovya, pan!*'

'*Nastrovya, pan!*' she repeated the toast eagerly.

Together, watched by an amazed aide who didn't think that a slip of a girl like this sniper could drink that much, the two of them swallowed the fiery spirits, their cheeks beginning to glow, their eyes sparkling, as they drained it down steadily, until finally Chuikov was finished, followed a second later by the girl.

Tipsy now, Chuikov swayed to his feet. 'Comrade sniper,' he bellowed, 'Death to the fascists! Victory to the Soviet Union!' With all his strength he flung his water glass at the wall, where it shattered into a hundred gleaming shards.

Carried away by the excitement of the moment, the girl did the same, crying, '*Victory at Stalingrad. . .!*'

1

'Stalingrad!' Colonel Katulov said simply, reining-in his big grey mare as the group of officers breasted the hill, while the weary infantry of the 333rd Punishment Battalion, known as the 'gulag rats', toiled up the rest of the steep slope.

Major Boldin, the battalion's second-in-command, gasped. He had fought over two continents ever since he was seventeen, and since the Fritzes had invaded Mother Russia in the summer of the previous year, he had seen more than enough of slaughter and horror; but he had never viewed anything like the scene stretched out below in the curve of the Volga.

The great city was ringed with fire, great orange balloons of flame exploding all the time, while the city itself, hugging the serpentine bends of the Volga like some monstrous caterpillar, belched huge spouts of flame and debris as shell after shell struck home. The noise was ear-splitting; a hideous man-made cacophony that seemed to strike the awed onlookers like a physical blow.

'God in heaven!' the bespectacled Vulf gasped in awe. 'It's how I visualize Dante's hell!'

Colonel Katukov turned round and looked coldly at the pale-faced lieutenant who affected the horn-rimmed glasses of the pre-war university teacher. '*Tovarisch mladshi-leitenant*,'* he snapped in that cold, crisp manner of his, his grey eyes piercing Vulf, 'that is not hell! At this moment you are being privileged – and the rest of that gulag scum up there' – he indicated the first

* Second lieutenant

weary 'rats', burdened by forty kilos of equipment, who were now breasting the height – 'to catch a glimpse of paradise. That is Stalingrad, a holy place, which has stopped every enemy effort to cross the Volga these last three months or more. Down there the fascist beast is bleeding to death.'

His words ended abruptly as a colossal yellow fireball exploded only fifty metres away, uprooting the snow-heavy firs, snapping them as if they were matchsticks and setting the wood alight immediately.

'Comrade colonel,' Boldin said coldly, while the other officers bent low over their horses' heads, trying to calm the trembling beasts and avoid the red-hot, fist-sized fragments of steel which flew everywhere, scything down anything that came in their way, 'I think we could leave the history of Stalingrad for a safer place, don't you?'

Katukov, as erect in his saddle as if he were reviewing a peacetime parade, gave him one of his grey stares, then nodded his head. 'Company commanders take charge of your companies. Ensure that there is a senior sergeant posted with a machine-gun to the rear of each company.' His harshly handsome face contorted into a bitter sneer and Boldin could see just how he still hated the command that Beria, the head of the Secret Police, had forced on him in the summer of 1941.* 'I don't want my jailbirds running away before they have a chance of redeeming their worthless lives by dying for Mother Russia.'

One company commander went red with shame, another looked down, the other two glared back at their CO, naked hate in their eyes for this 'Greenhat'† who had dragged them from Stalin's jails, the notorious Gulag Archipelago, and expected them to die for the dictator who had condemned them to that living hell.

Boldin nodded slightly. The four of them raised their

* See *The Gulag Rats* for further details.

† Soldiers' name for the feared Secret Police troops, the NKVD.

hands to their fur caps in salute.

Katukov did not even seem to see them.

Shrugging their shoulders, the four captains tugged their horses round and began to trot back to their awe-stricken companies to carry out the CO's orders.

Katukov turned to Boldin and Vulf. 'You two will come with me,' he said, his tone a little warmer now, for although both of them were gulag rats themselves, he had come to rely and trust in them ever since that great battle in defence of Moscow when they had first come together.

'*Comrade, can you hear our voice? . . . We know it. You must hear it! At this dear hour of our lives. Our first thought goes not to our sons, or to our mothers, but to you, dear comrade Stalin . . . .*' Desperately the skinny civilian with the dew-drop hanging from his red beak of a nose read out the poem of praise to the Soviet dictator. All the while whistles shrilled, red-faced NCO's bellowed orders and the lines of pale, nervous reinforcements filed down the river bank towards the waiting barges. The NKVD machine-gunners stood ready to mow down the first man attempting to desert.

The three officers of the gulag rats tethered their horses and joined the long line of heavily laden infantry who were about to embark on the nightmare journey across the Volga, the *politruks** everywhere now, attempting to calm them down with ferocious zeal, reading out exhortations to hate the enemy and be brave, distributing pamphlets entitled, 'What a Soldier needs to Know and How to Act in Street-Fighting' that were dropped into the snow. Even the most naïve recruit knew that there was a fifty-fifty chance he would never even reach Stalingrad.

Katukov was seemingly unmoved by the chaos and fear all around him. Instead he lectured the other two as they shuffled towards the waiting barges on 'the drill', as

* Political commissars

he called it. 'We'll land over there,' he snapped, indicating the smoke-covered far bank. 'There is a cluster of moorings behind the Red October and Barrikady Plants, which are pretty safe. However, the Fritzes have a look-out post on Mamaev Hill, up there. They'll spot us, naturally, and let us have the full weight of their artillery.'

'Naturally!' Vulf echoed sarcastically.

But, as always, sarcasm was wasted on Colonel Katukov. 'If we can get by that area, we're relatively safe,' he continued. 'If we're hit, on the other hand, over the side and swim for it.'

Major Boldin smiled wrily. 'A swim in the Volga in November, comrade colonel,' he commented. 'I think I prefer the Fritz artillery. . . . But if we do have to go over the side, colonel, where do we rendezvous afterwards?'

'Yes,' Vulf added, his curiosity overcoming his fear, 'where *are* we going, comrade colonel?' he grunted as one of the *politruks* dug him in the ribs to hurry him along into the barge. 'And what *is* our mission?'

'The rendezvous I can tell you,' Katukov said, as the *politruks* began to pack them in the barge like sheep being led to the slaughter. 'We are to report to General Chuikov's headquarters to the rear of the 284th Division.'

'And the mission?' Boldin urged, as the whistles shrilled and sailors in red-striped shirts and floppy, beribboned caps started to toss the cables on to the shore.

Katukov shrugged. 'That I do not know, *tavorisch major*.'

Vulf, pressed up tight against the back of a squat Siberian infantryman, who stank of rancid butter and black *mahorka* tobacco, shook his head with difficulty. 'Typical,' he said to no one in particular. 'The gulag rats are going to be right down in the shit with their booters again.'

The barge quivered. Its screws raced furiously. The

water churned in a wild white fury. And then they were off. The journey across the Volga had commenced. Next to Boldin, a white-faced youth with curly hair and frightened eyes started to pray. Major Boldin could understand why.

'The fascists have taken every single decency away from you! Everything! Liberty, justice, happiness, truth, the beauty of life itself! Give what you have left. Give your lives if necessary. . . .' The *politruk*'s face strained with the effort, but still he kept a wary finger on the trigger of his pistol.

No one listened. Everyone's gaze was now fixed on the Manaev Hill, which loomed up out of the fog of war. There was no doubt that the Fritzes were watching them. But would their observers be able to call up their artillery before they had passed out of sight?

Boldin swung a glance behind him. There were eight or ten barges chugging stoutly in their wake, packed to the gunwales with reinforcements, their frightened mass praying, clearly audible above the thunder of the barrage. He bit his bottom lip. The barges would make a very tempting target for any Fritz artilleryman who knew his stuff. With difficulty, he freed one hand and undid his tight collar. In case he had to make a jump for it, he didn't want to be strangled by the damn thing. Vulf caught the movement and did the same. Boldin flashed him a gleaming smile with his stainless steel teeth and whispered, 'Courage, little brother.'

'Everybody in the battalion knows I'm a devout coward,' he answered with an attempt at bravery and tucked away his precious horn-rimmed spectacles.

Now as they came ever closer to the danger point, the whole group of *politruks,* positioned around the rails to prevent anyone jumping overboard prematurely, broke into a fervent chant, like monks babbling their prayers, their eyes wide and wild with fear too. '*Into battle for our holy homeland. . . . Love of country is* stronger than death. . . . *The officer's order is the soldier's law of iron. . . .'*

There was a great rending, tearing sound which drowned the chant.

'*Fritz eighty-eight*!' someone screamed wildly.

Fifty metres away, the hundred-pound shell struck the water. The river erupted. Water drenched them and the barge rocked wildly as if struck by a sudden tornado.

That single shell seemed to act as a signal. In an instant the air above the Volga was filled with flying steel. Flame spurted everywhere. Great balls of orange fire started to explode among the barges, whipping the water into a wild, white fury, sending the craft reeling crazily from side to side. The first barge was hit. A body hurtled through the smoke and smashed against the leading craft to burst like a ripe melon. Abruptly the boiling water was full of screaming, drowning men.

Boldin jammed his elbow into the back of the man in front of him so that he would make room. Hastily he pulled off his boots and slung them around his neck. Katukov, his face now grim, hesitated only a minute and then as the obscene, stomach-churning whine of the German multiple mortars began to fill the air, he did the same. The reinforcements began to panic. Here and there a pistol cracked as a crazed soldier attempted to go over the side. Hoarsely the *politruks* cried above the tremendous racket, 'Stand firm, comrades, for God's sake, stand firm!'

Another barge took a direct hit. It broke in half immediately and went down like a stone, bearing its cargo of dead men with it, leaving a solitary soldier on the surface trying desperately to swim after the lead barge, although both his legs had been severed. His cry for help ended in a gurgle of water as he went under.

A German phosphorus shell landed on the barge directly behind theirs. It exploded in a burst of blinding, incandescent flame. Like a great roaring blow-torch, it hissed the length of the barge, ripping the flesh off the trapped soldiers, turning them into hunched, blackened pygmies in an instant, leaving the craft to zigzag wildly about the Volga with its cargo, completely out of control.

Major Boldin had had enough. He grabbed Katukov by the shoulder. 'Katukov, it's over the side!' he yelled above the howl and whine of the German shells.

'But the example,' Katukov began to protest, no fear in those cold, grey eyes of his.

Boldin cut him short with an angry snort. 'Damn the example!' he roared and ducked as their barge heeled under the impact of several tons of water smashing into its side. 'It's only a matter of seconds before they hit us. I don't want to be slaughtered purposelessly like a sheep in a pen! Are you coming?'

'*Horoscho,* I come!'

'After me, Vulf,' Boldin commanded and shoved his way forward.

The civilian with the red dripping nose drew his pistol, his eyes a mixture of fear and contempt. 'Ah, the gulag rats are the first to leave the sinking ship, eh? What else can one expect from treacherous scum like you? I –'

With all his strength, Boldin jammed his elbow into the man's skinny face. Something snapped. The civilian screamed thinly and went reeling over the side to hit the foaming water with a splash.

'Report me to Old Leather Face,* you shitty civilian!' he cried contemptuously and dived neatly over the side the next instant.

Vulf followed, then Katukov. Treading water, Boldin waited, then cried, in complete charge of the situation now, 'Right, after me! Keep together. Anyone tries to grab you in the water, smack him under the nose with the palm of your hand. *Davoi!*'

Swimming strongly , his big, almost brutal shoulder-muscles rippling under the material of his tunic, he struck out for the shore, leaving the barge to sail on to its inevitable destruction.

* Contemptuous nickname for Stalin

Gasping, spluttering, spitting out river water, and shaking with the cold, the three of them squatted on the sand bank, the river behind shrouded with burning smoke through which came the awful screams and pathetic cries for help of the wounded and the drowning.

Carefully Vulf put on his precious horn-rims and peered owlishly at the muddy bank which loomed up some twenty metres away. 'What now?' he asked.

Boldin looked at Katukov, who frowned but said nothing. Boldin forced a smile, in spite of the icy cold. 'We might be within our own lines and we might be in theirs. But either way, it's no good sitting here. Another five minutes and we'll be frozen solid.'

'Agreed,' Katukov said and loosening the pistol in his holster began to walk to the edge of the water. They followed and started to wade cautiously through the shallows towards the bank.

There Katukov halted. 'I'll go first,' he ordered. 'Who knows what our people might make of you two. 'He drew his pistol and indicated their uniforms which, like those of the other gulag rats, were devoid of badges of rank and unit insignia.

Vulf forced a grin. 'Agreed, comrade colonel. It's hardly likely that our own boys would shoot a Greenhat – at least not from the front!'

Katukov glared at him and began to clamber up the bank while they crouched there, dripping water and shivering, weapons at the ready.

Five minutes later Katukov was slithering down towards them once more, his face grim, and Boldin knew without his saying that they had come ashore in German territory. 'Fritzes?' he whispered.

Katukov nodded. 'Yes, there seems to be a heavy artillery battery up there. Can't make them out clearly in this damned smoke. But they're Fritzes all right.'

Vulf looked at Boldin, but said nothing. Boldin knew what the little intellectual was thinking. If the two of them fell into German hands, they would get the usual kicks and blows, but that would be it. The Fritzes would send them back to the POW cages. With Katukov and his damned green-cross cap badge, it would be different. The Fritzes always shot NKVD men and they might well shoot them, too.

Katukov made his decision. 'We'll bluff it out. In the smoke they'll not be able to make out our uniforms clearly. If they do, we'll make a run for it.'

Boldin nodded his agreement and Vulf frowned. In spite of the treatment Boldin had received from the NKVD in the gulag and the fact that they had helped to destroy his whole life, his military career, even his marriage – for his wife had committed suicide after his arrest, and his boy had vanished into one of the Stalin scholar schools – he couldn't betray his commanding officer. Boldin the gulag rat would lay down his life for the stern-faced NKVD colonel if called upon to do so.

Stealing up the steep bank as quietly as they could, the three of them crouched there momentarily, eyeing the Fritzes through the drifting smoke as they fed shell after shell into their howitzers. The slight wind brought snatches of commands in German towards them and every fresh explosion slapped them in the face with a hot wave of acrid burnt air until Katukov commanded in a whisper, 'Come on. This way!'

Time passed leadenly as they worked their way along the river bank, their slow progress punctuated by the regular thump-thump of heavy guns and the high-pitched whirr of German machine-guns sending red tracer hissing across the river like angry hornets. At another time those spandaus would have drawn the three men's curses, but not now. That distinctive, frenzied, hysterical sound told them that they were still within German-held territory. Now they began to creep through German outposts. Time and time again they froze at the occasional German voice or the sudden flare hissing into the grey-smoke sky to hang there for what seemed an eternity, bathing everything below in its eerie, unreal light.

Creeping behind Boldin, pistol held in a hand that shook badly, Vulf whispered, 'For God's sake, comrade major, how much longer? I can already feel the stuff trickling down into my right boot!'

Bolding grinned. Vulf was a card. 'Not much, little brother.'

In the front, Katukov hissed sternly, 'Be quiet, the two of you. Listen!'

Katukov cocked his head to one side and the others did the same. A well-remembered sound was coming from somewhere to their right. There was no mistaking the slow metallic chatter like that of an irate ancient woodpecker. It was the Red Army '05 model machine-gun all right.

'Our lines, colonel?' Boldin queried.

'Right, comrade major,' Katukov answered, advancing again, body bent as if against a strong wind, pistol at the ready, face tense. Boldin knew why. This would be the most dangerous stage of their little adventure. Front-line soldiers were notoriously trigger-happy. Even if they did manage to break through the Fritz lines, they would still have to contend with their own people out there somewhere. In this chaos, with vision reduced by the smoke and fog to about ten metres, the infantry might well shoot first and ask questions afterwards.

Carefully, they started to skirt a collection of ruined apartment houses, working their way to the sound of that old-fashioned machine-gun. To their left a Russian direct hit ripped the fog of war apart with dramatic, electric suddenness and they glimpsed pieces of metal or body flying into the air. A horse slammed into the ground directly in front of them, followed by a barbed-wire entanglement, its posts still attached to it, so that it looked like a huge net flung by some sea-giant to entrap them. Vulf gulped audibly and stepped over the carcass of the dead horse. '*Boshe moi!*' he said in a little voice, 'What in the name of all that is holy will come down next?'

Now they could catch fragmentary glances of their own

positions between the gaps in the house walls before they disappeared again in the smoke which billowed up like foam: a lunar landscape of churned-up brown craters against the white of the snow, rent apart time and time again by rust-red spurts of angry flame. It looked to Vulf like the end of the world. Wordlessly, they started to mount the stairs of an intact stairwell, knowing that they might well be able to get to the other side through the second floor without being seen by the Fritzes dug in around the building. On tip-toe, like children out to play some prank on their unsuspecting fellows, they crept up the stairs, their hearts beating like trip-hammers now, their hands, gripping their pistols, wet with sweat.

'*Hände hoch!*' The challenge cut into Vulf's back like a knife. He swung round.

A big German stood there, eyes blood-shot under his helmet, heavy, pugnacious chin covered with stubble, rifle in hand.

Instinctively Vulf lashed out with his foot. The German howled with pain. His rifle dropped from his nerveless fingers and clattered to the floor while he reeled against the wall.

Boldin's pistol cracked. The German was swung round by the impact at such short range. He fell screaming over the rail to slam to the floor below like a sack of wet cement.

'*Davoi!*' Katukov yelled, knowing now that it was no use attempting to conceal their presence in the house as cries of rage and alarm shot up on all sides. They had stumbled into a hornet's nest of enemy soldiers.

A German tried to bar Boldin's escape. Boldin smashed his pistol against the man's face. Blood shot from the soldier's smashed nose. He went down howling with agony. Boldin slammed his heavy boot into the man's contorted face and ran on. Two Germans sprang out of a side room, firing their rifles from the hip as they came. Slugs howled off the walls. Plaster trickled down on the Russian fugitives like grey snow. Katukov snapped off a shot to left and right. Both men went down, as if pole-axed.

Boldin stumbled on a loose plank and nearly fell. It saved his life. To his right, a bare-headed Fritz with a machine-pistol clasped to his hip, ripped off an angry burst. The slugs stitched a smoking line of holes just above his head. Behind the major, Vulf pressed his trigger. The bullet caught the German squarely in the chest. He slapped back against the wall, as if propelled there by a gigantic fist.

To their front now lay a large shattered window. Through it, Katukov in the lead could see the red flag with its dearly loved hammer and sickle, waving weakly in the faint breeze. It was the Red Army's line. 'This way,' he gasped and bolted forward, head tucked between his shoulders like a footballer, ignoring the wild shots which whined off the walls on all sides, pocking the plaster with ugly little spurts of blue flame.

Boldin and Vulf rushed after him. Boldin felt a dozen bullets tug at his uniform and the sudden, passing heat on his face as they cut the air close to his cheeks. Still he ran with the last of his strength, gasping leathern-lunged like an ancient bellows, knowing that it was now or never. If they didn't escape through that window, the Fritzes would trap them.

Katukov hesitated only momentarily, then, with a great roar, a compound of rage, fear and anger, he went through. Vulf hesitated.

'Jump, you little shit!' Boldin cried in anger. He lifted his boot and levelled a great kick at Vulf's baggy breeches. He flew through the window to slam down hard on the brick rubble fifteen metres below, followed by Boldin. And then the three of them, bruised and bleeding, were up and running for their very lives towards their own positions, cheered on by the Red Army men standing up in their trenches now, waving their helmets like excited spectators at some sports contest, followed by the frustrated fire of the Fritzes, cheated of their prey this one time. They had done it. They were now in Stalingrad!

2

The Red Army's engineers had blasted a T-shaped tunnel on the cliff side of the west bank of the Volga to the rear of the 284th Infantry Division, boring twenty metres below the surface to make the tunnel safe against anything but a direct hit with a heavy-calibre shell. This was General Chuikov's fourth headquarters in the seven weeks he had commanded the army defending Stalingrad.

Now, drinking hot tea laced with vodka, warming their frozen hands on the glasses, Major Boldin and Lieutenant Vulf waited outside in the dirty snow, watching the hectic traffic in and out of the tunnel while Colonel Katukov sought an interview with the army commander.

In spite of the languid, apparently bored manner of the elegant, pale-faced staff officers grouped at the entrance, catching a breath of air and smoking their cigarettes in holders, little Vulf could see that all was not well in Stalingrad. The couriers who kept appearing from the front were mud-stained, their uniforms ragged, sometimes red with blood, as if they had been forced to run the gauntlet of enemy fire to reach the HQ. And their eyes revealed everything – they were wide and wild, the eyes of men who were plain scared.

Vulf pressed the last few drops of precious lemon juice into his tea and said softly, so that the staff officers at the entrance couldn't hear him, 'The situation at Stalingrad doesn't look particularly healthy, Boldin. I think General Chuikov has problems.'

Boldin nodded his agreement, taking his gaze off the pitiful line of wounded filing past the tunnel, some of them barefoot in the snow, all of them terribly emaciated, with the blinded men bringing up the rear, hanging on to each other's belts helplessly. 'Yes, you're right, Vulf, Vassili Chuikov looks to me as if he's in a fix here.'

'And thousands die for a matter of prestige,' Vulf sneered. 'On the one side, the German dictator Hitler wants to capture the city because it bears the name of his hated rival Stalin, and on the other, Old Leather Face must defend it to the end so that *his* Stalingrad does not fall into Fritz's hand. Because of that, all Russia bleeds.' He spat contemptuously into the snow.

'What treacherous thoughts,' Boldin said mildly. 'It would be back to the gulag or worse for you if the NKVD heard you spouting such disloyal sentiments about our beloved leader.'

'I shit on the NKVD!' Vulf grunted and spat again.

Boldin smiled slightly at the little man's outraged look. 'You know, little brother, if fate had had it otherwise, I might well have been in command here this day instead of Vassili Chuikov.'

'What do you mean?' Vulf looked up curiously at the big major with the bold eyes and handsome face, marred only by a slight, bitter droop of the lips which indicated a disappointed man.

'Chuikov was my second-in-command in the Far East that year when the NKVD arrested me and dragged me off to the gulag.' He paused suddenly and remembered once again that nightmare march to the camps, the new prisoners dying by the score, urged on by the Siberians on their ponies, their bull-penis whips flaying the backs of those still able to march. 'Yes, he was fortunate enough to be sent off to Chungking soon afterwards to report on the Chinks. He escaped the Red Army purges that way. Besides,' he smiled softly, 'the good Vassili is a true proletarian. A peasant and a communist who commanded a regiment at the age of twenty-five in the Civil War. He has all the right qualifications for a Soviet hero. Still,' Boldin paused momentarily, 'if I had been sent to

China to watch the Chinks instead of Vassili, who knows who might be commanding in Stalingrad today?'

Vulf touched the big major's arm softly. 'The past, Boldin, the past,' he whispered. 'Besides, thank God you are not in command. Look at that!'

He indicated the tall figure of a young colonel staggering towards the entrance of the tunnel like a drunken man, leaving a trail of blood behind him on the snow, croaking, 'My regiment's gone . . . gone. . . .'

Hastily the group of staff officers grabbed hold of him by the arm and forced the hysterical officer to sit down in the snow, while they summoned the sentries to take him away. General Chuikov could not be troubled by such hysterics.

The sentries led the colonel away, still croaking 'My regiment's gone'. If he was lucky, they'd take him to the nearest field hospital; if he was unlucky, it would be a quick bullet at the back of the head in the shelter of some wrecked building.

'Poor bastard,' Boldin said and then straightened up. Colonel Katukov was striding across the snow in a great hurry.

'Hello, where's the fire?' Vulf whispered, hastily swallowing the last of his tea.

'We'll soon find out.

Some twenty metres away from them, the big colonel halted and waved. '*Davoi!*' he called, 'General Chuikov will see us. He's given us fifteen minutes!' He emphasized the time as if they were being granted a great honour. 'Come!' Imperiously he turned and strode towards the entrance of the tunnel HQ.

Vulf shook his head in mock wonder. 'Crap said the king and a thousand arseholes bent and took the strain, for in those days the word of the king was law,' he sneered, but dutifully enough he followed his big friend in the colonel's wake.

Chuikov rose from behind his desk, his blouse so

unkempt and devoid of decorations that he might well have been taken for a common soldier, and extended his unbandaged hand to Katukov. 'Welcome, comrade colonel. I am glad to see you here in Stalingrad.' They shook hands and Katukov, his face flushed with pride at his reception by the man who was a triple Hero of the Soviet Union, turned and said, 'My officers, Major Boldin, my second-in-command, and Second Lieutenant Vulf, the battalion intelligence officer.

Chuikov thrust out his hand. 'Comrade marshal' he gasped, mouth dropping open stupidly, hand suddenly suspended in mid-air. 'Why . . .?'

'No, comrade general,' Boldin said tonelessly, his face revealing nothing, though inwardly he was enjoying the look of absolute surprise on his former second-in-command's face. 'No longer marshal, just a simple major of infantry – and a gulag rat to boot.'

'*Da, da, ya ponemyu*' Chuikov stuttered, recovering his pose, 'I understand.' He indicated to his aide to bring glasses and vodka. 'Sit down, the three of you,' he ordered.

Mildly amused, Boldin did so with the rest, noting that even one of the most powerful men in the Red Army dare not be seen shaking the hand of a gulag rat – they were indeed the outcasts of the Soviet Republic.

Chuikov waited until the aide had poured the glasses full of the fiery spirit, then dismissed him with the command, 'Fifteen minutes. Then you're back. Understood?'

'Understood, comrade general.'

Immediately the usual toasts were over, Chuikov got down to business, undisturbed by the fact that the sirens were sounding their shrill warning that the German dive-bombers were on their way once again. 'Comrades, our position here in Stalingrad is intolerable . . . but not impossible. The hand-to-hand fighting for the factory has consumed battalions, regiments, even whole divisions of my 62nd Army including Gurtiev's 308th

Infantry division.' He looked sharply at Boldin.

Instinctively Boldin nodded in response to that look; he knew General Gurtiev. They had studied together at the Frunze Military Academy.

'The whole division was massacred at the battle for the Barrikady. They went in eight thousand strong and came out with two hundred and fifty survivors.' The pugnacious general stopped for a moment and allowed the information to sink in.

Outside the Stukas hurtled from the sky above Stalingrad, their sirens howling hideously. Everywhere in the Soviet-held part of the shattered city the flak guns started to bark.

'Not only that, comrades, but reinforcements and supplies are terribly difficult to get through by day, as you know yourselves – to your cost.' He indicated their damp, muddy uniforms. 'Now my observers tell me that ice sludge is beginning to drift into the Volga, so that until the ice stops moving and forms a solid bridge there will be difficulty in bringing supplies and troops across even at night when those damned Fritz artillerymen on the hill can't spot the barges.' He sighed and added, 'Intolerable, comrades, but not *impossible*, as I have already said. He took the bottle and refilled their glasses with the pepper vodka.

A moment or two passed while his guests placed salt in the web of skin formed by stretching out their forefingers and thumbs, licking it, and then downing the fiery spirit to the acompaniment of gasps and coughs.

Chuikov wiped his lips with his bandaged hand and Boldin caught a glimpse of the scabs and lesions which ran the length of his forearm. He realized that Vassili must be under tremendous strain in spite of his outspoken, abrasive manner.

'So, comrades, that's the bad news,' Chuikov continued, his eyes sparkling with the drink now. 'This is the good. Yesterday Comrade Stalin informed me that the Red Army will commence its great offensive to beat the

Fritzes on the Stalingrad front at zero six-thirty hours on the morning of November nineteenth exactly two weeks from now.'

Katukov gave a little gasp and even Vulf looked impressed.

Chuikov chuckled, obviously pleased with the effect of his surprise. 'Yes, comrades, Operation Uranus, as the attack is code-named, will sweep the Fritzes from the Volga and set them off running to their own accursed homeland for good. 'He reached into his desk drawer and pulled out a blood-stained map. 'This,' he anounced, spreading it out on the desk in front of them, 'was taken from the body of a German staff officer last week by one of our girl snipers.' He winked suddenly. 'A very pretty one, too.'

Colonel Katukov frowned and Vulf told himself that the NKVD man was a puritan. He had been forced to accept the vodka because the army commander himself had offered him it, but he didn't like strong drink. Nor did he like the reference to the woman.

'We are absolutely certain that it is not a plant. Intelligence confirms much of the detail it contains. Now, look here, we have the German Sixth Army under von Paulus around to the west of Stalingrad, in this natural land bridge between the rivers Don and Volga.' He swept his bandaged hand across the map, criss-crossed with a rash of blue and red crayon marks. 'In this area he has concentrated practically all his combat divisions for the purpose of capturing the city. Clear?'

'Clear,' they answered in unison, voices firm and decisive, though all three of them were wondering why Chuikov had revealed the details of the top-secret offensive to them. What had all this got to do with the gulag rats?

'Now von Paulus has stationed most of his supply dumps needed to feed, clothe and arm those divisions on the far side of the Don to the west where it makes that large loop before curving southwards to the Sea of Azov.'

He pointed to the area with his forefinger.

Outside there was the thud and crump of the Stukas' 250-pound bombs landing all around the entrance to the tunnel. But the general did not seem to notice as he studied the map, ignoring the concrete dust drifting down like thin snow on his bowed shoulders.

'As is, of course, clear to you, comrades, cut von Paulus off from those supplies and his vaunted Sixth Army will wither away just like that!' he snapped his fingers contemptuously. 'Add to that cutting-off of his supplies another thrust from the south, and von Paulus is trapped. Sooner or later he and his three hundred thousand soldiers will surrender and tamely march into the POW cages.'

A bomb landed close by and the bunker shook violently under its impact.

'Three hundred thousand soldiers!' Chuikov repeated the figure, obviously undisturbed by the near miss.

Even Vulf, a born sceptic, was impressed. With German troops virtually at the door of his HQ, half his army dead or wounded, his own headquarters under aerial attack, the tousled-haired general talked of tremendous victories; it was some performance.

'Now then, comrades, Party Secretary Comrade Stalin has ordered that the first priority of Operation Uranus is to cut the Fritzes off from those supplies, then the pincer movement will follow. But comrades, where should that particular thrust take place? I can tell you that it is easier to pinpoint where the two pincers should link up. Here at the bridge across the Don near Kalach.'

Boldin and Katukov nodded their heads in agreement. The only bridge across the Don in the whole area was the most obvious place. They could see, too, the reason why Chuikov found it difficult to make a decision about where the attack on the supplies should start. The Don was simply too full of curves and bends where a determined enemy could hold out or even launch a counter-attack across the river into the Russian flank.

'However, this captured map,' Chuikov continued, 'has helped us to make our decision where we should jump off. According to it, most of that area is held by Dumitrescu's Third Rumanian Army. From what we know of them they are poorly led, poorly armed, the Fritzes regard them as more of a burden than anything else, and the rank-and-file have no stomach to fight for that decadent, skirt-chasing king of theirs. Obviously the Rumanians are the weak link. So it has been decided that our attack on November nineteenth should be launched across the Don between Serafimovich and Kletskaya – here and here.' He held up a finger in warning. 'However, can we be sure that there are only Rumanians in the area? We have lost the Fritz General Heim's Forty-eighth Panzer Corps, an elite formation, and although our Fifth and Twenty-first Tank Armies which will spearhead the attack are good formations, they are no match for Heim's tankers.' He paused and let his words sink in.

From outside there came the sound of muffled cheering. Obviously the gunners protecting the tunnel HQ had brought down one of the gull-winged dive-bombers.

'It is therefore imperative comrades, that we know *now* if it is only the Rumanians who bar the way for us on our drive to Kalach.' He looked from one face to the other. 'It will be the task of the 333rd Punishment Battalion to find that out.'

As if he had been listening behind the door waiting for exactly this moment of shocked silence, the elegant aide appeared and, springing to attention, bellowed at the top of his thin voice, 'As commanded, I take the liberty of reminding the comrade army commander that fifteen minutes precisely have passed.'

Chuikov rose to his feet.

The three officers did the same.

'You will be supplied with German uniforms,' Chuikov said, giving them no time to recover from their shock. 'You will cross the River Don tomorrow night. It has all been arranged. You will reconnoitre the area as described and you will report directly to me.' He touched his bandaged hand to his dark, curly hair. 'Comrades, you are dismissed.' He slumped down at his desk and immediately began working on his papers.

Numbly, the three gulag rats allowed themselves to be led outside by the elegant aide, blinking in the sudden grey light, like sheep being led to slaughter.

It was only when the aide had left them with the information that the general's personal launch would take them back across the river that Vulf cried, 'But in the name of all that's holy, do you know what the Fritzes will do if they catch us in their uniforms?' His eyes, desperate and wild, flashed to the sky, as if he were appealing to God himself.

'Yes,' said Katukov in a voice drained of emotion. 'They'll shoot us.'

3

The giant oaks trenched the darkening skyline like the teeth of an upturned rake. The opposite bank of the River Don lay still and apparently empty. Admittedly the peasants and *kolhoz* farmers had fled long ago, but there were men over there all right, frightened, desperate, savage men – just as the watchers crouched in the snow were frightened, desperate and savage.

'This is the narrowest stretch of the Don,' their young guide, a former collective farmer from the other side, now a volunteer for the Red Army, told them.

Behind them, the dogs made uneasy by the whisper of the wind in the oaks started to bark and howl at the silver crescent of the moon which cast its spectral light on the gulag rats crouched everywhere in the reeds and snow.

'Quieten those damned hounds!' Katukov snapped angrily. 'At once!'

Vulf doubled away to carry out the order. The officers resumed their study of the opposite bank.

'If you would care to focus your glasses at ten o'clock, comrade colonel,' the ex-farmer said in that slow, polite manner of the Don people, 'you'll see one of their outposts covering the tunnel.'

Katukov and Boldin did so and the tall helmets of the Rumanian Army came into focus.

'They'll be little problem once we're across,' Katukov grunted. Behind them, the howling of the special dogs had ceased. Boldin told himself that for a city man, Vulf had a way with animals. He actually seemed to like the half-wild Alsatians which were going to cross the river with them.

'At two o'clock, comrade colonel,' the boy said hesitantly, 'they've got some armour – next to that ruined barn.'

Obediently, the two officers swung their night glasses round. A handful of light tanks, outlined in stark black against the faint silver light, swung into view.

'Hmm,' Boldin commented, 'I doubt if they're going to be able to start them easily in this cold – it's freezing the eggs off me!' He shivered dramatically. 'But if their cannon are manned, they certainly could make goulash out of the battalion emerging from the tunnel in dribs and drabs.'

'Agreed,' Katukov said, lowering his binoculars. For a few minutes he appeared sunk in thought, wreathed in a gloomy silence, while the rest waited for his decision. Across the river a red flare hissed into the sky. It hung there, bathing the gulag rats who had frozen into immobility in its unreal, glowing blood-red light. They tensed, waiting for the first snarl of a machine-gun, but none came. They had not been spotted. The Rumanians were nervous; the flares were just a routine measure. The flare dropped to the water and died with a small hiss, leaving them blinking their eyes in the sudden inky darkness.

'We'll do it like this,' Katukov said. 'Boldin, you take the lead assault party. In that uniform, you might fool the Rumanian outposts long enough to be able to deal with them before they start firing and waking up the whole damned Third Rumanian Army.'

Boldin, in an ill-fitting German major's uniform, nodded his agreement. 'I'll do my best, comrade colonel.'

'Then I'll follow with Vulf and the dogs. I'll head straight for those light tanks. If I fail to capture them, we'll have to use the dogs. . . .' He turned to the ex-farmer. 'All right, comrade,' he snapped, 'let's be on our way.'

'Yes, comrade colonel . . . and comrade colonel?'

'Yes?'

'Can I go with Major Boldin's party?' the boy drew a long, wicked-looking knife from the side of his boot, his innocent child's face suddenly contorted into a wolfish grimace, dark eyes blazing with hate. 'I have a score to settle with those Rumanian swine.'

'Yes, little brother, you can go with Comrade Boldin. 'He laid an almost fatherly hand on the boy's shoulder. 'But don't do anything foolish and dangerous. Mother Russia will have need of you and your kind in the years after this terrible war.'

Boldin shook his head in mock wonder. Was the harsh-faced NKVD man a sentimentalist at heart after all? Then they were gone, stealing into the silver gloom like grey timber wolves intent on their prey.

The stench of the tunnel underneath the Don hit Katukov an almost physical blow in the face. He blanched and hesitated. '*Boshe moi!*' he cursed thickly. 'What an evil stench.'

The guide smiled and stepped forward, hissing carbide lantern held up at the ready. 'It is two hundred years old, comrade colonel. They say that Stenka Razin, the Cossack leader, had it built, on his way to take Stalingrad.'*

'Hmm,' Katukov grunted, tying a handkerchief round his mouth and nose, 'it smells like it.' He indicated with a nod of his head that the guide should enter, then turned to Boldin. 'Off you go, comrade. Try to get through their positions with the least possible noise.'

'I will, comrade colonel,' Boldin answered, telling himself that he'd need the devil's own luck to be able to do that.

Time passed incredibly slowly. There was no sound save the drip-drip of the water from the ancient stone roof, the pad-pad of the dogs behind them, and the occasional scurry of clawed feet as the rats, their

* A legendary bandit who captured and held Stalingrad in 1670.

shadows magnified frighteningly on the walls by the flickering light of the lantern, scurried for safety at their approach.

Boldin, unimaginative soldier that he was, felt uneasy and not a little scared at the thought that he was deep below the Don in this ancient tunnel – what if the roof gave way? – and to take his mind off his fears, he talked to the boy who was leading them. 'What kind of men are these Rumanians, little brother? I know nothing of them.'

'Pigs!' the boy snarled and then relented a little. 'Their officers treat them like dirt, comrade major. They're all corsetted, perfumed fools who strike their soldiers for the slightest thing, and in their turn the soldiers take it out on us. I understand, but I also hate.'

Their guide's eyes blazed with fury and Boldin shook his head a little sadly. This damned war, he told himself, was turning the average Russian soldier into a ruthless, heartless killer. God knows how such people would ever find their way back to a normal quiet life once there was peace again. *Peace*, said a sudden little cynical voice from the deeper regions of his mind. What kind of peace can you expect, Major Boldin? For you and the rest of the scum, pimps, parasites, politicos who make up the 333rd Punishment Battalion, peace will mean only one thing – providing you manage to survive the war, which is hardly likely – back to the camps!

'Comrade major,' the boy's excited voice cut into his gloomy reverie.

'Yes?'

'Up there . . . that's the exit.' He held his lantern a little higher so that Boldin could see the dark, shrub-fringed hole that lay some twenty metres ahead.

'*Horoscho!*, Boldin snapped, everything forgotten now. 'Douse the light, boy.'

Hastily the youth did so and, depositing the lantern on the floor, reached for the long knife tucked down the side of his boot.

'Listen,' Boldin hissed to the men clad in field-grey all around him, 'make as little noise as you can. I aim to get close enough to the Rumanians' first position to use our knives.'

'Yes,' the boy whispered eagerly, 'cold steel –'

'Shut up!' Boldin interrupted him brutally. 'All right, follow me and I'll sabre the eggs off any man who gives our position away!'

They emerged into the silver gloom, strung well out, each of the rats clasping a knife, bayonet, or assault-spade, its edges ground until they were razor-sharp. Hardly daring to breathe, they began to work their way towards the first Rumanian posiion. They passed through a copse of snow-heavy firs, moving each frond carefully with their hands in order not to dislodge the snow resting on it. Boldin paused momentarily to take his bearings, sniffing the air like a wild dog, sensing the faint odour of garlic, stale sweat and black tobacco which indicated the presence of men to his right.

Like predatory animals stalking their prey, they crept towards the unsuspecting Rumanians, chatting softly with one another in the lazy manner of sentries all over the world, who knew they had a great deal of time to kill. *Fifty metres . . . thirty metres . . . twenty-five . . . twenty . . . fifteen*. . . . Ever closer. . . .

At ten metres, Boldin indicated that his force should break into two groups. He would take the first group to swing round behind the enemy position; a senior sergeant would advance directly towards it.

They set off once more, bent double, hardly daring to breathe, their hands gripping their weapons wet with sweat. *Five metres to go!* Boldin, his brow lathered in greasy sweat in spite of the night cold, could see the Rumanians' outlines quite clearly as they stood with their backs resting against the sandbags, unaware that their last moments on this earth were rapidly drawing near. He drew a deep breath and tried to calm the fluttering of his heart. He was getting too old for this sort of thing, he told himself.

Still the Rumanians continued to chatter softly in their melodious-sounding language, so soft and feminine. *Four metres to go!* In another instant, he would be able to reach out and grab the first soldier by the throat and silence any cry of alarm he might attempt to make. *Three metres!* Boldin tensed for the final dash forward.

Then it happened. Behind him the boy stumbled on a rock jutting up above the surface of the snow. The chatter ceased. The Rumanians swung round, machine-pistols and rifles at the ready, faces contorted with fear in the silver gloom as they spotted the intent figures advancing towards them. Boldin knew that it would be no use attempting to bluff them. They would shoot first and ask questions afterwards.

'*Davoi!*' he cried and dived forward.

Scarlet flame split the gloom. Next to him the boy screamed shrilly. The knife clattered from his fingers and he fell face forward into the snow, dead.

The rats streamed forward, screaming, knives, bayonets and spades gleaming in the moonlight, and flung themselves at the surprised Rumanians. In a crazy confusion, Russian and Rumanian tumbled to the ground, grunting obscenely like wild animals, even fear forgotten now.

A tall soldier who stank of garlic swung his riflle butt at Boldin. The major dodged just in time. His knife flashed wickedly the next second and the Rumanian went down, blood seeping through the fingers tightly clutched to his ripped-open throat. Bolding sprang over his writhing body. Another Rumanian had thrown down his weapon and was clambering over the parapet in a desperate attempt to escape these blood-crazed killers who had appeared so startingly out of the night. Boldin's big hand fell on the Rumanian's shoulder and heaved. The Rumanian lashed back with his elbow. Boldin gasped hard as it connected with his stomach.

The knife fell from his fingers with the shock. Again the Rumanian attempted to clamber over the sandbags and escape. Desperately, Boldin, almost doubled up and gasping for breath, grabbed at his foot. The Rumanian came tumbling down on to him. Together they fell to the ground in a confused mêlée, smashing their fists at each other, savagely attempting to gouge one another's eyes out. Boldin's fingers sought and found the writhing Rumanian's neck. He grabbed and held. The Rumanian's spine arched like a taut bow-string, strange gurgling cries coming from his throat as he writhed and twisted, attempting to break that brutal grip. Boldin held on, feeling the Rumanian growing weaker by the moment *'Die, you bastard!'* he grunted fiercely through gritted teeth, knowing he couldn't stand the strain much longer.

'Die!'

As if in response, the man's body went limp and Boldin staggered groggily to his feet. He heard, only vaguely, the thin asthmatic whine of an engine being started with difficulty in the freezing night air.

At the exit to the tunnel, Katukov heard that first desperate whine clearly enough. 'Get the damned dogs, Vulf!' he bellowed as one of the tank machine-gunners opened up and sent a wild burst of red and white tracer hissing in their general direction.

'The hounds – quick!'

The dog-handlers didn't wait for Vulf's command. Instantly they slipped off the chains. The heavily laden Alsatians darted forward across the snow as they had been trained to do, hurtling onwards, barking ferociously, ears pricked back, tails low as they ran to their deaths.

The machine-gunner spotted the dark shadows racing across the surface of the snow. Instinctively he knew they meant him no good. He ripped off a hasty salvo in their direction. Dog after dog went down howling pitifully and Vulf thrust his hands to his ears to drown out that terrible sound. But the others raced on and Vulf watched with horrified fascination, as the leading Alsatian squirmed its way underneath the tank.

The prong projecting from the heavy pack-mine on its back triggered off the charge immediately. The tank reeled back on its rear bogies in a thick crump of bright flame like a wild horse being put to the saddle for the first time. Sickened, his throat full of hot vomit, Vulf saw the dog sail through the glare and vanish.

Just behind, the frightened driver of the next tank pressed his foot down hard on the accelerator. The engine roared into violent life. He slammed the gear into reverse, smashing through a little straw *isba** behind him, careening off a third tank that wouldn't start, while its gunner swung the turret round, spitting fire from the m.g. at the half-wild hounds which were everywhere.

Dog after dog rolled over, yelping pitifully, but still the rest came on. Vulf hid his eyes. He could look no longer on this sickening dog-hunt.

Five munutes later it was all over. The dog-handlers were filing slowly back into the tunnel with the survivors, while in the snow the bodies of the dead, so cruelly massacred, both man and animal, started to stiffen rapidly in the night cold.

Vulf gulped hard and tried not to look at the dogs sprawled in the snow in front of the burning tanks. 'Boldin,' he said, 'they are like the gulag rats – animals to be slaughtered at the command of that monster in the Kremlin, cannon-fodder both of us, powerless to determine our own fate.'

Boldin pulled out his precious flask of vodka. 'Here, little brother, drink,' he commanded. 'It is not wise, just now, to think of such things. There will be another time one day and things will change.' But even as he

* A small hut.

uttered the words of comfort to his old comrade, he knew he was lying. There would never be any change in Russia. Their fate had already been sealed.

A moment later they had gone, stealing into the shadows. . . .

4

The 333rd Punishment Battalion was not the only unit engaged in clandestine operations that cold November night. Some fifty kilometres away in the ruins of embattled Stalingrad, a small group of soldiers in the field-grey of the Wehrmacht were also conducting an armed reconnaissance into no-man's land, the home of deserters and criminals, and the snipers of both armies.

Every man of the volunteer force knew that even at night the Red Army posted snipers among the grotesque mess of tangled steel and shattered brickwork that had once been a prosperous workers' settlement. Cautiously, they advanced to the site of the wreck which had been pinpointed from the air the previous afternoon, the young officer in charge praying they would find the Storch before the moon rose any higher.

Behind him von Friedel's batman, who had been ordered to go along with the volunteer patrol to identify his master, whispered, 'I can smell something burnt over there – at ten o'clock, *Herr Leutnant.*'

The young officer sniffed the air. There was, indeed, a faint smell of burnt metal and oil. 'This way,' he ordered softly.

Every man's nerves tingling anxiously, they crept forward again, eyes narrowed, trying to pierce the gloom, bodies tensed in anticipation of the first hard thwack of a steel-tipped slug.

'There!' the batman hissed.

'Yes, it's the plane all right,' the lieutenant agreed, 'or what's left of it. You, you . . . and you, come with me. The rest of you form a perimeter defence.'

Swiftly, the little group began to examine the burnt-out plane, fumbling in the dark, while around them the rest of the patrol went to ground, ready to do battle if necessary.

'The pilot,' one of the infantryman said. 'Over here, *Herr Leutnant*.'

Hurriedly, the officer knelt down beside the corpse, which in spite of the freezing cold, had become bloated with gas. Reluctantly the officer turned over the stinking body, trying not to hear the sighs that came as the gas escaped from the dead man's mouth. For an instant, he clicked on the little torch strapped to his tunic. The swollen, green face looked up at him with unseeing eyes. The tunic bore the flying eagles of the Luftwaffe. 'Yes,' he confirmed the identification, 'it's the pilot all right.' He switched off the torch. 'But where in heaven's name is von Reichel?'

Meanwhile, the soldier checking the wrecked interior of the plane reported, 'Nothing left, *Herr Leutnant*. Just a bit of burnt paper. Looks as if it might have been a flight map.'

'*Gut*. Stick it in your pocket, Heinz. The rest of you spread out now. Von Reichel's body must be here somewhere, unless they captured him.'

Wishing this macabre business was over, the young officer, together with the shaking batman, who had spent his three years of war in higher headquarters, began to search the snow-heavy bushes in a circle around the wreck.

Five minutes later they found what they sought: a rough mound of fresh earth, laboriously carved out of the frozen soil. Swiftly, the infantrymen unbuckled their entrenching tools and started to dig, knowing that every minute they spent in no-man's land increased the risk of their being discovered.

It didn't take long to find the corpse. Obviously the Russians or whoever had buried the missing man had been in a hurry too, for von Reichel was covered by only a few centimetres of soil.

Trying to ignore his own revulsion and knowing that he had to do it if he didn't want to lose face with his hard-bitten stubble-hoppers, the young officer cleared the rest of the earth away from von Reichel's face and then flicked on the blue light. 'Is it your officer?' he demanded.

The batman, obviously terrified out of his wits, gulped, 'I think so . . . but he looks different than when I . . . .'

'Yes, soldiers usually do when they're dead,' the lieutenant said cynically, his revulsion overcome by contempt for this rear-echelon stallion who had never heard a shot fired in battle. 'Well, is it him, or isn't it?'

'I don't know exactly,' the man quavered. 'But he had a big mole on his right hand . . . at the back.'

'Holy shit!' the officer moaned, but he remembered General Stumme's precise order to him before the patrol had set out. With a sigh, he fumbled in the cold earth for the corpse's right hand, freeing it with difficulty. 'Is this it?' he asked, holding up the dead man's hand.

'Yes, yes,' the batman answered hastily. 'That's the mole, *Herr Leutnant*.'

'You sure?'

'On my oath, sir.'

The lieutenant flicked off the light. To their right an owl hooted softly three times. It was the agreed-upon signal. Trouble was brewing. 'Come on,' he hissed urgently. '*Los!* Let's make steam. The Ivans are out there. . . .'

'Certainly looks very odd to me, *Herr General*,' Colonel Franz, Stumme's chief-of-staff, said thoughtfully.

The middle-aged general said nothing. Instead he dipped the end of his cigar in looted Crimean brandy and sucked on it reflectively. Outside, telephones rang and typewriters clattered as the staff prepared plans for a new attempt to crush the last Soviet resistance in Stalingrad.

'The pilot shot through the back of the head but unburied, and the plane burnt. But von Reichel buried. Very strange,' Colonel Franz continued. 'I mean, since when have the Ivans shown such respect for our dead as to bury them, especially in no-man's land. And alongside the aircraft, too. General, I think they got von Reichel's map, and this is a fake to convince us they haven't.'

Stumme nodded a little sadly. 'I tend to agree with you. They've got it and that means they know our complete dispositions.' He sighed. 'I am afraid we'll have to inform the Führer HQ.'

Colonel Franz looked at him gloomily. 'Heads will roll, general. You know that the Führer has ordered strictly that no officer carrying top-secret maps should go anywhere near the front?'

'I know it well, my dear Franz.' General Stumme gave him a parody of a smile. 'The head which will roll will be mine.' He picked up the phone. 'Operator, connect me with the Führer HQ – *at once*,' he barked.

General der Panzerwaffe Stumme had just signed his death-warrant.

Hitler patted Blondi, his Alsatian bitch, fondly on the back. 'Sometimes, Linge,' he said to his tall SS valet who accepted the lead dutifully now the exercise period was over, 'I agree with the Great Frederick – the more I see of people, the better I like dogs.'

'Yes, *mein Führer*,' Linge said solemnly.

Hitler patted Blondi on the back once more and then turned and walked back to his headquarters through the tall pines which sheltered 'Werewolf', as the Ukrainian HQ was called, from prying Soviet eyes.

The staff was waiting for him in the simply furnished log blockhouse which was the operations' room, and an irritated Hitler could see immediately that they had made no progress in the 'von Reichel affair', as it was now being called at the HQ.

He stalked by the high-ranking officers with their

purple-striped breeches and bemedalled chests and sat down at the head of the table. Without ceremony, he snapped, 'They've got his maps, haven't they, eh?'

Wooden-faced Field-Marshal Keitel, whose heavy chin looked as if it might have been cast in a foundry, said unhappily. I think so, *mein Führer*.'

Hitler's face contorted in a sneer. 'You *think* so, my dear Keitel.' He poked a thumb at his own chest. 'I *know* so! Have not the Reds a standing order that any captured German officer with the purple stripe of the General Staff down his trousers is to be treated like a king? They know, the NKVD, how to get information out of our people when they've captured them. Believe you me, those Red sadists could make even a mummy talk!'

One of the younger officers ventured a smile and Hitler froze him with a threatening look. On this particular November afternoon, the Führer was in no mood for joking. 'Our men in the Gestapo could learn a thing or two from the NKVD.' Hitler sighed. 'All right, I have already instigated court-martial proceedings against General Stumme. As corps commander he takes the final responsibility for the failings of his officers. Agreed?' He looked around the circle of well-fed faces.

Not one of them dared contradict him although they knew that this meant the end for a gallant officer who had fought bravely for Germany since 1939.

Hitler gave a cynical little smile, and told himself that he had tamed them, these fine officers, with their aristocratic ways and fancy manners. He had them in the palm of his hand. 'Good, then we can assume the worse. They know our exact dispositions. So what will the Reds do?' He answered his own question. 'I shall tell you, *meine Herren*. They will first select our weak spots. What are they?'

Again he answered his own question. 'Our Allies, the weakest link in the chain, those wretched Rumanians and Mussolini's shocking spaghetti-eaters.'

There was a mumble of agreement from the staff and

cunning-faced Colonel-General Jodl, Hitler's chief-of-operations, said, 'With permission, *mein Führer*, I would suggest the left flank.'

'Exactly, the Rumanian Third Army – the weakest spot in the whole front, gentlemen.' Hitler tugged the end of his nose thoughtfully. 'Now the Reds know our exact dispositions down to the level of division, we can expect them to do the following in order to relieve the pressure on Stalingrad. They will resort to their usual tactic of infiltration, probing for the best spot for a major attack. When they have found it, they will reinforce and build up rapidly and hit us hard with massed armour. Now we can't rely on the Rumanians to be able to recognize what the Reds are up to – their divisional staff officers are hopeless. No, gentlemen, we must have German troops up there in the north.'

'The barrel is empty,' Keitel replied hastily, preparing Hitler for the surprise Jodl was soon to spring on him. 'Our reserves are exhausted. Paulus's Sixth has eaten them all up completely.'

'Nonsense!' Hitler said sternly and Keitel's face flushed. He lowered his big, wooden head like a naughty child criticized by a village schoolmaster. 'Of course there are reserves. Order a comb-out of the army's rear echelon staff, taking only five per cent of the men employed – *supposedly* – there,' he sneered, 'and I wager you could form a new whole army. But no matter. I don't demand a large force. Just a highly mobile, experienced, motorized combat group, led by a resolute officer with extensive experience on the Eastern Front.' He leaned forward, giving them the full benefit of his confident, hypnotic eyes. 'I want the Führer's Fire Brigade dispatched to the Rumanians this very day. They'll do the job if anyone can. And I want them provided with the highest authority so that they can act completely independent of both Paulus and Dumitrescu. The Führer's Fire Brigade has not let me down yet, gentlemen,' he added with a smile at their surprised looks – they hadn't realized that he knew the nickname given to Harsch's elite hunting commando. 'And I doubt if it ever will.'

He started to rise to his feet, but Jodl interrupted him with a polite little cough, '*Mein Führer*,' he said carefully, as Hitler sat down again, 'we of the staff have been considering von Paulus's position in Stalingrad for three days now. In the light of a probable attack on our left flank, which if it only partially succeeded would cut Paulus off from his supplies so that the Luftwaffe would have to feed his men from the air, a very unlikely proposition –'

'*Um Himmelswillen!*' Hitler angrily interrupted the white-faced general. 'Don't be so damned long-winded! What do you want to say?'

'*Mein Führer*, why not withdraw from the Volga and abandon Stalingrad before it is too late?' Jodl blurted out his suggestion.

Hitler stared hard at the general while all round there was a shocked silence as the staff waited for the explosion which was sure to come.

But when Hitler spoke at last, his voice was soft and reasonable, yet there was no mistaking the determination and authority behind his words. 'Colonel-General Jodl, I would sooner take that pistol you bear at your side and blow a bullet through my brains than abandon Stalingrad.'

Jodl opened his mouth as if to speak, but Hitler waved him to be silent.

'There will be no arguments, Jodl. My mind is made up. There will be no withdrawal from Stalingrad as long as I am alive. Ensure that the Führer's Fire Brigade is given its marching orders immediately.' He rose to his feet. 'Gentlemen, I wish you a good afternoon.' Hitler strode out as his staff stiffened to attention.

For what seemed a long time they remained standing thus, like actors at the end of the first act of some nineteenth-century melodrama, until finally Jodl relaxed and said in a quiet little voice, as if he was talking about the state of the weather, '*Kameraden*, if the Ivans get through, it will mean the end of Stalingrad and four hundred thousand soldiers.' He hesitated a fraction of a second. 'It could well mean the end of Germany, too....'

5

The going was murderous. Doubled up against the wind that howled across the steppe at a hundred kilometres an hour the gulag rats toiled up the steep slope, each man blanketed in an icy cocoon of swirling, vicious white snowflakes.

They had been marching for three hours now, straight into the heart of the great snowstorm, the flakes penetrating every gap in their uniforms, making clumsy icy clumps of their boots, blinding them, whipping their crimson, streaming faces cruelly with razor-sharp particles. But still Katukov, marching at the head of the long strung-out column, would not allow his weary officers to halt the battalion.

'We must be well away from the Don by the time the Rumanians discover what happened at the river', he snarled angrily when Boldin had requested a stop.

'But comrade colonel,' Boldin had shouted his protest, 'I doubt if the Rumanians will venture out in this kind of weather, and if we go on much longer like this the men will begin falling out!'

'Then we will see what happens when that eventuality arrives,' had been Katukov's reply.

Now that eventuality had arrived. A senior sergeant from the rear company came staggering up out of the white, whirling fog, wheezing for breath like an ancient asthmatic, to report that five men had already fallen out and were refusing to move.

Katukov's expression did not change. 'Vulf,' he commanded, 'keep the companies moving. Boldin, you come with me.'

Together the two officers, their bodies bent against the wind, worked their way along that long line of human misery, the men not even turning to look at the passing officers, each one too preoccupied with his own wretchedness.

Captain Simonvitch, the commander of D Company, was waiting for them in the snow. At his feet were a handful of men some on their knees as if they were praying, others slumped full length in the snow, eyes closed, so that a causal observer might have thought they were asleep – or dead.

'I've tried everything to get them on their feet, comrade colonel,' he said anxiously, his eyes liquid with pain behind the pince-nez he wore. He had been a secondary-school teacher before one of his pupils had denounced him to the NKVD and he had been sent to the damps. 'Threats, pleas, promises,' he wrang his begloved hands like a mother over a naughty child.

Katukov ignored him. Standing there with the wind whipping his greatcoat against his tall, skinny frame, hovering above the fallen men, he cried, 'You are not to fall out, you scum, till I tell you to do so!' He aimed a kick at the nearest rat.

Boldin saw Simonvitch wince as the boot thudded into the fallen man's ribs. The ex-teacher felt for his rats. Indeed he treated his mixed collection of crooks and political prisoners like the kids he had once taught in happier days.

Pitifully, the wretch slumped in the snow raised his head, eyes blank of all emotion, even fear, and croaked, 'Can't go . . . on . . . finished . . . can't go on . . . .' He was too exhausted to complete the sentence. His head dropped once more.

Katukov raised his voice so that they could all hear. 'Listen, you parasites, I am not going to risk the success of this mission for rats like you. I know you – you'd sell your own mothers for a glass of vodka. None of you are going to spill your guts to the enemy if they find you.' He dropped his hand to his pistol-holster.

Simonvitch looked up at him in sudden alarm. 'What are you going to do, colonel?' he asked.

Katukov did not even look at the anxious captain. 'I'm going to give you up to three, and then anyone who is still not on his feet I'm going to shoot.'

'Colonel!' Boldin protested. 'These men are exhausted. You can't do this to them!'

'I can do exactly what I want, Major Boldin. My word is law. I have power of life and death over the scum which I have the misfortune to command.' Expertly he flicked off the holster catch and drew his pistol. '*One!*' he said loudly.

None of the wretches sprawled at his feet stirred.

'*Two!*'

Still there was no movement.

'*Three!*'

Katukov hesitated only an instant. Without appearing to aim, he jerked back the trigger. At his feet the man who had been kicked screamed with agony as the bullet, fired at such short range, blasted a huge hole in his back. His hands grabbed two handfuls of snow and he squeezed them hard in his death throes. His head lolled to one side and he was dead.

'In the name of God, you murdered him!' Simonvitch screeched. 'Murdered him in cold blood!'

'*Ruki nazad!*' Katukov commanded, using the old order from the gulag.

Shocked, Simonvitch placed his hands behind his back, as if he were a prisoner again, waiting the next order of the Greenhat in charge of him.

Katukov stepped over the dead man. 'All right, you have seen I am not making idle threats,' he said, his voice harsh and biting. 'Now, who is next? I warn you, I'd rather shoot every last one of you pigs than leave you here.'

The threat worked. Swaying like drunken men, their faces gleaming with white crystals that hung in thick profusion from eyebrows and moustaches, the exhausted men staggered to their feet and stumbled after the battalion.

Katukov watched them go for a minute, then turned to Boldin, putting his pistol back in its holster as he did so. 'Well?'

'Nothing,' Boldin said. His face revealed nothing of his feelings. With his foot, he started to push snow over the dead body. It would keep the wolves off for a while.

They came across the abandoned farm crouched in a group of firs sparkling a bright white in the gleaming new snow an hour after the snowstorm had stopped. By now even Colonel Katukov had had enough. After an officers' patrol – the officers being the only ones with any strength left – had ascertained that the tumbledown, straw-roofed farmhouse and barn were empty, he gave the command for the gulag rats to settle there for the night.

Now the fires were blazing everywhere, with the gulag rats warming their millet porridge over the flames, standing in weary lines to hold their canteens for a few minutes at the fires. Others were already slumped in the dirty straw, rolling cigarettes and drinking cold tea from their water-bottles, chatting softly with one another.

Boldin and Vulf, sipping in silence the last of the little intellectual's vodka mixed with cold tea, watched the ghost-like queues as they filed past, each face lit for a moment in the glow of the fires. It was a strange pageant of tough, rough, bearded faces: the faces of saints and sinners, Boldin couldn't help thinking, but gulag rats all, whatever their past crimes, condemned to sacrifice their lives out here in this white waste – for what? For Stalin, the man who had sent them to the camps, or for Mother Russia, the country which had created them? Boldin's brow creased in a worried, thoughtful frown. The same old questions had plagued him ever since he had allowed Katukov to recruit him from the gulag. He had still not found an answer after all these months in the line.

Glinka, the red-cheeked battalion comedian who affected an old-style drooping Cossack moustache which he called his 'tea-strainer', was going on about food in his usual cheerful manner. 'For *me*, comrades, food does not need to be of top quality like the Red Army throws away as waste. No, I'm so hungry most of the time, I could eat your smelly boots, Sasha, and wash them down with snow water!'

But this evening not even Corporal Glinka could raise much of a laugh. The march through the snowstorm had been too exhausting and the future out here behind the enemy lines too uncertain. The mood of the men lying in the straw was depressed. Indeed a couple of them were singing softly that melancholy soldiers' song 'The Dugout' with its sad, sentimental words of nostalgia and foreboding:

The flame flickers in the narrow stove.
On the log the resin glitters like a tear
And the accordion in my dugout
Sings to me of your eyes and your smile.
You are now far away, far away,
Between us there are hundreds of kilometres of snow.
You are so far, I cannot come to you
But death is outside, four paces away.
Sing, accordion, sing, defying the blizzard.
Call, call again for the happiness that has gone astray.
It is warm in this cold, cold dugout
It is warm with my undying love.

Boldin drained the last of his tea and vodka and told himself that there was something else, too. In spite of their exhaustion and depression, the rats were angry at the events of the afternoon. If Colonel Katukov pushed them much further, he could well have an open rebellion on his hands, and out here deep behind the Rumanian lines all the Greenhats in the world would not protect him from the gulag rats' wrath. He sniffed and dismissed the gloomy thought.

'Wipe the dewdrop off yer hooter, Sasha, or award yourself the Order of the Red Snot! By God, if you could see yersen in a mirror, comrade, you'd never comb yer hair with the light on ever agen!' Glinka laughed uproariously at his own joke.

Boldin buckled his water-bottle on to his belt, 'Vulf, give them thirty minutes more and then order the fires doused. They can be seen kilometres away.'

'*Horoscho*,' Vulf answered dutifully.

Five minutes later Boldin had settled down in the dirty straw next to Katukov, who sat there with his boots off to reveal that his foot-bandages were pink with blood – obviously the march had been too much even for is iron constitution – making a last study of his map by the fading light.

'Tomorrow?' Boldin asked.

Katukov raised his head and grunted, 'The same as today, I should expect, though now we are coming out of the hills, we can anticipate collective farms, inhabited by our own people. If they are patriots and not working with the fascists, I shouldn't be surprised if they couldn't give us the information we need about the presence of the Fritzes in this sector.'

'*If*,' Boldin said a little cynically. As cruel as the Fritzes had been, they had given the peasants back their land, taken off them by Stalin in the early thirties. Most of them, as a result, worked with Fritzes. 'How much further to the bridge at Kalach, colonel?' he added a moment later.

'Forty kilometres or thereabout. Two days' march in these conditions, Boldin.'

The big major looked up at the icy glitter of sky through a hole in the roof. It looked as if the storm had passed. The sky was cold, but clear. 'Yes, you could be right, colonel. With no more snow, we might do it.'

Katukov drew his greatcoat about him. 'We *will* do it,

comrade major,' he said coldly. 'Has not Comrade Stalin himself said recently that today an officer's order is an iron law. They obey . . . or they die! Good night.'

Katukov turned over and dragged his greatcoat over his ears. A minute later he was deep in an exhausted sleep. But Boldin could not go off so easily, in spite of his exhaustion. Whatever the solution to his question – did he serve Stalin or Russia? – might turn out to be, he knew his primary duty at this moment was to his men. Only he could prevent Katukov sacrificing their lives unnecessarily. From now on, he told himself, thinking of the NKVD colonel's last words – 'they obey, or they die' – he must be alert. As long as he lived, there would be no more shootings of helpless men lying in the snow.

At last sleep overcame Boldin. He, too, started to drift, barely hearing the soft crunch of the sentries' felt boots in the snow and a long, long way off a strange hissing sound, which he told himself must be in the wind. . . .

6

'Major!' the voice hissed urgently.

Boldin woke with a start. He stared wide-eyed into the gloom.

Corporal Glinka's face came into focus, the frost particles glittering in his eyebrows and moustache. 'What's going on?' Boldin said thickly and wiped a sabre-scarred hand across his scummed lips.

'There's somebody out there.'

'What!' Boldin sat up, suddenly very awake. 'Fritzes?'

'*Ya na snayu*,' Glinka shook his head. 'I don't know. All I know is that they're not our people.'

Hastily, Boldin pulled his boots from beneath his head and thanked God that they hadn't frozen up this time. 'Tell me, what gives?' he whispered urgently, pulling them on.

'Well, comrade,' Glinka said a little hesitantly, 'you know Glinka's guts – they're allus empty.'

'Get on with it!'

'I was on sentry patrol, comrade, when my hooter started to twitch, my belly began to growl, and the old jaw-water flooded my chops. Someone out there somewhere was cooking real meat, *real meat!*' He emphasized the words again, as if they were of vital importance.

'So old Glinka –'

'I'll tell you what old Glinka did,' Boldin interrupted him, hastily slipping into his greatcoat and buckling on his pistol holster. 'He left his post, an offence punishable by death on front-line service, and set off to look for the source of that cooking, eh?'

Glinka looked up at him, his head cocked to one side

in the comical manner he had and said, 'My family was always known as 'the locusts' back home before we got sent to the camps. There was nothing to stop us when we scented vittels.'

In spite of his tension, Boldin grinned. 'All right, locust, what did you discover?'

'There's a camp out there. Ski troops to judge by the skis parked everywhere, all set up in nice little tents like a lot of shitting Young Pioneers,* cooking their *real* meat as if it grew on trees, with not a care in the world. There was even one of the greedy swine singing as he filled his mean guts.'

'What language?'

'None that I could identify, comrade,' Glinka said, suddenly gloomy. 'All that *real* meat. By the Holy Virgin, it's enough to sicken a fellow of humanity! It really is!'

Boldin laughed softly and pulled on his fur cap. 'Come on, locust, we'll go and have a look at these *real* meat-eaters of yours.'

Silhouetted against the silver light of the stars and the dying flames of their cooking fires, Major Boldin could just make out the soldiers who were now beginning to creep into their four-men tents, while a handful of others, sub-machine-guns slung over their chests, were spreading out around the camp at an officer's order.

Occasional snatches of conversation drifted across the snowy steppe, but all that the men crouching there in the firs could make of it was that the language wasn't Russian. With frozen fingers Boldin adjusted his night glasses in an attempt to make out the strangers' uniforms. But in that light he could not distinguish them until he spotted the tall plume rising from the hat of the officer issuing the orders to the sentries. 'Of course,' he said, 'the Alpini.'

Next to him Glinka whispered, 'What lot are they,

* Soviet Youth Organization

comrade? I thought the English were on our side?'

Boldin laughed. 'No, they're not English, they're Italians.'

'Oh, Musso's boys,' Glinka said, a little relieved. 'They tell me that lot takes their boots off so that they can run faster.'

Boldin shook his head, the smile gone from his face. 'Not those Italians, Glinka. They're Mussolini's elite, the mountain troops. They won't run so easily, believe you me.' He made a hasty count of the number of tents, assessing that each one could hold four men. As there were over a hundred of them, he estimated swiftly that the Alpini were in half-battalion strength. He had seen enough, 'Come on, Glinka, come on. We'd better get back and inform the colonel.'

Glinka pulled a face. 'That's why I woke you, comrade major. You know that Greenhat. He'll be after them like a skinny dog after a fat bone.'

'Perhaps, but there's no other way. As soon as it's light, they'll spot us anyway, and we wouldn't have much of a chance if they come after us on skis.'

Glinka nodded. 'Oh, well,' he whispered, as they started to crawl back the way they had come, 'there might be a bit of grub left over for us in the morning over there.'

Boldin shook his head in mock wonder. 'One day,' he said, 'that skinny gut of yours will be the death of you.'

It was nearly dawn. To the east, the dull white of the sky was beginning to give way to the faint pink of the winter sun still hidden beyond the horizon, but already beginning to flush the snow a dramatic blood-red.

For two hours, the gulag rats had been crawling into their positions until now they surrounded the unsuspecting Italian camp. Their anger and foreboding of the previous day was forgotten at the prospect of the loot and other pickings they might find in the enemy tents.

Together with Katukov, Boldin and Vulf surveyed the

tented camp. Apart from the sentries who were now beginning to gather wood for the morning fires, the Italians slept on. 'They must think this is peacetime,' Vulf commented cynically. 'I wouldn't be surprised if they didn't have a danmed bugler to sound reveille.'

'As far as they're concerned,' Boldin said, 'they are deep behind their own lines. Why should they take more than normal precautions against partisans, if such creatures exist in this part of Occupied Russia?' he added for Katukov's benefit.

The grey-eyed colonel frowned at him, but made no comment. Obviously he knew, too, that most of the local peasants supported the enemy; there were no partisans in this part of the Don Basin. 'Remember, no one is to escape to report our presence behind the Rumanian lines. Clear?'

'Clear,' the other two answered dutifully.

'The main thing is to keep them away from those skis of theirs. Once they get them on, we've lost them.'

'Don't worry, comrade colonel,' Boldin reassured him, 'we'll see they keep away from the boards.' He rose to his feet. Behind him was his group of Volga Germans, all of whom spoke the German dialect of their peasant forefathers who had come to Russia at the invitation of Catherine the Great in the eighteenth century. 'Shoulder your weapons,' he ordered. The men did as he commanded.

Vulf looked at Boldin as if to say, shall I come with you, little brother?

Boldin shook his head and glanced at Katukov who was now engrossed in the scene to his front. Vulf nodded his understanding. Boldin's look read: 'Keep your eye on the Greenhat; ensure that he doesn't sacrifice the rats unnecessarily.'

Slowly the little group of rats in their German uniforms began to plod across the snow straight towards the tents, while behind the snow-dunes their comrades waited in tense anticipation, knowing that if anything went wrong with Katukov's plan they were dead men.

It seemed to take the Italian sentries an age to spot them. Indeed, they were only fifty metres from the first tent before a sharp voice cried, '*Alto!*'

Boldin halted. Behind him, his men did the same. A dark-faced man with a great beak of a nose was staring at them hard, sub-machine-gun levelled in the direction of Boldin's grey-clad chest.

Boldin tried to forget that one wrong move and the little Italian could rip him apart at that range. He drew himself to his full height and called as haughtily as he could, '*Italianer, sprechen Sie deutsch?*'

'*Como?*' the sentry asked, obviously uneasy in the presence of what looked like a German officer. '*Que dice?*'

'*Offizier . . . bringen Sie mich zum Offizier*,' Boldin barked in his best German officer manner. '*Warum stehen Sie noch da?*'

'*Si, si, prego*.' The sentry dropped his weapon a little and indicated they they should advance closer.

'Get ready to run,' Boldin commanded out of the side of his mouth, 'and then hit the dirt – *quick!*'

Striding forward as if he were Hitler himself, Boldin advanced closer to the camp, noting that more and more Italians were emerging into the new day, shivering and slapping their arms about their bodies, their breath a thick grey on the icy air. Now the piles of skis were only a matter of twenty or thirty metres away. They were going to pull it off.

It was just then that an officer came out of a tent to Boldin's right. He paused there, more wide awake than his men, the look of suspicion on his face obvious even at that distance. He opened his mouth to order something. Boldin knew they had been discovered. He didn't wait for the Italian to sound the alarm. Instead he bellowed, '*At the double, comrades!*'

His men needed no urging. They knew what was at stake. They pelted forwards towards the piled skis as the first wild shots erupted and the Alpini were flinging themselves down for cover in the snow.

Now all around the camp the rats rose from their hiding places. Their bayonets flashed in the first slanting rays of the new sun. '*Urrah!*' they cried bravely, and started advancing through the knee-deep snow in the very same instant that Boldin and his Germans flung themselves down around the skis and, panting crazily, began to answer the Italian fire as best they could, slugs striking up flurries of snow all around them.

Teniente Goldwasser knew instinctively that the companies had run into bad trouble. He had just been strapping on his ski boots in the tent that none of his brother officers would share with him because they maintained he was a Jew – which he was, though for his own safety he always stated that he was from the South Tyrol where half the population had German names and were German-speaking – when the confused firing had broken out, punctuated by hoarse cries and commands in a language that could only be Russian. He didn't hesitate. Loosening the pistol in his holster, he dragged his skis from beneath his bedroll – like any other Jew living in a fascist country in the year of 1942 he was prepared for any emergency – and started strapping them on, while the cries in Russian grew louder and louder. Then he was ready. With his knife he slashed open the back of the tent. He gasped at the sight of the Russian infantry stumbling clumsily through the deep snow, men falling here and there all along their line, but still coming on all the same, as if nothing could stop them.

Teniente Goldwasser was no hero. He had joined the Alpini because he was an expert skier and liked to ski, and because the uniform was very attractive to the prettier daughters of well-off middle-class families in the capital. Looking round the centre of the camp, he saw immediately that his comrades were trapped. There were already Russians surrounding the skis. Bodies lay writhing and moaning in the snow everywhere.

Now it was every man for himself. *Sauve qui peut.*

Goldwasser seized his poles. There was a slight downward slope behind his tent. It would give him the opportunity to gain speed almost at once. He took a deep breath, counted to three, and then with a grunt thrust himself forward. There was no going back now.

The advancing Russians saw him almost at once, the lone figure hissing across the white surface of the snow, escaping the confused fighting of the camp. 'Stop him!' the cries went up on all sides.

Half a dozen Russians kneeling in the snow began to pump fire at the man whizzing at them. Desperately, Goldwasser zigzagged from side to side, exerting all his skill, his body crouched low as he swept ever nearer, the bullets tugging and plucking frighteningly at his uniform.

Angrily Colonel Katukov took aim, feet spread apart, hand clasped on his hip, as if he were on some peacetime firing-range. The pistol jerked in his hand. Goldwasser yelped with pain and staggered alarmingly.

There was a ragged cheer from the gulag rats. 'You've got him, comrade!' Simonvitch yelled.

The men kneeling in the snow ceased firing. The Italian was obviously finished.

Goldwasser knew he wouldn't get a second chance. He straightened up immediately and thrust forward with all his strength, forgetting the burning pain in his arm where the Russian bullet had struck him. A bearded, angry face under a fur cap loomed up directly in front of him. Hardly aware of what he was doing, Goldwasser struck out with his ski pole.

The gulag rat screamed shrilly and went reeling back into the snow, the cruelly spiked pole sticking out of his eye, and then Goldwasser was through, careening crazily down the long slope ahead with his one remaining pole, the bullets striking up the snow behind him to no purpose. . . .

* * *

They were slaughtering the survivors now. In silence Boldin and Katukov watched as the rats, most of them a little drunk on the looted Chianti, streamed after a half-naked Alpini, yelling drunken obscenities, as the little Italian cut in and out of the tents. And then they trapped him. . . .

'Animals,' Simonvitch said thickly and turned away in disgust, tears gleaming behind his pince-nez. 'Revolting animals! What gets into men like that?'

Vulf shrugged cynically. 'Booze,' he said. 'What else do you expect, my tender-hearted friend? They are the gulag rats after all, aren't they?'

Boldin ignored Vulf's comment, just as he ignored the burly gulag rat with the tattooed face of the professional criminal who, with one booted foot planted on a dead Italian officer's chest, was expertly extracting his gold teeth, one after the other, chuckling with delight at his good fortune. The men were brutalized beyond words. Could one expect them to be any different after the years in the camps and these last two years at the front? They had been conditioned to kill in the most bestial way, and all of them knew in their heart of hearts that that was how they would end themselves sooner or later.

With disgust and disdain written all over his face, Boldin turned to Katukov and asked; 'What now?'

Katukov took his grey gaze off a gulag rat attempting to saw a dead Italian's finger off with his bayonet in order to obtain the golden wedding ring it bore. 'What do you mean – what now?' he demanded.

Boldin shrugged carelessly, as if the matter really didn't matter very much to him, but still it had to be faced up to. 'One of the Italians got away. Undoubtedly he will report to some authority sooner or later.'

'Report what?'

'That his force was attacked by troops wearing German uniforms. Even the stupid Rumanians will be able to work out what such a disguised force is doing so far behind their lines. Result: they'll come looking for us in force.' He nodded at the harsh, blue winter sky with not a snow-cloud in sight. 'Perfect flying weather. They'll have their spotter planes up within hours of that Italian's contacting his own people.'

Katukov bit his bottom lip as if he had just realized the full impact of Boldin's words.

'There is still time, comrade colonel.'

'Time?' Katukov echoed.

'Yes, to turn back. We don't stand a chance in hell if the planes find us out here. It'll be a massacre.'

'Impossible!' Katokov snorted. 'We haven't finished our mission yet. We do not turn back until we reach that bridge and complete our reconnaissance of the terrain.'

'Dead men don't do much marching.'

'Nonsense,' Katukov said, 'we'll find cover by day and march at night. Soon we should come across our own civilians – they will provide the hiding places we will need.'

Boldin shrugged. 'As you command, comrade colonel.'

Five minutes later they set off again, an insignificant black worm of men trailing across that infinite, sparkling white plain with a drunken Glinka singing happily, '*Oh, dear comrades, oh, how I'm gonna enjoy being dead . . .*'

7

'The place is inhabited, all right,' Katukov concluded.

'Yes,' Vulf agreed while Boldin continued to study the collective farm in silence. 'You'd think it was peacetime down there, comrade colonel.'

Boldin was tempted to agree. Smoke curled lazily from the little brick houses that surrounded the long low farm of the kind built in the early thirties when Stalin had ordered the collectivization of Soviet agriculture, killing millions of *kulaks* in the process. Boldin could hear the soft lowing of the cows within the barns and a cock crowed triumphantly somewhere. It was indeed all very peaceful, as if the greatest war in history were a million kilometres away and not a mere hundred.

'All right,' Katukov commanded, 'we move in and spend the day there. We march again tonight.'

The company commanders doubled-off back to their companies to carry out the big colonel's orders and Katukov turned to Boldin and Vulf. 'We go in alone. We speak German just in case . . . .' He didn't finish the sentence, but the other two knew well what he meant. A place like that couldn't thrive so peacefully unless it was under German protection.

Ten minutes later their guess was confirmed when dogs and excited children started to stream up the road to meet the column. In their midst a tall man bore the traditional gift of bread, flanked by two pretty girls with braided hair and in peasant costume, carrying bowls of milk.

'But they can see we're Fritzes!' Katukov snorted in exasperation, not wishing to believe what he knew was true: the peasants were indeed colloborating with the enemy.

'Perhaps they're really partisans,' Vulf said, tongue in cheek, enjoying Katukov's discomforture, 'just waiting for the right moment to attack us.'

Katukov flashed him an angry look. 'We'll play their evil game for a while,' he said through gritted teeth. 'But by God before we leave this night, they'll be taught their lesson! I'll root out these traitors once and for all!'

'*Willkommen, Kameraden*,' the big civilian bearing the bread and salt said in heavily accented German, while the two pretty girls gave a little curtsy to an icy-faced Katukov.

While Boldin and Vulf hid their grins, the civilian tore off a chunk of bread, spread some salt over it in the traditional fashion and handed it to Katukov to eat. '*Essen*,' he commanded.

Katukov choked the piece down and accepted a drink of milk from one of the girls who smiled up winningly at him.

Boldin and Vulf accepted their food and drink too, and Boldin said, this time in Russian, 'Thank you, comrade. Your name?'

'You speak good Russian,' the civilian said, accepting the fact without wonder in the peasant fashion. 'My name is Dudinka, comrade. The people have elected me to be their headman, now that our *natshalnik** has run away.' He gave them a good-humoured smile, as if they knew why he had run off. 'But come comrades, we have room enough to shelter you from this cold. Our food is limited, though.'

'Don't worry,' Boldin reassured the peasant with the strong, generous face, 'we have food enough to supply ourselves.'

'That is good,' Dudinka said, obviously relieved. He turned to the children, who were staring at the soldiers wide-eyed and open-mouthed, 'Hurry, you little brats!

* Boss.

Be off with you and warn your mothers to get the kettles boiling. Our German comrades will need hot water for their tea!'

Katukov gave a strangled moan at the words 'German comrades', and a grinning Vulf thought the big crimson-faced colonel looked as if he might have a heart-attack at any moment. 'You poor bastards,' he told himself as they started to march towards the farm, their approach heralded by the yelling children running towards the houses and the barking dogs which had appeared suddenly everywhere. 'Katukov's going to toast your balls for this, by God he is!'

'That was our *natshalnik*,' Dudinka said, pointing a calloused finger at the man standing in front of a gleaming new tractor in the centre of yellowing photograph. 'He picked up his heels and ran off when you Germans were over a hundred kilometres away, the bastard!' He spat contemptuously on the floor of the former chairman's office.

Boldin sipped his scalding tea and surveyed the photograph. In spite of its poor quality, he could see that the party official who had run the farm for Moscow had never missed a meal in all his life, unlike the ragged peasants with their wicker-work shoes who now thronged the square outside, chatting with the soldiers and serving them hot water for their tea from great steaming cauldrons.

'He had no neck, like all those Party bosses,' the peasant said. 'All he did was read *Pravda*, talk on the telephone,' he indicated the old-fashioned instrument on the desk, 'and drink tea *with sugar!*' He emphasized the words, as if they were the height of decadent luxury.

Boldin smiled. 'What happened when the Fr – when we Germans came?'

'It was not too bad, comrade. They hanged one or two of the little *natshalniks* who were in the Party. A couple of them got drunk and raped widow Zhukova, though I don't suppose she minded much. I wager she hadn't had it these twenty years and more than once she's offered one of the farm lads a few kopecks to come and help her out.' He winked knowingly at Boldin, who grinned back at him. Boldin liked the big peasant with the grizzled hair and weathered face of a man who had worked hard all his life in the outdoors.

'And then?'

'They went away and left us to get on with things the best we could. So the others elected me. But I'm no *natshalnik*,' he added hastily. 'I just organize the plant. Now each and every one of us farms for himself like we did in the old days before that monster in the Kremlin entered our poor lives.' Boldin handed him a cigarette and he nodded his thanks. 'I know not what kind of man your Hitler is, but I tell you this, comrade, there is nothing more precious than freedom! Poor we are, but we are free.' He lit the *Kasbek* cigarette with a flourish and breathed out a stream of blue smoke. 'I think it is better to be dead than not free, comrade.'

Boldin turned away hastily so that the big peasant should not see the look on his face at that moment.

'So, so,' Katukov said, as Boldin reported his news, 'the Fritzes came and went and left the treacherous swine in peace. And have there been Fritzes here since?'

'No, apparently not. Occasionally a few Rumanians have passed through, demanding food and the like, but when the peasants could show they had little more than eggs and a few scraggy chickens – they'd hidden their cows and horses, needless to say – they passed on and left them in peace.'

Katukov frowned out of the window at his men chatting to the peasant girls or lounging in the square, smoking their cigarettes and eyeing the little *isbas* as if they were calculating how much loot the poverty-stricken thatched houses might possibly contain. 'In peace,' he echoed. 'Yes, that's just what those *kulak* pigs would like, eh? To be left here to feed their miserable faces on the fat of the land, trying to forget what is happening outside, while the Soviet Fatherland bleeds to death and millions of brave soldiers die for them!'

'For *them?*' Vulf snapped, his weak eyes blazing behind the thick hornrims. Boldin flashed him a warning look.

'We Russians are not dying for common *kulaks* like that, comrade colonel,' he said with surprising boldness. All round, the company commanders tensed.

'What do you mean, comrade lieutenant?' Katukov barked.

'I mean, they, we, all of us – we're dying for one thing only! We're dying for Old Leather Face. It is as simple as that, comrade.' He stared defiantly at Katukov. 'I don't think you are an unintelligent man, although you are a Greenhat. You must understand *that!* We are all being sacrificed in the name of greed, power, ambition – the greed, the power, the ambition of that man in the Kremlin!'

Katukov did not react in the manner that the officers expected. He did not explode or roar with fury at the little red-faced intellectual, whose skinny chest heaved violently, as if he had just run a great race. Instead he said, his voice icy but calm, 'Comrade Vulf, I know you were sent to the gulag because of political crimes –'

'Yes,' Vulf sneered, 'I told my students that the sun didn't exactly shine out of Stalin's arse, or words to that effect. If you can call that a political crime!'

Katukov ignored the interruption. 'But I had thought that you had conquered that, overcome what one might call the follies of youth. I see now that I am wrong. You are as opposed to our great Soviet system *now* as you were in that year of 1939 when the judges were wise enough to sentence you to ten years in the camps. You are just as much a traitor as those peasant swine out there. The only difference between you and them is that they are traitors to our beloved Soviet Fatherland with their bellies, you do so with your head – and that is far, far more dangerous.'

'And what are you going to do about it, Katukov?' Vulf said boldly, too carried away with anger to be afraid now.

Katukov remained icily calm. His hand dropped down to his holster. 'What we of the NKVD always do with traitors, Vulf. I can – and will, if necessary – shoot you.' He made the threat with a voice that was completely devoid of emotion.

Vulf laughed suddenly and Boldin felt a cold finger of fear trace its way down his spine at that strange sound in that place. Vulf was deliberately challenging Katukov. This was the moment of truth.

'My dear Katukov,' he said very grandly, 'how many Greenhats are there here in this God-forsaken place?'

'What in three devils' name is that supposed to mean?'

'This! There is only one of you. There are eight hundred of us. The odds are slightly in our favour.'

Katukov looked down at the skinny little Vulf from his great height, and although Boldin hated all that he stood for, he could not help but admire him. The colonel was completely unafraid, in spite of the fact that he had to know that Vulf was right. 'So that's it, is it?' he said coolly. 'You are relying on that scum out there, are you, *Comrade* Vulf? You think they are going to support you.' He swung round on the other officers who stood there, faces frozen, holding their breath expectantly. 'Or any of you others, for that matter, eh?' He laughed scornfully. 'You think there is honour among thieves, Vulf. Well, you're wrong. Badly wrong.' He flashed a glance at his watch. In an hour it would be dark. The former collective farm had outlived its usefulnesss. He could act now and show these rebellious swine how vain their hopes really were. Without another word, he strode to the window and ripped it open, sending the snow showering everywhere.

'What are you going to do, comrade colonel?' Boldin asked in alarm.

Katukov ignored him. Instead he leaned out and cried: 'Hey, you scum!'

Everywhere heads turned in his direction. Senior NCOs threw away their cigarettes and snapped to attention.

'They have vodka here, hidden, of course, and they have food!' Katukov cried. 'Take it!'

There was a low cheer from the gulag rats and a moan from the civilians present, followed by cries of protest and fear.

'The women, too, they're yours!' Katukov yelled. 'Do with them what you will. But afterwards, destroy everything. Two of you to a house, smash everything! Windows, doors, gates, chairs, pots – *everything*. Leave them nothing. Not even a pot to piss in!'

A cry rose on all sides as the gulag rats broke ranks, streaming into the narrow lanes between the houses and the farm, pulling out their bayonets and entrenching tools as they ran, slashing at picket fences and smashing in doors and windows. Children screamed and ran for cover. Women fell to their knees and prayed for mercy. But there was none to be had. Everywhere gulag rats flung women to the ground, tossed up their skirts and raped them.

They found the collective's supply of vodka, great fifty-litre carboys in wickerwork cases. With their rifle butts they smashed off the necks and grunting mightily poured the fiery spirit down their throats, the liquid running down their unshaven chins and staining the front of their blouses.

Drunk now, they began to splash kerosene from the farm's store on to the straw roofs of the *isbas*. When the peasants tried to stop them, a rifle butt smashed into the protestors' faces put an end to their cries.

The first wisp of grey smoke streaked upwards, becoming scarlet angry flame almost instantly, hissing from roof to roof, the straw crackling wildly. The drunken soldiers staggered backwards, their faces seared by the tremendous heat. Above them, black smoke thrashed and writhed, swinging evilly to the horizon.

Mesmerized like the rest, Boldin watched as a lone figure ran screaming towards the soldiers, a hayfork in his hands, zigzagging in between the dying on the ground. It was Dudinka, the man who less than a couple of hours before had told him it would be better to be dead than unfree. '*No!*' Boldin called aloud, feeling the nails of his right hand bite deep into the palm of his other hand. 'No, don't do it, man!'

But it was too late. Dudinka lunged with his hayfork in the way he had been heaving hay on board the hay-cart these last forty years. A gulag rat holding an empty can of kerosene screamed shrilly as the six prongs sank deep into his back. His can fell from nerveless fingers and he sank to his knees, head bent as if he were in prayer. The prongs came out gleaming bright, wet-red in the wild light of the ever-growing flames.

The rats were on Dudinka before he could strike again, smashing their rifle butts into his big body. Vainly the civilian tried to keep on his feet. To no avail. They hammered him to the ground, and he disappeared beneath their flailing feet. Boldin turned away, sickened.

'So you see, *comrades*,' Katukov sneered over the word, 'if you want to kill me, you will have to do it without the aid of that drunken scum out there.' He jerked his head contemptuously at the gulag rats now being kicked into the column once more, their faces sullen and hangdog after the destruction of the village which still burnt softly in the background, the crackle of the flames punctuated by the sobs of the abused women and the moans of the wounded. 'They are out for themselves, each and every one of them. The only thing which keeps them together is fear – fear of me!'

Boldin was overcome by an overwhelming loneliness,

the desolation of the winter world and himself. Around him his fellow officers looked numbly at their boots, not able to face that coldly triumphant face.

Katukov raised his voice. 'All right, we go, *comrades*. But remember this, from now onwards in Punishment Battalion 333, it is march or croak. . . . *Forward!*'

BOOK TWO

The Bridge at Kalach

1

'Champers, Igor!' *Obersturmbannführer* Harsch ordered his Ukrainian batman, who had been watching the removal of the bullet from *Teniente* Goldwasser's arm with fascinated eyes.

'*Mais non, mon colonel*,' Duclos, the Fire Brigade's doctor protested, dropping his surgical scissors on to the table of the little peasant cottage which housed Harsch's HQ. '*Il est blessé.*' He tapped the bandage lightly and immediately it stained pink.

'Perk him up, I shouldn't wonder,' Harsch said lightly and with his one hand swung the broken infantry sword that he had carried with him now for three years of war.

Igor came in, rubbing the snow off the bottle of champagne and began pouring out three mugs of bubbling, pale-yellow liquid.

Harsch accepted his eagerly. 'Champers, best drink in the world, gentlemen.' He raised his mug, 'Up the cups,' he toasted, 'the night's going to be cold! *Prost!*'

'*Prost*,' the other two said a little reluctantly and sipped their champagne, watching the big scar-faced SS officer with the cropped hair drain his as if he were very thirsty.

'So,' Harsch said, picking up his sword again and swinging it to and fro happily, 'your companies were attacked by a group of Russians. You are sure they were regular Russian troops and not those damned, sneaking partisans?'

'*Jawohl Obersturmbannführer*,' Goldwasser said in his thick Tyrolean German. 'They were in uniform.'

'Good. How many?'

Goldwasser shrugged, winced with pain, and wished

he hadn't. 'My guess would be about a battalion. They swamped the Alpini – and there were four hundred of us.'

'I see.' Harsch nodded to a waiting Igor. The squat Ukrainian, who was one of a dozen different nationalities which made up the Führer's Fire Brigade, refilled the mugs.

For a while the three of them drank in silence while outside the storm howled and the drivers of the half-tracks turned over their motors once again to prevent them freezing up in the bitter cold. Harsch told himself that his men would need an extra ration of *schnaps* before the night was out. Then he walked over to the table, on which was spread his map, and stared down at it hard, swinging the broken sword, which was his habit when he was thinking.

Now as he stared down at the map of the Don Basin, covered with a rash of blue and red pencil marks, the pieces of the jigsaw puzzle began to make some sense in his mind. The Ivans who had attacked the Alpini had to be the same ones who had swept through the Rumanian positions on the Don; only half an hour before the wounded Goldwasser had staggered into their camp, the Luftwaffe had reported one of the freed farms burning in the middle of the steppe.

He put the blade of his sword on the map and traced an imaginary line along it, from the Don to the spot on the steppe where the farm had been. Yes, they had to be the same Ivans. But where were they heading? He frowned, following the course of his sword-blade until its jagged edge rested on the River Don once more, close to the small town of Kalach. Of course! The link between the Rumanian Third Army and von Paulus's Sixth – *the bridge at Kalach!*

'*Meine Herren*,' he said briskly, 'I think we shall call an end to the doctoring for this night.'

Duclos put down his mug. 'We march, *mon colonel*?' asked the former French army doctor, who had volunteered for the SS from a POW camp.

'Yes. I think I know where those Ivans are heading – and I want to be there before them.'

Goldwasser straightened up in his chair. '*Obersturmbannführer*, would you take me with you?' He hesitated, his mind a mixture of fear and hatred at the outrage the Russians had committed on the Alpini. 'I have a score to pay back.'

Harsch opened his mouth to refuse, then he laughed in that cynical manner of his and tucked his empty sleeve into his belt in preparation for the move. 'Why not, Goldwasser, eh? The Führer's Fire Brigade is a home for half the rogues of Europe. Might as well have a Jew in it as well!' Laughing uproariously, the big one-armed SS officer drained the last of his champers and went out into the howling night.

Obersturmbannführer Harsch had lost his arm in the abortive drive on Moscow in December 1941. His company had been ambushed by a whole regiment of Siberian riflemen. For ten hours he had held them off and then, with a handful of survivors, he had broken out of the trap, his shattered arm hanging by a few shreds of flesh. They had begun the long trek through the snowbound countryside trying to find the broken, retreating German army which had attempted to capture the Soviet capital and failed.

On the first day of that terrible trek, five of his men had died of exhaustion and he had sawed off the arm with an infantry bayonet, his teeth biting into a cartridge to prevent him screaming out loud and revealing their position to the Russian scouts who seemed to be everywhere in the whirling white waste.

On the second day, two of his men went mad with the strain and a third wandered off, his end announced by one lone shot; on the third day the remaining two men killed themselves in a suicide pact and he was alone and weaponless save the broken sword that had belonged to his grandfather. For two further days he staggered, and in the end crawled through that desolate Russian wilderness, the cruel white world glimpsed through a red mist of agony, half-conscious most of the time. Finally he was picked by a paymaster and his staff who had gone back in the wake of the retreating army to loot the war chest left behind by one of the infantry divisions.

Three months he had lain in the Charité Hospital in Berlin while the great Professor Sauerbruch himself had attended to his self-amputated arm and lesser surgeons had removed his frost-bitten toes. 'I mean, what use are the damn little pinkies anyway?' he had said easily when Sauerbruch had revealed to him that the green, suppurating, stinking pieces of flesh would have to go. 'At least, *Herr Professor,* I'll be able to take a size smaller in shoes now.' Then he had been discharged into a military world which apparently no longer needed his services.

For a month he had hobbled around Berlin on his canes, with the Knight's Cross of the Iron Cross at his throat, trying to obtain a new command, being dismissed politely but firmly everywhere as unemployable at the front.

Himmler, the chief of the SS, had even suggested he should request his release from the Black Guards and apply to run one of the stud farms for willing German maidens and the 'blonde beasts' on leave from the front that he was currently setting up in suitably remote areas of the Reich. They were to provide the Führer with 'the master race of the future'. . . .

'Pimping for those plain-faced horrors of Hitler maidens!' he had exploded to his cronies of the surgical ward afterwards, '*Gott im Himmel*, I'd rather offer my arse to you lot of vaseline merchants than that!'

But that eventuality had not come about. In the summer of 1942 when the casualties on the Russian Front began to run into hundreds of thousands, someone on Himmler's planning staff came to the conclusion that not only Germans were 'Aryans', but also Belgians, Dutchmen, Norwegians, even Frenchmen and Belgians too – Ukrainians as well, if one closed an eye to those high slavic cheekbones which marked a 'sub-human' and 'third-class citizen'.

By the end of July 1942, *Obersturmbannführer* Harsch found himself in command of a battlegroup of new SS men, recruited from over half of Europe, its ranks filled with eager, bold youths, desperate to die in the great 'European crusade against the Soviet animal'.

And die they did, in half a dozen bold missions behind the Russian lines which made the headlines in the daily newspapers back in the Reich and gained for Harsch and his new command the nickname, 'the Führer's Fire Brigade'.

This, then, was the man that Hitler had sent out, unwittingly, to stop the gulag rats: big, tough, cynical, an officer who knew he would not survive his war, just as his grandfather and his father had not survived their wars before him; but an officer who would sell his life and that of his men dearly. . . .

2

Obersturmbannführer Harsch was not the only one that night who was interested in the whereabouts of Colonel Katukov and his vaunted gulag rats. Many hundreds of kilometres behind the front, the Soviet dictator, Stalin, faced his greasy-haired chief of secret police, Beria, and asked that overwhelming question – the one that was being asked everywhere that first week of November 1942 in the offices of the *Stavka*:* 'Are the Fritzes backing up the Rumanian fascists or are they not, Comrade Beria?' He sucked at his curved pipe and looked at his fellow Georgian with those dark, cunning eyes of his. 'What news do you have of this Colonel . . . Kutukov of yours?'

Beria dabbed his brow with his cologne-soaked handkerchief, as scared of the dictator as were the young virgins Stalin was in the habit of dragging from the streets of Moscow – 'the green fruit', he called them. 'Little, comrade secretary,' Beria confessed in an anxious voice.

'How little, my dear comrade?' Stalin asked, his voice silk-soft, his eyes twinkling in that avuncular manner depicted in the standard portrait of him that adorned every Party office wall and 'House of Culture' throughout the Soviet Union. 'Be so good as to tell me, comrade.'

Beria extended his hands outwards in the Georgian fashion. 'I must confess that since he and his battalion broke through the Rumanian fascists' line on the Don, we have heard nothing from him.'

* The Supreme Soviet Command

'Do you think he has gone over to the Fritzes?' Stalin asked, bending forward in the throne-like chair that glittered under the great czarist candelabra above his head. 'After all, his command consists of known traitors.'

Beria shook his head with more confidence than he felt. His own word was all-powerful in Russia, but he knew the pock-marked dictator had more power than he would ever possess. The executioners with the heavy pistols could appear the moment Stalin clapped his hands together. 'No, comrade. He is a strange one, not at all your typical NKVD man. . . . But one thing is certain, he has ambition, an appetite for glory.' He smiled suddenly at the memory of the day he had summoned the tall, grey-eyed colonel to his office in 1941 and ordered him to form the gulag rats from the scum of the camps* to defend the hard-pressed capital. 'Oh yes, glory means more to him than his very life, that one.'

Stalin, sucking at his pipe, considered the information. Finally he said, 'Time is running out, comrade. We must hurry your Greenhat along. What do you think would do the trick, eh – a bauble for the breast or pepper up the arse?' His eyes narrowed cunningly as he stared at Beria and left him to make the decision: medal or bullet.

Beria screwed up his face and tried desperately to out-think the pock-marked monster facing him. Katukov was loyal, he knew that well enough. That one would never falter in his duty in spite of the fact that his command was composed of criminals and traitors, but cut off behind enemy lines there was no one with the knout to make him move more quickly.

'Time is running out,' Stalin said once again.

Beria made up his mind. 'Comrade, I am sure that we can rely on Katukov one hundred per cent, but just to ensure that he realizes the full urgency of his mission, I shall send him an emissary.'

'An emissary?'

* See *Baptism of Blood* for further details

'Yes, from Smersh.'

Stalin beamed. 'Smersh, eh. So it is to be the bullet after all, Beria?'

Beria nodded slowly, knowing that his hand had been forced. 'Yes, comrade, if necessary, it will be the bullet. . . .'

Now north of the Don, the Red Army continued their build-up. At night long trains steamed into the make-shift stations from Moscow and even from the Urals, laden with fresh troops. Heavy artillery by the hundreds, thousands of tanks, tens of thousands of fresh horses for the cavalry were brought in on flat cars on the lines running to Serafimovich and Kletskaya. Tirelessly, the *politruks* worked on the men of the attack armies, infusing them with the necessary fanaticism they would need to lay down their lives for Stalin, as undoubtedly many thousands of them would. Each new reinforcement was paraded before the banners of his regiment to receive his rifle or sub-machine-gun in a formal ceremony. The brass bands blared, martial songs were sung by the soldiers' choirs, and Party officials read out fiery speeches on the vital need for devotion to the Soviet Fatherland to the ranks of grey-clad soldiers standing to attention in the deep snow, their breaths fogging on the icy air.

As the men and materials moved inexorably towards the new front, German intelligence could not fail to see their spoors. Reconnaissance plans spotted the new concentrations, Russian deserters told interrogators of the arrival of new divisions from the east, deep-range Rumanian patrols beyond the Don brought back reports of the ever-increasing build-up. But the commander of the Sixth Army in Stalingrad, von Paulus, seemed unmoved by the news of the Soviet build-up brought him by his intelligence officers. Indeed, as that first week of November 1942 drew to a close with the danger of a catastrophe looming ever larger, he issued a self-satisfied proclamation to his weary troops. It read:

The summer and autumn offensive is successfully terminated after taking Stalingrad. . . . The Sixth Army has played a significant role and held the Russians in check. The winter is now upon us. . . . The Russians will take advantage of it. It is unlikely that the Russians will fight with the same strength as last winter. . . .

Behind his back at the Sixth Army HQ, staff officers told each other the Old Man had to be crazy. The Sixth Army could probably tackle the Russians whatever their strength, but weren't its flanks guarded by third-class troops from the Axis armies? What if the Ivans hit them? That week, the gentlemen with the purple stripe of the staff down their elegant breeches shook their heads in disbelief and commented, 'Friedrich von Paulus seems to be whistling his way past the graveyard. . . .'

And in their freezing trenches, the bearded, emaciated infantry stared bleary-eyed across the shell-pitted snowy waste of no-man's land and waited for the inevitable.

Beneath ten metres of earth and concrete, General Chuikov waited too. Two whores had set up a little light housekeeping to the rear of the bunker in a tiny room, its sole furniture an army mattress on the dirt floor, a hissing kerosene lamp which burnt twenty-four hours a day and an old gramophone on which they played the same record time and time again as their officer customers came and went, came and went.

Chuikov tolerated the whores, though he was wont to say in his tenser moments, 'Those bitches are only waiting for the Fritzes to come and give them the pox, too!'

He waited, listening to the exotic music of a continent he would never see, scratching his eczema, drinking moodily most of the day, and asking himself that same old question over and over again: *Where were the gulag rats?*

3

'The bridge at Kalach' Colonel Katukov announced proudly, as if the double-span bridge down below represented something of value. But then Boldin supposed it did. The gulag rats had marched through more than a hundred miles of enemy-held territory and had discovered the information that Chuikov wanted so vitally: there were no significant German fighting units on this side of the Don. The positions the Red Army would attack were held entirely by second-rate Rumanian troops. In silence, the two men crouching in the windswept firs surveyed the area of the key bridge with their glasses, holding one free hand above them so that they did not sparkle in the bright winter sunshine and give their position away.

To the left and right of the bridge's exit on the far side of the river there were sandbagged positions which housed light flak cannon, obviously for use against attacking dive-bombers. Beyond, there was a small collection of little wooden huts grouped around a large stone building which, to judge from the flag flying stiffly in the breeze above it, was the Fritzes' HQ. On their side of the river there was a single sentry, muffled up in a greatcoat with a scarf tied around his helmet, who, hands in pockets and rifle slung carelessly over his shoulders, stamped his feet and watched some comrades of his on the far side throwing snowballs at each other like overgrown schoolboys.

'Rear echelon,' Boldin commented contemptuously. 'They're having a nice old time of it down there, aren't they?'

Katukov did not answer, his lips moving as if he were counting.

Boldin sniffed and dismissed the Fritzes. 'Well, comrade colonel, we've got a long haul in front of us back to our own lines. I suggest we get started and make the most of the darkness. It'll be dusk in an hour, once that sun goes over the hills.'

Katukov continued to count and Boldin could see that while he did so he was thinking hard. Finally the colonel said, 'I make them out to be about hundred. And we are eight hundred. We outnumber them by eight to one.' He lowered his glasses and looked at Boldin, as if the numbers were of some significance.

'Yes. So?'

'What if we decided to disobey orders, Boldin,' Katukov said slowly.

'Disobey orders?'

'Yes. Why run the risk of being attacked on our way back to our lines and the chance of not being able to pass on the information that the Sixty-second Army needs? Why not do it this way: capture the bridge and pass on the information by their radios – the Fritzes always have radios, even the smallest of their units.'

'Capture the bridge!' Boldin exploded, his eyes incredulous. 'But today's only the tenth of November. The attack doesn't start until the nineteeth. We couldn't hold it that long, colonel! That bridge is of vital strategic importance for them. Once they know that we've got it, they'll fall on us like a ton of bricks.'

'But do they need to know, Boldin?' Katukov said calmly. 'We are wearing German uniform and we have enough German-speakers in our ranks. Once it is in our hands, we would allow things to carry on as always so that there would be no suspicion of what had taken place. After all, it is a small, insignificant garrison at present. Why should there be any kind of superior officer coming to inspect the place who might become suspicious, eh?'

Boldin opened his mouth to protest again and then he stopped, bottom lip drooping a little stupidly. There was something to Katukov's sudden plan. In the two or three days it would take them to reach their own lines, there was a distinct possibility that the enemy air force might spot them – with disastrous results. For all he knew, the Rumanians were already searching for them, warned by the fleeing Italians or anyone who might have escaped from the burning collective farm.

'I am sure, Boldin,' Katukov appealed to him, 'that we can play-act without suspicion or danger until the curtain for the real spectacle arises on the ninteenth.' He smiled coldly, obviously pleased with his plan and his metaphor.

'There are problems,' Boldin said guardedly.

'Probably, but they can be worked out. Boldin, you know as well as I do that one third of the art of soldiering is simply knowing one's job; another third, the possession of good, sound common sense; the final third is luck. Frederick the Great, the Prussian, once said he had no use for officers who had no luck.' His voice rose. 'Boldin, I have had luck the whole way so far. I know I am going to be lucky again, I can feel it in my very bones.'

'Comrade colonel, that might well be,' Boldin commented coldly. 'But it won't be *your* bones that will suffer if anything went wrong down there, it will be those of my gulag rats.'

'That may well be, but Boldin give me this victory, *please*.'

Boldin could see the naked greed in Katukov's eyes and told himself the Greenhat still craved as much for glory and recognition as he had done the very first day they had met.

'I am no longer young, Boldin. I have devoted my life to the Party cause, and I am still a mere colonel in charge of a bunch of criminals. Time is running out and I must have success if I am to make general before this war is over.' There was no mistaking the note of pleading in Katukov's voice.

'All right,' Boldin said. 'We'll give you your success, but promise me this.'

'Anything!'

'If you do get promotion to the rank of general and are given another command, you will recommend me as your successor in charge of Punishment Battalion 333.'

'Of course, of course, little brother,' Katukov answered eagerly. 'I did not think you had that kind of ambition.'

'I haven't,' Bodlin said coldly. 'I am a gulag rat and I will remain one, with one loyalty and ambition only – to look after my men and ensure that their lives are not tossed away worthlessly.' He held out his hand. 'Promise?'

Katukov took it and pressed it hard. 'Promise.'

Unwittingly Colonel Katukov had just signed his own death-warrant.

With dramatic suddenness, the pale yellow ball of the winter sun flashed one more time on the whipping aerials which marked the Fritzes' radio shack and disappeared beyond the hills, plunging the steppe into inky darkness. It was time to go. 'All right,' Boldin whispered, 'boats out!'

The men needed no urging. They had been hiding in the reeds at the edge of the river for two hours now, directly opposite the radio shack which was the attackers' first priority, even before the bridge itself. It had to be secured before the operator could signal what was happening at this lonely little steppe village. Silently, their equipment muffled, their boots covered in rags, they pushed out the rough canoes, abandoned a year before by some unknown fisherman when the Germans had first marched this way and, using their entrenching tools as paddles, started to propel the ugly little craft across.

In the bow of the first, Boldin cocked his head to one

side and listened with bated breath for the first sign that the Fritzes had been alerted to their presence. But none came.

From the huts there came shouts and cries, but Boldin knew that it had nothing to do with them. The Germans were having their dinner in spite of the fact that it was only three-thirty in the afternoon.

Five minutes later the bow of the canoe ground to a stop in the snowy, muddy reeds of the other bank. Boldin flung a glance at the stark black silhouette of the bridge some 300 metres to their right. The sentry and the gunners had not moved, and the barrels of the flak cannon still pointed skywards. They had landed undetected. Hastily he cupped his hands around his mouth, now bare of his precious false teeth, which were wrapped in a handkerchief and safely stored in his trousers' pocket, and cawed three times in the fashion of the wild birds of the steppe.

From behind them on the other side of the river came back the answering signal. Now Katukov would moved the rest of the battalion to both sides of the bridge. Once his flare signalled they had taken the radio shack, he would double forward, the gulag rats using the stone pillars beneath it to cross and surprise the gunners.

'Follow me!' Boldin hissed. 'Remember they *must* not send a message out to their people.'

Behind him Corporal Glinka grinned evilly and whispered. 'Don't worry, comrade major, they won't.' His long curved knife gleamed a dull silver in the faint light. 'First I'll slit me a Fritz's throat and then I'll cut me a big piece of that salami of theirs. My guts are doing flip-flops at the very thought.' He belched in anticipation.

'Watch some Fritz doesn't cut a piece of your salami off,' Boldin warned. 'Come on!'

In silence they stole forward, ignoring the noise coming from the houses where the Fritzes were feeding, intent solely on the radio shack. Already it was blacked out for the night so that its occupants could not see the killers approaching them over the frozen snow, slinking from shadow to shadow like grey timber wolves. Whatever little noise they made was drowned by the chatter of morse, broken occasionally by a burst of static or metallic voices from far away.

At the edge of the hut, Boldin hissed to Glinka, 'All right, take three men and slip round the other side to check if there's a back door. I'll take the front.'

'*Horoscho!*' the ever-hungry NCO whispered, his face serious and alert now.

On the tips of his toes, Boldin, followed by the rest of the little group, crept round the front of the radio shack, the hand with which he held the long combat knife wet with sweat.

Still nothing moved inside and the chatter of morse continued unabated.

Now the front door was only an arm's length away. In an instant Boldin would reach out for the rough knob, turn it and careen inside, with the old cry on his lips that he had used so many times in house-to-house combat these last terrible months, '*Hände hoch!*'

But that wasn't to be. Just as he reached out to turn the knob, the door opened! A knife of yellow light slid out into the darkness. A big man with his braces dangling, a handful of torn newspaper in his hand, stood there blinking at the sudden inky light, obviously attempting to locate the site of the latrine.

Boldin, frozen in the shadows, heared him draw in his breath and knew instinctively they had been discovered. '*Hey –*'

Boldin dived forward, knife at the ready, bringing the big man down with the force of the impact, the cry of alarm dying on his lips as he fell heavily into the frozen snow.

But in spite of his size, the German signaller reacted more quickly than Boldin anticipated. Just as he raised his knife to strike the lethal stab, the German smashed his doubled fist wildly into the Russian's face. Boldin was dazed for a moment. He had a blurred impression of the German's brutish face shivering before him then he recalled the danger the mission was in if the Fritz succeeded in breaking loose.

With all his strength he brought his body to bear on the German's. The long knife held tightly to his right hip slid into the Fritz's guts. He heaved wildly, his spine taut as if he were racked by the throes of passion. Grimly Boldin held on to him as the man tried frantically to free himself of that terrible blade of steel. Boldin's other hand clamped over the German's mouth to drown the strangled cries coming from his throat. Abruptly the German went limp, his head flopped to one side. He was dead.

Gasping as though he had just run a great race, his whole body trembling, for Boldin could never become accustomed to killing in this manner, he staggered to his feet, swaying wildly as he did so.

Glinka loomed up at the other side of the open door. He eyes fell on the bloody weapon in Boldin's shaking hand, but he made no comment.

Boldin nodded.

Glinka acted straight away. His boot slammed against the door and smashed against the side of the wall. The next instant Glinka sprang inside. A scream. A yell. A harsh command in Russian and then Boldin was inside with the rest.

A fat, pale-faced German lay moaning on the floor, holding his pudgy white hands to his stomach, through which trickled bright red blood. At the radio, a tall skinny fellow was standing bolt upright, his hands extended to the full limit, as if he were trying to reach the sky, mumbling in a panic-stricken voice, '*Nicht toten Kamerad . . . nicht toten. . . . Ich bin Kommunist . . . .*' And sitting calmly at the table, Glinka was cutting himself a thick slice off the salami he had surmised would be in the shack with his knife, its blade still dripping red with the blood of the fat German.

Boldin shook his head. 'You could have at least wiped the blade, Glinka,' he commented.

'Adds to the flavour,' Glinka said easily and then turning on the skinny German cried. 'Shut up about communists, Fritz! I eat *them* for breakfast.'

The skinny German shut up like a clam.

The flare hushed into the night sky and burst with startling suddenness, bathing the bridge in its red-glowing eerie light.

It was the signal. Boldin had captured the radio shack successfully. Katukov waited no longer. He rose from the reeds, pistol in hand, and yelled, 'Attack!'

'Attack!' The officers down at both sides of the bridge echoed the excited command. NCOs' whistles shrilled.

'*Urrah!*' the gulag rats roared in a deep, unified bass and started forward.

The sentry on their side of the bridge raised his rifle. But he never had a chance. The tide of rushing, crying men swamped him. He went down, trampled to death by their racing feet. At the gunpits, the terrified crews whirled the handles of their 20mm flak cannon furiously, trying to bring the barrels to bear on the running men who had appeared so frighteningly out of nowhere. To no avail. In a flash the gulag rats were among them, bayonets and entrenching tools flashing, hacking, gouging, chopping. It was over within seconds and the rats raced on, leaving the gunpits filled with dead men.

Katukov ran at the head of the little group, including Vulf, detailed to capture the HQ, knowing that if he weren't there, his prison scum would massacre every German they found.

On all sides now there was confused fighting in the darkness.

The startled Germans opened up from the windows of their huts or attempted to close with the Russians in the tiny streets. Scarlet flame stabbed the blackness. Men screamed and tumbled to the ground. No quarter was given or expected. When Russian and German clashed, they fought to the death, trampling and kicking the men at their feet, crazy animal grunts issuing from their throats.

A stick grenade sailed through the air in front of Katukov. '*Duck!*' he cried urgently. The grenade exploded in a flash of angry purple flame. Shrapnel zinged through the air. The blast hit Katukov across the face like a blow from a flabby fist. Behind him one of the rats howled in agony and dropped to the ground. Katukov raced on.

A German in long, drooping underpants appeared at the door of the HQ. Katukov pressed the trigger of his pistol. The German slammed against the door and started to trail slowly down its length, his false teeth bulging absurdly from his mouth. Katukov sprang inside. A sergeant stood at the far end of the corridor, rifle held indecisively in his hands, as if he did not really know whether to make a fight of it or surrender. Katukov made up his mind for him. His pistol cracked again. The NCO sat down abruptly, rocking back and forth, his shattered kneecap cradled in both hands like a mother comforting a sick child. Katukov sprang over him and wrenched open the door.

A fat officer with an open tunic cowered at the far end of the room, his meal still steaming on the table, a stained napkin tucked into his collarless shirt. It could be no other than the commander of the little force defending the bridge. Calmly Katukov walked over to the plate and taking up the chop which lay there, took a large bite of it, then apparently not satisfied with the taste, sprinkled some salt upon it, before saying in his best German, 'You will not be touched if you obey my orders exactly.'

The German swayed and then fainted clean away. Katukov grinned.

He had done it. For better or worse, the bridge at

Kalach was in the hands of the gulag rats.

Ten kilometres away, Colonel Harsch, chewing idly on a piece of hardtack smeared with ersatz honey which made up his first meal of that day, snapped to the half-track driver, 'Turn off the engine.'

Obediently the Dutchman did so, although it would be the very devil to start again in this biting cold. Harsch cocked his head to one side and stared at the faint, flickering pink of the horizon. Who could be firing this far behind the front? he asked himself. Unless some damn fool of a Rumanian general had ordered a night exercise. It would by typical of those powdered, perfumed fools who simply didn't know how to treat the average, ragged-arsed stubble-hopper.

'*Stoi?*' Igor asked, crouched next to him in the half-track.

Harsch picked up his broken sword and then laid it down again. He could hear nothing. 'Night exercise, I think.'

'Enough boom-boom,' Igor said and resumed his chewing of the hardtack.

At the green-glowing controls, the young Dutchman looked enquiringly at Harsch.

Harsch nodded. 'False alarm. Start her up again, cheesehead. My eggs are freezing up rapidly.'

Obediently, the Dutchman did as he was ordered. The engine, surprisingly enough, started at once and hot air wafted into the steel compartment once more. Harsch returned to his iron-hard biscuit and honey. He'd let the men rest a little longer. Then they'd push on again, Another hour and they'd be at the bridge.

Now all was silent again save for the soft ticking of the engines, the wind breathing icily across the limitless steppe and the crunch of the men biting into the biscuits.

4

Chuikov read the signal while outside the Stalin organs thundered yet again, bringing the bombardment of the German positions at Stalingrad to an end for this particular November day. He looked up and stared momentarily at Commissar Khrushchev with his bald, high pate and Commissar Malenkov, his face like a soft pudding. Hard as he was, he had to force himself to embrace the man every time they met. His nose sank into the political commissar's fat, round face like going into a half-inflated balloon whenever he had to submit to the man's cold, clinging embrace. Then, by way of setting the cat among the pigeons, he passed the message first to Krushchev and not to Georgi Malenkov, who was Stalin's personal watchdog at his HQ. Nikita Khrushchev and he were bitter rivals, and that master of intrigue knew that Malenkov would gladly report any of his mistakes to the dictator in Moscow.

Krushchev read the message slowly, while Malenkov craned to get a look at it over his shoulder. Chuikov, sitting back in his chair, watched both of the politicians to see how they would react. In the room at the back, the two whores still played that damned gramophone of theirs. Chuikov told himself he would have to stop them soon.

'So,' Khrushchev said and handed the message to Malenkov, who did not bother to read it again but instead said in an icy voice, 'Is that all you have to say, comrade?'

Chuikov sat back in his chair and waited for the fur to fly.

'And what do you wish me to say, comrade?'

'Well, there we have the sauce, don't we!' Malenkov's face flushed a hectic, ugly red as it always did when he was angry.

'How? We know now that there are no Fritz troops within the Rumanians' area. That is what these gulag rats were sent out to discover. They have completed their mission successfully.'

'Have they?' Malenkov persisted, and Chuikov knew well what he was thinking. The same thought had occurred to him immediately he had read the rest of that damned fool Katukov's message: '*Have seized bridge at K. Intend to hold until link-up takes place.*'

'What does that mean, Malenkov?' Khrushchev asked. He knew that Stalin had not yet forgiven him for the disaster at Kharkov that spring when the Red Army had lost 200,000 troops because he, Khrushchev, had urged Stalin to ignore warnings of disaster and press the assault; all the same, his obstinate peasant nature would not allow him to back off in front of this monstrous bloated pig from Moscow.

Malenkov extended two thick, hairy sausage-like fingers. 'Two things. One, the Fritz interception service might well be attempting to decipher that message at this very moment, and it won't take them very long to discover where the bridge at K is. Then all hell will be let loose there. Two, what if one of those rats lands in German hands? How long do you think it will take them to make him sing like a yellow canary? Not long, I wager. And what then?'

Chuikov thought it was time to intervene. 'I shall tell you, comrades – the Fritzes will know where we intend to attack on the nineteenth.'

'Exactly,' Malenkov said self-righteously and threw back a lock of greasy black hair which always hung down his low brow. 'Our whole plan will be in the bucket then.'

Khrushchev looked worried. Yet like the peasant he

was, he could think on his feet; it was an attribute which had saved his life many times in the years since the revolution and one which would make him the master of all Russia in the next ten years. 'Then we must order that fool at Kalach to withdraw immediately,' he snapped.

'I have already attempted to do so, comrades,' Chuikov said.

'*Attempted?*' the two political commissars echoed in surprised unison.

Chuikov nodded a little unhappily. 'My signals office had just started sending when it was hit by a Fritz 88mm shell.' He scratched at his diseased hand, gritting his teeth a little with the pain. 'By the time other operators were able to go on the air to replace them, they couldn't raise Katukov'

'That could mean that the Fritzes are already on to them,' Malenkov said eagerly.

'It could mean anything,' Chuikov said. 'Maybe he has gone off the air deliberately. Maybe his set has a defect. Maybe the interference in this area plays a role. After all, there are hundreds of radio sets operating here in an area smaller than that of Moscow. As I said, anything could have happened.'

'At all events, Moscow must be informed at once, and that fool colonel of yours must be punished,' Malenkov snapped, angry that the opportunity to blacken Khrushchev as the person responsible for this failure was slipping from his grasp. 'Now we must give Comrade Stalin a chance to make the correct decision before it is too late.'

'Correct decision?' Chuikov asked.

'Yes, what decision?' the other political commissar added his voice to that of the general.

Malenkov smirked at the two of them, glad to be able to score at last. 'The decision whether the whole counter-attack between Serafimovich and Kletskaya should be cancelled or not. . . .'

'Well, Boldin?' Katukov demanded, his boots off as he lay on the commandant's bed and sipped his breakfast tea complete with lemon, for an ample store of them had been found in the HQ.

'Everything's running very smoothly,' Boldin reported. 'A bunch of Rumanians came through on their *panje*-wagons heading for Stalingrad. A busload of German leave-men, as drunk as howitzers, came the other way heading for the railhead and leave in the fascist homeland.' He shrugged easily. 'So far, so good. Nobody seems to have tumbled to the fact that all is not well at Kalach.' He indicated the window with a jerk of his thumb to the spot where the commandant, dressed in his best uniform, wandered up and down the street, saluting and smirking wildly, knowing that if he pulled any tricks, Glinka, hidden in the HQ's look-out tower, would blow his brains out with his rifle. 'And our tame Fritz is doing very well. He must have been in the theatre.'

Katukov nodded his agreement. 'You see, my dear Boldin, my plan did work out well after all. Now they know the situation at Stalingrad, and I'm sure the commanding general is very glad to have this little Trojan Horse planted firmly at a key spot in the Fritz positions. It will be useful, very useful, later on.'

'Perhaps,' Boldin answered non-committally, 'though I wish we were still in radio communication with Stalingrad. Who would have thought that that long-nosed German bastard would pull a trick like that, knocking out our radio operator and destroying the radio? Ah well, he's one Fritz less to worry us.'

Katukov's smile vanished. 'Yes, Boldin, and that fool out there assures me that they did not have to report in by radio to their authorities or anything like that. So the failure of radio contact is no problem as far as the Germans are concerned.'

'All the same,' Boldin said, 'I'd like to know what our people are doing. There is – ' He stopped abruptly.

'What's the matter?' Katukov asked, sitting up suddenly.

Boldin didn't answer. Instead, he hurried to the window.

The commandant had stopped his posturing and was standing in the centre of the snow-covered street, hand half-raised to his cap, staring up to the bridge where the gunners were hurrying to their positions on the flak cannon.

'*Shit, thrice-times shit!*' Boldin cursed.

And this time Katukov, hastening towards him, did not need to ask why his second-in-command had cursed. There was no mistaking that squeaky, rusty rattle. Armoured vehicles were approaching the bridge from the other side of the Don – and they could only be enemy ones.

Colonel Harsch cursed the Dutch driver who had stalled the command half-track just as it had begun to take the climb that led to the bridge. The damned cheesehead had failed to change down in time and the engine had refused to take the strain in a too-high gear. Now the blonde-headed driver swore, red-faced, at the ignition, while a grinning Duclos in the medic half-track rattled by them on his way to the bridge. 'Heaven, arse and cloudburst, man!' Harsch roared and slapped his sword against the steel side of the vehicle. 'For God's sake, sort it out!'

Angrily Harsch dropped over the side and stared up the road towards Kalach. His next half-track came roaring round the bend, its driver ramming home low gear, the troopers packing its deck grinning at their commander's discomforture. Suddenly Harsch forgot his anger as his gaze fell on the commandant whom they had met briefly on their way into the Don Basin.

The man was striding up and down the street like a damned wooden puppet saluting briskly to left and right, saluting even before the slovenly clad soldiers raised their hands in greeting to him. There was something else strange about Kalach and its defenders. All of the soldiers wore the precious Russian *valenki*, the felt-lined boots of the Red Army which were so greedily sought after by the German *Landser*, where had these rear-echelon stallions obtained them? In his own command only a quarter of his men had them. What was going on in Kalach?

Suddenly Harsch made a decision. He sprang into the middle of the road, sword upraised.

Groetjean, the big Flemish driver of the leading half-track, hit the brakes hard. The carrier shuddered to a stop only a metre away from the lean figure of the CO, almost skidding into the ditch on the frozen snow. Behind it the others rolled to a stop. Now the only vehicle moving was that of Duclos, clattering over the metal bridge in low gear getting ever closer to the suddenly stationary soldiers on the other side and the fat fool of a commandant poised there with his pudgy fist half-raised to his cap saluting nobody like an absurd waxwork figure. . . .

'*They know!*' Boldin said grimly, lowering his glasses.

Next to him, Katukov took his eyes off that lean, handsome young German standing in the middle of the road, what looked like a broken sword in his one hand, and knew Boldin was right. '*Damn, damn, damn!*' he cursed. For a moment or two he was too paralysed to act, but then Boldin's urgent question made him realize the urgency of their situation. 'Do?' he echoed Boldin's query. 'They're stalled on that road! Quick! To those two flak guns down there. At that range, we might have a chance to knock them out. Come on, Boldin!'

Frantically, the two officers clattered down the stairs from their observation post in the HQ tower, scattering astonished rats as they ran, crying to the gunners, who were not yet properly awake. 'Fire . . . fire at the Fritz bastards. *Fire!*'

'*Duclos!*' Harsch yelled as he saw the men rushing for the twin flak guns at the far side of the river and knew instinctively what was going to happen. 'In God's name, reverse . . . *reverse!*' But Duclos, unable to hear above the roar of the tracks as the half-track clattered ever closer to the other side, just smiled and waved.

The doctor was twenty metres away when the frantic gunners at the first flak cannon finally brought down their twin-barrelled weapon to ground level and Duclos's driver realized that something was wrong. He slammed on the brakes. Duclos, taken by surprise, slapped against the cab. The driver rammed home reverse, just as the first wild slugs from Kalach came howling off the steel plating. Duclos saw their danger. He seized the cab machine-gun and swung it from left to right, scything down running men everywhere, while the driver started to roll backwards, the half-track zigzagging from left to right.

'Come on, come on!' Harsch cried in frenzied excitement, gripping the sword in a white-knuckled hand. 'Come on, you bastard, get back . . . *get back!*'

The flack gun opened up with an hysterical screech. White, glowing 200mm shells hissed through the air by the hundred. The half-track reeled under the impact. Great gleaming silver holes appeared abruptly along its length. White smoke started to pour from the shattered engine. Still, somehow, it continued to roll backwards, the dying, blinded driver jerking the wheel back and forth, the strength ebbing out of him, as if a tap had been opened.

Now the crippled half-track was only a matter of metres from Harsch's end of the bridge. They were going to do it, he told himself, as behind him the rest of the *Kampfgruppe* started to scuttle backwards to the safety of the bend, their machine-gunners sending streams of red and white tracer hissing across the Don at the men on the other side.

With a resounding crash the half-track slid, suddenly

completely out of control, across the bridge and buried its blunt snout in a heap of brick rubble.

Harsch groaned. They hadn't a chance now. Two flak guns concentrated their cruel fire on the crippled half-track. It disappeared under a hail of flying white shells. Harsch beat his sword against the side of his own vehicle in blind rage, then he, too, was swinging himself over the side as the flak cannon turned their fire on the last half-track.

The battle for the bridge at Kalach had commenced.

5

The half-track crept slowly up the narrow winding path that led from the river towards the stark black outline of the trees, tinged every now and again by silver when the moon appeared from behind the scudding clouds. Behind them on the other side of the Don there was the faint rattle of Harsch's own vehicles, the three half-tracks of the HQ group, as they made their way to the cover of the forest in which they would hide till dawn.

Goldwasser scanned his front carefully and then whispered to the French driver, '*allez – advance!*'

The young Parisian gunned his motor – unnecessarily loudly in Goldwasser's opinion – and then took the incline. A moment later they were on the river road heading straight for Kalach, with Goldwasser asking himself whether or not he had been a damn fool to have volunteered for this dangerous mission. Naturally it had been his idea to float a half-track across the Don way down below the bridge, out of earshot and sight of the Reds. Harsch, the one-armed German, had called his idea '*kapital*' and had slapped him on the back exuberantly, saying, 'Well, Goldwasser, I can tell I've got a Jew in the Fire Brigade now. They always come up with something!'

Perhaps it had been that which had prompted him to say, 'With your permission, *Obersturmbannführer*, I should like to take charge of the mission.' Here he was, a Jew, leading a dozen young cut-throats from all over Europe, who were the sworn enemies of his race. If he had not been too scared to consider the situation, he would have found it ironic.

Harsch had been able to see the irony of his position – a Jew in charge of a dozen SS men. His parting words had been, as his men had towed the rough-and-ready float back across the Don by means of a rope, 'Bring me back one prisoner, Goldwasser, and I'll apply to *Reichsführer* Himmler for permission for you to join the Black Guards. Hell, we might even form a Jewish Brigade!' And roaring with laughter at his own cynical humour, Harsch had staggered back to the trees where he and his group would hide.

Now they were on their way and once again Goldwasser ran his mind over the details of the plan which should bag them the prisoner whom Harsch needed to find out the details of the Reds' mission in the Don Basin. To the east of the bridge on the road they were presently taking was an isolated *isba*, which housed, or so it appeared from Harsch's study of the place through his binoculars that afternoon, a company HQ or something of that sort. With a bit of luck they would be able to surprise the staff housed there, pick up the most senior officer present and be off with him before the Reds had woken up to what was happening. At least that was the plan, but as Goldwasser told himself with a certain sinking feeling, in the Alpini they had always maintained that a plan was like a horse designed by a committee – it always turned out to be a camel!

Captain Simonvitch sniffed the night air and told himself it was going to snow. Somewhere a wolf howled at the sickle-moon. But Simonvitch did not hear it; his mind was too occupied with the state of his company. That afternoon, after a tally of the stores found in the captured village, Colonel Katukov had ordered that from now onwards until they were finally relieved by the great counter-attack, there would be a ration of 400 grams of bread, a canteen of oats to cook their *kavka* and 100 grams of salt pork per day. It did not seem much to feed the hungry men of his command, and besides, as he had explained to Katukov, 'My men need greens or something containing vitamin C. Otherwise they'll get scurvy and their teeth will fall out.'

Katukov had replied with a coarse laugh, 'Then they won't be able to eat so much hard-tack, and the ration'll go further!'

Simonvitch shrugged. People like Katukov simply didn't realize that soldiers were just like schoolchildren; one had to be fussing after them all the time or they'd get into trouble. Then hitching up his pistol-belt and forgetting the matter, he began his nightly round of the company sentries, the only company commander in the 333rd Punishment Battalion who would leave the roaring comfort of the great green-tiled ovens of the *isbas* to do so on such a cold night.

The Frenchman turned off the half-track's engine and now all was silence save for the howl of the wind in the trees in which they had hidden the vehicle.

'Do you think you'll be able to get it started again when we're back here?' Goldwasser asked a little anxiously.

'*Bièn sûr*,' the driver said. '*Regardez!*' From behind his seat he brought out a small can, punctured with holes and half-filled with earth. Taking a jerrican, he carefully poured about a litre of precious gasoline into the earth and with his bayonet began to stir the mixture into a thick goo, while Goldwasser watched puzzled. Finally, he achieved the right consistency and shoved the can underneath the half-track's engine. He scratched a match and threw it into the can. It ignited at once and soft blue flames started to flicker upwards. 'Dangerous,' he said in accented German, 'but effective.'

Goldwasser shook his head in admiration. These young toughs in whose company he now found himself seemed to be able to master every situation; he would never have dreamed of trying to keep a motor ready to start in that manner.

Five minutes later the little group of SS men were nearing the edge of the village, stealing from shadow to shadow, the only sound being the soft squeak of their own sock-covered boots on the frozen snow, the wind drowning whatever noise that came from the darkened huts. Nothing stirred. They could not even detect a sentry. It seemed as if the plan was going to work without trouble. Silently Goldwasser, the lead, said a prayer that it would.

'Sentry,' hissed one of the SS men to the right of Goldwasser.

The rest froze into immobility. Goldwasser heard his heart thumping away like the brass band of the Alpini on revue day in front of the King and Il Duce. 'Where?' he asked in a thin, strangled voice.

'There, somewhere,' the soldier whispered back, 'I can hear the red pig snoring.'

'What are we going to do?' Goldwasser asked a little helplessly.

'Take him,' the man who had reported the sentry hissed. 'Leave it to me, lieutenant.'

Cautiously hugging the silver shadows, the little patrol advanced towards the sound of the snoring, their boots making hardly a sound. Twenty metres . . . fifteen . . . ten . . . five. Abruptly the snoring ceased. Goldwasser felt a shiver of fear run down his spine. The sentry was waking up!

They froze. Before them they could make out the man, a bearded Russian, with his rifle clasped between his arms, as if he were cradling a precious child. The sentry opened his eyes. They could hear him yawn. Then he saw them, the men crouching there in the shadows who had not been there when he had gone to sleep. They heard his sharp intake of breath. In an instant he would shout out.

'Get him!' Goldwasser heard himself hiss.

Two of the SS men shot forward. One of them smashed the side of his hand against the man's mouth.

The other kneed him cruelly. The sentry's breath fled from him in an anguished gasp. He started to fall forward. His helmet tumbled to the ground. Goldwasser caught it in the very last moment. As the sentry's bent neck lurched past him, the first SS man brought his clenched fist down in a brutal blow. The Russian hit the snow, unconscious, just as Captain Simonvitch came round the corner doing his rounds with his stupidly cheerful, 'Damnable cold tonight, sentry, wh – ' He took in the situation at once. '*Alarm, alarm* – '

Instinctively Goldwasser pressed the trigger of his pistol. Simonvitch's cry of warning ended in a scream of pain as the slug smashed into his chest. He went reeling back, clutching the wound with wet, red fingers.

The Frenchman, sweating and cursing, drove the ten-ton monster as if he were back at the wheel of the taxi he had had in Paris before the war. He swung the half-track's wheel back and forth, while the tracer zipped through the air lethally, and over at the bridge, the Russians loosed salvo after salvo after the fleeing raiders.

They smashed through a fence. A group of Russians skidded like ice-skaters to a stop in front of them. Immediately they crouched and began firing. Standing up on the deck one of the SS men fanned the air with his hands and plunged down dead on his comrades. Another lobbed a stick grenade at the Russians. They flew apart and the half-track rattled on.

'*Savoiai!*' Goldwasser cried, yelling out the battle-cry of the Alpini, carried away by the wild excitement of this strange chase in the middle of the night.

A flare exploded in a blinding flash of brilliant white light to their front. Unable to see for an instant, the driver smashed into a small thatched-roof hut. With a burst of crashing glass, they were through, the bullets howling angrily off their metal sides. A second later the roof collapsed with a thunderous roar. 'Shit, driver,' one of the SS men yelled above the rattling tracks and snap-and-crackle of small-arms fire, 'what's this – a bleeding mystery tour!'

The sweating Frenchman took his hands off the wheel for a moment, 'You can drive it if you like, cheesehead!'

'No, no!' the cries of protest came from all sides.

'*Sales cons*,' the Frenchman cursed to himself and concentrated on driving again.

They shot through a small garden, smashed down the picket fence on the other side, and swerved into a narrow, tree-lined lane. A Russian loomed up out of the trees. Before anyone could stop him, he lobbed a grenade into the half-track. It exploded with a tremendous impact in those confined quarters. Goldwasser heard the shrapnel hissing through the air all round him. Men screamed and went down everywhere. Then they were out of the lane and a terrified Goldwasser recognized the road they had come in on. 'To the right, driver!' he screamed. '*À droit*.'

'*Merde!*' the Frenchman cried and swung the wheel round violently.

A bunch of squat Russian infantry sprang up from the ditch. Goldwasser swung his machine-gun from left to right. Gasping, he scythed them down, bowling their bodies to left and right as if they were puppets at the hands of a crazed puppet-master.

They were through. Crazily they rattled into the darkness, bearing with them a cargo of dead and dying in the blood-filled back of the half-track – and the vital prisoner.

6

'You can go – he'll survive.' With his broken sword, Harsch waved away the medical orderly who had been patching up the wound in Simonvitch's shoulder. He examined his prisoner for the first time, noting that the small, skinny man bore only the insignia of an officer, but otherwise no means of identification. Harsch indicated that Goldwasser should hand the Russian the bottle of *Moskovskaya* vodka, which stood on the ration crate.

Simonvitch nodded and took a hearty gulp of the fiery vodka. Harsch considered the fact. Probably a former political prisoner, he told himself, and some sort of intellectual to boot to judge by the fact he understood German. It should make his task easier; that type broke quickly.

'All right, that's enough,' he commanded and Simonvitch handed the bottle back to Goldwasser, staring up at the handsome blonde SS officer with frightened, short-sighted eyes. 'Now then, captain. I want to ask you two or three simple questions. Answer them quickly and I promise you that I'll have you in the nearest Rumanian hospital for proper treatment for your wound.'

'What sort of questions?' the prisoner asked hesitantly in German, his accent strangely familiar to Harsch, though at that moment he couldn't place it.

Harsch smiled at him. With the Russians, he knew, once they began talking they usually continued to do so. This one had started. 'First, your unit.'

'The 333rd Punishment Battalion,' Simonvitch answered, staring at his felt boots.

'Ah, the redoubtable gulag rats,' Harsch said. 'I've heard of you. From the concentration camps, aren't you? And yet heroes of the Soviet paradise, always ready to sacrifice your lives for the little Father up there in the Kremlin who sent you to them in the first place. Very curious.' He swung his broken sword, while Simonvitch remained silent. 'Second question. Why did you take the bridge at Kalach?'

Again Simonvitch answered the question without taking his gaze from his boots. 'Because our fool of a colonel ordered us to.'

Harsch grinned. 'It is common in all armies, Ivan,' he said and winked at Goldwasser. 'We are all led by fools. But that isn't exactly the answer I wanted. Perhaps I should phrase my question differently. What was the mission of your battalion so deep behind Rumanian lines?'

For the first time the prisoner did not answer. Instead he looked up from his boots, first at the handsome German and then at the dark-faced, hooked-nosed Italian, allowing his gaze to rest on the Alpini officer's face as if the look had some significance. Goldwasser dropped his gaze, oddly embarrassed.

Harsch gripped his sword more firmly and pressed the broken blade against the Russian's arm – hard. Simonvitch screamed. Blood began to trickle through the thick serge of his blouse. He stared down at it aghast. 'I asked you a question, Ivan,' Harsch said as calm as ever, while Goldwasser licked suddenly dry lips.

'I'm not answering,' Simonvitch said, his short-sighted eyes liquid with tears.

'It has cost me eight good men to capture you for the answer to that question,' Harsch said evenly. 'I'm not going to allow you to deny me it.'

'You can do what you like,' Simonvitch said, trying to keep his voice level. 'But I won't speak.'

'I wonder . . . I wonder.' Harsch raised his voice, 'Igor, take your countryman outside and let him have a little think about his decision.'

Igor spat on the floor of the tent. '*Buka!*' he cursed, and pushed Simonvitch in front of him.

The prisoner flung a last glance at the two officers. '*Nuzi smerti, nye budet*,' he snarled and went.

'What did he say?' Goldwasser asked, worried by the turn of events.

Harsch laughed. 'It can't be worse than death. A vain hope I am afraid, *teniente*. It is.'

'What?' Goldwasser said, already knowing what the answer to that question would be.

'Torture!'

'You couldn't!'

'Of course, I could – and *can*.' Harsch looked down at him. '*Mein lieber* Goldwasser, we're in Russia, not the Vatican City. We torture, they torture. It is a way of life out here in this God-forsaken wasteland.' He smiled a little grimly. 'My grandfather and my father would have been horrified, but then they did not have to serve a Hitler or fight a Stalin. Times have changed and the customs of war, too.' He sniffed. 'Besides, your own Duce is not averse to using the rubber truncheon and somewhat large doses of castor oil to get information out of his prisoners, they tell me, eh?'

Goldwasser said nothing and Harsch clapped him on the back. 'Don't take it to heart, old fellow. We'll have that Ivan singing like a canary before the hour is out.' But there *Obersturmbannführer* Harsch was wrong for once.

Five kilometres away at the other side of the river, the winter dawn came slowly, as if reluctant to throw its warming light on the war-torn countryside, Boldin and Katukov surveyed the situation and took stock of their assets.

Together they watched for a while as the gulag rats collected the dead of the night's raid and carried them to the river where the fast flowing water soon bore away the bodies; the earth was too hard to dig graves and both officers knew the men would soon need all their strength for other and more important things. Then Katukov took Boldin's arm and led him away so that they were out of earshot of the soldiers. 'He'll talk, I suppose, Boldin,' he said.

Boldin knew immediately to whom the colonel referred. 'He's a bit of an old woman, typical schoolteacher, comrade colonel, but he's tough all the same.'

'But he'll talk,' Katukov persisted.

Boldin nodded. 'We all do in the end.'

'So that alters our situation somewhat, doesn't it?'

'Yes.' Boldin looked across the river, the fog drifting away from its surface now in ghostly wreaths, as if he half-expected to see infantry already there.

'What do you think will happen?' Katukov asked.

'They'll bring up infantry, of course,' Boldin said coolly as if they were back at staff college and they were discussing some sand-table tactical problem. 'If they can get the Rumanians to co-ordinate correctly with them, they'll put in an attack from both flanks simultaneously. But naturally that won't happen straightaway. The way the Rumanians move, I'd give them another twenty-four hours. Dawn tomorrow morning is my guess.'

'Mine, too, Boldin,' Katukov agreed. 'But before then we can expect enemy air attacks. Dive-bombers, probably. They won't want to destroy the bridge itself if they can help it, but they'll want to soften us up for the infantry attack.'

'Yes.' Boldin looked at his watch. It was nearly seven. The sky was beginning to brighten more rapidly, illuminating the shell-stripped trees along the river bank so that they looked like gaunt outsize toothpicks. 'By the time Simonvitch spills the beans and higher headquarters has been informed, it will be midday. The fly-boys won't want to miss their precious lunch, so it could be at least two o'clock before they're airborne on their way here. Just time to give us thirty minutes of their steel eggs before it grows too hazy – and back to the mess for

English high tea, complete with serviettes.'

'Don't be so damned frivolous! The situation is very serious, Boldin, you know.'

'I know, comrade colonel,' Boldin answered cheerfully. 'But life is far too serious to be taken seriously, they always say.' The smile vanished from his tough face and he was very businesslike. 'Where do we establish our positions, comrade colonel?'

'*Madre de dio!*' Goldwasser exclaimed in horror.

The Russian prisoner's naked body was smeared with blood, both eyes were almost closed, his face a mass of black swollen bruises and his right kneecap showed white through the black caked blood of the open wound there.

Simonvitch flicked open his eyes and was aware again that he had talked. The squat Igor who had done the torturing had finally broken him. He had talked, then fallen into unconsciousness.

Now he awoke with that terrible betrayal uppermost in his mind. And he was dying and knew it.

'*Zhid?*' he asked in Russian through cracked, bloodied lips. '*Zhid?*'

Goldwasser swallowed hard and, looking down at the Russian's tortured body, saw that he was indeed circumsized; that had been the reason for that significant look before the torture had commenced. 'Yes,' he said softly, 'I'm a Yid too.'

Simonvitch attempted a smile and failed miserably. With a weak wave of his hand, he indicated that Goldwasser should come closer.

The Italian officer did so. 'What do you want?' he asked.

'Pistol,' Simonvitch croaked. 'Jew, give me your pistol. . . .' He put his forefinger weakly to his forehead and made the motion of pulling a trigger. 'No, brother, you . . . you shoot me.'

Goldwasser recoiled with horror. 'Kill you!' he

exclaimed. 'I couldn't . . . no, I couldn't do that!'

'Brother, you must!' Simonvitch, his eyes flickering wildly, clutched Goldwasser's hand. '*Palshalsta* . . . please.'

'No, no,' Goldwasser said, 'I couldn't, even if you are a Jew, too. I simply couldn't!'

'Then I will.'

It was Colonel Harsch standing there at the entrance to the tent, sword tucked into his belt, his one hand hovering at his pistol holster.

'You?'

'Yes, why not. One has to be in good shape to commit suicide, you know? The little fellow was brave, but in the end he talked.' He shrugged. 'It was to be expected.'

'Shoot!' the man on the floor croaked piteously, arms extended in a gesture of supplication.

'Oh, my God, I can't stand this!' It took Goldwasser all his will-power not to break down and cry. Blindly he blundered by the tall blonde SS officer into the cold air.

An instant later a single shot rang out and Harsch left the tent, placing his pistol back into his holster a little awkwardly. 'I don't know what you Jews say over your dead,' he said gruffly. 'But he was a brave little bastard, so say something.'

Without another look at Goldwasser he strode away and began to stare purposefully at the sky for the planes which would soon come. . . .

7

Nothing!

Nothing happened. Neither the infantry nor the expected dive-bombers arrived at the bridge at Kalach. The gulag rats extended their positions into the apple orchard to the east of the bridge, piling the snow up high, urinating over the cracks before smoothing them with their entrenching tools so that the frost would turn the snow into impenetrable ice. Boldin and Katukov surveyed the hundred-metre-high bluff on the western side from which had come the rattle of the German half-tracks. But nothing stirred there. An uneasy quiet had descended upon that part of the steppe. '*Boshe moi!*' Boldin cursed, lowering his glasses and blowing on his frozen fingers, 'you would think that the damned war had gone home and got into bed.'

And as the hours crept by with no sign of the Germans preparing for an attack, Colonel Katukov could only agree with him.

Half a kilometre away, huddled in the freezing tent together with Goldwasser, a moody Harsch was asking himself the same question that puzzled the officers of the 333rd Punishment Battalion: *what was going on*?

With Operation Uranus less than six days away, Josef Stalin had suddenly got cold feet. Malenkov's message had broken his confidence in the success of the flank attack. Behind the blacked-out windows in his Kremlin apartment, he paced the floor in his high boots, alternatively sucking his curved pipe and running its mouthpiece through his drooping, dyed moustache while barrel-chested Marshal Zhukov, his chief military adviser, watched him helplessly.

Stalin paused only to moan, 'Now the Fritzes'll know everything . . . *everything*, Zhukov!'

Inwardly Zhukov cursed the damned obscure colonel and his gulag scum who had captured the bridge and caused all this fuss, but outwardly he maintained an air of impressive calm, knowing it would be up to him to somehow convince the dictator that all was well. Nothing, not even foreknowledge of the offensive, could prevent it being successful now. All that long evening he had worked on Stalin, giving him a controlled, dispassionate recital of the facts: the thousands of tanks that made up the Russian Fifth and Twenty-first Tank Armies, the 3500 guns which would herald the attack with an hour-long bombardment of the Rumanian positions, the hundreds of thousands of infantrymen ready to follow up the armoured breakthrough. But still the dictator remained unconvinced, knowing that if he failed this time it might well mean the end of his regime.

Two thousand kilometres away at his mountain retreat, the Berghof, in the snow-bound Bavarian Alps, Hitler also remained strangely inactive, in spite of the warnings that had now reached him of the Russians' intentions. He dallied with his mistress Eva Braun, enjoyed his peppermint tea and cream cakes in front of the huge blazing fire, and whiled away the long evenings listening to Wagner and Lehar on the gramophone, expounding his theories to the toadying Borman and the rest of his cronies on everything from the superiority of the baked potato over the boiled one, to the inability of the average French woman to produce a boy child suitable for the infantry.

Hitler that November seemed strangely settled, already beginning to make plans for his future life in peacetime. For he was convinced the great Reich he had created in the last three years would endure. Did not his armies rule over 300 million people and over territory stretching from the French Atlantic coastline to the foothills of the Caucasus, and from the northern capes of Norway down to the yellow sands of Libya? Occasionally his military staff managed to get him into the conference room and attempt to explain the true state of affairs on the Don, but Hitler did not seem really interested by the threat to the Rumanian and, of course, Paulus's Sixth Armies. He would peer at the maps through his steel-rimmed spectacles, ask the usual questions about the weather and what Luftwaffe groups were operating in the Stalingrad area. But otherwise he did nothing.

He had reached the zenith of his power. In his fanatical heart he was convinced that nothing could dethrone him now.

It was while the generals, both German and Russian, waited in this strange hiatus, knowing what should be done, but with their hands tied by their political masters, that a very slight, very pale civilian presented himself at Chuikov's underground headquarters and asked politely if he could see the general.

The elegant staff officers lounging at the door of the tunnel, enjoying a minute's rest from the strain of directing the battle which still raged in the ruins of Stalingrad, laughed in the little civilian's face and told him this day Chuikov wasn't even seeing full generals; he had too much on his plate. That was until the civilian pulled out his NKVD identity card with the six letters written in bold red underneath the photograph, 'S-M-E-R-S-H'.

'*Smersh!*' the senior man exclaimed, his ruddy face suddenly pale and frightened. It was the first time he had ever met a member of that organization, dreaded throughout the Soviet Union, but like everyone else in Russia he had heard of it. Hurriedly he strode into the HQ tunnel. One minute later, General Chuikov was facing the little civilian, studying the man while he waited for him to state his reason for appearing so strangely in the middle of a battlefield.

The civilian had straight, lustreless black hair, the high bony forehead of an intellectual and flat, dark, impenetrable eyes. His eyes together with the pencil-thin black moustache which came down below his cruel-lipped mouth gave him an almost oriental appearance. But it was his hands that caught Chuikov's attention. They didn't seem to belong to that skinny, slight body: they were monstrous things, heavy-knuckled and covered with thick black hairs, and they hung almost to the man's knees when he stood up. They were apelike and frightening; the hands of a killer. The man from Smersh smiled suddenly and an instant later it was as if he had never smiled in all his life. 'I suppose you are wondering, general,' he said in a dull, but somehow ironic voice, 'what I am doing here in this place?'

'Yes, I am somewhat,' Chuikov answered uneasily, scratching frantically at his bandaged fingers wet with the sticky moisture of his weeping eczema.

'It is concerning this – er – Colonel Katukov.' His eyes looked at Chuikov lifelessly above that trick moustache, as if he were not really interested in the Hero of Stalingrad, just his own words, which had to be selected with great care. 'I would be grateful if you could let me have the latest information you have on him and his battalion.'

Inwardly Chuikov breathed a sigh of relief. At least the matter had nothing directly to do with him. 'There's nothing much I can tell you, comrade – ' he hesitated, but the man from Smersh did not supply his name, 'except that he disobeyed orders by taking the bridge at Kalach. We have reason to believe that the Fritzes already know what his mission is, due to this vain-glorious foolishness. But they have not yet acted – '

The man from Smersh held up his hand and Chuikov stopped speaking immediately, as if he were a simple soldier and not a full general of the Red Army.

'I'm not interested in the larger issues, just the situation at the bridge, general.'

'I see,' Chuikov said hastily, though he didn't.

'How far is this bridge at Kalach from here?'

'Three . . . four hours,' Chuikov hazarded a guess. 'But why?'

The man from Smersh poked one of his monstrous hands at his eye and rubbed the eyeball as if he were tired. 'You will supply me with a troop of your best commandos,' he said, not answering Chuikov's question directly, but then the men of Smersh never felt constrained to answer anyone's questions, however highly placed that individual might be, save perhaps those of Beria, and he, too, if the rumour were true, was a little afraid of his Smersh operatives. 'They will slip me through the Fritz lines and turn back.'

'Slip you through the Fritz lines!' Chuikov exclaimed incredulously. 'But what . . . what to do?' He looked in red-faced amazement at the slight civilian.

The man from Smersh tittered; it was a strange, uncanny sound at that moment, and it made the small hairs at the back of Chuikov's neck stand erect with fear. 'Nothing very much, comrade general. Just to do my duty as a Smersh operative.' His voice hardened suddenly and his dark eyes gleamed. 'I'll just kill the bastard, that's all. . . .'

8

In the thin yellow November sunshine, Corporal Glinka delicately picked the lice out of the seams of his grey Wehrmacht shirt and laid them on the barrel of the flak cannon, only half listening to Sergeant Sviechka's account of his last encounter with a female before he had been sent to the camps in 1939. 'Well, I managed to get her arse-curtains off without too much trouble,' the bearded NCO with the cross-eyes was saying, 'and of course, yer must remember in them days they had really frilly ones, with lace and everythin'.'

'Shut up, sergeant,' one of his listeners protested in a high mock falsetto, 'you'll have me coming down my leg in half a minute, you dog!'

The other members of the guncrew laughed softly, enjoying the sun, the story, this time out of war. Glinka placed another dead louse on the barrel and said, 'Sleep tight, my little German louse. Your Hitler will pray for you, now you have fallen for Fatherland and Führer.'

'But then the trouble started when I tried to cock my leg over her hams and mount her,' Sviechka continued. "You musn't", she cried. "I must conserve my strength for Stalin and the completion of the Five-Year Plan. What would the Little Father say?" '

The others rocked with laughter at the bearded sergeant's imitation of the unknown woman in that peacetime wheatfield so long ago.

'So I said to her in anger, "Didn't you know that your 'Little Father' fucks little boys?" . . . . Oh, did that do it! Up she was in a flash, frilly knickers in her hand, running through the corn, her skirt up in her haste showing all her arse – and I must admit comrades, it was a big one, as big as any hundred rouble mare, and then, was the watch in the bucket! A couple of thousand Greenhats jumped on me, pounded my butt into the shit with their clubs and hauled me away in chains. Next day the NKVD magistrate sentenced me to twenty-five years in the gulag. . . . Wait for it, comrades,' he held up his big horny hand. 'Not for what you think, but for sabotaging the Five-Year Plan!'

The others expressed their disbelief, as Sergeant Sviechka anticipated they would.

'Yes. Apparently my remark sent the bitch into such a state that she couldn't drive the combined harvester that summer so that made it a serious case of economic sabotage. Hence the twenty-five years.'

He sniffed and tugged the end of his stub-nose. 'The last I heard of the big mare, she was running a Fritz brothel – for their officers who fancied little boys. So much for Stalin's loyal virgin.'

They laughed again and Glinka raised his head from the lice-hunt to say mockingly, 'Come off it, Yuri, everybody knows you only like sheep.'

Once more the men laughed and Sergeant Sviechka said coarsely, '*Job tvojemadj!*'

'Can't, Yuri,' Glinka said easily, 'she's had a Moscow metro train up there these – ' He stopped suddenly and looked upwards.

The others heard the noise at the very same instant. All eyes swung to the winter sky. And there they were. Three Stukas hovering above the bridge like great sinister crows. The Fritzes had begun to react at last.

'Now listen you pomaded warm-brother of a flyboy,' Harsch said over the field telephone. 'I want your boys up there at the double and give the Ivans a taste of your square eggs.'

At the other end of the line, his cousin, *Geschwaderkommodore* Ritter von Heide, commander of the

Richthofen Wing, tut-tutted in that affected manner of his, and at that moment Harsch could imagine him screwing the monocle, which he didn't need, a little more firmly into his pale yellow eye. He then replied, 'But my dear crippled fellow, one can't go around starting private wars like this. Fat Hermann wouldn't take kindly to it one little bit.'

'*Quelle horreur!* One can't speak like that about our illustrious commander, *Reichsmarschall* Hermann Goering.'

'He can go and shit in his field-marshal's hat'.

'Tut-tut, this present unpleasantness has really coarsened you. I do declare that you'll never be received in a Berlin *salon* again. Your language is frightfully coarse. That comes of joining such a working-class unit as the armed SS!'

'Stick your salami in yer own rear entrance and give yourself a cheap thrill.'

Von Heide gave a whimper of delight. 'I say, old chap, you are really surpassing yourself. That's a good one! Can I use it?'

Harsch grinned. His horse-faced affected cousin was a card. 'You may. Now what about a few Stukas?'

'What's it worth to you, cousin? If I'm going to get myself put up against the nearest wall when this business comes out and have my turnip shot off, I want to know that it was worth it.'

'Champagne?' Harsch suggested.

'How much and what quality?' von Heide snapped quickly and Harsch could almost scent his greed over the field telephone.

'A case for every Stuka crew. A case for you, naturally. Brut . . . Château Rothschild.'

'*Zucker!*' his cousin breathed over the field telephone. 'A dream, though one would hate to think what the Führer would say – a Jewish champagne, what next?'

'He'll never know. If you have inhibitions, send him some regulation-issue peppermint tea to brighten his miserable existence.'

'Enough, enough treacherous talk,' Ritter von Heide said hastily. 'Walls have ears you know. What do you want?'

'I have a nice little bunch of Popovs trapped down here at Kalach, a hundred kilometres or more behind our own lines. But seemingly nobody wants to know of their existence. So, as I said earlier on, I've decided to start a small private war with them. For it, I need your daring young flyboys in their Stukas to give me cover when I cross the Don.'

'I see.' His cousin absorbed the information and then said, 'You did say Brut . . . Château Rothschild?'

'I did indeed.'

Good, then you've got your Stukas. Over and out!'

'Over and out!' Harsch echoed, a smile on his lips, asking himself if wars had always been fought like this. A minute later he decided they had.

'*Alarm . . . alarm . . . .*'

The cries ran from man to man. NCO's shrilled their whistles. Officers shouted commands while above them the three black-painted Stukas hovered above the running men like great sinister hawks.

Abruptly, as Sergeant Sviechka's flak-cannon started to pump a white glowing stream of 20mm shells into the sky, the flight-leader flung himself out of the sky. Hurtling downwards, sirens screaming hideously, engine howling in wild protest, the Stuka came straight down at a lunatic speed, the flak flashing by it and exploding in little balls of brown cotton wool. On and on it came. Would it never pull out of that crazy dive?

Just when it seemed the Fritz had to crash into the bridge, the pilot jerked back the stick. The Stuka seemed to stop in mid-air. Later Glinka would swear he had seen the rivets falling off the dive-bomber as its fuselage shuddered and trembled under that tremendous strain. Suddenly a myriad deadly black eggs tumbled rapidly from its sky-blue belly and hurtled to the ground. A pattern of explosions rippled along the snow-covered fields on both sides of the bridge, appearing brown against the white, like the work of a gigantic mole. Fist-sized, red-hot chunks of metal whizzed everywhere. Next to Glinka on the chattering flak-gun, Sergeant Sviechka howled in agony. Glinka, his brow wet with sweat, glanced over at him. Yuri's bearded face seemed to be slipping slowly down to his chest like molten wax, leaving behind a noseless, eyeless, gory red something. Without another word, Yuri fell to the ground – dead.

But Glinka had no time to worry about his running-mate now. The second German was coming down at 400 kilometres an hour. Hurriedly he pressed his eye to the sight again. The twin barrels began to chatter furiously once more. The sky all around the black, diving plane was peppered brown. Still it came on. Again the whole world seemed dominated by that ear-splitting, terrifying scream of the Stuka's twin sirens, followed a moment later by the howl of the air brakes as the pilot wrenched the plane out its dive and the hundred-pound bombs whistled down on the gulag rats' positions.

This time the German was more accurate. The bombs straddled the orchard positions, smashing into the ice strongpoints, flinging dead and dying rats on all sides. High above the battlefield, the flight-leader watched the destruction with pleasure and told himself he'd earned his case of 'frog lemonade'.

Now the last plane came hurtling down. But he was not to be as fortunate as his fellows. On all sides machine-gun and flak fire concentrated on the lone German, white curving tracer filling the air like thick flying hail.

Suddenly the Stuka was hit. Pieces of black metal started to fly from it. Desperately the German fought to keep control. The left wing broke off. It began to flutter to the ground like a great metal leaf.

'*We've got him . . . We've got the Fritz bastard!*' the gulag rats roared with delight and ceased firing to watch the end of the stricken German plane.

It was dramatic. Thick white glycol fumes pouring from its crippled engine, the pilot fighting to the very last to keep it on an even keel, it hit the ground on the west bank of the Don. Somehow the pilot righted it – for a couple of seconds. At 400 kilometres an hour, it ploughed through the thick snow, throwing up a huge white wake behind it. A tyre hit a rock. It burst with an explosion as if an 88mm had just blasted off. The Stuka lurched and shimmied. It swiped a fir. The fir snapped in half and the Stuka swung completely round, the pilot dead over his shattered controls. Next moment it disintegrated as its bombs exploded – one great, blinding white flash that had them blinking their eyes violently and then it was gone, festooning the trees all about with pieces of debris.

Glinka took his eyes off the lone wheel wobbling across the snow and said in an awed voice, 'God Almighty, what a way to go!' And then he remembered the other two planes and cried, 'All right, you slack-arsed shit-shovellers, let's get at it! *Davoi!*'

But the other two Stuka pilots had had enough. Abruptly they were off, winging their way eastwards once more, followed by a hail of angry but ineffectual fire from the gulag rats until Boldin cried, 'Cease firing . . . cease firing . . . Save your ammunition, men – ' His words ended in a cry of alarm.

From the other side of the river, an ancient Skoda tank was slithering down from the German-held heights, followed by a cautious group of infantry in the khaki of the Rumanian Army, each man bent as if advancing against a strong wind.

Obersturmbannführer Harsch was putting the second phase of his private war into action.

The Rumanian lieutenant with the weak, affected, pale

face and pencil-slim moustache, which looked to Harsch as if he painted it on every morning in front of his shaving miirror, had wandered into the little half-track laager, an hour after Harsch had extracted the promise from his cousin that the Stukas would cover his operation. The Rumanian hadn't spoken any German, but with the help of Goldwasser's Italian, which had certain similarities with Rumanian, and a lot of exaggerated gestures, they had discovered that the little Skoda tank was having engine trouble and was being taken to some Rumanian workshops for repairs, escorted by a platoon of infantry as protection against partisans.

'That's *his* story, *Obersturmbannführer*,' Goldwasser said a little contemptuously, while the Rumanian sipped Harsch's last bottle of champagne, his little finger with its manicured nail extended affectedly. 'My guess is that he's just bugged out from the front, knowing what was to come.'

'Exactly my own supposition,' Harsch said, smiling winningly at the young officer in his elegant tailored uniform and gleaming riding boots, complete, for some reason or other, with spurs. 'But that little Skoda could come in very handy, Goldwasser.'

'Perhaps, but I can't see our perfumed friend getting himself involved in anything even slightly dangerous.'

'Probably not,' Harsch agreed. 'But you know these Rumanian cardboard soldiers do tend to lead from the rear. If I could assure him that he wouldn't have to do any fighting himself, but just keep his peasants moving in the general direction of the Popovs, we might pull it off.'

'What are you going to bribe him with? There is no more champers.'

'Have a good look at him, my clever little Jewish friend. What kind of chappie do you think he is?'

Goldwasser sniffed. 'Like *that*, is my guess.'

'My guess, too. A typical warm-brother . . . . Goldwasser,' Harsch smiled again at the simpering Rumanian, 'would you be so kind as to leave my HQ for a few moments? I should like to talk to our dear Rumanian friend under – as it were – four eyes.'

Bewildered and a little hurt that he was being excluded from Harsch's confidence, Goldwasser had left and stood outside in the snow, watching the ragged Rumanians in their tall fur hats, chattering away in their own tongue. He did not wait long.

Exactly five minutes later, Harsch came out of the tent with his arm round the shoulders of the Rumanian officer to announce that the lieutenant was prepared to attack the bridge with his tank and infantry – naturally from a safe distance.

'But how?' Goldwasser asked when they were alone again. 'What was the bribe you used?'

'Me,' Harsch said simply. 'He's never had a German arse before. Obviously the idea excited him greatly. Apparently it will give him some degree of social status among his own kind in Bucharest. It's not every day that a Rumanian homosexual gets a chance to fuck an Aryan beast, what!'

Goldwasser shook his head in mock wonder. The big SS colonel was as crazy as his men.

Now shouting threats and encouragement at his peasant infantry as they crept down the steep bank behind the roaring Skoda with its 37mm cannon switching from side to side suspiciously, and occasionally hurling rocks at those who shrank back, the Rumanian lieutenant directed his 'attack' from behind a safe boulder, his mind full of things other than battle.

But the tank did the trick, however cowardly and undecided the infantry were. Its first shell went hopelessly wide, exploding harmlessly on the far bank, but its explosion was sufficient to panic the gulag rats at the western exit of the bridge. They started to pull back, firing as they withdrew, but pulling back all the same, deathly scared of those whirling tracks which could churn anyone unfortunate enough to fall beneath into a bloody pulp within seconds.

Boldin saw the danger at once. At the moment this was only a withdrawal, but the withdrawal could easily turn into a full-scale retreat. He had seen it happen before when infantry out in the open had been attacked by tanks.

'Vulf,' he cried to the little intellectual who was watching the scene with horrified interest, 'get the Fritz stovepipe. Quick!' For a moment it seemed as if Vulf had not understood. Then he remembered the meaning of the words; it was the Fritz soldiers' slang expression for the primitive Wehrmacht bazooka. He pelted into the little house where they had placed the weapons captured from the Germans guarding the bridge.

Panting, Vulf thrust the long, clumsy-looking anti-tank weapon into Boldin's hands. holding on to the rockets himself. 'What are – '

'Come on,' Boldin cut him short and started to run towards the bridge where the flak-cannon were firing all-out over the heads of the retreating soldiers, with the 20mm shells howling off the tank's sides in white blurs like ping-pong balls. 'Glinka,' he roared above the frenetic chatter of the cannon, 'try to drop your shells on to the infantry behind, and in the name of God, don't shoot us in the back!'

'Try not to comrade major,' Glinka said and raised his sights. 'It'd be the first time I've shot a major – one of ours, I mean.' He spat over the barrel.

Crouched low, the two officers ran forward, brushing the retreating infantry to both sides as they clattered on to the bridge, ignoring the bullets coming from the Skoda's turret as the gunner realized that these two men were not running away, but were intent on fighting.

Boldin grabbed a rocket and thrust it home. 'Fire at the turret-slit, Vulf,' he yelled above the rattle of machine-gun fire. 'Try to confuse the shit!'

He dropped to one knee, the rumbling Skoda a hundred metres away, a twentieth-century David facing up to an armoured Goliath. Hardly sighting the weapon flung across his right shoulder, knowing that if he didn't knock the Goliath out the very next second he'd be dead, Boldin fired.

A crack, a two-metre scarlet flame and the heavy black projectile was hurtling towards the Skoda, rotating crazily, trailing angry red sparks behind it. Crump! The Skoda reared up on its rear bogies and slammed down again with a tremendous thud that shook the very earth. One track slipped off like a severed limb. The tank, out of control, smashed into the side of the bridge and then slowly, very slowly, the gun barrel started to sink like the dying head of some primeval monster.

A minute later the ragged Rumanian infantry were fleeing for their lives, throwing away their weapons in their crazed fear, simply brushing aside the young handsome officer as he tried to stop them streaming on to the steppe beyond and vanishing for good.

Five kilometres away, as the last half-track was successfully manoeuvred from the rough log raft, Harsch correctly interpreted the sudden end to the fire-fight beyond the forest. 'I have a strong feeling, my dear Goldwasser,' he said, watching the men clamber on board their half-tracks in preparation for the last stage of their drive, 'that our Rumanian allies have received a bloody nose from the Popovs.'

'I expect you're right,' Goldwasser agreed as the fierce snap-and-crackle of rifle and machine-gun fire gave way to single shots and then died away altogether.

'Anyway,' Harsch said cheerfully, slapping his sword against the side of the half-track as a signal for the driver to start up and pleased at the success of his stratagem, 'now my pure Aryan arse is safe for a little while longer . . . . Carbide!' he cried.

'Carbide,' the code-word for 'start' ran the length of the little column and the first half-track began to roll. The third phase of *Obersturmbannführer* Harsch's private war had commenced.

On the outskirts of Kalach, the little civilian relieved himself of his heavy rucksack and, taking out his binoculars with those fearsome hands of his, focused them with interest on the scene below.

The man from Smersh had arrived. . . .

BOOK THREE

The Man from Smersh

1

The man from Smersh had been killing men – and women, too – since he was eight, a barefoot orphan from a godforsaken steppe village, one of the thousands of such children which the Civil War, the famine, and the warring armies, Czech, Russian, German, Japanese, French, American, Polish and all the rest, had swept into the cities.

It was not very surprising that he had begun murdering at that tender age. In that year of 1918, little girls sold themselves to men who could have been their grandfathers for a hunk of bread and a bowl of beans; boys who were belt-high to the soldiers did even worse things to keep themselves alive. But he could neither pander nor pimp. Instead he learnt to kill.

On the whole, it had been easy. He was a gentle, mild-mannered quiet boy, in spite of his ragged clothes and dirty face, who no one suspected when he came up to the Cheka* HQ with his scraggy mongrel dog, which he left tied up outside while the feared policemen fed him with sweet cakes and spoonfuls of honey. The bomb tied to the bell of the poor creature killed the lot of them half an hour after he had left.

It had been equally easy with the Red general who had given him a kiss on the forehead and invited the polite little boy into his private room. Whether for sexual reasons or just out of pity, the man from Smersh never found out, for the general did not live much longer after that invitation. He had plunged the razor-sharp dagger he had concealed in his ragged sleeve deep into the

* The first Communist secret police organization.

man's fat belly and ripped hard upwards. The general was dead even before he had slipped out of the window.

In the end the Cheka had caught him and the rest of the White terrorist band for which he had worked so successfully; it had been inevitable as the Communists had started to get the upper hand everywhere. But unlike the rest of the band who had soon been blown to eternity by heavy mauser bullets in those notorious cellars in Kiev, he had survived. The Cheka chief had taken a fancy to him.

Of course, there had been the usual sexual unpleasantness which had put him off that form of relief and entertainment for good. Now what always excited his fantasy was violent death. The perverted Cheka chief had ensured that he had been trained and educated. It had therefore seemed natural that he would become one of the first ten recruits to the NKVD's newest department, Smersh. An angry Stalin had ordered Beria to set it up in the mid-thirties to take bloody revenge on the ever-increasing number of Communists who had become disillusioned with the Dictator and the Party.

They had been great days for him. He had murdered men – and women – all over Europe, travelling first class, dining in the best restaurants, staying in four-star hotels, seeing a world that he had not imagined could possibly exist. Then he had loved his job.

Once he had killed a traitor in Switzerland who had become a religious fanatic – often the case with those who had found the Communist god had failed them. He had dressed himself in a priest's soutane and broad-brimmed hat and met the traitor in a lonely walk where he had bent on his knees to receive a blessing. He'd received it all right: he had pulled the Mauser from the sleeve of his soutane and as the treacherous fool had knelt there humbly, he had blasted the back of his head off!

In Paris, he had shot an old pederast of a Secret Service general, who had defected, as he lay in a drugged sleep in the arms of some naked young French pavement artist.

Once he had even managed to get inside one of the new Fritz concentration camps and drown a renegade German Communist leader, who was suspected of betraying Comintern secrets to the fascists. He had plunged him inside the great forty-seater latrine. Beria had awarded him the Red Star for that job.

In early 1940 he had fallen from grace. He had been sent to Mexico to deal with the arch-traitor Trotsky once and for all, and put an end to his flood of anti-Stalin propaganda. But he had been detected attempting to break into his villa and only escaped by knifing one of the guards and thus raising the alarm. The job of driving the ice-pick into the Jew's skull had been left to the effete Belgian who now languished in a Mexican jail: a thought which still gave him some pleasure.

But the great days abroad were over. Now it was Soviet citizens who couldn't be silenced legally that he had to deal with. The Molotov Cocktail through the letterbox of the well-known Jewish surgeon suspected of being a Zionist; the hand-grenade fixed to the ignition of a Finnish Communist's car who was thought to be supplying information to the British Secret Service; the knife job on one of Beria's former mistresses who had threatened to 'reveal all' in a letter to *Novy Mir*; the hammer-blow on the head of the Latvian hunger-striker.

More than once he had thought he might ask for transfer to some other department of the NKVD, perhaps out to the camps, far away in Siberia where he might be able to rehabilitate himself in the eyes of Beria. But he found he could not exist without the thrill that killing gave him; the knowledge that in his hands lay the power of life or death over virtually everyone in the Soviet state. He reasoned that however unimportant or humble his new 'cases' (as he always called them) were, the fact that he was one of the handful of men in the

USSR able to execute made him important, very important indeed. He stayed with Smersh.

Now on this chill November day, with the leaden clouds beginning to build rapidly, promising a snow-storm before the day was out, the man from Smersh considered how he was to tackle his present 'case'.

His professional pride and Beria's strict orders that the death of Colonel Katukov had to be publicly demonstrated to his soldiers so that they realized what the price of disobedience was made it impossible for him to kill the officer by means of a rifle with a telescopic sight. He would have to get so close to the 'case' that it would be inevitable that his soldiers would be involved. The question was: how would they react? They were a long way from Moscow here, and there were many of them. Would they calmly accept the fact that their colonel had been condemned to death in the capital and he had come from there to carry out the sentence?

Of course the man from Smersh knew that most of them were *tshestyni vor*, professional criminals, who owed allegiance only to themselves. But what of the rest, the kind of gulag rat he detested most: the anti-Communist, the ones who hated the Soviet system which had made him what he was? Would they tolerate the execution? He pondered the question in his little cave hiding-place. Finally, he decided that first he would make a reconnaissance. Veteran of half a hundred murders as he was and supremely confident in himself, he was no fool. First of all he had to find out how the land lay before he dealt with the 'case'. Slipping into his rucksack and shouldering his rifle, he set off for the orchard below as the first gentle flakes of snow began to drift down.

The man from Smersh was on his way for his own particular date with destiny: he was going to his last killing. . . .

'Germany, Germany without everything . . . without

butter, without meat. Even our little bit of jam, the Admin eats,' Obersturmbannführer Harsh sang softly to the tune of 'Deutschland über Alles', swinging his broken sword to keep time as the half-tracks nosed their way through the ever-thickening snowfall towards the Russian-held bridge.

Now the snow was hitting the half-tracks' windscreens like a wall of white flak so that the drivers were forced to reduce speed in order to be able to see the road ahead. In this kind of weather, Goldwasser, crouched shivering next to the singing SS officer, told himself they could bump right into the Red positions without warning. As the snow fell in solid sheets, as if some God on high were determined to blot out this war-torn world for ever, Goldwasser wondered what Harsch would do. As if he could read the Italian officer's mind, Harsch leaned over, pressing his mouth close to Goldwasser's ear, for the wind had now reached hurricane force, and bellowed, 'Don't worry, my little Jewish friend. I'm not going to attack in this weather. Even the Führer's Fire Brigade is not that *meschugge*.'

Goldwasser smiled at the use of the Yiddish word for 'crazy', and bellowed back, 'Then why don't we stop now, *Obersturm*?'

'Because this storm provides excellent cover. We can get right into the Popov positions without being discovered. The wind drowns the noise of the engines.'

'And then?'

'And then, my dear Goldwasser,' Harsch gave him an unholy smile, 'as befits two gents and officers, you and I will do a little recce.'

'Recce?' Goldwasser asked, feeling a cold finger of fear trace its way down his spine so that he had to shudder.

Harsch yelled, 'Yes, we'll recce their positions for the morning attack *personally*.'

Goldwasser groaned.

'I remember the crazy bastard once running through the whole camp naked,' Corporal Glinka recounted. He had a salt herring sticking out of his arse, shouting he was a mermaid! That was when the *telpluschka* arrived from Moscow with a fresh consignment of prisoners for the gulag. God, he must have put the wind up them! But he was like that. I remember the time that he promised he'd eat the commandant's pet dog if somebody would give him his tobacco ration.' He sighed at the memory. 'Those were the days, brothers. They'll never come back now.'

Vulf huddled next to Boldin, a blanket wrapped around his head, snorted '*Djavell!* That corporal must have had over his hundred.* Those were the days!' he sneered. 'Fun in the camp! Fun in the *telpluschka*!' He tapped his forehead. 'Absolutely, totally crazy!'

Boldin nodded absently and wished the snowstorm would end so that he could get outside and check their front. The Stukas and the attack by the Rumanians had obviously been the prelude to the main assault. But where was it? What had become of those SS and their half-tracks who had attacked them on the first day? Had they called off their attack because of the weather, or was there something else behind it? The thought worried him in spite of knowing that there were little groups of unfortunate gulag rats hidden in their ice-made positions out there in the raging storm. Not that he could see them in spite of the fact that it was still daylight; the storm was too intense.

'I remember the first time I saw the door of the *telpluschka* open to admit us prisoners,' Vulf was saying, 'I was nearly knocked over backwards by the stench. It hadn't been cleaned out from the last lot of prisoners so that the shit was knee-deep on the floor. They'd fed them rotten fish soup for three days and they'd died like flies from diarrhoea and choking on their own vomit,

* The vodka ration amounted to 100 grams; hence 'had over his hundred' meant drunk.

and now we were expected to undergo the same process. What a mess! Out of the seventy prisoners who set out with me, only twenty of us made it. Every day we shoved out ten or more dead when we halted at night for fish soup and more fish soup!'

'It's always been that way in Russia, little brother,' Boldin said, remembering how he had first gone to war in the large wooden goods wagon back in 1916 and how he had been transported to the camp in one after his disgrace twenty-odd years later, a marshal of the Soviet Union reduced to a 'faceless one', a mere number on the NKVD's arrest list. In the Czar's time then and Stalin's now. The *telpluschka* have always taken us Russians either to die in battle for the tyrant or to slave to death for him in some damned camp.'

Vulf nodded. 'I suppose you're right, Boldin.'

They fell silent again, listening to the howl of the wind and the patter of snowflakes on the little window of the *isba*.

'I think the Fritzes have got their arses in the bacon slicer,' Glinka said changing the subject. 'They got a bellyful this morning and they've buggered off. Besides, the Fritzes are easy put off by a couple of odd snow-flakes.' He jerked a dirty thumb at the window, now almost packed with wet snow. 'They run for cover as soon as they see a bit o' white.'

Boldin smiled and wished he had Glinka's confidence. The Fritzes were out there somewhere, he could almost smell them, but where? – that was the question. And then he had his brainwave. 'Listen, you rats,' he announced, sitting up suddenly, 'you've been running off yer mouths too long, doing nothing while your com-rades freeze their eggs off out there in the orchard.'

'Hard shit,' Glinka said. 'It'll be our turn tonight.'

'But till then, I've got a little job of work for your delicate lily-white paws.' Boldin said, taking a bullet out of his spare pistol magazine and then pulling out his combat knife. 'I'm going to show you how to make a deballocker that will really sit – so watch carefully because you're all going to be making them in five minutes' time. After all, we have to make our Fritz friends feel really warmly welcome if they chance to come stumbling through our positions this night.' Gritting his teeth, he scored his knife across the nose of the slug and then repeated the score in the other direction to form a cross. The deballocker was under construction.

2

The clatter of the half-tracks was almost drowned by the howling wind. The infantry walking on both sides of them as they advanced through the whirling snow were bent like old men, their uniforms whipped tight against their skinny bodies, the snowflakes clinging to their faces so that every few moments they had to wipe their eyes clear in order to see where they were going.

Now it was nearly dawn, the time, Harsch knew, when the Popov outposts were most likely to be dozing, especially in a storm like this. After all, who in his right mind would attack in weather like this? Only the Führer's Fire Brigade, he told himself wrily.

His plan was simple. It had to be under such conditions. The half-tracks would stick to what was still left of the road, while his grenadiers came in on both flanks, working their way through the Popov positions which he and Goldwasser had reconnoitred two hours before. When he judged they were in position, his red flare would be the signal for a bold, quick attack – for which the Führer's Fire Brigade was famous. With luck he would roll up the Popovs, in spite of their superior numbers, before they knew what had hit them.

The forest on both sides of the road had begun to thin. The wind howled straight across the steppe and, unprotected by the firs now, it made their progress even more difficult. The countryside was dead, as if it had been abandoned long ago to this cruel snow. They filed by a dead cow, already half buried by the snow, its legs sticking rigidly upwards so that it looked like a tethered barrage balloon.

Harsch narrowed his eyes to slits and peered through the whirling flakes. With difficulty, he could just make out the smudge of the new trees, the orchard, in which lay the main Popov positions on this side of the bridge. He tapped the driver on the shoulder and he slowed down even more. 'Bail out!' he commanded.

Like the veterans they were, the grenadiers rolled over the sides of the still-moving half-track, bodies held low so that they didn't present too big a target, and dropped into the snow. Harsch, gripping his sword, followed equally expertly for a man with one hand; and more awkwardly, Goldwasser.

A minute later the line of half-tracks, now occupied only by the driver and the gunner manning the 20mm cannon, disappeared into the snowstorm. Harsch waited till the last one's tail convoy light had vanished, then commanded, '*Mir nach!*'

Unslinging their weapons, ready for action, the grenadiers started to file after the big colonel up in the lead, with Igor slightly to his front and Goldwasser at his side.

The minutes passed. There was no sound save their own harsh breathing and the howl of the wind. In front Igor stumbled on, his head bent, sniffing the air like a tracker dog. 'He can *smell* Popovs, that one,' Harsch explained to Goldwasser. 'In this shitty weather, I'm glad of him. He won't let us stumble into some Popov shit heap.'

Goldwasser mumbled something, and Harsch said, 'If I survive this war, I'm going to take Igor back to the Reich with me. With him I won't need to keep any expensive hunt – '

His words were interrupted by a slight, dry crack like the breaking of a brittle twig in high summer. In the brief flash of blue light, Goldwasser caught a glimpse of Igor, screaming until his screams were drowned by the snow, clutching at his crotch and falling.

Harsch sprang forward. He turned his servant over. Igor lay there gasping like a stranded fish. Hastily

Harsch thrust the blade of his sword into Igor's mouth to prevent his tongue curling backwards and choking him.

'Here,' Harsch commanded while all around him the grenadiers crouched, their weapons at the ready, eyes peering through the snow to their front, 'take the flash. Let's see what happened.'

Goldwasser pulled the little torch off the lapel of Harsch's tunic and clicked the switch.

In the circle of faint blue light, he could see from Igor's face that the little Ukrainian was dying. His eyelids were flickering rapidly and his nose was already beginning to take on that cream-white, pinched look of the dying.

'Run it over his body,' Harsch ordered. 'Let's see what hit him.'

Carefully, Goldwasser did so and then he gasped with shocked revulsion. 'In God's name!' he began and couldn't continue.

'A deballocker,' Harsch said bitterly. 'Since our little recce, the Ivan bastards have slipped out and sown a deballocker minefield.'

'But what is a . . . deballocker.'

'Something only those Popov pigs could think up,' Harsch snarled, stroking the dying man's forehead, as his body heaved now with the final agony of death. 'A dum-dum bullet attached to the cartridge and a spring. Step on it and you're circumsized more thoroughly than any of your rabbis could do it.'

At his side, Igor's head fell to one side. Gently, very gently, Harsch drew his sword out of the dead man's mouth. 'He wasn't a bad bastard,' he said and closed his servant's eyes for good.

'What now?' Goldwasser asked, shuddering at the thought of the terrible death which lay just in front of them.

'Don't worry, Goldwasser, I won't let you have your thing docked any shorter. Now it's going to be up to the half-tracks. We'll make our way back to the road and follow them up.'

He rose to his feet and pulled out his Very pistol. Raising it, he cried the battle-cry of the armed SS – '*Alles für Deutschland* –' and pressed the trigger.

The signal flare hissed into the howling sky and burst into a bright, unreal light, bathing all below in its blood-red colour. The battle for the orchard had commenced.

'*Fritzes . . . the Fritzes are coming . . . .*'

The cries of alarm and fear pierced the howling storm as the half-tracks, racing at full speed, their cannon chattering, appeared out of the storm, heading straight for the forward posts.

What happened next was a massacre. The half-tracks simply rolled over the gulag rat positions, the drivers swinging their heavy vehicles round and round on the slick ice, catching glimpses of white, terrified faces below them, as they churned the occupants to bloody pulp, moving on to the next position, tracks red with blood. Here and there the rats had somehow managed to bury into the iron-hard earth and thought themselves proof even against the ten-ton half-tracks. They had not reckoned with Harsch's veterans. Blocking the whole top of the hole, they gunned their engines. Thick grey, choking smoke filled the pits. Clutching their throats, coughing horribly, the rats suffocated and the half-tracks clattered on to commence their deadly work once again.

Boldin, pistol in hand, firing at the white blaze of the attacking vehicles' flak-cannon, knew the position was lost. Already individual gulag rats were rising panic-stricken from their holes and positions, tossing away their weapons and beginning to run for the rear. It would be only a matter of moments before the whole position crumpled irretrievably. He had to rescue what could still be rescued. 'Vulf,' he called above the screams of the dying and the terribly mutilated men in the front positions, 'try to blind the drivers with your Very pistol . . . I must get the rest of them out. . . . Back off to Colonel Katukov's positions around the HQ!'

'*Horoscho!*' Vulf understood immediately. Crouching there, he fired his first red Very light directly at the nearest half-track. It burst on the vehicle's ugly metal snout. Red, blinding light shot up. The driver braked instinctively, thinking he had been hit by a bazooka-rocket and when he realized he hadn't, swung his vehicle round to escape into the white gloom.

Boldin dashed forward, kicking and slamming his pistol butt at the terrified gulag rats, snarling commands, snapping off wild, hopeless shots at the half-tracks whirling in and out of the stunted, snow-heavy apple trees like primeval monsters hunting their quarry. '*Back . . . back . . . in the name of hell, withdraw to the colonel's HQ*!' he yelled, blinded every time that Vulf spotted one of the marauding German vehicles and fired, bathing the trees in that glowing, unreal blood-red light.

Somehow or other he brought some order into the unholy mess. Firing as they went, the gulag rats started to back off. Boldin was everywhere, missing death by seconds time and time again, herding his men to the big, squat HQ, while the half-tracks pushed home their advantage.

And then suddenly, as was the case with all attacks, the steam went out of it. The firing and the pressure died away. Now could be heard the screams of the abandoned wounded as they died among the shattered trees of the orchard, as Harsch's infantry rejoined the half-tracks ro protect them from some bold bazooka man who had elected to remain behind and deal with the vulnerable armoured vehicles.

Sweating heavily in spite of the biting cold as he fought the survivors back to the centre of the battalion's defences, Boldin knew well that heart-breaking wail: an explosive bullet to the lung or something of that kind. The gutshot and the thighshot died easily; the blood had run out of them before they knew what had happened to their poor, mutilated bodies. But the lungshot and the headshot, they died slowly and horribly.

The little hairs erect at the back of his head, Boldin herded the rats through those scythed-off trees, ears full of those terrible cries, forcing himself by an effort of sheer will-power not to abandon the retreat and go rushing backwards to finish them off with the a shot.

Then they were flooding Katukov's positions and Vulf was helping him through the door into the warmth streaming out from the great green-tiled oven which dominated the colonel's room. And Katukov was saying, 'Now we are really in the shit, Boldin! Really deep in it up to our hooters!' as if he, Boldin, were responsible for the defeat in the orchard.

'So, this is our position,' Katukov said, his nerve recovered after the shock of that rout in the orchard, ignoring the thud-thud of the German flak-cannon against the thick walls of his HQ. 'We hold this place and a line,' with a borrowed bayonet he traced a line on the dust of the floor, 'up to the bridge, with both exits from it in our hands.'

Another burst of 20mm shells stitched a furious pattern on the wall outside and Vulf commented cynically, 'For a little while longer at least.'

Katukov ignored him. 'My estimate of their strength is that they are reinforced company size. We outnumber them considerably.'

'Yes, comrade colonel, but they've got armour of a sort and mobile cannon. All we've got is rifle and machine-gun power – and if I may be so bold to say so, we're bogged down in this place, whereas they've got mobility on their side!' Boldin said.

At the far end of the room, Glinka, pouring shredded tobacco on an open wound in his right arm by way of antiseptic, was saying contemptuously, 'When it comes to being shit-arsed smart, those rats up front are like the feller who carries a fork with him all the time in case it rains pea soup. They should have been expecting something like that after we'd spent half the shitting night spreading deballockers on both sides of the road. But no, they lay in their ice-palaces sawing wood, while the Fritzes sneaked up on them and gave them the real old purple shaft – right up the arse!'

Boldin smiled a little wearily. Glinka's assessment of the situation wasn't exactly staff college, but it served well enough. They had been caught napping. Now the question was: what should they do?

Katukov seemed to be able to read the big major's mind for he said, 'I propose a counter-attack to restore our positions in the orchard. We must keep the Fritzes as far away from the bridge as possible. That is essential.'

'With what?' Vulf asked.

Again Katukov ignored the question, but Boldin didn't. 'Colonel,' he said sombrely, 'a counter-attack against those mobile flak-cannon would be sheer suicide. They'd slaughter us. The attack would come to a standstill within five minutes. Quite purposeless,' he ended, without emotion. 'We don't stand a chance.'

'And what do you suggest, *marshal*?' Katukov emphasized the old rank with a sneer.

'Marshal or major,' Boldin controlled his anger, 'I'm giving you a simple soldier's thoughts on the subject.'

'They are?'

'Twofold. Either we try some sort of surprise flank attack and catch them off guard, or – ' he hesitated.

'Get on with it, man!'

'We abandon the position tonight as soon as it's dark. They haven't the infantry to stop – '

'Abandon the position!' Katukov cut in brutally. 'What are you saying, Boldin?'

'I think I made my meaning quite clear, comrade colonel,' Boldin said coldly. 'I have backed you up so far because I thought you might be right and have a chance of succeeding. Now I don't think you have. Sooner or later the Fritzes will bring their full weight to bear upon us and our effort will have been for nothing. All that will result from it is that another eight hundred *matkas* somewhere back there to the east will weep for dead sons – to no purpose.' He shrugged expansively. 'All to no avail.'

'But in thirty-six hours the great offensive will start,' Katukov protested. 'It is vital to its success that we hold the bridge till then.'

'*If* it starts,' Vulf said.

'My concern is my gulag rats,' Boldin added his final words to the discussion.

Katukov stared glumly at the ground.

At the far end of the room Glinka was saying, as if to emphasize the problem, for their food was beginning to run out too, 'Brothers, I'd sell my arse for a piece of good sausage now – even *bad* sausage. I'm that god-damned hungry!' Nobody laughed. It was a sign of the mood they were in.

Katukov raised his head. 'Boldin, give me one more chance.' He looked at Boldin, eyes pleading. 'Let me have that last counter-attack. If it fails, *you* decide.'

Boldin looked at the big colonel, his face tortured with emotion.

'All right,' he made his decision. 'One last time. After that, Katukov, I give the orders. . . .'

3

'What will the Fritzes do, little brother?' Boldin asked, trying to out-think the Germans somewhere out there in the howling storm.

'Am I Jesus?'

'If Jesus were a little four-eyed homosexual, yes!' Boldin said with a short laugh.

Vulf didn't share it.

'My guess is that they will attempt to cut us off from the bridge,' Boldin went on. 'After all, that is the important thing – the bridge.'

'So?' Vulf asked, a little annoyed by the reference to his sexual habits and this tactical rambling which didn't interest him one bit.

'When will the Fritzes make an attempt, where will they be at the time and how can we turn the situation to our advantage? Three small questions with – '

'Large answers,' Vulf beat him to it.

'Exactly.'

'As far as they are concerned,' Boldin said, thinking aloud, 'we're as good as prisoners tied up in this place. They can contain us with a handful of infantry and make the dash for the bridge with their half-tracks.'

'Oh, Boldin,' Vulf groaned, 'what does that damned bridge really matter? Do you think anyone will give a damn about it in a couple of days' time? It might rate a couple of lines in *Pravda* in due course, but that'll be about it. Somebody might read them – after they've read the details of the latest ration issue, of course.'

Boldin laughed shortly. 'I suppose you're right, Vulf, you little cynic. Why do wretches like us, the scum of the camps fight and die for that piece of architecture out there? There'll be no glory in it for us. You can be sure your *Pravda* won't mention that it was captured and held by the gulag rats. That honour will go to some Guards regiment or other.' He shrugged. 'But I suppose it's in the blood – of an old soldier like myself, I mean. We fight for the sake of fighting.'

Again Vulf grunted and lapsed into silence, leaving Boldin to his deliberations.

At the other end of the room, Katukov was thinking hard, too. He had come to the same conclusion as Boldin that as soon as visibility improved, the Fritzes would rush the bridge with their half-tracks; it would be a typical bold German tactic. But in doing so, as always with the *Blitzkrieg* methods the Fritzes favoured, they would offer their flank, yet what could the gulag rats do with that open flank? The only heavy weapons were on the bridge and they had used the last of the rockets for the captured 'stove-pipe'. How could infantry armed only with rifles and machine-guns stop armour? And then he remembered the old days of the revolution and he had it. He stood up abruptly. 'Boldin,' he called, startling the men slumped dozing on the straw-covered floor, 'Molotov Cocktails!'

Boldin clicked his fingers excitedly, then his smile vanished as quickly as it had appeared. 'But where do we get the gas from, colonel?'

Katukov had his answer ready. 'The Skoda. It must have at least half a tank full of gas.'

Boldin snapped into action at once. 'Glinka, you rogue!'

Glinka woke up reluctantly from an exciting dream in which he had been sitting at a table groaning under the weight of succulent hams and tender roast chicken. 'Yes, comrade major?'

'Glinka, you are the greatest rogue in the battalion. If anyone can get something – before it gets lost, it is Corporal Glinka.'

Glinka looked down at his hands. 'Things just seem to stick to them, comrade,' he said. 'Can't explain how it always happens to poor old Glinka.' He sighed, as if the cares of the world weighed heavy on his shoulders.

'All right, *poor, old* Glinka,' Boldin said, amused by the broad-backed rogue, 'I'm going to give you the chance of doing some official looting.'

Glinka's eyes narrowed, while Katukov frowned, displeased at the manner in which Boldin was handling this business. One didn't joke about such important military matters. 'What do you mean exactly, comrade?' he asked suspiciously.

'Glinka, you know that Rumanian tin can out there?'

Glinka nodded.

'My information is that it contained some very nasty Rumanian sausage. Someone reported that he could smell bacon in it, too. It's all yours – if you can bring back all the gas the tank contains.'

'So that's it, eh, comrade? I thought it was too good to be true. You want me to stick my bacon in the slicer to bring back the gas, eh?'

Boldin laughed. 'Glinka, I could order you, but I'm not. I'm dangling a bit of bait in front of your greedy optics to make you – er – volunteer.'

Glinka considered a moment or two. He knew from past experience that tank crews turned their vehicles into mobile stores. The ordinary stubble-hopper had to hump all his stuff; as a result he didn't carry much. Not the tanker. Anything he could lay his oily paws on was pushed aboard; after all he didn't have to carry it. He licked his lips greedily. Those Rumanians were reputedly great chow-hounds. 'All right, comrade major, I am ready to volunteer for this hazardous mission with my section.'

'What!' came the cries of alarm from his men lying in the straw, We didn't volunteer, corporal!'

'Of course, yer did,' Glinka said easily, reaching for his machine-pistol. 'Yer were just too shy, that's all.

Now move those lazy arses of yourn! Find what buckets and cans you can – come on, get the lead out!' He turned back to Boldin, grinning from ear to ear. 'Do you think Old Leather Face'll award me the Order of Red Salami for this one, comrade major?'

Katukov glared at him.

Five minutes later, Corporal Glinka was gone into the raging snow storm. Boldin would never see him again. . . .

Back in the house, the others settled down to wait.

The little patrol battled through the snowstorm, chewing the extra ration of biscuit that Boldin had allowed them, encouraged at regular intervals by Glinka's 'There'll be Rumanian brandy for all the canned goulash!' as they fought against the wind, heading in the general direction of the bridge.

They blundered into their own positions around the twin flak-cannon at this side of the bridge and nearly got shot by a trigger-happy sentry, who was startled by their sudden appearance out of the swirling white flakes. They were saved by Glinka's quick: 'Shoot me, yer son-of-a-whore and I'll jam yer rifle so far up yer arse that yer tonsils pop!'

There they halted for a few minutes to get their breath back and warm their frozen limbs by the fire which the gunners had got burning in the gun-pit. Then they set off again, now in battle formation as they passed their last post on the other side of the bridge, straining their eyes for the first glimpse of the wrecked Skoda.

Glinka stumbled over the snow-shrouded body of a dead Rumanian soldier and called, 'Over here, brothers! Come on. Follow me!'

A couple of minutes later they blundered right into the little tank and while Glinka pushed aside the dead gunner and began to search eagerly for food and drink, his patrol filled their cans and bucket with the precious petrol they would need to make the Molotov Cocktails.

But Glinka was in for a disappointment. All he could find in the confused mess of the wrecked tank was a dried-up piece of sausage, heavily spiced with garlic to disguise the cheap horsemeat that it was made from. Miserably he swallowed it, telling himself that there had to be some food somewhere. His stomach was doing back-flips with hunger, rumbling menacingly like an angry lion, and when Corporal Glinka's stomach did back-flips, there was trouble brewing, unless the 'inner pig-dog', as he often called it to himself, was satisfied.

He sniffed the air, finishing the rest of the horsemeat sausage hurriedly before the others discovered him eating, listening to their hushed chatter as they emptied the Skoda's tank. Suddenly his eyes lit up. There was no mistaking it. Somewhere out there in the flying white gloom there was hot, frying pork-belly. His trained nose twitched. There was no doubt at all. *Frying pork-belly made of real pig!*

He rose hastily and wiped the back of his hairy hand across his wet lips so that the rest of the patrol would not be able to see the 'food-wake', as he called it, and clambered out into the storm. 'Listen, you barn-shitters, make tracks and get back to the HQ,' he ordered.

They looked up at him, their faces wet with snowflakes. 'Where's the chow?' one of them asked.

'Don't you worry about that, arse with ears!' Glinka rapped, excited beyond measure by that wonderful smell of frying pork. 'Leave the worrying to Corporal Glinka. That's what he's paid for.'

'But you promised!' someone objected.

'Do you want a knuckle sandwich?' Glinka said threateningly, doubling his fist into a small steam-shovel. 'Start counting yer ivories if you do.'

'But you said – '

'Listen,' he drowned the protest, 'if I find anything you'll get your share. Now off you go. I'll follow yer up. Move it!'

Reluctantly they started to trail away, bearing their

heavy burdens until the storm swallowed them up. Glinka chuckled, telling himself that some idiot of a Rumanian peasant had got himself a lump of meat out there and was indulging in a little bit of private chow-time. It would be as easy as falling off a log. He slung his tommy-gun and pulled the long knife out of his felt boot. Crouching low, sniffing the snow-filled air at regular intervals, he started to trail that delicious odour.

The man from Smersh crouched in the low cave, considering his situation while he ate. He had just consumed one of the special cans of soup which Churchill had sent from England for the use of Russia's partisans. When you pulled a cartridge in the middle, the can heated of its own accord. Now he was roasting a large piece of salt pork on a spit above the solid-fuel cooker which could fold up into his pocket – again a gift from that whisky-swilling plutocrat in London.

He had been witness to the Fritz half-track attack which had stopped him in his attempt to break into the gulag rat position and carry out Beria's orders. Now he wondered what he should do next. He had no wish to clash with the Germans. He did not fear them. But he was realist enough to know that he had not the power over them that he had over his fellow countrymen. Everywhere in Soviet Russia, the very name 'Smersh' had a paralysing effect on his fellow countrymen. In Russia, he could walk into any community and dominate it. But not with the Fritzes. He cooked his meat, listening to the sizzle and splash of the fat as it dropped on the cooker, and discussed with himself in the fashion of lonely men, what he should do. It was thus that Corporal Glinka discovered him.

'Russian?' he asked, standing there at the entrance of the cave, knife in hand, greedy little eyes fixed on the cooking meat.

The man from Smersh jumped with surprise and

then, trying to check his jingling nerves as he saw the uniform, answered, 'Yes . . . yes, I am Russian.'

Glinka lowered his knife. 'Nice bit of pig-meat you got there, comrade,' he said, his mind too full of food to ask what a civilian was doing out here, cooking a prime piece of pork.

'Do you want some?' the man from Smersh asked, recovering quickly.

'Can a duck swim?' Glinka said eagerly, the saliva trickling down his bearded chin now. Whatever doubts he may have had were overcome by the delicious scent of food and the strange civilian's polite, mild manner; the man couldn't be dangerous.

The man from Smersh handed him the spit and said, 'Help yourself.'

Glinka reached over eagerly and with his knife sawed off a chunk of the meat. 'Better than getting yer leg over a fat-titted whore,' he gurgled and bit deep into the meat, letting the grease run down his chin.

'I wouldn't know,' replied the man from Smersh, taking in the tattoos on Glinka's fingers and the blue marks on the back of his neck with the legend 'Chop Here'. The man was obviously a professional criminal. All the signs were there. 'What is the situation over there?' he asked.

'Shitty, decidedly shitty,' Glinka answered, mouth full of pork.

'What do you mean?' the man from Smersh asked, telling himself that the firing he had heard early on had been that of the Germans or Rumanians after all. He had been right not to go into the gulag rats' camp.

'We expect the Fritzes to attack with armour as soon as this snow stops. That's why we were just near here. We were getting gas for Molotov Cocktails.'

'Your colonel intends to defend the place then?' the little civilian asked.

'Yes, he's a hard-arsed bastard, that Katukov. Typical Greenhat,' Glinka answered, gnawing at the meat. 'Hey, how did you know – ' Glinka's startled query ended as the thin wire cut deep into his throat. He died with his mouth full of uneaten pork. Presumably it would have been the way that Corporal Glinka, the comedian of the 333rd Punishment Battalion, would have wanted to die.

4

Silence!

The thump-thump of the flak cannon against the walls of the HQ had stopped at last.

Men looked at each other significantly. From above, in the look-out tower the sentry cried, 'The snow's letting up, comrade colonel.'

Katukov stared at Boldin. 'This is it, then?'

Boldin nodded grimly. 'Yes,' he said, 'we'd better get off.'

He turned to the gulag rats, armed with the crude petrol bombs, who were to be covered by the rest. 'Don't take any stupid risks,' he warned. 'Throw the things and then go to ground straightaway. Clear?'

'Clear,' they answered, knowing that they were potential suicide candidates.

Now from the direction of the orchard where the Germans were came the rumble of engines starting with difficulty in the cold dawn air.

Up in the watch-tower the sentry cried excitedly, 'I think I can see them, comrades.'

Katukov, who would hold the house in case the Germans did make an attack on it, swept a quick look round the men posted at the windows and nodded his satisfaction and then, surprisingly for that unemotional man, stuck out his hand to Boldin. 'Good luck, brother,' he said.

Shocked into silence by the gesture, Boldin took it and then his group was out the door. Little Vulf, who was to remain behind, was shaking his head and telling himself not many of them would survive the next hour. He attempted to fix the look on Boldin's bold, broad face in his mind's eye in case he never saw him again; and then Boldin, too, was gone into the last flakes of snow.

The ten half-tracks burst out of the orchard at widely separated points and then, as prearranged, formed up into a large open arrowhead with Harsch's own vehicle in the centre and directly beyond the point so that he could control the attack by hand signals if necessary. Satisfied that they were all in their positions, Harsch pumped his one arm up and down rapidly three times, the infantry signal for 'at the double' and then they were off, a steel wedge of racing, roaring vehicles heading straight for the bridge. Almost immediately the two flak guns some 500 metres away opened up. White tracer shells started to curve through the grey air towards them, gathering speed every instant.

Goldwasser flashed a look at Harsch, holding on the best he could as the half-track rattled and swayed over the rough ground. There was no fear on the German's cruelly handsome face, just excitement, boundless excitement.

Wham!... wham!... wham!... Goldwasser ducked instinctively, as a salvo of shells pumped a line of gleaming holes the length of the half-track. But still it raced on through that hail of fire.

Now the air was full of searing purple flame, the acrid, choking stink of burnt cordite, whirling copper shell-bands and fist-sized pieces of flying metal. A half-track was hit in the engine. It rolled to a stop, smoke pouring from the shattered motor. Immediately the grenadiers flung themselves over the sides and dropped to the snow, their weapons chattering.

The wild drive continued. They burst through the thin line of defenders who scattered immediately, throwing away their weapons in panic. Next instant they went down screaming under the flailing tracks of the armour, bodies pressed flat like cardboard in the snow.

Now the lead half-tracks were firing flat out themselves, their fire concentrated on the two flak guns holding the bridge only four hundred metres away. Fountains of snow and earth spouted up in great rolling clouds all around them and a terrified, yet mesmerized Goldwasser could see the tracer slugs howling white and red from the steel girders of the bridge. Still the flak guns kept firing, though their gunners were badly rattled now and their fire was scattered.

'*Heaven, arse and cloudburst!*' Harsch cried exuberantly, waving his broken sword. 'This is the life, Goldwasser, eh?' He grinned down at the white-faced Italian. 'Don't worry, my friend, you can only die once – and think – you can give your life for Adolf Hitler! What a –'

His words were drowned by the rending crash of one of the half-tracks, its windscreen a spider's web of smashed glass, its headless driver sprawled over the shattered wheel, slamming into one of the little *isbas*, completely out of control, scattering dead and dying men in its wake.

Harsch frowned and in a more subdued voice said, 'Two gone, eight to go.'

They raced on. Now the bridge was only 300 metres away.

'Here they come,' Boldin hissed, wiping the sweat off his hand and taking up his bottle again.

All around him in the ditch, his men did the same. Behind them, the second line, armed with rifles and tommy-guns, prepared to cover them.

Boldin narrowed his eyes. The half-tracks were rattling across the rough, snow-heavy ground at an amazing speed. In a minute they would be almost parallel with them, at perhaps fifty metres' distance. The trick would be to rush them, fling their homemade bombs and duck; and Boldin had no illusions about how many would survive that wild rush.

He began to count out loud. '*One . . . two . . . three . . . four.*' His men tensed. '*Five . . . six . . . .*' They lit the rough wicks that led into the deadly mixture. '*Seven . . . eight . . . nine!*' The half-tracks were almost upon them now. '*Ten . . . FORWARD A-T-T-A-C-K!*'

And then they were up, crouched low, racing for the nearest half-tracks, screaming loudly while behind them their comrades sent a stream of covering fire over their heads. The Germans spotted them almost at once. The grenadiers raised themselves up above the protective steel sides, knowing instinctively what the men running towards them across the snow were attempting to do.

A soldier next to Boldin screamed and stumbled into him. He pushed the wounded rat to one side. Fortunately. Next instant the bottle he was carrying burst into flames, streaming its fiery contents all over the unfortunate man, turning him immediately into a human torch.

Harsch saw the danger at once. He dropped his sword and placed his hand, fingers outspread, on the top of his helmet, the infantry signal for 'rally on me', crying furiously, 'Back off. Great crap on the Christmas tree – *Back off!*'

Too late!

Already the first bomber had got within throwing range, staggering through the falling bodies of his comrades who were going down on all sides, braving the wall of fire being put up by the desperate grenadiers. Screaming obscenities, he lobbed his bomb at the half-track in the very same instant that a burst of schmeisser fire ripped open his chest and sent him staggering backwards.

The bomb burst with a soft plop against the side of the half-track, splashing gasoline everywhere which ignited immediately. In a flash, the grenadiers were ablaze, the deadly, searing flame burning the length of the vehicle like a gigantic blow-torch.

Boldin in the lead, fighting his way through his dying

men, screaming with agony as they fell, clapping bloody hands to ruined faces, chests, limbs, reeled back at that tremendous heat, his nostrils assailed by the sickening stench of burning flesh, as the terrible flames shrivelled the trapped, screaming grenadiers into charred pygmies, as the half-track careered on, trailing flames behind it.

Out of the smoke and flame came another. He didn't hesitate. Ignoring the slugs cutting up little spurts of snow all around his running feet, he pelted within twenty metres of the half-track so that he could see the pale-faced young Germans with their silver SS runes and death's-head badges and flung his Molotov Cocktail. Next instant he flung himself headlong into the snow, the burst intended for his chest missing him by millimetres.

The bomb exploded against the half-track. The driver bailed out, leaving the screaming grenadiers to their fate. A couple of them fell over the side and began running in panic, their bodies wreathed in the cruel, voracious flames until finally they fell and the flames consumed their agony-racked bodies.

Now the half-tracks started to veer off to the left away from the bomb-throwers, and Harsch told himself he knew the signs; the steam was going out of his attack. In a minute some fool of a driver would throw in reverse, slam into the half-track behind and the panic would start. Even in the elite Fire Brigade, such things could happen. Fire terrorized even the best-trained veteran. He had to do something before the rot set in.

'Driver . . . move it!' he bellowed above the confused racket all around. He flashed a look at the man. It was Adolfo, 'the Führer's Spanish Bastard', as the swarthy volunteer was called in the Brigade. '*Vamos andando!*' he yelled, pointing his broken sword to the left flank of what was left of his flying arrowhead.

'*Si, si,*' Adolfo yelled back and swung his wheel half left with a snarled '*Hijos de puta!*' at the bomb-throwers.

'What are you going to do, *Obersturmbannführer*?'

Goldwasser cried, holding on for grim death as the half-track heeled wildly.

'Take over the point myself! They'll follow me. I'll get them away from those damned Popov bombers. Come on, Adolfo, *carbide!*'

A bomber loomed up out of the fog of war. Harsch's gunner pressed his trigger. The man's stomach was ripped apart. He stumbled away, dragging his guts across the snow behind him. Another bomber came into view. Again the machine-gun chattered frenetically. A sudden line of holes etched themselves across the Russian's chest. The bomb fell from his nerveless fingers and exploded on the ground. The half-track clattered through it and Goldwasser's nose was suddenly full of the stink of singed hair – his own.

Now the other half-tracks started to swing towards Harsch's as he urged his driver to take the lead. Weaving in and out of the slower ones, Adolfo swung the ten ton vehicle from side to side, as if it weighed ten hundred-weight, brilliantly avoiding a collision at the very last minute. Now the bridge was only 200 metres away, and in front of them there were only the two flak cannon and a handful of Russian infantry. It looked as if *Obersturmbannführer* Harsch was going to capture the bridge at Kalach at last.

5

Steel flew everywhere.

A yellow-white spurt of flame at 100 metres' range and the half-track just behind Harsch's disintegrated. In a series of glowing red lumps of metal, what was left hurtled across the bridge road. The body of a grenadier slammed against the side of Harsch's half-track and burst like an over-ripe melon. Goldwasser screamed with absolute fear as hot blood drenched him.

The tracks clattered on to the hard-packed snow. The flak cannon was only fifty metres away now. Harsch could see the crew, their faces contorted with fear, flinging shell after shell into the rack in order to stop this metal monster that was heading straight for them on a collision course. A stream of 20mm shells scythed the half-track. Behind Goldwasser, a grenadier went down, arms flailing. Goldwasser began to blubber like a little child.

Twenty-five metres! Harsch saw the loader throw down the shells and start to pelt for the other side of the bridge. The half-track rocked crazily. The left track shot off. '*Cono!*' Adolfo screamed and fought the half-track which was swaying from side to side like a drunkard.

Ten metres! The gunners scattered wildly. Like a steel mountain, the half-track, filled with dead and dying men, towered above the flak cannon. The stink of explosive and hot oil filled the air. There was a great rending crash. The half-track came to an abrupt halt. Adolfo smashed against the windscreen, teeth flying out of a suddenly blood-filled mouth. Slowly, terribly slowly, the gun and the half-track began to tilt, a mixture of wrecked, tangled metal and chunks of mangled bodies.

A lone gulag rat, crazed beyond measure, attempted to rush the stalled half-track. He slipped on the shredded flesh and blood and fell. Spitting out his teeth, Adolfo let him have a burst with his m.p., lisping, '*Maldito sea la madre!*'

The gulag rat rolled over and lay still.

A second half-track made the bridge – and a third.

At the second flak gun the crew fired one last tremendous burst. The half-track driver flung up his hands in agony. Completely out of control the half-track shot clean into the air and plunged into the Don. An obscene belch of trapped air and it had gone for good. And then the Russian gunners were fleeing for their lives. Colonel Harsch's men, what was left of them, had pulled it off at last. The bridge at Kalach was in German hands once again.

The man from Smersh was not very expert on matters of war, but he recognized that even with the handful of men at Harsch's disposal and the three battle-scarred half-tracks now blocking both ends of the bridge, the one-armed Fritz making his dispostitions down below was in a good position. His men were protected by their armour, however small their number; it would be a tough nut for the gulag rat renegades to crack without heavy weapons. That is, he told himself, if they didn't simply fade away now that the Fritzes had got through.

He squatted at the entrance of his little cave, surveying the bustling Fritzes through his binoculars, wondering what he should do. Now he was cut off by the Fritzes from the man he had come to kill. Should he simply turn about and make his way back to the Russian positions in Stalingrad, leaving his mission uncompleted? Almost instantly he rejected that solution. He had had one failure; Beria wouldn't tolerate another. And he had no illusions about what would happen to a Smersh man who incurred Beria's displeasure. The Smersh killers knew too much. It would be a bullet at the back of his skull.

He considered the matter thoroughly while the big Fritz officer moved back and forth across the bridge, followed by a smaller officer in a uniform which he couldn't recognize, preparing for the counter-attack that he obviously expected the gulag rats to launch.

He and his men were SS, he knew that. He knew, too, that they fought to the very end. They had no alternative. Invariably the Russian infantry slaughtered them if they fell into their hands. But how steadfast, he asked himself, were they when they were leaderless? Would they stand and fight if he killed their officer?

The man from Smersh squatted there and thought out the problem.

Harsch was flushed with victory though he knew now from his own count that he had taken heavy losses. In all, he had only sixty men, including the wounded, to hold the bridge. Still, he was confident that with the protection of the half-tracks and the firepower they provided, he could do so until relief arrived. For finally Hitler had decided to act and an armoured infantry battalion was on its way from Paulus. According to the radio operator who had received the somewhat garbled message, it was expected to arrive at the bridge by nightfall.

'Let us say at dawn tomorrow, my dear Goldwasser,' he had commented. 'One must always take the statements those field-greys of the Wehrmacht make with a grain of salt! Goldwasser had seen from the look on the SS officer's face that the thought that they would have to hold out here till the following morning did not worry him particularly.

Now his preparations were complete and his men were enjoying their first hot food for the last twenty-four hours, cooking cans of 'Old Man', the standard meat ration reputedly made of old men, on their entrenching tools held over a petrol-and-earth fire. Harsch and

Goldwasser surveyed the big Russian HQ, with the dead lying in confused, frozen heaps in front of it.

'Wonder what's going on over there?' Goldwasser asked thoughtfully, lowering his glasses.

'Yes, me too,' Harsch said. 'They are strangely silent. It's unlike the Popovs. They usually make a great deal of noise before they counter-attack, especially after the political commissars start firing them up and they've swallowed their battle ration of vodka.'

'Perhaps they're not going to attack after all?' Goldwasser suggested.

'It would be a pleasant thought. But what else can they do? Now for them it's either piss or get off the pot. The only alternative they have is surrender – and,' he grinned, 'thcy'd hardly do that to the armed SS. No, my friend,' he accepted the steaming can of Old Man handed to him by Adolfo gratefully, 'they'll counter-attack all right.'

But *Obersturmbannführer* Harsch was wrong. All the fight had gone out of the gulag rats. The beating they had taken at the hands of the Germans had been too much. Now the survivors and wounded lay in the dirty straw, smoking or staring numbly into nothing. All was silence save for the low moaning of the wounded. Even Boldin, the indestructible, slumped in despair, gazing at his blackened hands.

Colonel Katukov frowned. Outside all he could see were shattered bodies, the gory litter of war. All was black, white, blood-red; it was the landscape of absolute despair. He took his gaze off the steppe wolves, knowing that the god of war had finally removed his mask and that the flood gates of ruination had been opened. Yet he still had to act. He couldn't just give up. He must inspire his worn out, savagely beaten scum to one last effort. *He had to!*

He turned slowly and stared around at them lying down on both sides of the room, hardly moving even when the lice started to bite in the heat that came from the green ceiling-high oven. Their bearded faces were hollow-cheeked and had a waiting, wolfish impassivity which came from hardship and want. 'Comrades,' he said simply, using a word that he had never thought fit to apply to the 'scum' from the camps in the long months he had commanded the gulag rats. A couple of heads were raised. The rest remained bent. 'All through history, our land has been defeating invaders,' Katukov continued quietly. 'Our land and our people. Even the Tartars and the Golden Horde couldn't beat us, although it took centuries to break them. But in the end we Russians smashed them all. Livonians, Lithuanians, Poles, the Teutonic Knights, the Swedes, the French. We've always conquered in the end – and we will conquer the Germans, too.'

His words died away hesitantly, but more heads were raised now and Boldin was looking at him curiously, his weary brain trying to understand what was taking place.

'I know you are weary, hurt, desperate even,' Katukov continued, 'but can't you make one last effort? Not for *Stalin*, not for *me*. But for our Russia. For our comrades who are dead out there, who have died all these months since last June for Russia.' Katukov swung his burning gaze around the long room, as if willing them to rise to their feet and obey him. 'Whatever you may have once been, criminals or politicals, you are still Russians. You were conceived in Russian bodies, bred on the fruit of Russian earth, schooled in the Russian tongue.' His voice hardened. 'You have a duty to Russia and to yourselves, to *your* dead, *your* wounded, *your* maimed! You can't overlook that fact, try as you will. And what is that duty, comrades?' He raised his right index finger, his face glowing, his eyes searing their amazed faces. 'I shall tell you. Your sole duty is to carry that bridge. Nothing else. To rise up from the very pit of hell itself. To keep on till death – and beyond death. To take that bridge, rip it from the hands of the obscene fascist beast and give it back to Russia!' He paused, his big chest heaving with the effort of that burning intensity, his eyes noting with a great surge of hope that here and there the weary men were stumbling to their feet and Boldin, their real leader, was fumbling for his equipment. 'It won't be long now, comrades. Then the Red Army will come sweeping down to our aid, a matter of mere hours. But when they come, comrades, we must be waiting for them down at that bridge – even if there is only one of us left – but we must be waiting. *We must!*' He attempted to say more, but the rest of his words were drowned in cheers and suddenly he was in the middle of a mass of men who cried and swore and clapped him on the back, the hated and feared Colonel Katukov. Thus it was that that single dry shot at the bridge was not heard in the wild excitement of the long room.

'*Aee-i-oh!*' Harsch screamed with the absolute agony of it and staggered back against the side of the half-track, broken sword tumbling from his one hand, the fingers pressed up against his shattered right eye suddenly soaked in blood. Before Goldwasser could reach him, he sat awkwardly on the snow, gasping shallowly with the tremendous pain. High above him, the man from Smersh slung his telescopic rifle and doubled back to the cover of his cave before the German bullets started winging his way. He'd finished the Fritz off for good. He had killed enough men to know the signs of death when he saw them.

Goldwasser tried to prize away the fingers gently, but Harsch held fast as the first terrible wave of pain began to ebb temporarily. 'No good, Goldwasser,' he said weakly. 'This time the Redskin's gonna bite the dust.'

Up at the far end of the bridge his grenadiers started firing wildly in the direction from which the lone shot had come.

'What do you mean?' Goldwasser gasped.

'You . . . you're in the SS, Goldwasser, that's what I

mean,' Harsch's voice was getting weaker by the instant. 'I hereby pass on the command of the Führer's Fire Brigade to you.' He attempted a smile, but failed lamentably. 'What would Hitler say . . . a Yid commanding an SS unit . . .!' The blood was streaming down between his fingers now and dripping on to his camouflaged blouse.

'But what am I supposed to do?' Goldwasser asked in panic.

'The boys'll see you through. . . . Just hang on, Goldwasser.' Harsch's voice was very weak now. 'Hang on . . . till morning. . . . And listen, Goldwasser . . . .' The Italian craned his head forward so that he could hear. 'Once you're safe, take off. Back to Italy. . . . Take a boat from there . . . South America . . . as far as you can get . . . Europe's doomed, triple doomed. . . .'

Now the survivors of his elite command were gathered around their dying commander as he lay slumped there in the bloody snow, supported by the little Jew, his chest heaving now in sharp shallow gasps, his good eye almost closed.

'*Mala hora, buena cara*,' the swarthy Adolfo said with pride in this big blonde man whose very language he had hardly understood, but whom he had followed to death. He raised his hand in the Falangist salute.

It acted like a signal.

Frenchman, German, Belgian, Dutchman, Swiss, all of them clicked to attention and their hoarse young voices joined in that fanatical scream to a deity who had long since abandoned them. '*SIEG HEIL . . . SIEG HEIL . . . SIEG HEIL. . . .*'

On the ground Harsch's head fell to one side, his last words a faint, 'Damned untidy thing to do. . . .'

6

On the nineteenth of November 1942 at exactly 6.30 a.m. the pre-dawn gloom between the towns of Serafinovich and Kletskaya was transformed suddenly into a brilliant blaze of bright orange and ugly red flame as 3500 Russian cannon of all calibres erupted into violent life. Along the whole winter horizon the brazen lights flickered like angry blast-furnaces and the air was suddenly filled with that obscene, frightening sound of thousands of shells ripping the dawn stillness apart. It was the thunderstroke that opened a major offensive – one that changed the twentieth century. *The march westwards of Soviet Russia had commenced!*

Trapped in their straw-lined trenches and log-roofed dugouts, the fur-hatted Rumanians of the Third Army quavered, tight-lipped with fear, as the shells ripped up and down their lines, destroying them metre by metre. The front line, the second line, the reverse line, they all disappeared under the weight of that tremendous bombardment. Bunkers collapsed. Men died fighting the sliding soil. Others went crazy, shouting and singing like village idiots, dancing on their parapets until that whirling, vicious steel maelstrom swept them away. Shell-shocked soldiers screamed soundlessly with terror and buried their ears in their hands; mouths, dripping with crazed saliva, opened purposelessly. Everywhere the telephones whirred as excited, panicked staff officers called for aid. But there was none forthcoming.

One hour later precisely, the tremendous bombardment ceased. There was a loud, echoing silence which died finally in the furthest hills. But not for long. It was soon replaced by the ominous, but certain, rumble of tank tracks. Hundreds of them. Thousands of them. The Russian Fifth and Twenty-first Tank Armies were coming.

'*The Ivans are coming . . . the Ivans are coming. . . .*' The terrified cry rose everywhere as the first thirty-ton T-34s with the red star on their armoured sides breasted the heights and began churning their way across that lunar landscape, followed by the mass ranks of the Soviet infantry, their brass bands playing military marches, the soldiers linked-armed, goose-stepping towards the Rumanian positions in their thousands and hundred thousands, crying '*Urrah Stalino. . . . Urrah Stalino!*' Drill sergeants dressed their ranks with blows from their swords and the flag-bearers waved that gold and red banner which would bring fear one day to a whole continent as it headed steadily for the English Channel.

The Rumanians broke. It was to be expected. As the first T-34s burst out of the fog and snow, they leapt from their shattered trenches and started to run.

On all sides the frightened cry went up. '*Run for it! . . . run for it!*'

Priests and cooks, quartermasters and generals packed their trucks and sat in them frantic with fear, praying desperately that their engines would start at last. Then they were off, driving in every direction across that limitless white steppe. Anywhere away from that terrifying Russian steamroller. Corps commanders, soldiers of thirty years' experience, broke down and had to be carried to the waiting staff cars, sobbing like little children. Generals who had often enough in these last terrible years in Russia ordered their men to fight 'to the last soldier and the last cartridge' fled shamefully, leaving their troops to their fate. Others could neither flee nor fight; they were too paralysed by fear. In the end, when the T-34s were already rolling into their headquarters, they put their fancy little pistols into their dry mouths and blew their brains out.

Every man capable of moving was moving now. Even the wounded panicked, crawling across the snow after their comrades, crying piteously, 'Help me, comrade . . . help me. . . .' No one was listening. But they kept on, the blind using the eyes of the legless, the legless using the legs of the blind.

The Third Rumanian Army was broken. Now it was in full retreat, heading for the one bridge across the Don at Kalach.

By midday the Russians are deep into the Rumanians' rear.

By the hundred, the T-34s smash in the depots and dumps, their crews looting and drinking as they rolled, leaving blood and crushed bodies and burning, shattered equipment in their wake, their engines going full out, their tracks whining a triumphant song of victory.

A battery of self-propelled guns shell a Rumanian cavalry depot and roll through it, plucking at pieces of raw horsemeat and stuffing their mouths full of the bloody flesh so that the grinning gunners with their scarlet, dripping mouths and gleaming white teeth look like cannibals.

A reserve hospital is overrun. For a few moments all goes well, but then the tank infantry find the medical alcohol. The massive rape of the plump little Rumanian nurses commences. Patients are bayoneted on the operating table.

The brown horde sweeps all before it. Here and there a little group of Rumanians tries to stop them. To no avail. Red flares hiss into the grey sky everywhere, colouring the snow a blood-red hue. A barrage of unbelievable force sweeps over the heads of the stalled infantry. The mounting thunder of the bombardment flattens the handful of Rumanians. In an inferno of flames, flying rubble and earth, and explosions of impossible power, they are ripped apart, clawed from the very ground, whirled upwards to disappear for good in volcanoes of flame.

In the deeper dugouts the Rumanians hold out a little longer, but not much. To their front the forest burns as the whirling storm of steel rolls towards them. Men go mad. The dugouts sway to and fro like ships at sea caught in a sudden hurricane. The defenders' eyes are wet with crazed fear. They scream, but no sound comes. And then that terrible maelstrom swamps them too. In its wake, as it passes on, it leaves churned, steaming earth, littered with chunks of human meat.

A Guards' regiment appears out of the snow and mist, legs clad in gleaming jackboots stamping across the snow in perfect step, bayonets gleaming, big bodies proud and packed together, officers with silver sabres across their shoulders, flags flying bravely.

'Fire!' the Rumanian colonel cries desperately. His men are all former Iron Guards, the elite of the country. They fire at will.

The Guards are mown down like corn. They come on, automatically closing ranks as they do so, goose-stepping as proudly as ever. The Rumanians fire again. Tracer hammers into the Russians. '*Urrah Stalino!* they cry hoarsely and quicken their pace. A thousand bayonets flash as one. They are going to charge!

The Rumanian colonel throws away his pistol. The former Iron Guards break and run. The advance continues.

Between Chir and Kletskaya, General Mihail Lascar surrenders his four divisions, walking through a shattered cavalry unit into captivity.

Hawk-faced General Dumitrescu thinks of shooting himself, but instead the commander of the Third Rumanian Army, now a formation in name only, decides he must express his anger to higher headquarters at the way the Germans have let him down. 'Yes, gentlemen,' he cries in feigned rage at his elegant staff. 'The King must hear of this!'

General of the Army Dumitrescu is last seen heading for Bucharest in his gleaming Daimler. The end is not far off now.

It was the mobs of frenzied, unarmed Rumanian soldiers who had somehow managed to cross the Don, shell-shocked, hysterical, trickling blood from mouth, nose and ears, who first brought the news to the Sixth Army of just how bad the situation was. It travelled speedily through the army right up to Paulus's HQ. Immediately the general's intelligence officers began to work out the details. They were shocking. Of the Third Rumanian Army's seven divisions, four had been broken and captured, three had fled. There was nothing now to stop the Red Army sweeping across the Don and cutting off Paulus's left flank. A similar attack on the Rumanian Fourth Army to his right would end in the same way. Paulus's Sixth Army ran a serious risk of being cut off to the rear by a great Russian pincer-movement. Now the Russians were turning the German's own blitzkrieg tactics, perfected in France in 1940, against them. An immense débâcle of world-shaking importance lay before them if something was not done soon.

General von Paulus woke up at last to his situation. He knew that the Rumanians on his left flank were finished and he knew too from Intelligence that along a 200-kilometre front from Beketovka down to the shores of the salt lakes Sarpa, Tzata and Barmantsak that three Soviet armies were massed to attack the vastly overextended Fourth Rumanian Army. If he was going to get out, it had to be *now*! The signals requesting an urgent decision flew that morning from Army HQ to Army Group HQ to that of the Supreme Headquarters until finally they reached Adolf Hitler in the far-off Berghof.

Von Paulus waited and waited. Then finally Hitler's reply was there. He opened it with trembling fingers. If he had known then how much depended upon that signal, his skinny aristocratic body would have trembled, but he didn't.

Speedily his dark eyes ran across the message:

'Radio message, Number 1352.
TOP SECRET
Urgent!
To: HQ Sixth Army
Führer Order
Sixth Army will hold positions despite threat of temporary encirclement. . . . Keep railway line open as long as posssible. Special orders regarding air supply will follow!'

Wordlessly the tall general passed the message to his chief-of-staff, General Schmidt.

His eyes flew across it. 'But general,' he protested, 'how are they going to supply the army?'

'By air, it appears,' Paulus said looking down at his smaller companion, eyes blank of emotion, though his mind was racing crazily.

'A whole army of a quarter of a million men!' Schmidt exploded. '*Impossible!*'

'It's the Führer's order.'

'I shit on the Führer!' Schmidt burst out, exasperated beyond measure, his gross face flushed with rage. 'In the filthy weather we have here there isn't a hope in hell of supplying us by air. Look, it's snowing again. *By air!* general, *it's stark, staring madness!*'

'It's the Führer's order,' von Paulus repeated as if the words were part of some ancient liturgy.

The Sixth Army was doomed. As Churchill was to say, 'The hinge of fate had turned.'

7

The massed fire of the two half-tracks stopped the gulag rats dead. The first line was simply wiped off the face of the earth, disappearing into the smoke of the chattering 20mm cannon and hissing, massed machine-guns. The second line flung themselves to the body-littered ground, clawing at the snow with their hands, frantically trying to bury themselves, get away from that terrible merciless fire.

Katukov, his chest heaving wildly, blood pouring from a deep gash at his temple, dropped into a steaming hole next to Boldin, and gasped, 'We didn't pull it off . . . we didn't pull it off!' His head bent, that once proud man, as broken now as the scum who had followed him so bravely a few minutes before, sobbed as if his heart were broken.

Gravely Boldin patted his heaving shoulder. 'You tried, comrade, you tried,' he whispered, trying at the same time to place the strange rumble that was beginning to come from their rear. 'What can mere men do against armoured positions like that?'

Katukov continued to sob. He was a broken man.

Boldin bit his bottom lip. He had seen it before. Katukov's nerve had gone. He would never be any good any more. His days as a soldier were over. Colonel Katukov would never again command a combat formation.

Boldin flashed a look around the survivors of the second wave. They were absolutely beaten. Around their cracked lips, the flesh quivered and their eyes were glazed with an unnatural sheen. They would not attack again this day. The gulag rats were a spent force.

The strange rumble was getting louder, but Major Boldin was only just aware of it. Suddenly he was overcome by an unreasoning rage at the sobbing Katukov and the worn, exhausted men lying and crouching in the snow all around him. He forced himself to his feet, ignoring the first slugs that came howling his way from the German positions. 'On your idle feet, you shit--shovelling scum!' he roared.

No one moved. 'Comrade major,' someone protested.

'Couldn't get up a whore's drawers, even if she was lying on her back with her legs spread in the air,' someone else said wearily, voice full of bitter humour.

'You dogs!' Major Boldin cried, sobbing with rage, the slugs cutting the air around him, '*You rats of the gulag, do you want to live for ev –*'

Boldin stopped short.

Over the heights to their rear, there were running men in fur hats, locked together with trucks and horse-drawn carts – hundreds of them, thousands of them. Men flogging ponies furiously. Others grabbing for the running boards of the trucks. All shouting.

Sweating, swearing, screaming, the first of the drivers came closer, lashing their snow-caked ponies, already frothing at the mouth, the carts disgorging their contents as other soldiers threw overboard the loot of a year in Russia, leaving a trail of litter behind them over which the men on foot fell.

'Rumanians – *counter-attack!*' someone screamed.

Wearily the gulag rats grabbed for their weapons, knowing now that nothing could save them. There were thousands of the enemy out there. They would be swamped.

But they were not witnessing an attack, but a stampede as the Rumanians streamed by the open-mouthed gulag rats, shouldering them, pushing them out of the way, hardly aware they were there at all in their haste to get across the bridge, running for their lives, passing over debris, dreams and dead, over the tears of those who had suffered and died for this bit of Russian earth, with history following in their wake. For behind them roared the steel might of the Red Army, the armouured mass of the T-34s. The gulag rats would need to attack the bridge at Kalach no more.

Half an hour later it was all over.

Against the side of the bridge they were shooting the SS; they always did. Their last cries rang out in the language of all of Western Europe, as if the old continent was saying its good-bye. They were brave, banal and bawdy. '*Maricons. . . . Es lebe Deutschland. . . . De koffie ist klaar. . . . figlio di puttana. . . . Arschloch. . . . merde. . . .*' Western Europe died on that bridge that November day.

Not that the gulag rats cared or even listened. They celebrated. There was an accordion and vodka. They played the music and the Rats and the men of the Red Army danced together. Bags filled with delicacies were handed out to them, cakes smeared with chocolate frosting, chocolate bars, biscuits, tins of pork. Every new tank ploughing its way through the piles of Rumanian dead which lined both sides of the traffic-choked road, had packets of cigarettes for them and bottles of looted Rumanian red wine. It was a feast the likes of which the bearded, exhausted veterans had not seen these many years. But like all feasts it had to end.

And it ended with a shock.

The civilian with the straight, lustreless hair and the frightening, hanging hands covered with thick black hairs, wasted no time. 'Colonel Katukov?' he rapped.

Katukov looked up, his face still blank and wet with tears. he stared unseeingly at the civilian, backed up by the platoon of Greenhats armed with tommy-guns. He said nothing.

'Who are you? What do you want?' Boldin spoke for

him.

The civilian did not take his flat, impenetrable eyes off Katukov.

'Is this him?' he asked.

'Katukov? . . . yes.'

The man from Smersh held up his ID card with that dreaded name printed underneath it for all to see, 'S-M-E-R-S-H' as if that were explanation enough. 'Take him away . . .' he commanded.

ENVOI:
THE DESTRUCTION OF COLONEL KATUKOV

'The celebrated tale of the man who gave the powder to the bear. He mixed the powder with the greatest care, making sure that not only the ingredients but the proportions were absolutely correct. He rolled it up in a large paper spill and was about to blow it down the bear's throat. *But the bear blew first.*'

Winston Churchill
The Second World War

1

Katukov squatted in the corner of the big cell, watching one of the prisoners whittle the frozen black bread into equal portions. He was no longer hungry, but the others, a mixed bunch of deserters, cowards who had refused to attack, officers relieved of their commands because of incompetency, were desperate for food. They never took their eyes off the man carving and stabbing at the precious bread. As if it were very important to stay alive, Katukov told himself wearily. They would all hang or be shot by the NKVD before the week was out.

Katukov turned his gaze to the cone-shaped mound of excrement in the corner. It had risen slowly, recording the length of the condemned men's stay in the cell, and it was always black, the colour of the frozen bread, their only food.

Outside, the thunder of the guns had diminished and Katukov could hear the NKVD guards opening the doors of the cells further down the long corridor and crying, '*Skolko kaput?*'

'How many dead?' Katukov mused. They had three propped up in the shadows of the corner of their cell. At first some of his fellow prisoners had been for throwing them out, but Petrov, the general who had abandoned his division when it had been ordered across the Volga into the hell of Stalingrad, had pointed out that frigid temperatures within the cell would keep the bodies from decomposing for weeks and thus they would be able to get extra rations of bread. Katukov had sniffed, 'For weeks!' but the others hadn't listened. They had been too hungry.

So now he sat among the starving, the shit, and the dead, and mused on his fate.

There had not even been a court-martial. The man from Smersh had had him led into Chuikov's office and declared simply, 'Katukov, the man from Kalach.'

Helplessly, he had stared at Chuikov's seamed, tough face, but the commanding general had avoided his gaze. Instead he had asked of the man from Smersh, 'What is your decision?'

'Comrade Beria had ordered – ' the man from Smersh did not finish his sentence. Instead he turned his thumb down in the classical symbol. Chuikov had nodded. 'So be it.'

'But,' Katukov had begun and then he had closed his mouth and, head hanging miserably, had allowed himself to be led away. That had been the extent of his 'trial'.

Now he had been in the cell with these contemptuous creatures for five days. It couldn't be much longer before they came for him with that '*Davoi bistre*' which meant the end.

The man handed him his iron-hard piece of bread, holding his free hand underneath the sliver carefully, ensuring that any crumb that might fall off would not be wasted. Katukov thanked him gravely; he wanted nothing to do with these wretches. Hardly aware that he was doing so, he started to chew on the bread, his mind blank of all thought save for that one overwhelming question: *when?*

It was the same question that Boldin and Vulf were asking themselves, as they watched the hangman, 'The Tuliak' (he came from Tula) supervise the erection of the gallows half a kilometre from the cell where their former commander lay.

Behind them the din was tremendous as the bulldozers from America rattled back and forth, their cruel scoops biting into the piles of dead, German and Russian, raising them high into the air for a moment before depositing them in the great open graves like heaps of logs, whereupon emaciated German POWs with handkerchieves tied across their mouths started to sprinkle the bodies with quicklime.

Tuliak was not a small man. Indeed he stood just short of one metre ninety, with a chest like that of a carthorse. He was completely bald with a pair of unbelievably wicked eyes, blazing like searchlights above his vodka-thickened nose. Now he swaggered back and forth, chewing on a piece of dried meat, shouting his orders at the soldier carpenters, a small piece of rope between his reddened hams, playing with it all the time like a Moslem with his 'worry beads', as if it gave him a feeling of security, satisfaction, to have the tool of his trade always with him.

'A pig,' Vulf commented, 'a real pig.'

Boldin nodded, sizing up the hangman, wondering how they could get to him. Katukov had been vain, ambitious, and often harsh and cruel to that scum which he detested, the gulag rats. Still, he did not deserve to die in this ignoble manner – at the end of Tuliak's hempen rope. 'What did you hear of him?' he asked finally, raising his voice as a fresh battery opened up across the Don at the Germans now trapped in a dying Stalingrad.

Vulf shrugged. 'I don't know why you bother. But I will tell you all the same. Professional killer. Back in the bad times in the late twenties. Mostly women. Throttled them for food.'

Boldin looked at the hangman with his brutally muscled shoulders which rippled even through the thick, wadded civilian jacket. 'Pleasant sort of a fellow, eh, Vulf?'

Vulf nodded and shuddered as those red hams unconsciously twisted the rope once more, feeling for the knot which would be placed just beneath the victim's Adam's apple.

'How did the NKVD find him?'

'He got caught and was sent to the gulag. As you

know, Boldin, the so-liberal Soviet State got rid of the death penalty for murder back in those days.' He sneered. 'They only shot you for saying the sun didn't shine out of Stalin's arse or something as heinous as that. After a while Beria heard of his – er – talents, and selected him as the NKVD's chief hangman to be used when it was necessary to make a public example of some traitor or the like. Just as our former commander is going to be made one *pour encourager les autres*, as the frogs say.' He spat into the dirty snow. 'The pigs!'

'Yes,' Boldin said slowly, pondering Vulf's contemptuous words. 'So friend Tuliak was once in the gulag. . . . He knows the rules. . . . Hmm.' He took Vulf by the arm and led him away through the masses of fresh infantry laden like pack mules who were preparing to cross the Volga for the final battle with von Paulus's trapped Germans, now all but gone to ground in the smoking rubble that had once been Stalin's own city.

'What are you thinking, Boldin?' Vulf asked as they walked slowly towards the gulag rats' lines, guarded as always when they were out of action by surly NKVD men, armed with Maxim machine-guns.

Boldin did not answer his question directly. Instead he said, 'I know you don't like Katukov.'

'To be frank, I've *hated* the bastard with a passion at times,' Vulf broke in.

Boldin didn't seem to hear. 'But whatever his faults, Katukov is a brave man who has fought all his life for Russia, however misguided his other motives might have been.'

Vulf halted and looked directly at Boldin. 'Listen, have you had your hundred? How can we get Katukov out of a NKVD jail in the middle of this armed camp? Even if you could convince the rest of the gulag rats to follow you in the attempt, which I doubt, what good would those couple of hundred exhausted men be against the thousands of troops here? There must be at least two regiments of NKVD alone. Now tell me that, Boldin!'

The big ex-marshal grinned down at the little man, the thin rays of the winter sun sparkling on Boldin's stainless steel teeth, obviously amused at his companion's genuine anger. 'Who said anything about getting Katukov out of jail?' he said mysteriously. 'What do we need to do that for when we've got the Tuliak. . . .'

The Tuliak lay on a hard wooden bed next to the roaring tiled oven, his ugly face red with the tremendous heat. He prised a piece of meat from between his teeth with a bayonet. He was alone in the dugout although even general officers had to double up in the crowded rear echelon lines; but then he was the Tuliak of the NKVD. Ten minutes went by before he condescended to notice the two grubby private soldiers, devoid of any badges of rank or unit identification, standing just inside the blanket-covered doorway to the underground dugout. 'Well, what do you two evil maggots want?' he asked at last, swinging himself up from his bed and dropping his bayonet, instinctively reaching for that short length of rope.

'Not much, just a few words with you, Tuliak,' the bigger of the two soldiers answered. Calmly he walked across the room and, picking up the rest of the meat lying on the greasy plate, stuffed it in his own mouth, while his companion, holding some sort of bundle in his hand, grinned maliciously through his thick, horn-rimmed spectacles.

The hangman's mouth flopped open stupidly. He gasped hard, as if someone had just punched him in his fat overhanging gut. 'What . . . what do you think you're up to?' he roared in a vodka-tinged bass, his wicked, coal-black eyes blazing. 'Don't you red-arsed monkeys know who I am! . . . I'm not just anybody.' He stood up, towering even above the big private soldier and jerked a thumb at his massive chest. '*I'm the devil himself!*'

The man who had stolen Tuliak's supper was unimpressed. He swallowed the rest of the meat and said quite calmly, 'I'll show you something . . . devil.' He reached in the pocket of his earth-coloured soldier's blouse and brought out an object which glittered a bright silver in the wavering light of the candles that illuminated the dugout. 'Razor-blade,' he said and placed the thing in his mouth. He crunched hard and began chewing, almost as if he enjoyed it, while Tuliak stared at him, his brutish face a mixture of wonder and disbelief.

There was a trick of doing it without any harm but Tuliak did not know that. He was obviously impressed as the big soldier carefully spat out sliver after sliver of chewed steel, thrusting out his tongue at intervals to reveal it was whole, before finally reaching over and taking a swig out of the hangman's own bottle of vodka.

'What . . . what do you want from me?' he said, not as confident as he had been a few moments before.

'I have been told you are a good sort of fellow and like to help people,' the soldier who had chewed the razor-blade said.

'What?'

'You heard.'

'You cheeky arse with ears!' Tuliak thundered. 'Don't you know that even the felt-lice don't even dare move in the Tuliak's shitty drawers during the great man's rest hours and you barnshitters dare come in. . . .' His words drained away as he saw the object which the one with glasses was displaying inside the handkerchief that he had just unfolded. '*Boshe moi!* . . .' he croaked, 'is . . . is that. . .?'

'It is,' the little man said calmly. He walked across the dug-out and deposited it on the packing-case which served as a table.

'That . . . *that's a sawn-off cock!*' he stuttered stupidly. 'A human cock . . . .' He swallowed hard and stared down at the bloody piece of flesh which lay in the cloth.

The little man nodded. 'Yes . . . it could be yours.'

The Tuliak started back. '*Mine*?' he quavered.

'Yes, if you don't prove just how good you really are,' the big man said, making a cutting gesture.

The Tuliak shuddered. 'But who are you?. . . What do you want from me?'

'Sit down,' the big one said and he pressed the Tuliak back on to his wooden bench. 'I've got something to explain to you, little brother, something very important. If you wish to keep your salami, unlike the poor fool to whom that one belonged, you'd better listen and listen carefully.'

The Tuliak listened.

The man from Smersh was pleased with himself. Beria had signalled his congratulations. Perhaps there might be some of those first-class trips abroad for him again after all. Now he waited for the night train which would take him away from Stalingrad back to the comparative safety of Moscow. He no longer had any interest in Katukov. Chuikov would take care of him; he wouldn't dare fail.

Impatiently, he stamped his feet on the cold concrete and wished the goods train would make its appearance. Chuikov had reserved a whole carriage for him just behind the engine. There would be steam-heating and, knowing just how much the military brass feared Smersh, probably a hamper of food, vodka and wine as well. He eyed the common soldiers, most of them lightly wounded, who thronged everywhere, waiting for the train. What a miserable existence they led, he told himself and thanked a god he didn't believe in once again, that the Soviet system had given him the opportunity it had.

'Comrade!'

The man from Smersh spun round.

A common soldier was standing there under the faint blue light of the blacked-out platform lantern, grinning at him with a mouthful of stainless steel teeth, his right arm in a dirty, blood-stained sling. 'What do you want?'

he asked coldly, disliking being called 'comrade' by this dirty foot-slogger.

The soldier indicated the unlit cigarette, a roughly made compound of black tobacco and newspaper. 'A light, comrade.'

'A light . . . oh, yes' He had been about to refuse, but now the goods train was beginning to steam slowly into the station, its floodlight illuminating the snow-bound track, and he didn't want to be detained by the soldier's whining importunings if he refused. 'Here,' he fumbled inside his thick fur jacket and brought out a box of matches.

'Could you light it for me, comrade,' the soldier had the cheek to ask. 'Bit difficult with my one flipper, you see.'

'Damn. . . . All right, come closer!'

'Many thanks, comrade.' Obediently the soldier moved closer and, striking the match, the man from Smersh reached up to light the cigarette for the soldier.

It was then that he saw clearly the soldier's face, those bold eyes and broad cheeks. 'Hey aren't you – '

His scream of agony was drowned by the clatter of the goods train's locked wheels, as the razor-sharp dagger that Boldin had carried in the sling in the fashion of the gulag killer slid deep into his stomach. Then he was falling, falling, falling, his skin seared by the heat of the red-hot boiler before the great, gleaming, cruel steel wheel ran right over him.

A moment later Boldin had gone, slipping through the excited, curious, unfeeling mob of soldiers, disappearing into the night to where Vulf had the horse waiting for him.

The man from Smersh had committed his last murder. . . .

The battalions, to which the criminals who were now going to be publicly hanged had once belonged, were lined up around the gallows. They were formed in a hollow square, sunk in a hushed, dawn silence, the new snow falling softly on their bent, greatcoated shoulders.

On the raised platform with its twelve nooses, the Tuliak, arms crossed across his massive chest, waited impassively, head framed by one evil circle of hemp. The kettle drums rolled softly. The hangings could commence.

The senior NKVD officer in his green-cross cap, now powdered with snow, raised the charge sheet, his other hand grasping his sabre. 'Former General of the Infantry Petrov. Accused of cowardice in the field. Sentence – death by hanging!'

The kettle-drums started to beat quicker.

'Division Petrov – *eyes left!*' the NKVD officer rapped.

The two hundred or so men representing the division which the general had deserted snapped their heads to the left. Petrov, his head uncovered, chin thrown out proudly, hands tied behind his back, came stalking out into the cobbled courtyard, guarded by riflemen of his own division, his last escort. He was shivering, whether from fear or cold, no one would ever know. Guided by his former soldiers, he mounted the steps to where the Tuliak was waiting for him.

As the drum beat increased, the hangman untied his bonds and swiftly threw the noose over the general's head, adjusting the big knot so that it lay to the left of the victim's Adam's apple. The general waited impassively. The wind strengthened. More and more snow started to fall on his erect shoulders. The NKVD officer nodded to the Tuliak. He pulled the lever.

Snap! There was a startled gasp from the soldiers. Suddenly the general was dangling there, the rope twisting under the impact, his head bent grotesquely, his tongue hanging out of the side of his mouth like a piece of wet leather, his trousers at the front black with urine. General of the Infantry Petrov was dead!

Immediately the NKVD photographers rushed forward. Their flashes cut the gloom as they recorded the event for the Red Army's official newspapers. Even in this month of victory, those who wavered had been shown the dread results of such hesitation.

'Former Captain of the Guards Manitskov. Accused of military failure in the field. Sentence – death by hanging!' the NKVD officer read out, the snowflakes shrouding his shoulders now.

'No, no' the tall captain cried, 'I don't want to die. . . . *No, please don't!*'

The two guardsmen grabbed their ex-commander more firmly and half-pushed, half-dragged him to where the Tuliak stood waiting for him at the second gallows, arms crossed as before. The drum beat increased. Everywhere the soldiers dropped their eyes save in the Guards Regiment where again the soldiers clicked their heads woodenly to the left to observe the last march of ex-Captain Manitskov. The snow pelted down.

Thus the gruesome public hanging continued with wretch after wretch being dragged through the snow by former subordinates or comrades to finish dangling and swaying at the end of one of Tuliak's hemp ropes.

Now there were eleven of them swaying there, almost obscured by the flying snow which was coming down as if it would never stop again, as if God himself wanted to blot out that cruel misery below.

'Ex-Colonel Katukov of the 333rd Punishment Battalion!' the NKVD officer bellowed, the wind snatching at his words. 'Accused of grave disobedience in the field. Sentence – death by hanging!'

The drums rolled as two gulag rats, one tall and burly, the other skinny and undersized, dragged out the Tuliak's last victim, the big form somehow shrunken, his head lolling, as if he were already unconscious. Indeed a third gulag rat, a big fellow, whose features were obscured by the flying snow, hurried into the courtyard to aid the other two as they virtually carried their victim to the gallows.

'Punishment Battion – *eyes left!*' the NKVD officer

rapped and there was no mistaking the contempt in his voice at the craven manner in which Katukov, a former NKVD officer himself, was going to meet his death. A Greenhat was supposed to be above fear, at least in public. His contempt was reflected in the faces of some of the gulag rats as they watched their commander being led to his death.

Then finally the three gulag rats got him on to the gallows where they were forced to support him until the Tuliak had his rope around Katukov's bent neck. He rapped, 'Stand back there,' and pulled the trap hastily.

The dead man dropped like a sack of cement.

The hangings were over. The drums beat. The lone bugle sounded. Sabres flashed. Officers bellowed orders and the regiments marched off, their boots muffled by the snow, leaving the dead to hang there in the streaming white, a grim warning to all who might pass this way to the battle on the other side of the Don. Stalin's revenge was terrible. . . .

'Cheer up, colonel,' Vulf said, as the three of them squatted in the cover of a wrecked T-34, waiting for the goods train to come along the single line below, already blocked by the trees they had placed across it. 'It all worked out well.'

'I am no longer a colonel,' the man in the long civilian overcoat, complete with cloth cap, said sadly. 'I am nobody. A faceless one.'

Boldin did not take his eyes off the railway line, save occasionally to flash a glance at the green-glowing dial of his wrist-watch. The train heading out of Stalingrad with its freight of damaged weapons being carried to the repair workshops to the rear of Stalingrad was due any minute now. During the daylight hours the line was dead on account of the Fritz dive-bombers; the driver would want to get clear of the embattled city before it was too light.

The escape had worked out well. The Tuliak had been

convinced easily enough – after he had seen that sawn-off penis – that he was dealing with two killers who would take their revenge even if it meant their own death to do so; he had been in the gulag long enough to know the type. Thereafter it had been simply a matter of ensuring that Katukov would be the last one to be hanged. The Tuliak, scared out of his skin, had gone along with everything so that it had not been difficult for Vulf and himself to slip Katukov, the last man in the cell, a common soldier's cap, while they grabbed one of the three corpses there to take his place. The only hitch had been Katukov's weak protest, 'But I want to die. . . . I deserve to die. . . . I disobeyed orders. . . .'

Boldin's quick, angry, 'We're risking our lives to get you out of this hell-hole, Katukov, so don't play the fool!' had swiftly brought him to his senses. He had hurried after them as they had dragged 'Colonel Katukov' to his death.

Now they were carrying out the last stage of the escape. In a matter of minutes while the train crew cleared away the 'fall', they would slip Katukov on the train heading eastwards. He had a civilian pass they had taken from one of the dead and sufficient money to give him a start. Yet Boldin could see from Katukov's face that he wasn't happy.

'What will I do?' Katukov asked miserably. 'I know only the trade of soldiers. The army has been my life. . . . What will I do? The square, the discipline, the orders, the tramp of marching feet, the smell of polished leather and gleaming steel,' he rambled on numbly, 'it's been my . . . whole life. I know no other. *The flag* . . . .' He broke off abruptly.

Listening to the big, broken man, Boldin felt a sudden icy cold, the awful loneliness, the silence, the desolation of this winter world in which they all lived and it made him angry to feel thus. 'Dammit, Katukov,' he blurted out, 'that's all over, don't you realize? You're an outcast like we are outcasts. The system has condemned us! We have no home, no family, no fatherland any more! *No flag!*' He flashed Katukov a bitter look, his eyes blazing angrily. 'Katukov, you have become that which you have always despised and hated – now *you* are a gulag rat, every man's hand against you, condemned to wander across the face of a fatherland that does not want you until death finally and mercifully releases you from this living hell!'

'Me . . . *a gulag rat*?' Katukov quavered and somehow, though it might have been a trick of the grey pre-dawn light, his once proud face seemed to shrink, become hollow-cheeked, with the eyes suddenly cunning, almost shifty, yet bold and knowing like those wolfish prison faces to be found everywhere in the 333rd Punishment Battalion.

Five minutes later when the train squealed rustily to a halt down below, and the driver and his mate, used to this sort of thing, but angry at the extra work all the same, set about clearing away the logs, cursing at each other as they did so, Katukov stole into the rear wagon noiselessly and concealed himself expertly beneath the tarpaulin over a wrecked howitzer, as if he had been doing this sort of thing all his life. He had indeed become a gulag rat. . . .

A thousand and a half kilometres away, *Reichsmarschall* Hermann Goering thundered in his bombastic style over the airways, spitting out the words which no one in Stalingrad listened to any more; for now the thousands of hungry, weary, ragged Germans who were struggling out of their cellars and throwing away their weapons were prisoners. Stalingrad had just surrendered, making those pompous phrases that crackled over the loudspeakers, hung everywhere in the ruins, sound ironic, absurd, mocking.

Rising above all these gigantic battles like a mighty monument is Stalingrad. . . . One day this will be recognized as the greatest battle in our history . . . a battle of heroes. . . . We have a mighty epic. . . the struggle of the Nibelungs. . . . My soldiers, thousands of years have passed and thousands of years ago in a tiny pass in Greece stood a brave and bold man with three hundred soldiers, Leonidas with his three hundred Spartans. . . . Then the last man fell and now only the inscription stands . . . "Wanderer, if you should come to Sparta, go tell the Spartans you found us lying here as the law bade us". . . . Someday men will read; "If you come to Germany, go tell the Germans you saw us lying in Stalingrad, as the law bade us". . . .

But there would be few of those who surrendered this January day who would return to tell Germany what had happened. At the Univermag Building, 3000 moaning, cursing German wounded lay in a merciless wind that whipped through the shattered walls, with the helpless doctors placing the most seriously ill at the edge of the packed crowd so that they would die first from the cold.

Ringing the huge brick building on four sides was a stack of frozen corpses two metres high, past which the mournful, groaning lines of German prisoners in their thousands shuffled without a single glance. Lowing like cattle, dilapidated earmuffs over their ears, their heads wrapped in blankets, their faces blackened by beards and frost, they were urged eastwards by the little Siberians on their ponies who cracked their cruel, leaded whips whenever the long column appeared to be stopping, marching to their deaths.

Then the air was filled with another sound – the stamp of well-trained infantry going the other way. Hastily, the slant-eyed Siberians cracked their whips and herded their prisoners to one side. A new battalion with a difference. Next to Colonel Boldin, there fluttered the black skull-and-crossbones of the 333rd Punishment Battalion, reinforced and back to its old strength: 800 men from the camps, saints and sinners, faces set as they marched westwards to fight and die for the Kremlin tyrant who aimed to conquer the world.

Here and there some of the soldiers watched those dense ranks, following the big colonel astride his grey mare next to that sinister flag. Some of the watchers crossed themselves in awe; others spat and looked away as if they could not bear to see the scum of the camps; a few whispered in subdued tones, 'It's the rats, the gulag rats!'

But it was one of the slant-eyed Siberians, who gave them the name by which they would be remembered in Stalingrad long after the last one of them was dead. 'Not gulag rat,' he said in his strange Siberian sing-song. 'No, they . . . steppe wolves. . . understand.' He pointed a skinny finger at the soldiers disappearing up the street into the softly falling snow, '*wolves of the steppe. . . .*'

THE BERLIN BUNKER

James P. O'Donnell

Never before have the final, desperate days of Hitler and his closest followers been re-created as hauntingly as in *The Berlin Bunker*.

'Superb. Quite simply the most terrifying account of the nightmare and its end I have ever read' *Theodore H. White*

'Quite staggering . . . exciting and riveting reading' *The Bookseller*

£1·50

BAPTISM OF BLOOD

K. N. Kostov

Traitors, reactionaries, pimps, whoremasters, black marketeers, murderers and perverts – the worst the labour camp had to offer . . . they called them the gulag rats.

Punishment Battalion 333 was the roughest, wildest band of fighting men ever to draw blood. Yet they fought like the hounds of hell.

Driven by an embittered and sadistic commander against the Nazi push towards Moscow, the gulag rats face a desperate conflict of fury and brutality: their baptism of blood.

£1.25

COTTON'S WAR

John Harris

If it hadn't been for the shopkeeper in Heraklion, Cotton might never have been involved . . .

In the spring of 1941 the Nazis were storming their way through Greece. The *Loukia* was crucial to the British cause and the Greek resistance – and her cargo even more so. When the *Loukia* is wrecked in enemy territory, the British gathered together a handful of 'volunteers' for a dangerous mission of retrieval: two RASC men, some sailors, one German-speaking airman and Mihale Andoni Cotonou – otherwise known as Corporal Cotton of the Marines.

A superb story of action and character, *Cotton's War* is one of John Harris's most exciting war novels.

£1·10

ARMY OF SHADOWS

John Harris

France – Winter 1944. The long-awaited liberation is at hand.

The bombing mission had gone well. The crew of the Lancaster bomber began to relax. Then the Messerschmitt came out of the darkness, its guns blazing.

Of the nine-man crew only Neville and Urquhart survived, parachuting into the heart of occupied France. Now, for both of them, the testing time had begun: a time of peril as the fliers joined forces with the Army of Shadows – the men of the French Resistance – and entered a deadly game of cat and mouse with a ruthless and desperate enemy.

'John Harris writes about war as few men can. . . . With gathering speed, the story moves to a thundering climax – and a cracking good read it makes' *Daily Mail*

90p

HELL IS ALWAYS TODAY

Jack Higgins

'We're pretty hot on parking tickets, but not so good on maniacs who walk the streets on wet nights murdering women.'

Police morale is low. A callous, motiveless killer has the city in a stranglehold of fear as he casually selects his fifth victim. Even the whores are staying at home, and as public anxiety increases Mallory and Miller, the hard-pressed officers assigned to the case, realize their troubles are just beginning . . .

Not only a new corpse found in the driving rain, but, just to complicate matters, news of a dangerous criminal on the run.

85p

A FINE NIGHT FOR DYING

Jack Higgins

The body was dragged out of the English Channel in the nets of a local fishing boat. After six weeks on the seabed weighted down with seventy pounds of chain, there wasn't a lot left of gangland boss Harvey Preston – and what there was made Paul Chavasse's stomach lurch.

Special Branch had handed the case over to 'The Bureau': the little-known branch of British Intelligence that deals with only the most delicate and hazardous operations. And soon Bureau agent Chavasse finds himself involved on one of the toughest cases of his career as he uncovers a trail that seems to lead straight to millionaire Enrico Montefiore, a recluse who hides from the public gaze in a stronghold on the windswept marshes of the Camargue . . .

£1.25

TOLL FOR THE BRAVE

Jack Higgins

By the author of 'The Eagle Has Landed'

Ellis Jackson had woken up hugging a twelve-bore shotgun. In the next room, his mistress and his best friend lay naked on the bed, their heads blown to pulp.

Active combat, a Viet Cong prison camp and the callous treachery of his interrogator and lover, Madam Ny, had all taken their toll. Back in England, Ellis had finally cracked.

Or had he? Maybe things weren't as simple as that – in any case, Ellis wanted some answers. Making use of his highly developed talent for survival, he found them: and he proved he wasn't mad.

It might have been easier to take if he'd *really* been out of his mind.

85p

Scarface the Mother Jackal

Shen Shixi

ISBN 978-0-9937053-1-1

Written by Shen Shixi
Translated by Zheng Chen
Illustrated by Fang Cao Wen Hua

Publisher: Dennis Li
Book Design: Monica Miller
Proofreader: Mary Baylor

Printed and bound in Canada

Integrator International Education and Publishing Ltd.
11815 Cowley Dr. N Delta, B.C., Canada, V4E 1W5
info@caiiep.com
http://www.caiiep.com

ANIMAL FICTION KING SERIES

Scarface the Mother Jackal

Shen Shixi

Translated by Zheng Chen
Illustrated by Fang Cao Wen Hua

Integrator International Education and Publishing Ltd.
Vancouver

CONTENTS

THE GOLD-BACK JACKAL

They emerged from the thickets of wild marigolds on the hillside -- seventy or eighty of them, jackals of every size. They were heading in the direction of the hidden observation site that Champa, my Tibetan guide and I had built among the branches of a tree. These were gold-back jackals, peculiar to Gaoligong Mountains in Yunnan Province. I was delighted and promptly raised my new camcorder to film them. Jackals are a small mammal of the genus *Canis*, thus they are known as "wild dogs". They are medium-sized carnivores. In many places, common jackals are called "red dogs" or "red wolves", so named for their reddish-brown coats. In North America, there is a species known as silver-back jackal because of the layer of silver hair covering their backs. Several decades ago, a French naturalist explored the canyons of Gaoligong Mountains on foot, and apparently discovered a species of jackals with gold marks on the back and therefore named them gold-back jackals. Unfortunately, they are very rare and are only active primarily above the snow line beyond where most humans can live. Although the Yunnan Institute of Zoology repeatedly sent search teams into the area, they failed to find even a trace of the elusive gold-back jackals.

I could hardly believe my luck! I felt like some precious gold had fallen at my feet or I had found a bulging, well-padded wallet by the roadside. Gold-back jackals are indeed distinct from other jackals. The coat on their back has a thick layer of golden hairs, giving the effect of the animal wearing a gorgeous fur vest; thick black lines run down either side of their nose bridges, eyebrows, eyelids and ears, outlining them and giving prominence and dignity to the facial region. Creamy white hair at their heels makes them look as if they are standing in snow. However, what most intrigued me was the French naturalist's report of that gold-back jackals are social animals led by an adult female, whereas a young male, which lives with a small family as their basic unit, usually leads other jackal species.

Gold-backs' social structure is a rarity among their species, and therefore must harbour many little-known mysteries. They would be a perfect topic for my research.

Using the zoom on my camcorder, I clearly saw that the leader in front of the pack, as predicted, was a female. She was slimmer than the other females, and from her belly hung a dozen or so teats, which dangled and swung like little wind bells as she walked. I could see she was aged: the coat on her back had turned from golden-yellow to golden-red and was darker than the other jackals. The inked brush of time had blackened the hairs between her chin and neck; across her weather-beaten face, a deep scar ran between her ear and her mouth, making her long face look even more tired and careworn. I named her "Scarface".

About a hundred meters away from the tree we were hiding in, Scarface suddenly stopped, raised her neck and gave a soft howl. Then, like well-drilled soldiers receiving an order from a senior officer, all the jackals, including several juveniles, came to a halt. Some were poised to turn and flee; others seemed about to pounce. The jackals all looked at their leader, awaiting her next order. She flared her nose and moved her ears, noting any suspicious smells and sounds. I was a little nervous, thinking that perhaps she could hear the whirring of the camera motor, so I turned it off at once. Just then, I caught the sound of heavy breathing approaching from behind. I turned and was startled to see Champa, my Tibetan guide. He was the picture of anger; the blue veins on his neck stood out, he ground his teeth, and his chest heaved. He looked just like an angry leopard. Champa was carrying an old-fashioned shotgun, the kind that needed to be refilled with gunpowder before every shot. Aiming the barrel at the jackals, he was ready to press the trigger...

As a zoologist, I couldn't tolerate him killing these precious gold-back jackals. With no time to think, I grabbed his gun and lifted it upwards. Bang! With a loud crash, the shot went skywards. It hit the tree canopy, sending a shower of leaves into the air. Scarface gave a long howl and fled into the woods. The rest of the pack was at her heels, and in an instant, they had vanished.

"What do you think you're doing? How could you shoot at them like that?" I demanded.

"Evil jackals! Those evil jackals! I... I'll smash their heads in, and then I'll skin them alive to avenge my dog, Snow Queen!" Champa gnashed his teeth in anger, and his eyes glistened with tears.

That night, inside the camp yurt, Champa took a large swig of barley wine and recounted in an aggrieved tone, the story of the blood feud between the gold-back jackals and the two of them, himself and his beloved dog, Snow Queen.

2

FURY OF THE HUNTER

"Snow Queen was a hunting dog that I raised from a pup. Her coat was as white as the year-round snow on Gaoligong Mountains. So I called her Snow Queen. She was a pedigree Tibetan Mastiff. I suppose you know about Tibetan Mastiffs. They are the bravest hunting dogs in the world. For seven or eight years, Snow Queen accompanied me whenever I ventured into the mountain forests to hunt. Once, I got really drunk and lay down in a wood hut. Somehow, I don't know how, the hut caught fire, but I didn't realize it and I still lay on the bed, passed out. Snow Queen rushed through the flames, and dragged me out of the house by my clothes. I have no children, so she was like a daughter to me."

"Three years ago, when the highland barley was flowering and the bucks were growing antlers, I brought Snow Queen into the mountain to hunt. Halfway up the mountain, where the snow had not yet melted, a pair of jackals jumped out from a rocky moraine ahead. I fired a shot and it blew off half the skull of the female. Quick as a flash, Snow Queen rushed up and ripped off the tail of the male jackal. The male jackal howled and bolted. Afterwards, I carried the body of the female on my back, draped the male's big, fluffy tail around my neck and headed towards Spruce Plateau, where sika deer are usually found.

"We'd barely gone a few hundred meters into a bushy area when we found ourselves surrounded by a large pack of jackals. Clearly, the tailless male had brought back his gang to exact his revenge."

"Snow Queen was very brave. She charged into them to scare them away but there were too many of them. Afraid that she would lose against such odds, I whistled for her to come to my side."

"There's an old saying, 'Destroy the leader and the gang will collapse, and strike where it will most hurt.' I looked for the leader of the pack. It's been my experience that once you shoot the leader dead, the whole pack collapses into disarray.

Otherwise, no matter how many jackals you kill, not only will the pack refuse to retreat, but the pack will stalk you and fight you to the bitter end."

"It didn't take me long to figure out that the pack leader was actually a female! Yes, that's right, the one you saw today, the one with the scarred face. Back then, she didn't have a scar and looked much younger. When she saw us, she gave out long howls and short ones, a series of orders to the other jackals to bite me. I fired a few good shots at her, but she was so agile, dodging this way and that, that I was unable to harm a single hair on her head."

"I soon ran out of gunpowder as well. There was nothing to do, but to run for a yacca pine, some two hundred meters away. Jackals are fierce creatures, but they can't climb. If I could scramble up that tree, I'd be safe; as for Snow Queen, once I was up in the tree, she could run back to the camp to warn everyone. Tibetan Mastiffs are strong and can outrun jackals. She'd be able to elude them.

"I aimed blindly into the bushes where I could faintly see them, running as fast as I could towards the pine tree. I was there in no time. Then, I put the gun on my shoulder, roped the dead jackal onto my back, and began climbing the tree. Meanwhile, Snow Queen was barking at those jackals to prevent them from attacking me while I was climbing.

"Snow Queen was the most loyal of dogs. She would never leave me until I was entirely out of danger. The girth of that pine trunk was as long as two arms. It was a difficult and slow climb, thanks to the five-kilo shotgun on my shoulder and the 15-kilo jackal on my back. Many of the pack began whining, probably realizing that once I was up the tree they could do nothing to me. Their ugly wailing sounded like the crying of hungry ghosts."

"Just then, the lead female and the tailless male jumped out from a ridge and started running straight towards the pine tree. Snow Queen dashed up to head them off. The tailless jackal fought with Snow Queen, trying to stall for time, allowing the female to creep around to the foot of the tree. The female jackal jumped as high as she could, trying to bite my ankles and drag me down. I'd just got halfway up the tree and my feet were about two meters above the ground, within reach of her jaws. Hugging the tree tight with one arm, I pulled out my long knife with the other hand. Hacking the air with my knife, I managed to slash her in the face, which is how she came to look like she does now."

"Wounded, she cried in agony and fled. Then, I took my chance to climb a fork in the tree and sat on a long, horizontal branch. Just then, I heard a yelp from Snow Queen, and turned to see that tailless jackal was biting her neck. In a one-on-one fight, she would never lose: a Tibetan Mastiff can fight two jackals at the same time, but there were five or six jackals surrounding my dog. Some were biting at her legs and some at her tail, preventing her from moving at all. That tailless jackal was like an executioner when he sank his sharp fangs deep into Snow Queen's neck, and jumped and lunged at her, cruelly tearing at her neck. Fearless as she was among dogs, Snow Queen was hopelessly outnumbered by so many jackals. I know how hunting jackals operate: once they bite a vulnerable part of their prey, they will never relax their grip. Even mountain leopards and tigers fear jackals because of this dreadful trait."

"I wanted to shoot those two damned jackals and save Snow Queen, but when I shook the gourd containing my gunpowder, I knew that there was no gunpowder left. With just my knife, I couldn't possibly fight off those evil jackals. Not even if I had superpowers. I sat in the tree, witnessing my Snow Queen's neck being ripped apart. She was lying in blood. I'll never forget the helpless look in her eyes and her desperate cries for help. Up there in the tree, I felt as if her cries were piercing my heart, but there was not a thing I could do. Within minutes, Snow Queen was a pile of bones."

"For three years now I've been looking for those jackals. They're very cunning, and kept moving about, so I couldn't find them. To chance upon them today is truly a case of 'enemies meeting on a narrow road.' Just now, I saw clearly that that damned tailless male was still part of the pack. I give my word as a hunter that I will chop its head off. No, not just him. I'll kill every last one of them in memory of Snow Queen." As Champa swore this, he cracked his knuckles and his eyes burned with a vengeful fire.

CONJURING BANNER

Champa went back to the camp to fetch the jackal's severed tail. It was about 60 centimeters long and burned black at the end. It was stiff and spotted with white mold. Actually, it looked more like a filthy stick than anything else. Champa was an experienced hunter. Following the jackals' tracks, he came to a desolate ravine and hung the tail on a small crooked tree beside the path. The footprints left in the wetland indicated their presence in that ravine. He hung it just three meters high in a fork of the tree so it was clearly visible to the jackals, but beyond their reach.

"I'll have those evil creatures know that for every debt

there's a creditor, and I've come to exact the blood debt from three years ago," said Champa. His voice was cruel and cold.

There was nothing I could do to stop him. Unless you've lived among the hunters on Gaoligong Mountains, you'll never understand how deeply they love their hunting dogs. They treat them as family. Even when their bodies wear out with age, they will never kill them; nor will they abandon, abuse or put them out on the street. Instead, they keep on treating them as well as ever, looking after their pets in their old age and burying them with great ceremony. Once, when the beloved dog of an old hunter died, the man's grief was so acute he fell ill and never recovered. His last wish before dying was to be buried in the same tomb as his dog. Champa had witnessed his beloved dog being torn apart. For such a man of action and self-esteem, the memory of that scene coiled inside him like a snake, piercing his heart all the time. For a hunter who feels his honor is his life, the grief of losing his beloved dog was imprinted on his soul and inscribed in his memory. It could never be erased.

Of all the creatures of prey—jackals, wolves, tigers and leopards, Champa saw jackals as the worst of villains. They had mercilessly torn Snow Queen apart and had almost killed him. The jackals had only themselves to blame for being blamed; they had brought punishment on themselves. Of course, we might look at things from the jackal perspective: A jackal couple are walking in the mountains, when suddenly—*Pow!* Disaster strikes. The female has half a skull shot away, and the male's tail gets bitten off. Is that not an injustice? A tragedy even? Moreover, if they respond in kind—an eye for an eye, demanding blood for blood—is that so unreasonable?

However, I am a member of the human race. I cannot think only from a jackal's perspective. Since time immemorial, a human's attitude towards wild animals has been absolute and uncompromising. Humans are permitted to hunt and kill; resistance from animals is not permitted. If animals dare to fight back, they are considered treasonous, are branded as murderers, rounded up and killed without mercy.

That afternoon, Champa went back to the camp for rice, so I went by myself to the mountain stream to catch some red frogs, which would make fine specimens. While I was busy in this activity, I heard the faint howling of jackals coming from the desolate ravine. I immediately ran over there, crawled behind a rock halfway up the mountain and observed through my binoculars the most unbelievable scene. It was the gold-back jackals, led by Scarface. They had gathered under the tree where the jackal tail was hanging. Scarface raised her head, staring at the tail dangling above her head, her eyes full of concern and terror; the rest of the pack paced about restlessly like ants on a hot pan. The tailless jackal kept on jumping up at the disfigured remains, like a high jumper making repeated attempts to clear the bar. But he was no flying jackal; however hard he tried, the elusive tail remained beyond his reach.

Clearly, the pack recognized that the tail hanging on the crooked tree belonged to their own tailless jackal. It was the same tail bitten off three years earlier by the hunter's dog. Jackals are among the smarter creatures of the animal world, so they must have understood the implications of the sudden appearance of the jackal tail in the ravine that they frequented, and why it hung on the tree like a flag summoning the spirit of the dead.

It was a portent of imminent disaster, a secret order for their encirclement and extermination. Normally, when faced with a threat to their life, an animal's first reaction is to flee, especially when the threat comes from a human being. All things being equal, flight will be the first choice. However, I knew these jackals would not leave the ravine, at least not within the next month or two. The reason was simple: we were at the transition between spring and summer, a time of year in which, according to their life cycle, infant jackals are born. Some of the females must have given birth already and, unlike felines, canines cannot pick up their pups by the scruff of their necks and move them elsewhere. Field studies indicate that jackals usually give birth in a secret den or hole and remain there until their pups are three or four months old and ready to learn how to hunt. Until that time, the pack will never leave their territory.

The pack was disordered and restless until Scarface finally calmed them with several long howls. With heavy steps, they finally left the crooked tree, the tree that threatened them with such ill fortune.

KIDNAPPING YOUNG JACKALS

It was almost dark. Champa said he was going to hunt a pheasant to supplement our meals, so he left the field observation camp. Early next morning, while the dew was still lying about, he returned, carrying a bulging sheepskin sack on his back. He strode into the camp and threw the sack onto the floor. His square-set face looked tired, but happy. He said proudly:

"Hey. Take a look at what I've got!"

Inside the sheepskin bag, something live was wriggling. I untied the knot and was amazed to find eight jackal pups, which were still not weaned. They had dense coats, their backs had layers of soft and golden hair, and there were white hairs between their toes. Undoubtedly, it was a litter of gold-back jackals.

Champa recounted how he'd caught these little jackals. "Oh boy! Those jackals are so crafty. Their den is hidden at the end of the bushes and behind the moraine. I spent all night fumbling trying to it." Just after dawn, Scarface had led the pack away to hunt. "I fired a shot outside the den and scared away the two old jackals left behind to tend the pups. Then I put my hands into the den and picked them up as if I was gathering mushrooms."

How much courage it took to intrude into a jackal den, all alone and in the dead of night!

"Why did you bring them here? What do you intend on doing?" I asked.

With these pups in our hands, we needn't worry about Scarface and the tailless jackal coming here ever again." As Champa spoke, his eyes grew stern. His tough lower jaw twisted; he looked determined to kill.

I understood. He was going to keep these pups as bait and exact a terrible revenge. The plan was clever all right, but despicable.

"No way. Gold-back jackals have state-level protection. You can't do this," I tried to dissuade him firmly, motivated by my conscience and duty as a zoologist.

"What? You want to protect these evil jackals?" Champa's eyebrows shot up in shock. "Try finding any herder on Gamaer Grassland who agrees with you!"

"Gold-back jackals are wildlife. China has the *Wild Animal Conservation Law*, and it prohibits any act that harms them!" I took out the weapon of the Law, hoping to argue him out of such a reckless action.

"So what! So are mosquitoes, flies, cockroaches, and rats—all of them are wildlife. Are we going to protect them all?" Champa sneered in reply.

"This is completely different. Mosquitoes, flies, cockroaches and rats are harmful to humankind. In the past, they were classed as the 'Four Pests' to be eliminated, but gold-back jackals are as a rare, endangered species. They eat rodents like rats and wild rabbits, so they are useful animals and should not be hunted or killed indiscriminately." I argued from a zoologist's stance.

"What? Jackals useful? Hah! Now, you're being ridiculous!" Champa looked as amazed as if a tree had started talking. His eyes grew big, as he argued back, "If my fellow villagers heard what you just said, they'd spit at you. Most definitely. We, the people of Kaza Village, Han and Tibetan alike, loathe these evil jackals. We know them as vermin like rats, and the sooner they are wiped out the better."

"You are so wrong to say that," I told him.

"Damn! Oh, sorry, please forgive my crude language." Champa's face turned red and his chest heaved violently. He kept pulling at his hair. I could tell he was trying to rein in his anger and calm himself down. However, the words he uttered were still as hard as stone, "We, Kaza people have a saying that 'When friends come, reach for the good wine. When jackals come, reach for your gun.'" As for jackals and wolves, jackals rank as even more evil and hateful than wolves.

I certainly knew the common term, "jackals and wolves" as a synonym for bastards, but only as an idiom in Chinese daily life. It certainly could not be used to signify that these two animals are vermin that perpetrate every conceivable crime, that they are unpardonably wicked and therefore they should be cursed with festering boils on their heads and under their feet. Human prejudice against jackals and cultural differences also play a part in this point of view. However, I am not at all eloquent; my words came out stiff and clumsily. Having failed to convince him, I chose to keep silent for fear of truly offending him.

A while later, when Champa had calmed down a little, he drew a breath and continued, "You've never been a herder, so you don't know how formidable these jackals can be. They're so savage and sly and they do terrible harm to many herders. When a pack encircles a bullock, they jump onto its back and bite its tail, forcing the bullock's tail to stick up; then, they use their claws to poke into its back passage. Their sharp claws are like iron hooks that hook onto the bullock's guts and pull them out, and the bullock's insides fall to the ground, still bloody and warm, like a tangled hank of yarn. Once guts are pulled out, the bullock, no matter how strong, will fall to the ground and can't get up again. These evil jackals have more dirty tricks to play. When they have eaten a sheep, they keep its head and fur intact and drape it over another jackal to disguise it as a sheep. The jackals then crouch down low in the bushes until another sheep approaches the false one. Then, the jackals leap out and bring the poor creature down. On top of this, the jackal thinks lightning fast. They have an uncanny ability to anticipate their enemy's plans like a wizard outwitting a general and his army. No matter how clever your trap, and even if you cover the dirt with sheep footprints, a jackal will not step onto it; even if you rub lard on the trap and hide it in the thick grass, it will still sense something not quite right. Our village has set more than a hundred traps, but we've never caught a single jackal with them. Even if you fix a hunting net among dense branches and tether a frisky lamb under the tree, the cunning jackal can sense something amiss and, unlike other beasts, will never move to take the lamb and get itself caught in the process. In our community, the jackal is seen as a devil incarnate, as a wild and evil ghost reborn in this world. It's the worst thing in the world."

"Jackals are carnivorous beasts and of course they hunt all herbivores, cattle and sheep included. Using their claws to poke the anus and disembowel other animals, using sheepskin for disguising themselves as sheep... these actions are food-gathering skills. It's comparable to us using bows and arrows to shoot birds, and hooks to catch fish. You can't use that argument to conclude that they are evil beasts and should be killed." I tried my best to refute him. "As for them not stepping into the traps and never touching the bait under the hunting net, this just indicates how very clever they are and good at protecting themselves. Their understanding of how to protect themselves and their ability to survive in a very dangerous environment... how can these things be called crimes?"

"Bah! Why do you always argue for the jackals? Are you a relative of theirs? A friend of theirs? Perhaps you're their lawyer? Maybe their patron saint?" Champa fixed me with a surprised gaze. His mouth turned slightly up at the side and his face was scornful. "How can you compare humans with jackals?"

"Humans and jackals alike are inhabitants of earth and have the right to exist," I countered.

"There are lives and there are lives. It's like forest mushrooms—you've got the delicious edible Boletus and the Green cracking Russula, but on the other hand, you've got deadly poisonous ones like Gilled Toadstools and Sickener Russulas," Champa argued.

I debated further, "Scientists have concluded on the basis of field studies that the number of these jackals is already very small. Even if there are cases of stealing cattle and sheep from herders, they are rare, and they hardly pose a serious threat to animal husbandry. In actual fact, dissections of dead gold-back jackals show that their main food source is red snow hares, which are wild rodents."

Champa remained unconvinced. "Even if what you say is true, it doesn't prove that jackals shouldn't be wiped out. Red snow hare meat is delicious and their fur can be sold. If all the jackals are put down, the red snow hare population will increase and we can organize hunting teams to catch them. It's sure to make a profitable side-line, and perhaps we, Kaza people could soon be well-off."

Champa was as stubborn as a mule and convinced that only

he was right, so it was hard for me to change his mind. All I could do was sit on my hands and wait to see how he intended to deal with this pack of jackals.

The pups were a couple of weeks old and already able to walk. They wormed their way out of the bag and suspicious and curious, sized the two of us up. Initially, they were timid, and huddled up against one another, but before long, their irrepressible, mischievous, and energetic nature showed itself. Soon they were bouncing about and chasing each other around the camp. I made up a bowl of milk from powdered milk to feed them; Champa made a large basket from strips of pliable willow to keep them prisoners.

That night, the mournful howling of jackals in the surrounding forest could be heard inside our field study base. It was a shrill, hoarse and trembling sound; a sound that gave me goose bumps all over. It was a pitch-black, moonless night, but we could see the green lights of their eyes, circling in the dark night like will-o'-the-wisps. For sure, these jackals had returned to their den from hunting and discovered their pups missing, and their acute sense of smell had led them to our camp.

As a precaution against any animal attacks, we had dug a protective moat three-meters wide and two-meters-deep, and erected a stout fence with posts as high as three meters and with a diameter the size of a bowl. However ferocious these jackals were, they couldn't possibly get in.

During the second half of the night, several daring jackals did manage to cross the three-meter-wide moat and threw themselves at the fence. They poked their pointed muzzles through the gaps between the posts and howled a ceaseless cry that sounded like a stream of foul abuse and vicious curses. At the sound of the howling from the adult jackals, the pups in the wicker cage grabbed at the cage with their claws and bit at it with their teeth. The crying and yelling from the jackal pups only enraged the adults further, so they began head-butting the posts. Dong, dong, dong! It sounded like the beating of wooden drums.

Champa fired a shot over the fence to scare them off. However, within half an hour, they were back outside the camp, howling away.

"They can throw their weight about for two days at most. And then I'll send the lot of them to hell," Champa vowed.

Not until the first rose-colored rays of the morning sun emerged above the eastern mountain did the anxious rescue party withdraw to their ravine.

THE JACKALS EXECUTE

After being informed about the presence of a herd of wild asses along the southern Gaoligong Mountains, Champa accompanied me there, but after searching for a day and a half, we didn't find a trace of them and decided to head back. When we were passing the ravine at dusk, we saw those gold-back jackals again. They were gathered under the small crooked tree, on which the jackal tail hung. The adults had formed a big circle, facing inwards to the center where the tailless jackal was standing, the one whose tail had been bitten off by Champa's beloved dog, Snow Queen. With grave expressions, they gazed at the tailless jackal, all the time making strange, low sounds.

For his part, the tailless jackal trapped in the circle, yelled loudly and bared his teeth. I could tell he was nervous and fearful. The setting sun cast a ghastly shaft of bloody light into the woods.

I had never witnessed jackals behave so strangely: the way they surrounded this one individual with their pack looked like a public trial. The jackals forming the circle were playing the role of judge, while the individual at the center was like a defendant awaiting a sentence. If my hypothesis was correct, then the strange, low noises made by these jackals were the charges laid against the defendant, and roars of the tailless jackal were his attempt to defend himself against their accusations.

As a trained zoologist, I was attracted by this little-known phenomenon, so I observed them carefully through my binoculars.

Just then, Scarface raised her head and gave a long howl; instantly, the judges and the defendant fell silent and held their breath, waiting for the chief judge to pronounce sentence.

Scarface uttered three sharp howls. Howl! Howl! Howl!

Then the tailless jackal, standing upright until this point, trembled and knelt down. His face looked exactly like a defendant hearing his death sentence. The jackals surrounding him lowered their heads and looked downcast.

Suddenly, the tailless male rolled on the ground and jumped to his feet. The golden fur on his back stood up and his eyes glared fiercely. He acted like a cornered beast, howling madly and opening his mouth to bite the others around him. One of the females was scared into retreating a little, so a gap in the circle opened. He took his chance and jumped out, yowling as he dashed at full speed into the wild.

Plainly, he didn't accept Scarface's decision, and was lodging an appeal by force. When he jumped out of the circle and dashed away, his actions were in essence a form of prison-break and escape.

I thought Scarface would lead the pursuit party, like a posse pursuing the most wanted outlaw. However, I was wrong; she just turned her head, watched him, far away by now, and howled a long, sad and accusatory howl. The rest of the pack watched him retreating and howled wretchedly.

It sounded like they were begging the tailless jackal to come back. A moment earlier, those jackals had been subjecting him to trial; now, they seemed to be entreating him. I was baffled; not knowing what was going on.

I focused my binoculars on the escapee and found that the howls of Scarface and the rest of the pack seemed to be pulling at his feelings like an invisible rope. Despite himself, the jackal slowed down, ran a dozen meters further and finally stopped. He turned back to look at the pack. Unwilling to go back, but unable to continue, he turned his head and circled on the spot, torn by his inner conflict.

Scarface and the others were howling sorrowfully to the sky. Finally, the tailless jackal decided to go back. He walked slowly, as if trudging through mire, with every step taken requiring great strength. With lowered brow, his muzzle twitching and wrinkling, his mouth slightly agape, and tongue lolling, he looked abject, as if submitting to his due punishment. I was curious. Based on what I had just seen, he had not lost his freedom: he was neither detained nor hindered; furthermore, he would come back to the pack reluctantly. He could just leave without as much as a backward glance. The world was large and he could go wherever he chose. So why come back against his will?

Back at the tree, the other jackals surrounded him again and Scarface licked his forehead and ears, while some other females licked his body and legs. They seemed to be rewarding him like a hero returning in triumph. Without displaying even the slightest hint of pride, the tailless jackal only looked more pained and howled plaintively.

Later, Scarface put her face against his head and rubbed against it. My impression is that the way animals express their feelings is a little crude. Even when a male and a female are in love, such intimate behavior is not the norm. Apart from new mothers, who perform this act to shower love on their still blind newborns, jackals do not behave in this manner. It was my first time to see such tender and touching behavior between adult jackals. At the same time, four females, with swollen teats hanging from their bellies, licked his legs as if they had chosen one apiece. Every one of them was licking the same part— his knees.

After a while, Scarface buried the male's head beneath her chin, raised her own head toward the tail hanging from the tree before uttering a short howl. That howl was the signal for the most rarely witnessed execution scene on earth: those four females licking the limbs of the tailless jackal, suddenly bit him, just as they would do to a fleeing quarry.

The tailless jackal instinctively tried to jump out of the way of those jaws, but his limbs seemed nailed down and immovable. He yelled in pain, twisting and shaking his head, his eyes wide, jaws open and sharp teeth bared. The strange thing is, he offered no resistance and did not return bite for bite, though it would be easy for him to do so.

Those females were biting him viciously. Although I couldn't hear anything, I could feel their canine teeth gnawing at his bones, and could sense his knees being dislocated and his legs being broken. His body went into violent spasms.

Another howl came from Scarface, signalling the four executioners should release their grip and step back. The victim fell to the ground like a piece of sawed off wood. Every leg was broken and it was clear that he could never stand up again. He rolled about on the ground, howling in anguish.

The others stood silently in front of him, heads lowered and tails down. It was a scene of great sadness.

I couldn't figure it out. Why did they bite and cripple him if it made them feel so wretched? The last sunset glow on the mountain was fading into the evening light. Scarface approached the tailless male, her neck craned toward him, and then she regurgitated some pulp. The other females followed suit. I recognized this as a method of feeding peculiar to jackals. After catching their prey, the female swallow as much flesh as they can manage. Then, on returning to their den, they regurgitate the semi-digested meat to feed their pups. This is also called "fake rumination". The tailless jackal smelled that pile of pulp and turned his head away. He was dying, so how could he face food?

Several late returning crows alighted and perched, cawing, on the crooked tree. Scarface raised her head and howled at the tail hanging there before leading the pack off into the bushes.

The hanging tail, the hostage pups, that cruel punishment... Suddenly, I understood the connection between them. The tail that hung on the tree signalled to the jackals that someone was coming to avenge the Tibetan Mastiff they'd torn apart three years earlier, and the kidnapping of their eight pups soon followed this warning. The jackals had found where their pups were detained, but they could not rescue them. The tail on the tree was an icy, glimmering sword of vengeance suspended above their heads. Scarface, with all those hard years of experience behind her, was all too aware that jackals were no match for a human and could not possibly fight this avenger. Their only way out was to compromise, to concede. Since the avenger had hung that tail on the tree, it followed that he was coming after the tailless jackal, the original cause of the feud. For the sake of their eight pups, for the survival of their whole family, they decided to sacrifice the tailless jackal's life. Cruel? Absolutely, but a wise move too. Scarface had no heart for it, but she had no choice. That is why after his limbs were gnawed through, she howled mournful cries and fed him regurgitated mush as if she would with her own pups. It was a reasonable hypothesis in my view.

Once the jackals were far enough away, Champa and I came down the hill to the tree in the ravine. The dusk was thickening;

the cawing of the shadowy black crows and the groans of the dying tailless jackal created a kind of disturbing duet that echoed through the mountains. But as soon as the jackal spotted us, he stopped groaning and clenched his teeth. He knew we might appear, and he didn't panic at all. Though unable to stand up, the jackal tried as hard as he could to hold his head up and maintain his dignity as a beast. There was no terror in his eyes, and no remorse: just sorrow and resignation.

Champa pulled the rifle bolt and aimed the barrel at his head, cursing, "You bastard jackal, you never thought this day would come, huh? I'll take your head to avenge my Snow Queen!"

The tailless jackal still kept his head high. I figured he had known all along that things would end this way. When the pack surrounded and howled at him as if holding a trial, he had foreseen that he would face the hunter's ghastly muzzle. He didn't want to die. He had rushed out of the circle and had the chance to run far away. However, he had chosen to return to his pack, even though they were intent on killing him. This allegiance to his family overrode even his survival instinct. So after a moment's hesitation, he accepted the punishment imposed by his own kind, accepted what fate had arranged, and chose to exchange his own life for the safety of his whole family and the survival of the eight pups.

I felt a deep, begrudging respect for the tailless jackal then.

Bang! Champa pulled the trigger. A cloud of blue smoke came out of the muzzle and wrapped itself around the body ...

The crows cried in fear and flew off, like a burial ceremony's entourage.

"Champa, look, the jackal family has punished the tailless jackal on your behalf. You know why Scarface did this. It was a way of apologizing for what they did three years back." I patted his shoulder, "If enmity is not settled amicably, there is no end to it. You've avenged Snow Queen, so let's return their pups to them."

Champa frowned, thought about it and then shook his head. "No, when I buried Snow Queen, I swore to exterminate these evil jackals. I cannot break my vow. Yes, the tailless jackal was the culprit that killed my Snow Queen, but the others had a hand in the killing too. I saw those bastards tearing her apart piece by piece. I remember very well a female with a lopsided jaw, clawing out the guts while my dog was still alive; then, a male with black ears bit her heart, her still beating heart; several others ripped at her limbs when she still had breath... These jackals are wicked beyond all redemption. Even hacking them into a thousand pieces would not satisfy me.."

"Revenge breeds more revenge in a never-ending cycle. What

is past is past. Let it go!" I said, in an attempt to soothe him.

He kept silent and just kept on shaking his head. After a long while, he muttered, "The pups didn't hurt my Snow Queen. After my revenge, I'll raise them myself and release them into the wild once they're old enough."

6

SETTING FIRE TO THE GOLD-BACK JACKALS

Looked at purely from a hunter's perspective, Champa's scheme was an ingenious one, one that could wipe out this nest of jackals without exposing either of us to risk. At the end of the deserted ravine was the "sky strip," a long narrow pass just five or six meters across and quite overgrown. It was flanked by vertical cliffs that even the wildest monkeys could not climb. Situated at the end of the valley was a kind of chain bridge commonly found in northern Yunnan province. It was suspended between two mountains spanning a torrential river below. This chain bridge had a narrow deck of wooden boards that both humans and animals could barely walk on...

What the plan boiled down to was this: to scatter sulphur over the weeds at the entrance to the defile, and place the wicker cage with the eight pups in the middle section so that the jackals, on hearing their cries, would not hesitate to dash to their rescue; by entering the "sky strip," they'd be entering our trap. From the cliff, Champa would throw lighted torches onto the sulphur-strewn weeds. It was the dry season, so the withered vegetation would ignite easily and become a wall of fire in no time at all. Lately, a southwesterly wind had prevailed and the strong valley wind was blowing towards the Nujiang River. This meant that the jackals would surely flee towards the river, where hundred-meter-high cliffs awaited. The only way out was by crossing the chain bridge, but I was there long before, ready and waiting. Once the thick smoke rose, I would remove two of the wooden boards. Monkeys could cling onto the greasy chain with their hands and grapple their way across but jackals, having clawed paws, could not. They would either be burnt to death by the intense fire behind them, or fall into the river from the bridge and be swallowed up in the torrent. Not a single one could possibly survive.

Champa set about keeping his promise to save the pups. He tied a long hemp rope onto the puppy cage so that once the fire was set, he could haul it up the cliff and out of danger. He was an experienced hunter and everything went as planned. I saw a thick smoke rising in the air and watched the cage as hauled up the cliff inch by inch. Soon, I heard the jackals howling. I stood in the middle of the bridge and pulled out two of the wooden boards.

Within minutes, Scarface and the other panic-stricken jackals were at the end of the bridge. She saw me standing in the middle, then halted and looked around, clearly seeking another escape route. She soon realized that, being hemmed in by the cliffs, the chain bridge offered the sole way out. She gaped, her eyes staring, hackles up, and scar livid. She looked like a demon incarnate. She howled and ran at me. I knew she was trying to scare me off, so that she could lead the pack over the bridge to safety. However, I wasn't frightened; the bridge deck in front now had a three-meter-long void, leaving only two suspension chains as thick as a man's thumb. Unless she was a world champion long-jumper, she couldn't possibly leap across the chain bridge; unless she was a tightrope performer, she couldn't possibly cross the steep void via that slender iron chain.

Just as anticipated, she rushed at me, howling, but stopped short of the abyss. Craning her neck, she saw the Nujiang River rushing below and immediately recoiled in shock. This part of the river was abrupt and full of submerged reefs and rocks; the river ran like stampeding wild horses, thundering as it clashed against the reefs. The other jackals stopped here and turned as if hoping that they could return. They were crowded at the end of the bridge. They were also in a desperate fix, unable to go back and unable to go forward.

Dead twigs and withered leaves crackled in the fire and the flames leaped so high that the "sky strip" became a sea of fire. The wind fed the fire and the fire fed the wind in turn. Soon, the raging fire approached the start of the bridge. Within minutes at most, the flames would spread to the far end, where I was standing. I looked closely at several jackals nervously biting each other in despair. One old jackal, bald-chested, closed his eyes and walked on, trancelike, step after step, clearly keen to put an end to this undue, premature agony by stepping into the void and tumbling down into the river below.

Howl! Scarface cried to the sky and the chaotic pack quieted somewhat; those scrapping with each other stopped biting and the bald-chest jackal halted. Dozens of eyes turned toward Scarface, waiting for her to figure a way out.

She hurried to the center of the bridge and stopped at the point on the suspension chains where I had removed the decking. She stared at me. This time, her hackles were down; she did not bare her teeth at me in threat; nor did she try to jump and bite me. Quite the reverse was true: her look was submissive, her mouth closed, her bushy tail dragged on the ground and her neck was drawn in. Suddenly, she lay down, spread-eagled, jaw on the deck, muzzle upward and ears down. Her soft, vulnerable neck was exposed, and her tail swung weakly as she whimpered. She was a pathetic sight.

I had studied jackal behavior before. When two jackals fight and bite each other, the loser adopts a posture like Scarface's; it signifies an admission of defeat or surrender. In jackal society, once a jackal makes this surrender posture, the other will stop biting and give him a way out. In a contest between jackals, a victor can never bite an adversary that admits defeat. It is an important taboo. This jackal was exceptionally smart; she knew the pack was in a desperate situation, and that only I could rescue them. The rest of the pack followed Scarface's lead, prostrating themselves and showing their vulnerable necks, whimpering again and again.

My heart trembled. I wasn't entirely in agreement with Champa about his cruel, vengeful plan. It was so excessive, so extreme to exterminate these precious gold-back jackals to compensate for the killing of just one hunting dog. As a zoologist, I thought that it was my duty to protect these rare and

endangered wild animals. I reasoned that, since I had no grudge against them, I shouldn't be helping Champa kill them.

As the wildfire approached the start of the chain bridge, several balls of dry grass caught fire, and, carried on the wind, landed on the chain bridge with the agility of firebirds. One of the fireballs rolled onto Scarface's back and scorched her golden fur. She grimaced with the heat of it, but she still crawled on the ground and entreated me piteously. The fire was actually burning their flanks. If I didn't intervene to help them, the flames would force them into the rolling Nujiang River, and they would fall like tea leaves dropping into a pot of boiling water.

I didn't wait any longer. I took a piece of the removed board and extended it across the void. No sooner was it in place than the jackals stepped onto it, one by one, and ran into the forest on the far side. When the jackal family lined up to cross the bridge, Scarface remained on her stomach, still in the posture of begging for mercy, still whimpering.

Within two minutes at most, seventy or eighty jackals went over that board, across the bridge and on to safety on the far bank. Only then, did Scarface stand up and tread on the board to cross the void. As she passed me, she stopped, tentatively extended her muzzle and rubbed gently against my trousers, while uttering several howls. It seemed like a gesture of thanks for giving them a way out. Then, she ran swiftly across the bridge to pursue her family. The fire jumped out of the "sky strip" and onto the end of the bridge. It consumed the wooden deck entirely, but the gold-back jackals were long gone by then.

Later, I spun an unlikely tale and told Champa a lie. That the wires attaching the boards were too tight and that it had taken me ages just to lift out one board, by which time the jackals had run to the far side. Champa cast me a sceptical glance, heaved a heavy sigh and said nothing.

MOBBED BY WILD ASSES

Prior to our encounter, we had no idea just how fearsome wild asses could be when riled. They were a group of desperadoes. They kept chasing Champa and me, refusing to let us go.

It was in an area of flat pastureland in south of the mountains that we found them. In China, wild asses are listed as an endangered species and these creatures hadn't been sighted around Gaoligong Mountains for over twenty years. I was very excited to see them, so I hid in a bush and raised my camcorder to film them. From what I had read about them, wild asses are sensitive and timid animals, so the thought of having to take any precautions against them, never crossed my mind.

Wild asses are also gregarious animals and this herd was over one-hundred strong. It was the mating season, so several young males were taking little nips at each other, competing to win the best mates. With loud brays, they fought enthusiastically. I was able to film many great sequences. One black-neck female, seemingly intent on stardom, grazed her way into the bushes where Champa and I were hiding. She was close enough for me to touch her legs. From his sheepskin sack, Champa drew out a nylon rope, with a crescent-shaped piece of lead tied to one end. It was a typical bolas used by herders on Gaoligong Mountains. When catching a horse, they throw the rope forcefully at a horse's legs and the lead-weighted end gets tangled up in them, making the horse stumble. Champa winked at me and made a rope-throwing gesture. I understood. He wanted to knock the black-neck ass down. It wasn't a bad idea. Having a live wild ass would greatly assist my research, so I gave him the nod.

Champa stood up abruptly and yelled. Seeing a human appear out of nowhere, the startled wild ass reared up, and raised her foreleg hooves. At that moment, Champa raised his arm and threw the bolas in order to tangle her back legs.

A wild ass is just two-thirds the size of a regular horse, but its strength is by no means weaker. The black-neck ass jumped and ran forward as hard as she could; Champa was unable to stop her. He was dragged out of the bushes, and staggered down the slope after her. The other asses brayed in alarm, and ran away to watch from a safe distance.

"Help! Come here quickly!" Champa shouted to me, holding on to one end of the rope for dear life.

I put the camera down and rushed towards him. The ass was running down the slope very fast, and by the time I reached Champa, we were almost at the bottom of the hill. We spent an immense amount of energy pulling her and holding her down to the ground. I grabbed her neck and restrained her, while Champa hobbled her four legs. She was lying on the ground, desperately crying for help.

As we were busy grappling with her, the sound of asses braying suddenly came from all directions. I raised my head and gasped in fear: god knows where they came from, but these wild asses had us surrounded. A strong white-face male brayed as he ran back and forth, commanding the others to tighten the circle. Perhaps, because male asses are especially bold and irritable during the mating season, seeing us handling the black-neck female in such rough fashion, they wrongly took us for love rivals and intended to fight with us.

The worst of it was that Champa's hunting rifle, his Tibetan knife and my revolver, all our weapons were lying among the bushes at the top of the hill, as much as four hundred meters away from where we needed them. We were empty-handed and the grassy hill was devoid of even a rock to hurl at them.

"Ah!" Champa had hogtied the female ass. He stood up and waved his arms about, jumping up and down like a frog. He screamed as well. I knew this is what hunters do when they encounter wild beasts. They use this primitive display of strength to scare them away. This time it didn't work. The wild asses raised their front-hooves and brayed loudly. The noise of a single wild ass braying is so loud and sonorous that it is also known as the "braying ass." The sound of so many of them yelling together was all the more powerful, loud enough to waken the dead, and they instantly drowned out Champa's yelling.

The white-face ass charged with all his strength, reared up, his front hooves poised to come down on my head like a pair of hammers. If he succeeded, my head would be smashed in or I'd be knocked out. But Champa was sharp and agile; he threw the bolas and smashed the lead weight against the lips of the white-face ass. Maybe the bolas had broken one of its front teeth because it abandoned its attack on me and ran back to the herd.

Nevertheless, the attack by the white-face ass provoked the other males into following his example. As if keen to play the role of handsome hero coming to the rescue of their damsel in distress, they stamped the ground, their hooves drumming the earth, shaking their manes and tails and preparing to move in.

Far outnumbered and at a disadvantage, I gulped, "How about letting her go? Let's not invite trouble."

Champa realized the perilous situation we were in, so he had to untie the rope. The black-neck ass rolled, stood up and ran back to the herd, all the while caterwauling in complaint.

We had assumed that once we had released the female, the other wild asses would stop harassing and attacking us. Wrong. They still kept us surrounded. So we tried to make our way back up the hill. Provided we could get back to the cover of the bushes, grab our guns and fire several warning shots, we could definitely quiet these furious wild asses, scare them to death, and then drive them away. Champa waved the bolas and kept shouting; I waved my fists and kicked my legs in a martial arts manner. All the while, I kept yelling, trying to break through the circle.

When we were ten meters or so away from them, the white-face ass suddenly turned around. The others, previously facing us, also did an 180-degree turn to present us with their rear ends. I knew they weren't about to hold a behind exhibition—there is nothing remotely beautiful about their behinds; nor were they about to fart in unison and asphyxiate us. They were about to deploy their most powerful weapon—the backward kick.

When confronted by enemies, besides running away, horses have two methods of self-defence: one is "the forward stamp" and the other is "the back-kick". The so-called "back-kick" involves jumping and kicking back with the hind legs. The leg muscles of horses are very strong and their hooves are very hard, so the back-kick can inflict serious damage. I read a report once about how a leopard which tried to steal a foal and was knocked unconscious by a foal's angry mother. It took only one well-placed kick. In addition, there are many recorded examples of wild asses encountering wolves in the wilderness, and when realizing that they are unable to escape, they form an inward-facing circle, back-kicking together to counter the wolves' attempts to kill them.

It was quite a spectacle—a hundred or more wild asses kicking backward with the grass flying and the dust whirling about. Far from us escaping this circle, we were lost inside it, unable to tell one direction from another. The lips of the white-face ass had a large swelling from where the bolas had struck; his expression was fierce. He was arrogantly kicking his hind legs and braying loudly. Relentlessly, step by step, the wild asses were closing in; the circle had shrunk to just five or six meters across. At this rate, those hooves would be hammering down on us without mercy; our bodies would be kicked every which way before their hooves finally shot us through the gates of hell.

My spine tingled and my legs went weak; Champa's forehead was damp with sweat. If a zoologist and his hired guide were to die like martyrs in the line of duty because of a good kicking by asses, wouldn't this give people a great laugh?

Then, at this moment of peril, from the top of the hill came the sharp howl of a jackal. At this, as if hearing the tolling of their own death knell, most of the asses stopped kicking immediately, and looked around. I looked too, and was thrilled to see those familiar gold-back jackals crossing the top of the hill. Elated even, because field study records show that the natural enemy of the wild ass is neither the tiger nor the leopard, but the jackal. Wild asses can resist tigers, leopards, and wolves, by forming a circle and kicking backwards: but this tactic is entirely ineffective against jackals. In fact, it will only get them killed faster. When dealing with large prey, jackals have a distinct tactic that other beasts do not possess, and it is this: they can jump onto the behind of their victim, poke into its back passage with their claws and hook out its guts while the prey is still alive. The raised flanks of wild asses doing back-kicks undoubtedly make it easier for jackals to play this secret weapon.

This unusual hunting method is nasty and cruel, and it is probably an important reason for why jackals have such a terrible reputation. Anyway, wild asses fear jackals like mice fear cats. If the jackals rushed down the hill, these damn asses would bolt in terror. We were as good as saved. In fact, several timid female asses were already poised to flee.

Seconds passed. The jackals stayed where they were. Instead of charging at the wild asses, they just watched from their hill-top vantage point. When I looked again, I was dismayed to see that many of them had flesh and bones in their mouths, and their bellies were round. This meant they'd just caught prey and feasted on it. As with many carnivores, jackals are not vicious butchers and don't hunt for the fun of it. They hunt only to survive. Once their bellies are full, they lose all interest in pursuing and killing another creature. In other words, at this moment, they had neither the impulse nor the desire to attack these wild asses.

Scarface, who was in the lead position, shook the partially gnawed hare she was carrying in her mouth, gave a light howl and turned to leave. To her, a fight between animals on the pasture was too familiar to be of interest, not worth standing around to watch. The white-face ass seemed to know that these passing jackals were not going to intervene, so he started throwing his weight around once more. There were more hee-haws and more back-kicks. The rest of them felt their fear fade away and a renewed stirring of their fighting spirit.

Just two meters away from me was a female kicking backward, and though she didn't strike me, the dust and sand she kicked up was thrown on my face, and some grit got in my eyes. While I raised my hands to my face, rubbing my eyes, the white-face ass snuck up behind me. He bucked as if to kick me with his hind-hooves. If he kicked me, the best-case scenario would be that I would have some broken vertebrae; in the worst-case scenario, I would be killed. Champa noticed and sprung like an arrow from a bow, leaping to push me out of range. However, he wasn't fast enough to avoid injury himself, and his calf received a glancing blow. He gasped with the pain of it and could hardly stand.

I yelled to the jackals for help. I don't know where that idea came from: perhaps it was like a drowning man clutching at straws; but perhaps, deep down, I believed that Scarface was not a villain who would bite the hand that fed her. I had given her and her family a way out when they were trapped before so maybe she would help me out this time. However you looked at it, the jackals were our only chance of being rescued from being kicked to death by these crazed asses. I couldn't abandon our last hope.

I saw Scarface, just on the point of leaving, turn back again. She looked at the asses and raised her pointed ears to listen carefully. The asses had tightly hemmed us in, and the dense dust cloud they kicked up was blocking her view. Drawing on my last reserves of strength, I jumped up and waved my arms about desperately, trying to make myself visible through the dust.

My plea for life finally was heard. The gold-red fur on Scarface's back stood up in an instant; she spat out her kill, raised her head and uttered a long howl—a call to action. In rapid response, the others spat out the flesh and bones from their mouths, braced their relaxed bodies and howled, teeth bared, claws at the ready.

The wild asses got quiet again. They stopped kicking and looked anxiously toward the top of the hill. Scarface led the rush down the hill. Under the setting sun, the red glow cast over the jackals' back fur was like a flowing river of flame. Terror-struck, the wild asses fled, virtually as one; the encirclement collapsed instantly. Only the white-face ass and two young ones refused to admit defeat. They snorted and turned their backs on Scarface at the front of the pack, probably to give her a taste of their hooves. The white-face ass produced a back kick, aiming his hooves at Scarface's lower jaw. However, she was too fast; twisting from the middle, she dodged them, and hid herself between his two hooves, and even before they touched the ground, she jumped onto the flanks of the white-face ass. He probably knew about live evisceration by jackals, and was frightened witless. He jumped up and down as if on hot coals. Braying like crazy, he reared up and managed to shake Scarface off. He dared not fight on, but galloped away, his flanks marked with trails of blood, all made by a jackal's claws. The young asses fled too. The jackal pack howled again at the retreating backs of the wild asses, but pursued them no further. Their bellies were full and they had no need to spend their energy in chasing them.

THE JACKALS FORGIVE CHAMPA THE HUNTER

Rescued! Released! Exhaustion came after a sudden release of tension and I felt like collapsing. Gasping, I propped myself up while Champa used his sleeves to wipe the sweat from his brow, and rubbed his calf where the ass had kicked it. His calf had a huge bruise and his leg was already swollen.

Scarface approached to within six meters of me, wagging her tail in a friendly manner and crouched slowly onto the ground. Plainly, she had recognized me and had commanded the pack to chase away the wild asses. She had remembered the debt of gratitude she owed me because of my merciful act on the bridge two days before. I gestured to her that she should now leave with the pack. We were out of danger and no longer needed them. They were bloodthirsty predators, after all, and not the cosiest of companions to have around! Scarface got the message and stood up. She gave a howl to assemble the scattered pack in readiness to go back uphill.

As he passed by us, Bald Chest, that old jackal gave me a kindly look, a greeting of sorts. And then his eyes turned to Champa ... Suddenly, he jumped as if he had been hit and gave a terrible howl as if struck by to his heart. At this, every one of the pack, as if confronting their mortal enemy, raised their tails. The fur on their backs stood up; their faces became a picture of cruel brutality.

Shaken, I had no idea what next was about to happen.

Bald Chest ran up to Scarface and whispered for a while, muzzle to muzzle. Scarface's eyes went up at the corners, her muzzle twisted. Her face, so gentle a minute earlier, grew icily hostile. Her hard, predator nature now shone through. She fixed Champa with her cold eyes, lowered her body, straightened her muzzle and approached him cautiously, as if inspecting some highly suspicious, dangerous object.

My brain went into overdrive. I understood what was going on. Bald Chest must have recognized Champa as the hunter they had trapped up that pine tree years earlier, the man who'd hung the jackal tail on the tree. It was the same man who had fumbled into their den and kidnapped eight pups. The same man who'd used the pups as bait and almost forced the entire pack into the Nujiang River. The same man who nearly ended their lives... Scarface's eyes widened, and her nostrils twitched as she came closer, wanting to confirm all this with her keen eyesight and sense of smell.

It was all my fault. In my preoccupation in getting the jackals to save us from those crazed wild asses, I'd forgotten that Champa, my guide, had a blood feud with the jackals themselves.

Champa seemed to sense something from the pack's furious outcry. He jumped to his feet, fists clenched and eyes wide. He looked like an angry lion.

Hooowwl! ... Scarface uttered an angry howl at the sky. It was verification, confirmation, accusation. The response was immediate. The others surrounded us, showing their teeth and snarling ferociously at Champa.

Champa took to his heels and ran up the hill. I knew he was trying to grab the gun that was hidden in the bushes. Provided he had his gun, he could hold off their murderous attack for a while. But his leg was injured terribly so he could only hobble: running fast was an impossibility. Actually, even without an injury, he'd not have been able to reach the top and find his gun: before he moved a few meters, several jackals were already blocking his way. From behind him, Bald Chest and the female with a crooked mouth jumped onto his back and brought him down.

The rest swarmed in. Some bit at his arms, other bit at his legs; Bald Chest was going for the back of his neck and Crooked Mouth was clawing at his back passage, trying to pull out his guts.

Champa suddenly rolled over, and punched and kicked to push away his assailants. I rushed to help him fight off that bloodthirsty mob.

Whoa! A male tore one of my sleeves off. Zip! A female now

ripped off a trouser leg. I was keenly aware that Champa and I were empty-handed and no match for them. Our resistance was futile: it wouldn't be long before those sharp teeth and claws would have us torn apart.

Howl! Scarface howled solemnly and the jackals fighting with us jumped off. But they didn't go far. They had us penned in tight. Champa's clothes were torn too and his shoulders showed several bloodstains; but luckily, he'd not been seriously injured.

Howl! Scarface fixed her eyes on me. She waved her bushy tail and howled softly.

Howl! Howl! Howl! The other jackals also fixed their eyes on me. Some squatted, others sat or lay face down, but all adopted postures of offering peace and howled urgently.

I understood. Scarface had ordered the jackals fighting with us to pull back, not wanting any harm to come to me. For all that, she was a jackal; she knew the difference between mercy and hatred: she understood that one must reciprocate kindness and cruelty in like coin. Obviously, they wanted me to go, to get away.

Champa seemed to understand what was going on, so he pushed me and urged me to go. "Quick, out of here! It's not you they want. Go now!"

"No! I'm not leaving." I couldn't just abandon Champa to this fate. He had saved me more than once during our field study. One time, when I was chased by a swarm of hornets and had nowhere to hide, he drew them off by waving a branch at them for all he was worth, allowing me to escape unharmed, whereas he got stung all over, a dozen times at least. And just moments ago, he had gotten his leg injured while saving me from that back-kick by the white-face ass. I simply couldn't submit to the jackals and betray my friend in order to save my own skin.

The jackals kept at it, urging me to leave.

"Go on. Run for it! I'll settle the score from three years back. This has nothing to do with you." Champa made a loop with the bolas and gritted his teeth, "No worries. I'll break their damned necks!" As he said this, he tried to loop the nearest jackal to him, the one with the crooked mouth.

I knew Champa was a tough man of action and he didn't want me harmed.

"Champa, you're my guide, and I'm your boss, so you've got to listen to me." I grabbed the bolas, threw it down, and said in a commanding tone, "Lie on the ground and do exactly as I do."

I lay face down, spread wide my arms and legs, and raised my neck to expose my carotid artery, the most vulnerable of all the arteries.

"What are you up to? You want to make it easier for them? Are you begging them for mercy?" Champa asked in surprise. He was still standing, upright as a post, with the air of one who would not bend even if a great mountain fell on him. That was the kind of man he was; one who preferred to die rather than bend.

"Champa, please, please lie down. I'll explain later." I grabbed his feet, pulled him down and dragged him toward me.

The picture of Scarface begging me on the chain bridge had come back to me, inspiring me to use the same method to get us out of this fix. I knew that, in the jackal world, to lay prone means to surrender and renounce all resistance. To expose the vulnerable artery to the enemy is to allay his anger and induce him to abide by the most important rule in jackal society—not to attack a defenceless rival when honestly asking for peace.

On the chain bridge, Scarface had aroused my compassion with this posture. I intended to do likewise with her. She watched Champa and me and lowered her head thoughtfully.

Howl! Howl! Crooked Mouth and several other females with their swollen teats hanging from their bellies, caterwauled at her in fury. I guessed they were the mothers of the abducted pups, and for them, the pain of losing their kids were indelible, and must be avenged. Unhappy with Scarface's hesitance, they were urging her to inflict the harshest possible revenge on us, well, to be precise, on Champa. The others joined in. Their collective resolve was high; they were filled with a mutual hatred.

I was worried that Scarface might succumb to such intense pressure and give the order to attack: although she was their leader, she couldn't entirely disregard the pack's wishes. And indeed, she did raise her brow and her scarlet tongue slid over her dreadfully white teeth. She seemed to have every intention of attacking. So I hurriedly tilted up my lips as I'd observed jackals doing and yelled at the very top of my voice, "Don't do anything stupid! Hurt Champa today and I swear that I'll bring the hunting squad tomorrow and destroy every last one of you. This vendetta will have no end. But if you let us both go today, I guarantee I'll bring the eight pups back to you..."

Of course, she didn't understand human speech, but she seemed to read something from my sincere look and solemn tone. She lowered her brow and closed her mouth.

Crooked Mouth howled furiously and jumped up to bite Champa. At this, Scarface jumped onto Crooked Mouth, bashing her head against the jackal's middle in order to push her off Champa. Scarface howled a warning at Crooked Mouth, now rolling about on the ground: no one moves without my say-so! You don't want to mess with me! Crooked Mouth crawled away, shaking off the grass and dust and howling continuously.

Although I couldn't understand their language, her angry face and aggrieved tone indicated that she was expressing to the others her immense sadness at losing her babies and accusing Scarface of being partial to their enemy.

Several of the pack cast were discontent and glanced questioningly at Scarface. Two females waved their tails wildly, venting their anger, while two males stole up behind Scarface prepared to bite their pack leader. Maybe out of revenge, or perhaps emboldened by the idea that her pack would support her attack, Crooked Mouth sprang up again, fast as a whirlwind. When she was about to bite the back of Champa's neck, Scarface howled angrily, stopped her and raised a paw to claw her face. Crooked Mouth turned to dodge, but Scarface, at lightning speed, tore off her right ear in one bite. One side of her head was gushing blood. Crooked Mouth screamed and fled in panic.

Scarface gave a long, terrible howl to the heavens. The ear was still bouncing between her teeth and dark red blood smeared her muzzle. The pack was stunned into silence. Sensibly, the two hostile females stopped flicking their tails angrily about and the two rebellious males soon came back into line and crouched low in obedience.

Maybe, in the savage society of wild jackals, only with the harshest punishment can a pack leader maintain their firm authority. Scarface looked at us again and remained quiet for several minutes. Her eyes showed neither hostility nor hatred. They were just filled with resignation and sorrow. Finally, she seemed to sigh, then turned around and walked towards the top of the hill. The others left with her, following her obediently.

I watched them as they moved further and further away into the gathering twilight. Scarface moved slowly, spine bent, head down and tail dragging on the ground. She was exhausted, mentally and physically.

9

AWAY FROM HOME

That night, back at our field study camp, we showered and changed clothes, and Champa began to drink alone. After downing an entire bottle of strong liquor, he was completely intoxicated and began talking nonsense. He said that he wanted to go panning for gold in the Jinsha River, so he could buy a hundred Tibetan Mastiffs, train them to fight jackals and wipe every jackal off the face of the earth. Moments later, he would say that he wanted to buy a machine gun, so that next time he came across any jackals he could wipe them out in one fell swoop... *rat-a-tat, rat-a-tat, rat-a-tat.*

Hung over, he didn't wake up until noon the next day. When

he did, he came outside. He smoked his pipe of tobacco quietly, and then he shouldered the wicker cage with the pups in it and walked off towards the mountain. I asked where he was going and what he intended to do. Instead, he walked off without answering.

He went to that small crooked tree, put down the basket, and looked at the jackal tail, which by now had been hanging there for two weeks or more. He pulled out his knife and jumped up to cut the rope. That jackal's tail, that great symbol of revenge, fell to the ground. He opened the wicker cage and released the pups. The freed pups yapped gleefully and chased each other around the tree.

Champa pulled me aside and quickly hid us in the bushes at the top of the hill. Almost immediately, we heard the noisy howls of jackals coming from the gully. I looked through my binoculars. Yes! Those familiar gold-back jackals came out of nowhere and gathered under the tree. Several of the females pulled their newly restored babies to them and showered them with kiss after loving kiss. The pups played between their mothers' legs just like naughty little kids. It was a mother-and-child reunion that would touch even the sternest of hearts!

I scanned the scene carefully, trying to locate Scarface. There she was! She was crouching by a round rock, guarding a pup in front of her. The pup didn't look happy at returning to its family. It lay curled up among the fallen leaves. When Scarface put out her tongue to lick it, the pup only turned away. Scarface raised her sorrowful face and gazed into the sky.

Right then, we heard a jackal howling in the valley; a red shadow flew out of the gully and was at the tree in a twinkling of an eye. I zoomed in. Ah, it was Crooked Mouth, the one whose right ear Scarface had bitten off. She looked around anxiously, searching for something. Scarface saw her and relaxed her frown. She gave two howls and stepped aside. Crooked Mouth dashed up to the rock and saw her pup curled up among the leaves. In her excitement, her howl sounded different—joyful or sad. It was hard to tell. She bounded toward the pup and covered it tight underneath her, licking and cuddling for dear life, regurgitating food into its mouth. The pup livened up immediately and nuzzled its mother's legs affectionately

Of course, the pup curled up among the leaves was Crooked Mouth's own flesh and blood. After a while, Crooked Mouth finally calmed down and brought the pup to Scarface. With an abashed expression, she groomed the fur on Scarface's back as if apologizing for her rudeness and the offense she made the day before. In return, Scarface licked what was left of the right ear, as if apologizing for her harsh punishment. Several females came up to Scarface, some licking her neck, some grooming the fur between her toes and some snuggling up to her. They seemed to hold her in great admiration and respect. The pack was about to leave. When the other jackals brought the eight pups out of the gully, Scarface stood under the tree and gave three long howls before running to join them. I guessed she knew Champa and I were hiding in the bushes and was probably expressing her gratitude in the jackal manner.

Without warning, Champa drew an ox horn from his waist and blew it, his cheeks bulging. As the low and gloomy sound spread through the air, a row of human heads suddenly appeared from behind the rock ridge, about a hundred meters behind us; some wore felt hats, others kerchiefs, and others animal skins. Obviously, they were hunters who roamed the mountain forest. Champa raised his hunting gun, and as if in response to a pre-arranged order, they all raised their guns. I was shocked. Apparently, Champa had gone behind my back and asked these hunters to hide behind that ridge. They all carried firearms. Were they intending to wipe out the jackal pack as soon as they found their eight pups? This would be just too mean-spirited, too underhanded and too ungrateful. I was no hero, and I wouldn't dare block the dark muzzles of those guns with my own body. Besides, it wouldn't be a smart move to do that for a pack of gold-back jackals. All I could do was to protest feebly, "No..."

No one listened to me. Champa didn't even look at me. He pulled the trigger. Crack! A shot rang out. It was closely followed by the thunder of gunfire from behind the ridge, resounding through the valley. Before long, the air was choked with the pungent smell of gunpowder, which made me cough and left me breathless. I thought these gold-back jackals were goners, since they hadn't left the rock ridge and were still within sight of these hunters and within range of their rifles. If twenty or thirty guns fired together, at least ninety percent of the jackals would be dead or injured, cut down like scythed wheat. I couldn't help, but stand and watch them.

The strange thing was that they hadn't fallen; they stood there still, completely unharmed. They turned their startled eyes back behind them in amazement. Of course, I didn't think the jackals had some magic invulnerability that made them immune to spear thrusts and sword cuts like Buddha's indestructible guardian warriors; neither did I believe the hunters had suddenly became short-sighted or skew-eyed. I was beyond confused, baffled as to what was going on. Scarface gave a long, sad howl—the order to run for cover. In less than a second, they divided into several small groups that escorted their own pups and young, and scattered in every direction. Some headed towards the thick bush while others ran out of the gully. Bang! Bang! Bang! Champa, who was standing next to me, pulled the trigger again. So did the hunters. Only then did it become clear that Champa and the hunters were pointing their guns skywards, that the bullets were hitting the trees and causing the leaves to fall like green rain.

"What the hell are you doing?" I cried out, bewildered.

"I want the guns to tell these jackals they're not welcome. We hate them; we want them out of Gamaer Grassland; we want them to disappear from this land!" Champa's voice was resolute and decisive. He clenched his teeth and the blue veins in his neck stood out.

"But the jackals gave us enormous help. Without Scarface, we would have been smashed to pulp by those asses. But you..." I felt too sickened to continue.

"If it wasn't for that, I'd have sent them to the King of Hell long ago," Champa replied. "They did save me that once, so now I'm giving them a way out. We're even now. Jackals are savage, deadly and evil. They have to be driven out."

Now, I got it. Even though the jackals had saved us in our hour of need, even though Scarface had managed to stop the other angry jackals biting him that did not dispel Champa's hate and prejudice. Champa was a courageous and upright man; his belief system was to repay kindness with kindness and avenge acts of enmity. Because the jackals had rescued us, he had aimed his gun at the sky and not at them. But deep down, his hatred for gold-back jackals, the killers of his beloved dog, Snow Queen, hadn't disappeared, and the herders' hatred of the jackals had not diminished one iota. Therefore, this meeting was only to drive them out of Gamaer Grassland with gunfire. The force of tradition dies hard and rigid beliefs can injure many.

The jackals had disappeared completely, but Champa and the other hunters kept firing at the sky threatening and intimidating them, sending them their hostile message.

"Suppose they refuse to leave their home here, and remain on Gamaer Grassland? What then?" I asked anxiously.

"I owe them nothing now. This is a polite warning before we resort to force." Champa spelled things out as he looked into the stark white peaks of the Gaoligong Mountains. "If they stay here, for the peace and tranquillity of Gamaer Grassland, we'll organize a hunting party and wipe them out without mercy!"

I shivered at his words. Concerned about the jackals' fate, I couldn't rest easy, but I had no clue as to how the hatred between the jackals and the local herders might end.

"But they did help us, especially Scarface. That shows she's not evil." Champa, with some insight into my thoughts, whispered into my ear. "I don't want to aim my shotgun at Scarface's chest either, but for as long as they remain on the grassland, our cattle and sheep will suffer and the herders can't live safely. Even if God came down to earth, he couldn't change their terrible reputation. We simply can't coexist. We're like fire and water."

I said nothing. Silence was my only way to protest.

"You needn't worry about them so much." Champa paused a while before continuing, "That pack is savvy enough to know that shooting at the sky was a warning of our intent. They'll probably quit Gamaer Grassland tonight to find somewhere else they can live."

I hoped so. This would be the best way to avoid the bloody conflict between the local shepherds and the gold-back jackals. I secretly prayed for the jackals.

That night, I slept in Champa's yurt on a bed covered with warm Tibetan felt. I was exhausted, but exceptionally clear-headed. I kept thinking about Scarface and her pack of gold-back jackals. I was indignant at the wrongs done to them by humans. I was distressed by the misunderstanding and prejudice of the local herders, and I was worried about what would befall all of them. I tossed and turned, ruminating over every possibility and wondering what the future might hold.

Not until the cock's first crow, did my eyelids start drooping. I closed my eyes again and was on the verge of falling asleep when suddenly every dog in the village began barking, as if they were celebrating great festival. The dogs dashed up and down the street, barking in high spirits. I began to stir. I opened my eyes, wondering what was causing all the ruckus and excitement. Very soon, the dark night was lit up by pine resin torches, and I heard the footsteps and shouts of villagers. Someone outside the yurt yelled to us, "Come see, those evil jackals are moving out." I leapt out of bed, lifted the thick, yak-hide tent flap, and rushed out.

High in the azure sky, the moon hung like a bright silver plate, illuminating everything around as bright as day. Opposite the village rose Riquka Peak with its perpetual snowcap radiating silver in the moonlight, and its peak encircled by a silvery belt of thin clouds. Men and women, young and old emerged, gazing up at the mountain. I did too, and saw dozens of shadows moving slowly along the ridge leading to the mountain pass. Despite the wide valley that separated us, the white snow and moonlight enabled me to make out their silhouettes; their pointed muzzles, fluffy tails, short thick legs, rounded ears. They had a thick layer of fur on their backs, which gave off a golden light. One look was enough to tell: the gold-back jackals were on the move.

"The evil jackals are gone! Our cattle and sheep will be safe!"

Arf, arf, arf! Arf, arf, arf!

The people were cheering, the dogs were barking. The village was abuzz with noise and excitement. It felt like a victory party.

On the snow-covered ridgeline, the slow-moving silhouettes came to an abrupt halt. The one leading the party turned its head, raised its neck and howled at the Kaza village and at the lush Gamaer Grassland that stretched out at the foot of the mountain, bursting with green life. Although I couldn't see well enough, I was sure it was Scarface. Taking their cue from her, the other jackals raised their necks and started howling too.

Howl! Howl! Howl! Howl!

The biting wind from off the mountain carried their cries far and wide.

Jackals' voices are coarse and grating and their howls are hard to hear. So when the pack started baying at the moon, their chorus of discordant cries sounded like the crying, grieving and lamenting of some wretched ghosts. I shivered. They kept on howling, pouring out their painful melancholy.

They had lived on Gamaer Grassland for generations raising their young and were nourished by this fertile land, a land

providing happiness and troubles too. Jackals are territorial creatures, and much like other beings on earth, jackals are attached to their native land and most unwilling to leave their birthplace. But now, pressured and harassed by these humans, they were being driven away from the land where they'd been born and bred. I could only imagine their wretchedness. On the boundless snow mountain, a long journey and uncertain destiny lay ahead; where would they find a home? On this wide earth was there no place even for a pack of gold-back jackals? They cried and they wailed; they addressed to the heavens their rightful complaint against humans.

Among the howls, there was one that had a particularly sad and miserable quality. I believed that it came from Scarface. This elderly-sounding voice seemed to beg for mercy and forgiveness, to call for understanding and tolerance. I understood Scarface: this experienced old female had weathered the years; she was generous, benevolent and well disposed towards humans. Even at the last minute, before crossing to the other side of the col, she clung to the hope that a man could set aside his hatred and allow them to remain on their grassland.

And who would want to lead a wretched life far from home?

But when the howling stopped, the locals brought out guns, bronze drums, hunting bows and ox horns. Some fired gunshots into the air. Others beat their drums wildly. Still others shot arrows, and sounded their horns. From the barns, the yaks mooed, the goats bleated and the horses neighed. The village seethed with excitement. This was no friendly farewell party. It was a rowdy expulsion, a merciless exile, something in the nature of celebrating an armed deportation.

I focused on Scarface. She seemed to recoil as if from a heavy blow. Her silhouette shrank. It was easy to guess that she'd lost all hope. She threw herself to the ground, possibly overwhelmed with sadness. Minutes later, I saw her silhouette again. She stood up and continued toward the mountain pass. The pack followed.

Dozens of shadows were inching their way up the white slope. They moved slowly. The thin air, the thick snow and the steepness of the slope was taking its toll. Every step they made was laborious. Seen from a distance, they looked as if they were crawling across the edge. The sounds of guns, drums, crossbows, dogs and horns continued, urging them to leave now and never look back. The sounds of the villagers demanded their complete expulsion and every cry ruthlessly smashed their last hope.

Within half an hour, the jackals could no longer be seen in the wind-blown snow on the mountain pass.

The pass on the north side of Riquka Peak is the entrance to

Gamaer Grassland so, for them, walking over the col amounted to being swept out like some rubbish. It is snow-covered all year round, and summer is the only season without heavy snowfalls. Avalanches fall frequently from the peaks at either side. Raging storms block the gateway and can trap any animal and even the hardiest snow leopards cannot pass it. Indeed, man or animal regardless, it is safe only to walk in late summer. It's hardly an exaggeration to describe crossing the pass as harder than flying into the sky. The jackals would probably never be able to come back.

The villagers were ecstatic. Some set off firecrackers. They brought out their best spirits, drinking deeply and toasted each other for finally putting an end to the jackals.

Species diversity is extremely important for ecological balance; if one species disappears, it may well lead to profound ecological imbalance. In nature, there exists a biosphere, where one link is connected with another, and as with any chain, the breaking of one link can trigger a chain reaction and can endanger the entire life system, including humankind. If an ecological balance is rudely broken, disastrous consequences may follow. Knowing this, I couldn't share in their joy; I hid away in my yurt, heavy-hearted.

Champa came in, bringing with him a full bronze bowl of

barley liquor. He looked radiant with joy. "Days without jackals are grand feast days for herders. Come on. Drink this wine and toast to the permanent disappearance of jackals from Gamaer Grassland."

I shook my head, refusing the drink. "Don't rejoice too soon. Answer me this: what does 'Gamaer Grassland' mean in Tibetan?"

"It means grassland, the haunt of the jackal dogs," he replied.

"Precisely," I said. "Since ancient times, Gamaer Grassland has been a place where humans, gold-back jackals and other animals have co-existed. Now you've driven them out and broken the eco-balance. Who knows what trouble you've set in motion!"

Champa snapped back, "Don't you get on your high horse with me. How dare you lecture us and try to scare us! Without these jackal dogs, the grass will only be greener, the cattle and sheep will get fatter and the herders will get richer. You don't want to drink to our celebration? That's fine! You're not one of us anyway when all's said and done!"

After that declaration, he poured the wine on the ground and stormed out.

Whether Tibetan or Han, herders are honest and blunt speakers, but I didn't mean to deliberately offend him. I wasn't at all annoyed by Champa's rude behavior. If indeed it proved to be the case that a jackal-free Gamaer Grassland was better—that the grasslands would be greener, that the sheep and the cattle would grow fat, and that the Kaza would become richer herders, then I'd happily accept his outburst.

Sadly, I feared the reality would be just the opposite.

RABBIT DISASTER

After the jackals left, Champa's prediction proved true: Gamaer Grassland grew vigorous and strong for a time. Without the jackals, the only predators remaining were the sparrow hawks. However, these hawks only go after newly born lambs and they cannot seize cattle or sheep. The upshot was that the herders no longer needed to guard their sheep, and even the sheepdogs were not necessary. The yaks were left to graze freely and went wherever the pasture was rich, without the herders worrying about them meeting any misfortune. With their natural enemy expelled, the livestock had nothing to fear and grew fat easily. The sheep became so fat that you could literally squeeze oil from their flanks. The yaks grew strong and glossy; the skin was stretched drum-tight over their plump bodies. One ewe belonging to a Han herder even gave birth to twin lambs, a rare event on Gamaer Grassland, so all the villagers went to congratulate the man. Later, a Tibetan herder owned a yak weighing over eight hundred kilograms and the animal was rated the heaviest in the prefecture. The commissioner himself presented the creature with a large red rosette. It was a quite a sensation at the time.

What delighted the local herders most was how many more red snow hares appeared. Their numbers seemed to be growing daily. When the gold-back jackals were present, there were only a few red snow hares and they were seen only occasionally. Even when the herders went hunting after hares in the grassland with the assistance of their well-trained hunting dogs, even after a careful search, they could not produce one catch. However, after only three months without the jackals, red snow hares stopped being a rarity: they became an everyday sight on Gamaer Grassland. If you went to the grassland in the morning, picked some grass to make a hat to wear as camouflage, crouched down and kept silent, within a few minutes, you'd likely see the figure of a red snow hare hopping among the emerald-green bushes. When the herders and dogs spent just half a day on the grassland, they never returned empty-handed. It didn't matter how poorly they shot or how inept or clumsy were their hounds. They would always go home very pleased with themselves, carrying one or two hares on their gun barrel.

The meat of red snow hares may not be as tasty as beef or mutton, but as wild game, it does have a special flavor. Moreover, after being aired and tawed, their pelts can be sold at market. They're worth nowhere near as much as the skins of otters, winter foxes, and Asian golden cats, but even at a modest price, they can fetch more than enough for basic necessities.

Several Tibetan and Han herders in Kaza entrusted their sheep to their sheepdogs, and let their yaks roam freely on the grassland. This left them time and energy enough to hunt hares on the side. Their life felt free and unfettered.

Champa said to me, in a semi-sarcastic manner, "You said the ecological balance would be broken without those evil jackals. But in fact, life is far better without them. Anything you'd like to add?"

Indeed, I had nothing to say. I hoped that my prediction would never come true. However, science is science at the end of the day and the laws of science are beyond the will of man. What is bound to happen will eventually come to pass.

Four months later, things were different. The red snow hare population exploded. Previously, if you walked on Gamaer Grassland in the morning, the most active time of day for the hares, you needed to camouflage yourself, crouch among the bushes and wait in silence before spotting even one hare. But camouflage was unnecessary now. You just needed to walk in the fields and even the most short-sighted individual could easily find them. Previously half a day's search, even with a dog, would not necessarily result in a catch: you had to be lucky. Now, a hunter didn't even need to go in person. They just sent their hound there and within one or two hours, it would return with a half-dead hare in its mouth. One morning when several villagers went to the grassland in search of a missing yak, they fired shots into the bushes at random, and shot dead two hares. Even a boy playing on the grassland with an antiquated bamboo crossbow could dispatch several hares and bring them home.

Initially, the villagers did not see the population explosion as a sign of disaster. Quite the opposite; many thought it a wonderful thing and fondly imagined that more snow hares would make them an even greater fortune. I advised that before the hares ran rampant, measures should be taken as soon as possible to arrest their rapid growth. Champa gazed at me in amazement, as if I were a being from another planet. "Ah, are you afraid that extra money will bite your hand? Are you deliberately preventing us from being well off? It's a great thing that we've got more hares. We can create a special hunting squad to hunt just red snow hares. We can build a meat processing plant to cure the fresh meat and sell it to big cities like Beijing and Shanghai. And then, we can build a leather factory to process the skins, and make them into beautiful, fashionable clothes which everyone will value, then export them through foreign trade, and earn still more money, lots of it. All in all, more red snow hares is blessing! There's no downside."

Patiently, I tried to enlighten him. "Everything has a limit. More red snow hares are a good thing and they can generate extra income for Kaza herders. But that doesn't mean the more hares the better, because once the limit is crossed, a good thing can become a bad thing and can bring unexpected serious consequences. Anyway, as a zoologist I know about this. I've been reading about this for almost twenty years. You've got to believe me. I have no reason to hurt you. Why would I?"

"Their fur can be skinned and sold; their meat can be eaten; and their bones can be ground up to feed chickens and ducks. So tell me, why is it a bad thing to have more of them?"

"Red snow hares are rodents. They multiply very fast. They can produce three litters a year, with six to twelve leverets each time. When the leverets reach six months old, they can breed too. In theory, a pair of adult red snow hares can multiply to over ten thousand within two years. With all rodents, their teeth keep on growing throughout their life, and they have to shorten their two front teeth by nibbling so they continuously nibble at grass roots and bark. This is especially harmful to vegetation. Unless their numbers are curbed, they are extremely likely to strip the grassland bare. Another thing, if their corpses are scattered in the wild in large numbers, they're very likely to cause an awful epidemic ..."

"All right. You can't scare me." Champa interrupted crossly, "Kaza herders have been living here for generations and we never heard of the grassland being eaten bare by red snow hares. You're exaggerating. You say you've been studying for twenty years, so you must know these lines of poetry, 'Fires burn the grass, but do not kill; it grows again when the spring breeze blows.' The grass on Gamaer Grassland has never been exhausted; it can feed as many cattle and sheep as you can imagine. Many times, when the grassland was on the point of being burnt bald by wildfire in winter, spring rains turned it green again overnight. This grassland is a treasure bowl bestowed on us by Heaven. No one can spoil and destroy her, let alone a bunch of tiny hares."

Alas! My warning went unheeded. They would "shed no tears before seeing the coffin, not turn back before hitting the wall." I could do nothing for them.

Another two months on, and the population had increased exponentially, snowballing rapidly to the point where the villagers started to get worried.

I had seen Gamaer Grassland in winter: the pastures were golden yellow; groups of verdant spruces punctuated the boundless sea of flaxen grass, a brilliant expanse embellished by a thin scattering of white snowflakes and dotted with red euphorbia flowers. It is a gorgeous feast for the eyes. But now, those golden pastures were withered, bitten off at the roots by the nibbling teeth of countless hares; on the spruces, the bark had been stripped up to one meter from the ground, and they looked like a man's decaying limbs. It was winter, the dormant period, and the pasture grass had stopped growing. Even so, like a giant legion, the red snow hares were still grazing on it. It was only mid-winter, but they'd already eaten more than half of the grassland bald, exposing a large area of scabby, black earth. At sunset, ravenous hares emerged from crevices and holes in droves; within seconds, thousands of them were nibbling and wriggling on the grassland, a red terror to shock the eyes and chill the heart. It was the first sign of a calamity-in-waiting. At this rate, the grassland was likely to be a wasteland by the end of winter.

All the village men above the age of sixteen clamoured, and wanted to form a hunting squad to conduct an all-out campaign against the rabbits. And why wouldn't they? Winter was the slack season and there were few distractions for young adults; hunting was their favourite pastime; killing the hares would protect the pastureland and the eco-environment where herders lived. On top of that, it was a profitable sideline. All the dogs in the village came out with their owners to hunt red snow hares on the grassland. They brought out all of them—Tibetan Mastiffs, sheepdogs, foxhounds, males and females, big ones and small ones, fat ones and thin ones, old and young. Even the mangy ones were used.

The hunting squad left early and returned at night. Sometimes, when the hunters had to hunt late into the night, they simply slept on the grassland around a campfire. The dogs would chase after the hares at the smallest provocation. They never stopped pursuing them even when the rabbits were foaming at the mouth with exhaustion. The ferocious barking of dogs and cracks of gunfire continued all day long. The entire grassland became a huge slaughterhouse, the air thick with the smell of blood.

Champa took charge personally and acted as head of the squad. He was strong and valiant; he killed his target with every shot, and was well known as an excellent sharpshooter. He approached the operation quite astutely: he divided the squad into four smaller groups and made sure that the men closed in from all directions, just as they had when they expelled the jackals. However, the result was less than ideal. After a gruelling day, they managed to catch only a few dozen hares.

In the Cretaceous period, Gamaer Grassland was a vast expanse of water, but during the Cenozoic era, due to the collision and squeezing of the Eurasian Plate, crustal movement occurred and the area was pushed above the sea level, forming a flat, fertile grassland on what is now the Northern Yunnan Plateau. Even now, shell fossils can be found in its earth layers. Given its geologic history, the surface of Gamaer Grassland has pronounced features of marine geology. Large areas of former coral reef can be seen everywhere. Some of these coral formations protrude above the surface by ten to twenty meters; some lie dozens of meters below ground; some remain honey-combed like ant nests; others, weathered and silted up, resemble tumble-down walls. The reefs were formed underwater by the accumulation of calcium carbonate structures secreted by polyps called corals. These coral reefs occur in many different shapes, with large or small pores, caves and voids, which connect with one another.

Red snow hares do not burrow themselves, but take over these natural crevices and caves of the grassland and there they habitually live underground. The particular geology of Gamaer Grassland, with its gaping holes in the coral rocks, made it the perfect shelter for red snow hares. These hares have a keen sense of hearing and smell. On hearing the barking of hounds and smelling the gunpowder of shotguns, they would dive underground to their shelter among the caves and holes, spaces too cramped for the hunters and the bigger dogs to track them down. Although the smaller local dogs could almost get inside, they lacked the nerve to chase and fight the hares in the underground darkness. Often, the dogs would pursue a hare down for a few meters before losing their nerve and retreating. Back above ground, they squatted and barked angrily down into the caves. There was one slim and exceptionally brave sheepdog called "Along" that, in pursuit of a red snow hare, followed the hare into a labyrinthine cave system dozens of meters deep. Sadly, the sheepdog got lost and couldn't find its way out. When its owner put his ear to the ground, he heard his beloved dog barking, a sound of weeping and complaint. It took two days before the dog's bark finally faded away.

The grassland, which should have been a scene of glorious victory to hunting dogs, turned out to be a graveyard, where the living were being buried alive. Having witnessed how Along had died, the other hounds were even more reluctant to go down into the caves.

The crafty red snow hares used the underground maze, formed aeons earlier by coral reefs, as their shelter. They operated like guerrillas, popping up one minute and then, disappearing the next. They knew how to deal with the hunters and their dogs.

"They won't outwit me. I'll go get help from the villages nearby, borrow more dogs. Let's see how long these damned hares will keep on making trouble!" Champa banged his fist on the table.

That same night, Champa swiftly rode his horse to recruit help from several nearby villages, and two days later, several squads of hunters drove into Kaza, bringing with them more hunting dogs to wage another encirclement and eradication campaign. The simultaneous convergence of humans and dogs created a noisy and impressive spectacle: Gamaer Grassland became a sea of hunters and dogs.

But there were no stellar results. The daily kill was only about a hundred at most. With too many hunters from all these different villages, a coordinated command was next to impossible. Communication by ancient ox horn could not keep the parties in touch so confusion was inevitable. One Han herder from Kaza Village shot a Khampa hunter from Nafa Village in the leg by mistake; a Tibetan hunter from Songdian Village broke the arm of a Han herder from Qingdi Village, who was hiding in the bushes. And the dogs from different villages were even more difficult to handle than the humans: male dogs fought with each other; female dogs clamoured for favor, started fights and bit at each other. Many of the animals were hurt and the atmosphere got foul. The campaign lasted only a week. The outside reinforcements had to be withdrawn.

The hunting squad went out every day that winter. Though the overall results fell short of their mark, the actual number of hares caught was by no means small: the total killed approached eight thousand. However, this hardly made a dent in the rabbit's overall population. The golden pasture looked as if it was being scalped at a frightening rate. At dusk, a giant mass of red snow hares, thousands of them came swarming onto the grassland like a red tide, a horrific red terror.

Kaza Village was about one kilometre from Gamaer Grassland, located at the foot of Riquka Peak. Up until now, no one had ever seen red snow hares there. But in the late winter, the red snow hares were drawing close to the village because of either food shortage or territorial expansion. In the woods around the village, the trees' bark was mottled after being gnawed at by the hares.

Perplexed, Champa scratched his head as he surveyed the pile of dead hare bodies piled high on the threshing ground. "What the devil's going on?" he asked. "How come the more of them we kill, the more of them there are?"

I quoted his words back at him. "'Fires burn the grass, but do not kill; it grows again when the spring breeze blows.' Those lines apply to red snow hares as well."

"How can you joke at a time like this? I'm in deep trouble," Champa complained.

"I'm not making fun of you," I said. "The more of them you kill, the more they will reproduce, and the reason for that is simple. When one red snow hare falls, thousands of others rise."

"Which means?"

I explained to him seriously. "Your hunting squad may have killed a good number of them, but you haven't destroyed their reproduction mechanism. Their rate of reproduction is much faster than your kill rate. For their numbers to grow even when you're killing them is only to be expected."

11

BITTER RESULTS

Winter gave way to spring. The watery sunlight gradually intensified, branches greened, the layer of ice over the Nujiang River cracked, and the melted ice flowed away into the distance, babbling a song to springtime. Flocks of wild geese and black swans flew back to the grassland, having wintered over in the south.

Normally, at this time of year, Gamaer Grassland displayed itself at its best, like a beautiful, young model showing her finest gowns, with the continuous patter of raindrops providing the background music. The gray-brown grassland, transformed by the first spring rain, became dotted with light green shoots, which shimmered like the heavenly stars. After the second spring rain, thick grass would cover the land, robing the grassland in green gauze as fine as a cicada's wings. With the third spring rain, the grassland seemed like an enchantress in a close-fitting dress of emerald green, beautiful enough to take your breath away. After the fourth spring rain, the grassland changed again and wildflowers blossomed in brilliant purples and reds among the dark green grass as if the field was a noble woman dressed in full regalia, seated at a banquet.

However, this spring, Gamaer Grassland looked too hideous to bear. No sooner did shoots emerge than those greedy hares nabbed it. Just as a hint of greenery appeared under the melting snow water when the snow hares descended on it in the thousands and devoured every stalk.

The way red snow hares eat green grass is entirely different from how yaks and goats graze. The latter only eat the aboveground blades and never damage the roots. So, after a gentle watering by spring rain and a burst of spring sun, new blades can burst forth vigorously from their roots. In contrast, red snow hares are relentless robbers; not content with eating the above-ground blades, they also scrape up the earth to bite the roots off. Such extreme damage to the plant's root system inevitably prevents regrowth and the appearance of any new grass.

After four or five spring rains, brilliant sunshine bathed the land in light. But the Gamaer Grassland still appeared patchy and lacklustre. It was parched and brown in the east, but green in the west. Great swathes of bare earth were exposed. The wildflowers too seemed listless. Their petals went limp. They looked sad and withered, and for as far as the eye could see, the entire grassland looked downtrodden.

In the fall, the Kaza herders usually air their highland barley straw on a wooden stand called a "highland barley stand" which they use later as winter forage. This way, when heavy snowfalls limit the availability of rich pasture, they can chop up the straw finely and feed their cattle and sheep. Every household calculates their forage precisely, storing just enough to support what their livestock consume over one winter. By the time the spring thunder rumbles the earth, the forage is almost exhausted, and the livestock are moved onto Gamaer Grassland for a change of diet—to feast on the flourishing spring grass.

"The work of a year depends on a good start in spring." This old adage is particularly true for those who work the land. Sure, they see their animals through the winter on the dry forage, but the barley's taste and nutrition are not ideal and it does no more than maintain an animal's life. In spring, the grass is nutritious and the cattle and sheep thrive, putting back the weight they lost during the winter. So herders pin all their hopes on spring. Cattle and sheep bask in the warm sunshine as they munch the tasty and nutritious spring grass. Within days, their winter-thin bodies will turn glossy, their gaunt faces become radiant again and their lethargy is replaced by strength. Then, mating takes place, perpetuating the family line. More young are born and their populations flourish.

However, for the herders of Kaza this spring looked like a gateway to hell. The sparse spring grass on Gamaer Grassland was simply not enough to meet the needs of all of Kaza's yaks, cattle and sheep. The stored winter forage had run out long ago, leaving the herders nothing to feed their hungry cattle and sheep. This should be the fattening-up season, but these pitiful animals had too little to fill their bellies and quickly became emaciated. The shoulder blades of many yaks stood out, and the ribs of many goats were plain to see. Moreover, starvation made them lose their vigor: bulls and rams lost their libido; cows and ewes no longer gave birth. The stirrings of love that springtime brings were lost entirely.

The herders' livelihood depended completely on their livestock. Just looking at their stick-thin animals, the villagers furrowed their brows and they would sigh all day long. True, by catching some red snow hares, they had their rabbit meat and fur, but this could by no means compensate for the ruined grassland and the inadequate forage. The income from the meat and skins was paltry; for a small advantage, they were now suffering inordinately.

The greatest fear that stalked them now was that springtime is also the peak-mating season for red snow hares, a time when their number skyrockets. Red snow hares are mammals with a very short infancy. In other words, infant hares have fur even when still in the womb and can open their eyes the second after they come out of the birth canal. Once their fuzzy hair is licked clean, they can hop. After ten days of suckling, their incisor

teeth emerge, enabling them to browse tender grass, alongside their mother. Just two weeks into spring, a new generation of hares were bobbing around on the grassland. Looking into the distance, one could see a surging red tide. It made one's hair stand on end.

Even the pastures of Gamaer Grassland proved insufficient for their destructive hunger. Finally, something happened that left the herders shocked beyond all belief. One night, a group of hungry hares attacked a barn built beside the village gate and plundered some five hundred kilos of highland barley plus the rest that was stored in a little reed-built store. Soon afterwards, vegetable plots and orchards on the edge of the village received the same treatment. One night, two watchdogs, a black one and a brown one, heard noises and rushed to the vegetable plots, trying to catch the thieves in the act. But, they were outnumbered and the brown dog was bitten to death by the furious hares, and the fur of the black one was nibbled off. Fortunately, the dog survived, but it was bald all over.

The villagers were fearful now. Some said, "If things go on this way, it won't be long before they're eating up our homes." Others said, "Once the grass on Gamaer Grassland runs out, these red snow hares will become as vicious as jackals. They'll come for our livestock, and maybe even us!"

Champa tied his Tibetan robe tightly and bared one arm like an angry gambler. He held a torch high and yelled at the top of his voice. "I refuse to believe we can't get the better of these hares. Let's burn the damned creatures to death."

The herders mobilized themselves. Some collected cattle dung, some cut reeds and some cut firewood, preparing to launch a fire attack on the Gamaer Grassland. They built and lit fires everywhere. Unfortunately, being spring, there was plenty of rain and not much withered grass, so the fires could not set the prairie ablaze. The air was filled with a dense smoke, but the fire did not spread. Furthermore, the hares would dive swiftly into the holes underground and hide. The men worked for several days with little to show for their efforts. They had to give up this foolhardy strategy.

"Poison! Let's poison these damned pests!" Champa gnashed his teeth in anger.

So villagers went to the city to buy all sorts of rat poisons—zinc phosphide, Shoxin, Raticate, Castrix ... They mixed the poison with food and scattered the bait on the grassland. To poison the hares more easily, they also threw the poisoned food down into their coral caves.

The poison tactic worked quite well initially. Within a few days, the surging red tide seemed to ebb. There were dead hares everywhere, in mountain crannies, under the trees, beside the water and under the rocks. The furrowed brows of herders finally relaxed, and their forlorn expressions brightened. But, the jubilation lasted only a few days: things took a sudden turn for the worse. Red snow hares are quick learners. Having witnessed the pitiful sight of their own kind poisoned and dying, they soon realised that the food was a trap, and that there is no such thing as a free lunch. So the bait scattered by the herders remained untouched. Rabbits have a keen sense of smell, and the lessons they learned with their blood and lives, remained with them. On top of that, they shared information quickly. Therefore even though the herders used modern, expensive poisons and scattered them in the grass and caves, and even though the hares were hungry enough for their stomachs to gurgle and their eyes to dim, every one of them shunned those temptingly presented rat poisons smelling of lemon or chocolate. The hares were wise to the humans' tricks and they were going to let themselves be poisoned anymore.

The plan had to be abandoned. Worse, it brought unexpected and disastrous consequences. Before the strategy was implemented, to avoid any harmful accidents, every household was cautioned to take good care of their cattle and sheep and never let them roam on Gamaer Grassland when the poison was being used. The grassland was treated like a curfew and an off-limits military zone. But there were too many cattle and sheep for the number of pens available; besides, the herders of Kaza were not used to rearing livestock in pens, so, on top of the inadequate provision, they were lax in their habits. Unavoidably, due to the negligence of their owners, some animals snuck out of the crude hurdles. Their livestock ran to the grassland and swallowed the rat poison by mistake, dying in an excruciating manner.

As for the intended victims, some hares died in underground holes. Others expired in tree holes and in secret crannies. However, their bodies couldn't be cleared away fast enough. It was spring, humid and warm, and bacteria bred fast. Within days, the stench of decaying bodies filled Gamaer Grassland for a 50-kilometer radius. It was bad enough to scare off even the black crows, which scavenge on decaying corpses. A dreadful pestilence was inevitable. Yaks and goats, already enfeebled from lack of food, were too weak to resist. Several of them died every day. The hunting dogs helped search out the hares' corpses, but because the corpses contained poison, by holding them in the mouth, the dogs got poisoned too. Many of the villagers' animals died.

Misfortunes often come in pairs. After this series of setbacks, some herders moved away, unable to tolerate such a miserable existence any longer. There was a Han herder, by no means well off, with just four yaks and seven goats. When the pestilence raged, all his animals died, so he and all his family moved to the city to make a living. This was the first time ever in Kaza's history that a villager had fled because of famine. Faces were shadowed in gloom, the elderly spent their days wringing their hands, women spent their days crying, and men spent their days drowning their sorrows in drink. Some deeply superstitious herders started to burn incense to implore the gods for their blessing.

Champa was at his wit's end, and, now out of options, was forced to turn to me. Red-faced with embarrassment, he stammered, "Mr. Shen, it was all my fault. I didn't understand what you meant before. I never ... never thought. .. that this situation would get so serious. I didn't respect your ideas before. Please don't take what I said before to heart. You are a respected zoologist and surely, you can find a solution. Please help us wipe out these damned red snow hares. Please save Kaza Village!"

As Champa spoke, his eyes moistened and tears of regret welled up. As our folk wisdom observes, "For men to weep they must be deeply hurt." Champa must have been feeling terrible. It was he who had brought on the disasters that the Kaza herders now suffered. He carried a heavy burden of guilt.

I couldn't stand by and watch any further devastation. I am not such a mean-spirited person as to take malicious pleasure at Champa's predicament. Even though he had ignored my advice and sneered at me, I bore him no grudge. Moreover, as a zoologist, I felt it was my responsibility and duty to help the Kaza herders solve this crisis.

"There is a way out," I said, "but, whether you can accept it or not, I'm not sure."

"If it makes Gamaer Grassland green again, I'll do whatever you ask!"

"Then bring the gold-back jackals back," I said. My tone was definite, unequivocally clear.

"But ..." Champa winced as if his jaw ached.

I knew why he was dumbstruck. To local herders, jackals were demons. It was only half a year ago that they had chased them away, and now they were supposed to bring them back. They couldn't get their heads around the idea.

"Mr. Shen, surely you can think of other ways? How about a different predator for the hares?" Champa looked at me eagerly.

I shook my head.

In fact, after the first signs of the plague of red snow hares, I'd started to experiment with different ecological means to deal with the hares' rampant population growth. Inundation by one species, which poses a threat to human life, can be tackled in many ways, such as hunting, poisoning, contraception and the encouragement of natural enemies. The latter approach is the most natural, economic, scientific and effective, and causes the least pollution. In the natural world, creatures co-exist, and almost all animals have their natural enemies. Furthermore, the use of natural predators to eliminate or curb the population of a particular animal species is not only theoretically feasible; there are quite a few examples of it working in practise.

In the early 1960s, large tracts of orchards in California had a plague-like infestation of green aphids that fed on the flower buds of fruit trees. Despite the immense amount of pesticides used against them, the aphids still were not eliminated. Instead, the insects grew drug resistant and even their genes mutated. The aphids doubled in size, and as they did, their appetite doubled too. Having devoured the fruit tree flower buds, they proceeded to eat their leaves as well. The fruit farmers suffered serious financial losses as a result and turned to the scientists for help. An entomologist named John Boots introduced a green-eyed wasp from Mexico. It was a predator wasp, partial to eating many kinds of aphids. Within three months of their introduction, the fruit trees, nibbled bare by the green aphids sprang back into life.

Then, there was another case. In the 1970s, there was a population explosion of starlings in southern Canada. Huge flocks of them covered the sky, destroyed crops, and polluted city streets with their droppings. They seriously disrupted aircraft take-offs and landings too. Shooting at them, using poisoned bait to trap and kill them, and aiming ultrasonic devices to drive them away were all equally unsuccessful. In response, local scientists introduced dozens of pairs of highland falcons from Nepal, a raptor that feeds exclusively on small birds. Soon, the starlings disappeared.

Again, in the 1980s, a kind of fish called the mudskipper multiplied uncontrollably in the sea off Japan's Okinawa Island. The fish had little economic value. However, they did have a sucking disc on their body and could easily catch the more valuable fish such as yellow croaker, hairtail and chum salmon, which provided the livelihood for the local fishermen. Immense schools of them would attach themselves to their fishing boats and affect the boats' working. At first, the fishermen went all out to capture them, hoping to curb their numbers to a reasonable level. However, these ten-centimetre-long fish multiplied rapidly and the capture campaign took place in the middle of the flood season, so days of immense effort yielded almost no results. Then they brought in a dozen or so scuba divers armed with sound and light weaponry to dive deep underwater, hoping to disperse the schools of fish by using dazzling light, harsh sound waves and stun guns. The costs were enormous, but the results were minimal. Eventually, they found a solution and from a marine aquarium in Hokkaido, scientists brought in dozens of fish called "wolf eels" which feed on mudskippers. Fast swimmers with voracious appetites, they very soon dispersed the giant congregations of mudskippers.

Based on these successful practices overseas, I experimented with various ecological approaches to curb the malignant expansion of the hares. I went back to the Kunming Institute of Zoology and referred to the source index. I selected the sable, rat snake and hen harrier as my experimental varieties. The sable is a fast mover and its slim long body enables it to worm into narrow holes. According to field studies, sables eat various members of the rabbit family. Once they can track them, they can worm into any seam and get at the rabbits. Rat snakes are active underground and are capable of reaching any place that red snow hares can reach. When scientists dissected them, they found that rat snakes are particularly partial to newborns still wrapped in their amniotic sacs. Just like eating a soup dumpling so these rat snakes can consume an entire hare with one bite. These snakes need to eat one burrow full to provide one rat snake meal, so they are the true enemy of red snow hares.

The hen harrier is among the largest of the hawk family. Its eyesight is so acute it can spot rabbits hidden in the bushes from one-thousand-meters up in the sky. The harriers drop from the sky as silently as a falling leaf, snatch the back of the rabbit in their sharp talons and fly back into the sky. In many places, hen harriers are trained to hunt wild rabbits. Field studies show that when hen harriers are flying, wild rabbits are rarely seen above ground. I dipped into my own research funds to purchase three pairs of sables, a dozen rat snakes and seven hen harriers, and transported them a great distance to Gamaer Grassland.

To my great sorrow, the sables brought from the Great Khingan Mountains in northeast China fell ill with vomiting and diarrhea, dying within days of arriving in the grassland. The rat snakes from Shennongjia, in Hubei, central China, were unaccustomed to the colder weather on Riquka Peak and reacted adversely to the high altitude. They looked half-dead and spent their days under the rocks like monks in a meditative state. The hen harriers introduced from Bosten Lake, Xinjiang, in China's far west, suddenly, for no known reason, had a change of preference: the ubiquitous red snow hares failed to stir their appetites; they showed much more relish for the red jungle fowl raised by herders and had great fun trying to catch them. As a result, two were shot dead by angry herders, and the others flew back to Xinjiang.

It wasn't that I couldn't forgive Champa or that I had a special affection for jackals: they were the only way to save the grassland.

"Can you guarantee that bringing them back will definitely reduce the number of red snow hares? And that Gamaer Grassland will grow green again?" Champa fixed his bloodshot eyes on me.

"I can't say categorically. But the chances are better than ninety percent," I told him.

"But so many hunters and dogs have tried so hard to surround them, poison them and burn them. And every time, it failed. How can a few dozen jackals take them down?" Champa asked sceptically.

I had thought this matter through and carried out a survey. I also made an experiment and came to this conclusion: that although their number was small, these gold-back jackals could effectively stop the rapid reproduction of red snow hares, because everything can be vanquished and there is always a natural enemy. I consulted local chronicles at the county archive bureau and found that the number of red snow hares had never soared or ever caused any grassland devastation in local history. To me, this was evidence that gold-back jackals functioned like protective gods for the Gamaer Grassland. I caught eight pairs of rabbits and took them to Kunming where I kept them in a large wire cage that was used for experiments by the Institute of Zoology. Its interior mimicked the ecological environment of Gamaer Grassland: under the ground, ran a maze of coral rock; above the ground, lush pasture was planted. My monitoring showed that these red snow hares ate and slept well; they were active and mated frequently. Soon, the females were pregnant and gave birth on schedule; the survival rate of their young was one hundred percent.

It was now time for the experiment's second stage. I borrowed a pair of gold-back jackals from Yuantong Mountain Zoo and raised them in an animal enclosure next to the hares' cage. There was an iron grille between them, so they could see, smell and hear each other. The very second that the jackals saw the hares, their eyes brightened like light bulbs, flashing green. They rushed at the grille and howled threateningly. The odd thing was, at the very appearance of the jackals, the hares seemed traumatized, becoming dazed, foolish, and lethargic. They spent the day curled up deep down in their caves, and only dared sneak out for food when all was quiet at the dead of night. While grazing, they raised their plump ears to listen carefully. Like birds startled by the mere twang of a bow string, the slightest rustle of leaves in the wind would have the hares dashing back to their caves. Their appetite and weight dropped rapidly. Several of the does seemed to have melancholia and amnesia; their heads drooped and they often forgot to nurse their newborns. As a result, the babies starved to death, one after another, leaving only three survivors. At the height of their estrous cycle, the rabbit cage was devoid of all noise or passion. In this cold, asexual atmosphere, they remained as somber as monks and nuns. Only three pairs mated and only two females got pregnant. This experiment was powerful evidence that gold-back jackals are indeed the nemesis of red snow hares, and the trusted protectors of ecological balance on the Gamaer Grassland.

I told Champa the details of this experiment. He was a smart man and sighed in understanding, "I made a god-almighty mistake in driving the jackals out of Gaoligong Mountains. I admit it. Okay, you're the boss. Let's bring them back. Only..." His face wrinkled up like a prune, and he drew a deep breath, "How do I explain this to my fellow villagers?"

Indeed, this was a tough problem, since the villagers, Tibetan and Han alike, all equally detested the jackals and regarded them as demons capable of every kind of wickedness. Less than a year ago, they had been celebrating when they drove them away, beating drums, exploding firecrackers, blowing ox horns. And now they were supposed to invite the jackals back? Could we convince them to change their minds? The place was remote and isolated, culturally backward, and many locals clung to superstitions. Scientific explanations alone would not be enough to convince them.

Champa smoked seven bowls of tobacco in a row, saying not a word, but filled the yurt with smoke. After a long while, he raised his head from the cloud of smoke and said excitedly, "I've got it!"

As a zoologist, I didn't know whether to laugh or to cry at his idea. But it was brilliant idea, and the only workable one.

12

REGRET

Early next morning, Champa wrapped a leopard skin around his waist, and painted multiple colored stripes on his naked torso, using tree sap and watery mud. The overall effect was that he looked like a mutated zebra. He knelt down on the threshing ground and faced the towering and majestic Riquka Peak, his hands interlaced and mumbling some phrases. He seemed to be praying piously for something. This strange behavior drew the attention of passing villagers, who stopped and stared in curiosity. The children, loving any excitement, spread the news throughout the village, and it was not long before men and women, old and young left their houses and gathered at the threshing ground. They bent their heads together and whispered into each other's ears. By now, a huge, red sun was rising slowly from behind Riquka Peak. Bright sunlight suffused the snowy fog and morning mist, making it resemble a pink gossamer kerchief draped over the village. Champa gave me our secret signal to start. I raised the horsewhip that I was carrying and gave his back several lashes. I didn't dare put much effort into it; this was after all a performance, a charade.

Whoosh! Whoosh! Whoosh! The horsewhip fell on Champa's back and brushed off some of the pigment and dust.

"Are you hungry or something?" Champa turned back and muttered in discontent. "That was just a tickle. Do it for real!"

He wanted me to give him a fake beating like Zhou Yu did to Huang Gai before the Battle of Red Cliff way back in ancient Chinese history. All right, I'd whip him to my heart's content. I shook my wrist and the horsewhip danced like a venomous black snake.

Crack! Crack! Crack! With every crack, a track of blood appeared on Champa's back. There was an uproar. People were shocked by such a murderous lashing and didn't know what had gotten into me. They cried out that I was too cruel. Some pointed at my hand and berated me, urging me to put the whip down immediately.

The village head was informed about the situation. He rushed over, shoved me out of the way, and tried to help Champa to his feet. But, stubborn as a mule, Champa turned away and remained on his knees.

"Champa, have you lost your mind? What's going on?" the chief demanded.

Among the crowd, an old Han man with a long, angular face was very puzzled. He speculated, "Is he possessed by the ghost of a horse, so that only whipping can expel the ghost inside him?"

"It must be for the sins of a previous life!" An old Tibetan woman wiped away her tears.

Bowing repeatedly and reverently to Riquka Peak, Champa sobbed, "I have done wrong. Last night, the God of Mountains appeared in my dream and told me the gold-back jackals on Gamaer Grassland were used by him to guard his home and were then sent by him to the mortal world to help ordinary people and save them from disaster. But we treated them like vermin, like flies and mosquitoes. We hunted them, killed them and drove them away. We committed the sin of impiety. This inundation of red snow hares is punishment from the God of the Mountains. Well, it was I who insisted on driving them away. My offense is the greatest, and I must make atonement with my own blood!" At this, the onlookers could only gaze at each other, at a loss as to how to proceed. Several superstitious old folk immediately knelt, bowed towards Riqua Peak and started supplicating to the God of the Mountain for mercy. Their foreheads pounding the earth fervently.

To local herders, Riquka Peak is a sacred mountain; no other mountain has greater stature. It is also, where the gods dwell.

"So... so what should we do?" The village leader scratched his head and asked.

"The God of Mountains told me there's one way, and one way only to remove this bad fortune, and that's to ask the gold-back jackals back to Gamaer Grassland." Champa's reply was resolute and decisive.

To be sure, the village head prudently that all the villagers vote on this. So, beside the cairn of Mani stones situated by the village gate and used by pilgrims for ritual circumambulation, earthenware jars were set up, one black and one red. Every villager irrespective of gender and age took a yellow bean in their hand. They circled the Mani stone clockwise, while chanting sutras. Then, each threw a yellow bean into one of the two jars to vote: the red jar signified yes; the black jar signified no. When the votes were counted, the yeses won by a landslide: the red jar contained more than one hundred and seventy beans;

the black jar only thirteen. Finally, after the vote, the villagers of Kaza decided that Champa and I would go upstream together to find and bring back the lost gold-back jackals.

Although Champa had made the whole thing sound very mystical, and it seemed superstitious, the end did justify the means. We packed and left that same afternoon.

Our modest baggage included two air-dried red snow hares. These were gifts for the jackal pack. It was my belief that these special gifts would be a clear expression of our good intentions.

13

THE SMELL CARD

Champa and I crossed Gaoligong Mountains and walked for seven days and seven nights before eventually finding traces of gold-back jackals in a valley near Bailong Gorge in the upstream section of the Nujiang River.

The first clues we found were their droppings, and then a few wisps of golden hair in the bushes. Based on this, we concluded that there must be gold-back jackals in the vicinity. Predators have to be highly mobile in order to acquire food, and jackals have a range of about one hundred square kilometers so a random search would be quite useless. Having studied the routine activities of jackals, we came to a stream in Qinggou Valley and found several sets of jackal footprints on the wetland there. So we settled down nearby, waiting for the jackals to appear.

One habit that jackals have is that although they hunt for food everywhere, they will only drink water from only one spot. This means they may hunt within a range of one hundred kilometers, but will insist on returning to drink water only in this area. Once they've drunk water somewhere else, they are reluctant to abandon it and will return every two or three days. Water is the basis of life and all animals depend on it. Mammals with territorial awareness generally make their source of water the center of their hunting range.

The next evening, we hid in a grass nest beside the stream and watched for any signs of activity. A raccoon climbed from a hole in a big tree and straddled a branch. Its vigilant bright eyes darted this way and that. Having seen nothing suspicious, the raccoon swung its big five-hooped tail, and dove from the tree's high crown. Its plump body was hidden in the bushes, with only its black-brown back visible. The raccoon swiftly made its way to the stream, where it clung to a stone and remained there motionless like a silent fish hiding under a cool stone. A giant salamander crawled out of a dark, stone cave beside the stream, intent on unearthing worms or catching frogs beside the water.

However, no sooner had it reached the stone than the

lightning fast raccoon jumped onto it. The salamander's neck was severed before the poor creature realized what was happening. Then the raccoon, salamander in mouth, plunged it into the water to clean it, splashing the water about. After cleaning it, the raccoon put the salamander on the stone, tore off a piece of meat and cleaned it again before cramming it into its mouth to chew its tasty morsel. Given their fastidiousness, raccoons could easily be referred to as "nature's hygiene role model." After eating for a while, the raccoon suddenly became uneasy. It straightened up and turned its head left and right. Its rounded ears twitched listening carefully; its pointed muzzle trembled and sniffed, and its eyes looked fearful as if something horrible was approaching. Half a minute later, the raccoon put the remaining salamander in its mouth, and scurried away from the stream, retreating to the safety of the tree.

As a zoologist and student of animal behavior, it was not hard to conclude from the terrified flight of the raccoon that some fierce carnivore was approaching the stream.

"Quiet. Don't move a muscle," I whispered.

Very soon, there was a rustling in the bushes as an old male jackal furtively appeared. He jumped onto a small earth hummock and scanned the area. I recognized that this was a sentry jackal, performing a role similar to that of a scout in an army, who leads the way for the team and is in charge of exploring the best path onward. It was very quiet around the stream. The old jackal, having observed the stream for several minutes without finding anything abnormal, turned around and made several long howls into the bushes. Soon, seventy to eighty jackals of all sizes surged forward and ran to the stream to drink water.

I adjusted the focus on my binoculars: pale brown body, with a broad golden band down the back. Yes. It was the same pack of gold-back jackals that were driven from Gamaer Grassland. Look! That one with the missing ear is the female, Crooked Mouth. Scarface bit that ear off to stop her from harming Champa and me. Look again! There's old Bald Chest, looking much older than a year ago; even his neck's nearly bald now! Wow! That young male with a purple patch on his back I remember very well. A year ago, he was one of the eight pups taken by Champa. Back then, I joked that this pup looked like a purple-gold doll. Well, Purple Patch was a very imposing adult now!

And what about Scarface?

I scanned the area with my field glasses, but I couldn't find her. Just as I was getting worried, I looked closely and found that the one leading the group was Scarface. Next to her were a female jackal, which had two bushy green eyebrows, and two pups of who were about three months old. It seemed that

Scarface came late because she'd had been busy taking care of these latecomers. I was so relieved to see her. I had a fine impression of Scarface. She struck me as a wise jackal, an intelligent one that knew good from bad. As long as she was still in the pack and acted as the leader, we could hope that they would return to Gamaer Grassland.

Scarface took the green-eyebrow jackal and pups to drink water from the stream. Champa asked quietly what we should do. I whispered, "I'll go out and try to let Scarface know our good intentions. As for you, you just stay here. They dislike you, but they are friendly towards me. I'll go alone and give it a try."

"This is too dangerous. What if..." Champa was concerned for my safety.

I wasn't recklessly putting my life on the line. I guessed the chances of being attacked by the jackals was almost nil, provided I went alone. During this time, I'd been reviewing all the information about jackals I could possibly lay my hands on from both Chinese and foreign sources to better understand their habits and behavior. According to all the literature I read, of all medium-sized and large beasts of prey, jackals are the most in awe of humans and never have spontaneously attacked any human being. To date, there has been no conclusive case anywhere in the world of jackals killing or eating humans, so the probability of jackals attacking humans is lower than that of domestic dogs attacking their owners. On top of that, when I previously dealt with these gold-back jackals, I had saved them once and they had saved me as well, which made us friends already. I believed that they would not fail to recognize me. Provided they remembered, they wouldn't attack me. In humanity's lexicon, jackals may be the embodiment of wickedness but in the real world of jackals, they have never returned good with evil.

"But I'm worried that you appearing out of the blue like this will startle them," said Champa.

I had given this matter some thought too: would my sudden appearance scare them into running off? Bipeds like us couldn't possibly catch up with these four-legged jackals. If they did take off in fright, it would make it even more difficult for us to find them again. However, I sensed that, even if I did appear out of nowhere, they were unlikely to run off just at the sight of me. Even herbivores will not scatter without question, let alone fierce carnivores like jackals. When faced with sudden and abnormal movement, different animals demonstrate distinct behaviors. However, they have one behavior in common, and it is this; when alarmed, they first adopt a flight posture; next, they look back, prick up their ears to listen and sniff carefully to make a judgment before deciding between to fight or flight. This observation and judgment process differs from animal to animal. For some, the process takes just seconds; for others, it is longer, perhaps several minutes. Generally speaking, when something sudden and abnormal occurs, the observation and judgment process of fierce carnivores is longer than that of relatively weak herbivores.

The duration of this process also depends on the animal's observation distance. Every animal has its own distance of vigilance: for wild rabbits, it is about seventy meters, for egrets, about fifty meters, and for tigers, two hundred. If a sudden and abnormal movement occurs within that range, the animal's psychological pressure will rise and the creature will become highly tense. They may think, "This strange movement is too close to me. If it really is an enemy, it can spring at me in a second. I can't drop my guard. I'd better run. Of all the strategies, retreat is the best. Better run a thousand times in error than take one fatal risk." This way, they shorten their assessment process to the minimum.

On the other hand, if the sudden and abnormal movement is beyond the range of vigilance, it is within the limits of their psychological endurance, they are able to control their emotions in unhurried fashion. They may think, "I do need to guard against this strange noise, but the whispering of the wind and the cries of cranes doesn't make every single plant around me an enemy soldier lying in ambush about to attack. The source of this noise is still far off. Even if it does turn out to be my enemy, I still have enough time to escape. There's no need to fear. Let's see what it is exactly before reacting." As such, animals appropriately lengthen their observation and judgment process. I knew this rule, so why not take advantage of it?

Carrying one of the dried hares and moving like a silent snake along a ravine, I crept towards the windward side of the jackals. I estimated the distance between us was about a hundred meters. According to my ethology textbook, the vigilance range of jackals is about eighty meters, which meant that we were at a suitable distance apart, where they could see me, but not be frightened away.

By now, most of the jackals had drunk enough water. Some were lying at ease among the wild flowers, and others were playfully roughhousing each other. The mothers were licking their pups' coats. The males were looking for frogs among the vegetation...

I jumped out from behind the rock, leapt to an open space without any barriers between us, holding my hands high and uttering soft howls. I had deliberately chosen to go windward

of the jackals, so that the wind could carry my scent. Among humans, when two long-separated friends encounter each other, A may recognize B, but B may not remember A. In this case, A reminds B in a complaining tone, "No wonder they say that short memories go with big brains. I'm such and such a person! Have you forgotten me?" Thus, this self-introduction jogs B's memory. With a big "Of course, yes," of recognition, B makes profuse gestures of apology, and the old friends head off for a drink or two and renew their friendship. These gold-back jackals could not understand my language of course, let alone the verbal signals used by humans. They did not know my name, but they had an identification system for distinguishing between the familiar and the unknown; namely, scent. The jackal's sense of smell is ten times more sensitive than that of a human being: they have an ability to recall scents and use their sense of smell to explore the world. By standing and facing upwind, I hoped to introduce myself and remind them that I was a familiar old friend.

I uttered some soft yelps, mimicking the noises they make when they are happy and expressing my pleasure at seeing them again. I held my hands up high. In human society, this gesture means that the weaker is submitting to the stronger and begging not to be harmed. But, in jackal society, it was proof that I wasn't carrying a sword, spear, bow or arrows. I had no weapons to make them fearful; I came in peace; all I had were good intentions; and I wanted friendship only.

As anticipated, when I came out from behind the rock, the jackals stopped everything they were doing, their leg muscles tightened, and they were poised as if to run off at once. They turned their necks and stared. Dozens of jackal eyes were watching me. I stood very still. If I were to bend or move at this moment, they would turn and run away. We remained motionless and silent for a while. I noticed Scarface raising her jaw and tilting her muzzle to sniff. I only hoped that the wind would blow a little harder so my scent would carry quickly. Crooked Mouth, Bald Chest and young Purple Patch followed Scarface's lead and sniffed the air. Most of the others kept looking her way, awaiting orders. Scarface spent a long time sniffing, giving a short howl from time to time. She seemed to be wondering, "What's that scent all about?" Her leg muscles remained taut, her tail up, and she stayed poised for imminent flight. This meant she hadn't recognized me yet.

We'd met three times at most, and the last time was nearly a year ago. Though jackals do recall scents, it can fade over time. On top of that, I was a hundred meters away. I was windward of her, but the wind was not strong enough; with the gentle breeze, some of my scent was lost halfway. Sensitive as her nose might be, she could not tell for sure. Suppose Scarface failed to recognize my scent and ran off with the pack, what would I do? I broke out in sweat at the thought.

Just as I was feeling too hot to breathe and loosened my collar to get cool. Suddenly, I came up with a bright idea. I remembered that I was wearing this same denim jacket on my last encounter with the jackals on Gamaer Grassland a year back. For the last few days, I'd been climbing mountains and crossing rivers, sweating a lot. So my jacket was ripe with my scent, and this could help Scarface recall the past. I immediately took off my jacket, wrapped it around a stone and threw it towards them. This is my name card. Oh, please recognize me. The jacket flew in a graceful arc like a giant, grey bird and landed on a grassy area some fifty meters away, about halfway between us. I wasn't strong enough to throw the jacket the full one hundred meters.

Scarface looked at me warily and walked cautiously in my direction. Apparently, she was coming to check out my "olfactory name card." Sticking to animal protocol, I stayed where I was and awaited her verdict. She advanced fifty meters, took my denim jacket into her mouth and swiftly retreated to the stream to check it out with Crooked Mouth and Bald Chest. They dug their muzzles into the jacket, their noses flaring as they breathed in deep to check whether or not the scent was genuine. Then, one clawed at it and another tugged at it with its mouth. They tossed it this way and turned it that as they checked it inside and out, searching for strange, suspicious or dangerous scents. They were more thorough and rigorous than customs officers looking for contraband. All I could do was wait patiently.

After tossing the jacket about for a long while, Scarface finally gave her verdict. She raised her head and sent a long howl to the sky. Melodious and soft, it sounded like an all clear. The other jackals relaxed their tight limbs, gently lowered their tails, and loosened their flight-ready posture. Some jackals returned to their spots among the wildflowers to catch low-flying red dragonflies.

Scarface came alongside me. She squatted on the ground, resting her tail on her back legs.

Even an amateur zoologist could tell that the jackals recognized me as an old friend, and that I meant them no harm. So they let their guard down.

Thank God! Boy, I was relieved!

14

SEEING THROUGH A SCHEME

I kept my hands in the air, smiling and making jackal sounds as I moved cautiously toward the jackals by the stream. I couldn't be in too much of a hurry. Otherwise I would make them feel anxious. I was aware that human's persistent hunting and persecution of jackals has made them inherently vigilant against any creature walking on two legs. Even when jackals encounter those who have previously helped them, there is no show of intimacy similar to that of dogs when they see their owners. In the world of the jackal, one should never intend to do harm toward others, but one should always guard against others doing harm to oneself. I thought I'd had a very good handle on what they were thinking because, as I got nearer, Scarface kept on glancing at me. With every step I took, her ears twitched violently. I could tell she was uneasy.

When I was within eight meters of them, Scarface could hold back no longer. She sprang to her feet and directed a sharp howl at me. Her eyes were hostile. She had warned me not to come too close. For animals, as well as a vigilance distance, there is "an avoidance distance". The former relates to suspicious activity and potential risks; in other words, it is connected to natural enemies. Avoidance distance has to do with same species—competitors or friendly aliens that are beings unlikely to harm them. Suppose a goat is grazing on a hillside and notices an ox approaching. The goat knows that the ox will not hurt him so, in general, the goat will not mind and they will each graze as they wish. But if the ox comes within four meters, the goat will definitely turn and run. It will never graze shoulder to shoulder with the ox and always maintains a certain distance between them. This is called "avoidance distance". The term refers to the appropriate distance set to evade potential risks. Ethologists explain the avoidance distance as necessary because an animal has instinctive need for caution.

According to the textbooks, gold-back jackals have an avoidance distance of around seven meters. I was encroaching on their domain and the proximity to their fixed avoidance distance was bound to make Scarface nervous. But I'd thought of how to remedy my situation. As soon as Scarface howled at me, I immediately lay face to the ground and raised my neck to expose my carotid artery. This placating position is frequently seen among jackals and it means that one of them is willing to concede or acknowledge defeat. The hostility in her eyes gradually receded and she crouched low again. Crooked Mouth and Bald Chest also recognized me. They stood a dozen paces from me and waved their fluffy tails in a friendly greeting.

I sat down on the grass and looked at the jackals that surrounded me. They were much thinner than a year ago. Their shoulders stood out and their ribs were plainly visible; their bellies were flat and hunger flickered in their eyes. The only pups were the pair belonging to the green-eyebrow jackal. Evidently, the pack was not thriving. I observed many females of childbearing age among them. It was the height of the summer breeding season, but contrary to expectations, none showed signs of pregnancy. I looked again at Scarface. Her back fur was dusty and dull; her beard was brown and frizzy. The wrinkles on her muzzle and face was etched deeper and her scar had turned ugly and grey. She looked far more haggard than last year. Clearly, these jackals were not doing well.

I could imagine the barren nature of this land, deficient in food resources. The terrain was narrow, pinched in by steep high mountains in the north, and the natural moat of the Nujiang River in the south. These jackals were only surviving, and secretly I was pleased about that fact. I don't enjoy the suffering of others, but the reason I was pleased was that it gave us hope that we would be able to bring them back to Gamaer Grassland. Had they been expelled to a place where they found plentiful food why would they be willing to return to Gamaer Grassland? Suppose they had found comfortable caves to live in, caves that were warm in winter and cool in summer. If there was wide grassland for them to hunt in, countless cattle, sheep, pigs and rabbits for them to prey on, and endless mountain springs and streams as their source of water, why would they return? There were no flowering peach trees and green willows to feast their eyes on, singing orioles and darting swallows to accompany them, but would they still be willing to return to Gamaer Grassland?

All beings ceaselessly strive for a better quality of life. I knew that this was true of humans and it was true for the jackals as well. I took out one dried red snow hare and held it out to them. Instantly, like iron filings meeting a magnet, their eyes were drawn to the hare in my hand. Greed flashed in the eyes of the black-eared male I'd come across before; old Bald Chest put out his long tongue, begging; saliva drooled copiously from the permanently open corners of the mouth of Crooked Mouth ... Ah, here's your favorite food, a special delicacy; take it as a token of your homeland's invitation to return! I raised my arm and threw them the hare.

Gift giving can smooth the way. It works well in human society, and this small gesture could help to win over the jackals, too.

Wow! The jackals swarmed closely around the hare, fighting over this delicious gift.

Come eat! Enjoy! Once given a taste of their favorite food, wanderers will miss their beloved home, and will feel an urgent need to return. Come now! Enjoy! Once you accept these gifts, you'll be happy to return and will tamely follow us back to Gamaer Grassland.

Dozens of jackals jumped up to fight for the hare. Only Scarface remained where she was, and watched me thoughtfully. That was when Champa came running up from behind the rock. He crawled up to me and threw the other hare to Scarface. He pointed at her and quipped, "We should bribe the leader. These days, whatever the leader says goes. She's the head of the pack. We need her cooperation to bring all of them back to the grassland."

Scarface squinted. She glanced at Champa and me and then looked at the hare beneath her muzzle. She looked around several times. It was already dusk and the sky was dimming. Suddenly, her eyes flashed deep blue, as if a firefly had lit them. Then I remembered reading something in an ecological pamphlet describing the ecological habits of jackals: among these was their habit of squinting. It is not caused by poor eyesight. When they stare at something suspiciously and hesitantly, they narrow their eyes, and that indicates they are about take action. I shivered, fearing trouble.

My fear was not misplaced. Seconds later, she jumped and emitted a sharp, raucous howl. It was like an emperor

proclaiming a harsh edict. In an instant, the other jackals retreated like a tide from their tight encirclement of the dried hare. It lay on the grass, skin mauled, fur in tatters, but it had not been entirely eaten. The jackals looked at it longingly, mouths drooling with greed, but they didn't dare come forward and fight for it.

Clearly, Scarface had given an order forbidding them to touch the hare. They followed her order to the letter. Her word was law, her authority absolute, her discipline strict.

But jackals are jackals. They can't change their love of raw meat and fresh blood. Being unable to eat this delicious food was frustrating beyond description. There was yearning in the eyes of several jackals. They jumped around the body and were reluctant to go far.

Scarface jumped into the circle and made a circuit of it. As she moved, she emitted a series of modulated howls. When she howled, some jackals pensively moved away from the hare, while others seemed suddenly fearful and sprang far away from that temptation. Of course, I couldn't understand the exactly what those howls were saying, but it was a safe guess she was explaining to her subjects why they couldn't eat the hare. From her earnest look, I surmised that she was patiently giving them a lesson.

Most of them started walking away from the hare. Some moved quickly and others slowly, and soon they retreated into the bushes. Only young Purple Patch begrudgingly gave up this fancy dinner. He tried to hide among the cosmos flowers growing by the stream, so that when Scarface had her back turned, he crawled towards the hare, using the flowers as cover, and furtively gripped its leg in his teeth. His aim was clear. It was to avoid Scarface's surveillance and drag the hare off to a quiet place to scoff it down alone.

But Scarface was vigilant. No sooner had the hare been moved than she turned swiftly, leapt like lightning and sank her teeth into the thief's shoulder. His skin split open, exposing his flesh. He was forced to spit out the hare, screeching miserably and dashing back to the pack. Scarface was as firm in dispensing justice. There would not be any illicit thefts. As dusk gathered, the jackals gradually disappeared into the sparse bushes. Scarface was the last to leave. She drew back to the edge of the bushes, where she remained for a while, resentfully watching Champa and uttering several long, desolate howls, an expression of her pent-up bitterness and a recounting of their miserable sufferings. Soon, Scarface disappeared behind the thin curtain of night.

Champa and I stood beside the now deserted stream, and

looked at each other helplessly. Our attempt at bribery had failed. We felt wretched.

"That Scarface is really hateful. She doesn't want to eat the hare, fine! But she was a real bully to not let the others eat it!" Champa said indignantly.

"It's all your fault. I told you to stay hidden so why did you come out?", I demanded. "When Scarface saw you, she remembered you and the other herders driving them away, so she refused the gift."

Sulking, Champa defended his actions. "When I saw the jackals surging forward to fight over the hare you tossed to them, I thought it was all done and forgotten. But maybe one hare wouldn't be enough for them, so I came out to help you. I threw the whole hare to Scarface to apologize for what I did to her in the past. But she didn't appreciate my kindness. What else could I do?"

I heaved a deep sigh. Humans have always been hard on jackals. They slander them, wrongly blame them, hunt them and drive them away, so that jackals long ago lost their last bit of trust in us. Besides, humans and jackals use two vastly different information systems, so mutual communication is next to impossible. Therefore, Scarface would not readily trust us. The estrangement of humanity and jackals was formed generations ago; it would take more than a couple of red snow hares to change that.

"What do we do next?" asked Champa.

"We keep on looking. We hope against hope that our sincerity will move Scarface."

15

KEEPING A DISTANCE

Champa and I continued our search, following their footprints. Three days later, on a deserted sandbar beside the Nujiang River, we caught up with the pack again. But this encounter was even worse. I had barely tossed them the dried hare than Scarface howled and ran off with them without so much as a backward glance. During the next half month, we found them several times, but Scarface was stubborn. As soon as she saw us preparing to throw them the dried hare, she ordered the others to shun us, as if steering clear of poisoned bait.

To me, she was fairly friendly, allowing me to enter their avoidance zone and never howling at me fiercely. She just refused the gift. Champa was a different matter: she would gaze at him resentfully and never allowed him into their avoidance zone. One time, while I was taking a noonday nap in the shade, Champa discovered the pack in a nearby ravine. Thinking he'd let me sleep for a while, he didn't rouse me, but took the dried hares and made his way to the ravine to meet the pack on his own. No sooner was he inside the vigilant distance than he was spotted by the sentry jackal, which emitted a long, warning howl. Instantly, the jackals divided into two columns and surrounded Champa in an intimidating tight ring, jumping up and snarling at him, their teeth bared as if about to bite him. Fortunately, I woke up in a nick of time. I rushed down the ravine, yelling at Scarface as if I was possessed. When Scarface saw me, she dispersed the encirclement and led the pack away. Nothing came of the incident.

Clearly, Scarface understood our intention. She would not allow the pack to touch the dried hare, for fear that once they'd tasted food from back home, they'd start pining for the homeland, the grasslands. After tasting the delicious morsel, her pack might be seduced by our offerings to return to Gamaer Grassland. I wondered why Scarface snubbed our invitation and was unwilling to return with us. There were two likely reasons. Their traumatic expulsion of one year back remained fresh in her memory; the sudden, cruel behavior of humans was etched deep in her heart and she wanted no further dealings with them. She was all too wise now about how sly humans could be and suspected this might just be another of their dirty tricks. She feared that we were using the hares as bait to lure them back to Gamaer Grassland in order to trap them all at once. For her, our gesture of kindness could only signal yet another trap, another fraud, and a plan to exterminate them all at once.

On this planet ruled by humans, wild animals are the ruled. The way they deal with human beings can be compared to how common people deal with a tyrant. At any time, they might be wrongly accused of crime, causing their entire family to be exterminated. Of course, they had to be exceptionally prudent and cautious.

"That Scarface is such an unappreciative animal!" Champa gnashed his teeth in anger. "When Liu Bei, the founder of the great Han Dynasty, wanted to persuade Prime Minister Zhuge Liang out of retirement, it took only three visits to his mountain retreat. The two of us have called eight times, and these jackals just remain here and refuse to go back with us. They're harder to persuade than the Prime Minister. This is ridiculous!"

"Their anger runs too deep. They need time to forget the unpleasant past and start trusting us again. Don't push them," I tried to soothe him.

"The famine's getting worse by the day. The red snow hares are overrunning the grassland. We can't just wait." Champa snapped.

"So, what do you suggest?"

After pondering for a while, Champa came up with this idea: "How about we find their secret hideout. They've got two pups with them. So we sneak into their den at midnight, fire some shots to scare off the adults, put the two pups in a bamboo basket and carry them back to Riquka Peak. The adults won't leave them, so they're bound to follow us, waiting for an opportunity to rescue them. This way, they'll come back to Gamaer Grassland as obediently as an ox, being tugged by its master's rope. Once there, we'll let the pups go."

I shook my head repeatedly; his plan was just absurd. If we broke into their base in the middle of the night, it would be too dark for them to identify us as intruders and judge whether we came with good or ill intentions. In their confusion, they would well misjudge us and attack us in self-defence. In particular, any attempt to take the pups would arouse their protective instinct and Scarface and the green-eyebrow jackal would likely fight us to the death. Either way we'd be mauled to death or they would be shot. In either case, serious and deadly consequences would follow.

Champa then came up with another idea. "Mr. Shen, you saved Scarface once and she's grateful to you. When you see the jackals next time, can you bring the hunting net with you? Once you reach the proper vigilance distance, pretend you are ill, hold your stomach, roll on the ground and groan. Scarface will definitely feel bad for you and rush over to look after you. That's when you take your chance and trap her in the hunting net. Having taken the leader hostage, we'll have the advantage; we needn't worry any longer that they won't submit. They'll just obey and come back with us."

I rejected this angrily. "No! How could I abuse her trust in order to trap her? That would be shameful!"

"Tut-tut! These are jackals we're dealing with, not men. It's not shameful at all." Champa was offended, "So don't go slinging mud at me! In the first place, our motives are good. We mean no harm. We only want to lead them back to Gamaer Grassland. You've seen what a hellhole this is in comparison. What's so wrong about getting them to come back to their home and to a better life?"

I had nothing to say in reply. Yes, humans have long followed the path that "the end justifies the means," provided one's intentions are good. But I've always thought it unfair to play tricks on animals. Suppose, as Champa suggested, I did pretend that I was ill, and exploited Scarface's good nature to catch her in a hunting net. Could I could justify it to myself as "using my intelligence" to win victory? But is "using my intelligence" really that much different from scheming and being deceitful?

"Mr. Shen, don't be such an egghead," Champa continued. "And don't go forgetting that our fellows in Kaza are desperate for us to return. For every day we're holed up here, the grassland suffers even more. Fine, you're a zoologist, but you can't just consider animals' feelings and disregard those of human beings!"

My face burned with embarrassment and I didn't know what to think. Perhaps I really did need to change my point of view; maybe I should protect the interests of humans by using every trick in the book to deal with these gold-back jackals. Then I thought better of this; it just felt wrong. Champa's idea sounded like a kidnapping or blackmail plot cooked up by an underworld gang. And, putting aside any moral objections and the difference between humans and jackals, even if we went ahead with his plan, the results could very well be the opposite of what we intended. In the first place, if they saw their leader get caught, the rest of the pack would probably run for their lives in every direction. As the saying goes, "when the tree falls, the monkeys scatter." That would completely obliterate our plan to bring them back. And even if that didn't happen, kidnapping their leader and threatening them would not be a wise move since we were the ones who drove them out of the grassland to begin with. Any new tricks from us that would involve capturing their leader and coercing them into returning would just provoke even greater hatred before the old wounds had even healed. It would simply exacerbate their hostility. Why would they be willing to follow us back? When I explained my concerns to Champa, he had no reply.

"What would be good might be something along these lines... Suppose, when they're out hunting, they run into a wild boar, a black bear, or fight with some predatory wolves over territory. Then, we suddenly show up to rescue them. They will be so grateful and naturally will grow close to us. This will be our chance to bring them back."

"It sounds like a good idea, but we can't wait too long," said Champa.

16

BEES VS. JACKALS

Well, as luck would have it, we did get a chance to rescue them from great danger.

That afternoon, Champa and I spotted them again in an old grove, not far from the Nujiang River, so we quietly followed behind them. They came to a gingko tree, which are known for their great age and are considered living fossil trees. Then, Crooked Mouth, walking in front of the pack as the sentry, started behaving strangely. She began pawing the air with her front legs, straightened her body, pointed her muzzle up to the sky and howled continuously. Since she couldn't close her mouth, her howls were painful and sounded like a broken horn.

In response, Scarface, close behind her, crouched low, turned her face and also looked up at the sky. A second later, Scarface sprang up, throwing herself in the air, roaring and snapping as if some invisible airborne monster was threatening them. I promptly took out my binoculars and turned them toward the canopy of the gingko tree.

There were two mischievous gibbons up there, using a stick to poke an oval wild honeybee nest between the branches. They were lar gibbons, which in China are native to northwestern Yunnan. Their fur is sandy-coloured and they have white hands. Excellent climbers, they can also leap between trees several meters apart, in movements that are as swift and graceful as flying birds. The two gibbons were probably a couple, intimately hooking their arms over the shoulders of the other. One of the gibbons had hooked its feet onto a soft, springy branch while shaking the canopy of the gingko with its long arms, making the green branches and leaves tremble. The other held a stick, as thick as its wrist, and stuck it into that giant, dark brown nest. From its color and shape, I knew it was a hive of bees. These wild bees make honey that is first-class, golden-yellow, clear, fragrant and sweet. I watched these gibbons trying to knock the hive off the tree so as to get at tender honeycomb inside.

Scarface was under the tree, growling at them. She was clearly trying to make them stop stirring up trouble. Bees are vengeful insects. If their nest is destroyed, they will all emerge and bite the offenders with their poisonous stings. The jackals were just passing under the tree, and if the gibbons knocked down the hive right then, I didn't dare imagine the consequences.

Champa once told me a story about his father. As a young man, his father liked to hunt. Once, when his father was off with his dog hunting wild duck at a place called Shilanzi at the west foot of Gaoligong Mountains, he had the bad luck to encounter a group of wolves. While his dog held them off, he hastily scrambled up a large tree, but the poor dog was torn to pieces by the wolves. From his refuge up in the tree, he fired at them and killed seven of the wolves, but the rest would not retreat and circled the tree closely. With his ammunition exhausted, alone in the desolate mountains, he was in mortal danger. He could have died right there. However, just at that moment, he noticed a bees' nest, hanging on a fork in the tree. In a flash of inspiration, he pulled out his long knife and thrust his knife into the nest. Bang! The hive fell to the ground like a bomb and smashed open among the wolves. Thousands of agitated bees threw themselves on the wolves. Wolves can't move as fast as bees, so they were all stung. They screeched continuously, foaming at the mouth and rolling on the ground. Within just half an hour, the entire wolf pack and every bee in the nest were dead. Because of this trick, not only did Champa's father survive, but he also amassed dozens of wolf skins and generous amounts of superior honey that made him a tidy sum of money.

Scarface howled threateningly up at the gibbons. The others, understanding what was going on, picked up the pace to quickly pass the tree. Gibbons are apes, and as close relatives of humans, have a higher intelligence than other animals. They can examine and analyze facial expressions. When the two gibbons in the fork of the tree heard the jackals howling, they contemptuously looked down at them. Not only did they remain unintimidated by Scarface's jumping and howling; they actually poked the nest more forcefully. They certainly knew that jackals are unable to climb. They couldn't possibly jump up into to the canopy to bite them, so they felt invulnerable and fearless. *Hum!* You don't want me to poke this nest? So what! I'm going to poke it anyway. Let's see what you can do about it! In the animal kingdom just as among humans, there are ruffians and rascals, and there are troublemaking pranksters.

The giant honeycomb was teetering. Some bees flew out and buzzed around in the sky. This sign was the prelude to war. Standing on her hind legs, Scarface continued howling up at the gibbons, giving the other jackals the order to flee. They made off at once towards the bend in the river, leaving this dangerous place as quickly as possible.

However, it was too late. Through my binoculars, I observed the gibbons up in the tree stabbing at the dark brown nest with their stick. The nest fell off like a soft, ripe fruit. It had hardly hit the ground when the gibbons grabbed a flexible, springy branch and kicked off from the trunk with their legs, just as if they were playing on a swing, launching their bodies through the air like shooting stars. In the twinkling of an eye, looking like a gust of yellow wind, they flew through the canopy, and landed on a large tree opposite from where they once sat. The two gibbons, secure from pursuit by the bees, could now hide in a safe corner to sit out the war. Once the battle was over, they would return to enjoy the sweet, intoxicatingly fragrant honey, and then disappear without a trace.

As for the honeycomb, as soon as it was freed from the tree, it dropped like a body in freefall. It was surrounded by a dense ring of bees. Scarface gave a miserable howl and fled from the gingko tree. Smash! The mud-built nest plummeted right onto a large blue stone beneath the tree, and the impact made the clay explode into a mushroom-shaped dust cloud which instantly released thousands upon thousands of angry bees. They were seeking the culprit who had destroyed their home. The jackal pack had not managed to get far; they were running and jumping about in the grove , and the vines and grasses swayed and rustled under their feet. They looked like a group of outlaws on the run. The bees swarmed after them.

Generally speaking, animals flying through the air on wings will outpace quadrupeds running on the ground, just as a plane is always faster than a car. The bees soon caught up with the jackals. The swarm of bees, hanging over them like the sword of Damocles, soon darkened the head of every jackal. Bees are deservedly called the bravest insects in the world. Once they sting an enemy, they will die soon thereafter, so one might well say that every bee attack is an act of suicide. However, apparently careless of their own lives, they kept diving to sting the jackals, which were now running for their lives. They were intent on dying a hero's death.

For the jackals, it was catastrophic. They may be beasts of prey with sharp claws and teeth, but these are clumsy weapons against the stings of these tiny, nimble enemies. They were in the unjust position of having to take the beating. Crooked Mouth bit randomly at the air and did catch several bees. Although her teeth did cut the bees in half, they did not neglect to sting her lips and tongue before dying. As a result, her mouth became more crooked; just like an opened ring-pull can, her mouth simply could not close. She gave up the struggle and fled in panic.

The black-eared jackal raised his clawed pads to bat away the bees flying in front of him as if swatting at flies, but, far from killing them, he succeeded only in attracting more of them. Besieged, he was so frightened he bolted into the bushes. Old Bald Chest fled to the stony beach and crawled into a narrow crevice, where he wrongly thought he'd be safe in his "air-raid shelter." Bees can get into any small holes. They continued attacking him in the crevice; a moving target had become a fixed target. Two minutes later, he screeched and staggered out... Through my binoculars, I tried to identify Scarface among the fleeing jackals. There she was! She and Green Brow were sheltering the two pups. When the bees attacked without quarter, Scarface and Green Brow used their own bodies like an umbrella to cover the pups. When the bees eased off, the jackals kept on running, with the two pups between them.

The pack of jackals howled in agony as if they were being slaughtered. It was not just a question of physical torture for the jackals; it was mental anguish too. They hadn't provoked the bees, quite the reverse; they had tried to stop the gibbons from destroying the honeycomb. However, little good had that done them: the bees saw them as their mortal enemies and were trying to sting them to death in revenge. Alas, where was justice? Where was justice? The natural world has no court of law to measure the scales of justice. Injustices are all too frequent in the jungle, one animal being punished for a wrong done by another. Animals truly have nowhere to vent a grievance or redress an injustice.

The bees seemed experts in the art of war. Their legion split into several small teams to attack the jackals. They stung them head-on, tailed them very closely, intercepted them, opened a gap on one side, and trapped the dizzied and disoriented jackals in that old grove, some two hundred meters away from the cove in river. It was a total rout. The jackals rushed about like headless chickens, driven first to the east, and then to the west. They ran back and forth within a range of five hundred meters.

Champa whispered, "At this rate, they'll get stung to death."

Wild bumblebees are by no means the fiercest among bees. The stings of the black-tailed hornet (Vespa ducalis) and another kind of bumblebee are much harder and far more toxic. The sting of the black-tailed hornet is half an inch long and can pierce even the tough, thick skin of a bear, while bumblebee stings can kill even a strong yak, its limbs twitching before dropping down dead. The sting of the common bee is of weaker toxicity. One sting will cause the skin to swell and itch. Normally, it is not fatal, but multiple stings may cause fits, convulsions, and even death.

The jackals had been stung badly enough to lose their sense of direction; disoriented, they didn't know where to flee. Even if they were clear-headed, they could barely shake off the pursuing swarm. Even if they could fly or burrow, the bees would have followed them everywhere. For many four-footed beasts, wild bees of any variety are the worst adversaries to provoke.

When humans encounter bees, they find refuge by running indoors and shutting every door and window. If outdoors, they protect themselves by plunging their entire body underwater, using a hollow reed to breathe through like a snorkel. If there isn't a pond or river nearby, humans can save their lives by getting into a tree hollow or small cave and using their clothes to block the entrance. If a tree hollow or a cave can't be found, humans can fend off the bees by building a fire. At the very least, they can mitigate the attack by breaking off a tree branch and brandishing it randomly at the bees.

However, such defensive measures were beyond the capabilities of jackals, so they were helpless against the bees.

"Think fast. We've got to save them!" I told Champa.

"This...this is too dangerous. Those bees shouldn't be messed with," Champa mumbled hesitantly.

"If we help them now, Scarface is bound to feel grateful. Then we can achieve our aim of bringing them back to Gamaer Grassland," I urged.

This was the truth. If we stood aside when they were in peril, the jackals would probably have no place to escape and would be stung to death. If they were wiped out, it would be impossible to put an end to the dreadful plague of hares. In that sense, saving these gold-back jackals was like saving Gamaer Grassland and the herders of Kaza Village. Yes, we had to risk our lives. Concealed in a secret cranny, we'd not been discovered by the bees, but to stand up and move would invite instant trouble: the vengeful honeybees would throw themselves at us without a second thought. Even so, this moment would be an excellent chance to win the jackals' trust. It was a risk worth taking!

Champa frowned, closed his eyes and thought for a few seconds. Opening his eyes, he looked over the surrounding terrain and pointed at the Nujiang River, some three hundred meters away, saying, "There's only one way. We have to bring the jackals to the earth cave where we're camping and build a fire in front of it. This will scare the bees away."

To help us observe and follow the gold-back jackals easily, Champa and I had dug a hole or an earth cave in a sand wall beside the Nujiang River, and we spent our nights there. Although it was summer, the high altitude meant the wind on the river was still chilly at night. We had collected lots of dead branches and dry firewood the day before and piled them in front of our cave for cooking and keeping warm. This pile of firewood was our only existing source of fire.

It was a great idea, one born of Champa's rich experience in outdoor survival. No wonder he could make a living as a hunter in the mountain forests. I said, "Good, let's do that. We'll divide the work. You go ahead to the cave and make a fire and I'll try to draw the jackals over there."

In order to get to the cave, we had to get past the pack of jackals. We used our outer clothes to wrap our heads before jumping out of our hiding place. Sure enough, we had hardly gotten up when the bees came straight at us. We used our clothes to hide our faces and dashed for it. We scuttled off like frightened rats. Champa made for the cave. I rushed off in the other direction, toward Scarface.

Jackals are pack animals. They are highly disciplined and obey their leader always. Only if Scarface went to the river would the pack follow.

Since she needed to protect the two pups, Scarface was running slowly, stopping and starting. So I caught up with her quickly. I drove away the bees from above her head by swinging a branch, while shouting, "Follow me. Make for the river." Sadly, she didn't understand my language or intentions; she just rushed about at random. But when I swept the bees off her head, she looked gratefully at me. I tried to grab her by the scruff of her neck and pull her towards the river. Although the bees were attacking her, she never once dropped her guard. My hand had barely touched her neck when she dodged away and turned back to howl at me twice, in what seemed to be a warning: "I've had enough bad luck already. Don't you dare try taking advantage of me!"

The backs of my hands and my heels were badly stung. They hurt worse than the penicillin skin test I once had. I'd already hesitated too long. I couldn't afford to play games anymore and chase Scarface in this dangerous hide-and-seek. I had to lead her and her pack to the cave by the river.

My eyes came to rest on the pups. One was male—let's call him "Moustache Boy" because of the moustache-like tuft of brown hair between his nose and mouth. The other was female with limpid eyes like two expanses of autumn water. Let's call her "Autumn Water Girl". Scarface and Green Brow had done all in their power to protect the little ones, at the risk of getting savagely stung themselves. I concluded that the pups were probably the children of Green Brow, which made them Scarface's grandkids.

Suddenly, I had a eureka moment! If I took the two pups away, Scarface would be upset and follow me and that meant all the others would follow her to the cave. Of course, stealing the two pups right in front of Scarface and Green Brow would be like bearding a lion in its den—an extremely dangerous move. Dangerous though it might be, it was the only idea I could come up with. I was a desperate gambler staking everything on a single throw and I decided to take that risk. I took my chance when it came. When the bees relaxed their attack and Scarface tried to turn and run into a gully, I threw away the branch I'd been using to swat away the bees. Instead I reached out to pick up the two pups, and sprinted to the river. From behind, I could hear the infuriated howls of their mother and grandmother. *Howl! Howl!* The other jackals came running towards me, ignoring the bees. I knew I looked like a criminal, a child snatcher abducting kids by the road; Green Brow and Scarface ran close behind me, crying bitterly and loudly.

I'd almost made it out of the grove when I felt a sudden heavy pressure on my shoulder. I didn't need to look back to know that it must have been Green Brow jumping onto me. I didn't dare to look back, because if I did my throat would immediately be caught in her rank-smelling mouth. I put the pups on my shoulders and draped them around my neck and behind the back of my head. You want to bite me? You'll have to bite your own kids, though!

Of course, their mother wouldn't bite her pups, but she didn't release my back, either. She howled the most fearsome howl, loud enough to make me dizzy. At this moment, Scarface leaped between my legs, and used her neck to block my left leg and her tail to hook my right leg. What with carrying the two pups and having one adult jackal on my shoulder, I couldn't stand up for long. Blocked by Scarface, I stumbled and fell to the ground. Probably not anticipating that I would fall down, the effect of inertia would have thrown her above my head. But, agile as a gymnast, she straightened herself up in mid-air, and instinctively made a one-hundred-and-eighty-degree turn before making a perfect landing face to face with me. Her muzzle was within inches of my throat; her eyes signalled murder; her blood-red tongue cruelly licked her sharp teeth. I tried to shield myself with the two pups I was carrying, but she had my arm in her teeth, preventing me from moving. Green Brow brought her horrible white teeth toward my neck, aiming at my carotid artery...

I was sweating in fear. How could this neck of mine withstand the bite of those saw like teeth? It wouldn't take much effort on her part, just a small bite, to send me straight to the King of Hell. It was impossible for me to get away from her. If I tried biting her, my teeth were no match for hers. She could kill me with just one bite, but even with ten bites from me, the best I could expect was to take some of her coat. If this unreasonable jackal actually bit through my neck, it would probably be the world's most tragic and most farcical miscarriage of justice, with no chance for a future. I did not want to die a martyr for the cause of environmental protection, and it must have been completely from instinct that I suddenly lay on my stomach and exposed my soft neck. I had mimicked this jackal surrender move many times already, and it had always worked, effectively defusing every threat of attack. So, at this critical moment, I deployed this trick to save my life again. Green Brow's teeth, poised to bite, suddenly stopped moving; confusion filled her eyes; Scarface loosened her grip on my arm.

Although I escaped having my neck bitten, my backside suffered. I was wearing very thick jeans. While I was running, the flapping of my trouser legs had kept the bees away from my legs and behind; but when I crouched low and imitated the begging-to-surrender action, my hips were raised so high that my trouser crotch was stretched as tight as drum skin, accentuating every curve. As a result, the bees penetrated through my trousers and stung my backside. It was like multiple injections jabbing my muscles at the same time. I screamed out in pain. This startled Scarface and Green Brow and they both took half a step back. I hastened to my feet, which may have made Scarface think I was trying to make off with the pups. Howling, she leaped towards me, and fought for the pups in my arms. Her meaning was clear: hand over the pups if you want to live. On the point of tears, I begged Scarface:

"Please calm down now, and trust me. I'm not about to kidnap your babies. I'm here to save you. Follow me, please. I beg you!"

As further demonstration of my good intention, I put out my tongue and forced myself to lick the faces of the two pups. In jackal society, licking is the paramount ritual gesture of respect, love, and enduring friendship. Faking a smile, I tried to lick the pups lovingly and selflessly as hard as I could to prove how much I loved them. Kissing jackals was mortifying! It felt like kissing a shoe brush, their faces were that bristly. The muzzle of Autumn-Water Girl had some mucus, possibly snot. I swallowed it anyway. Moustache Boy's mouth smelled putrid which made me retch.

Who knows what it was that moved them: perhaps it was my misty eyes, maybe my non-stop piteous begging or maybe my affectionate licking. Scarface and Green Brow stopped their fierce and threatening howls; their cold and aggressive eyes seemed soften just a little. So I took my chance and dashed toward the river with them close on my heels, fearful of losing the pups. I figured that they sensed my good intentions or at the very least understood that I meant no ill since they did not jump at me as I ran nor used their tails to trip me. The rest of the pack followed Scarface.

Finally, I led them to the Nujiang River. Because of the proximity to Bailong Gorge, the terrain was high and steep, and the torrential river roared like thunder. In front of the cave, Champa had built a campfire from which billowed dense smoke; it was blown on the wind towards the jackals and me. As an old adage says, "Use hot water to destroy an ant nest and fire to burn the hive." Fire is the thing that bees fear the most. When met head-on by the dense smoke, the smoke-cured bees became less antagonistic, and no longer dive-bombed us so wantonly. I bolted through the dark smoke and into the cave, carrying the pups with me. Then I came out, waving my arms and shouting to the pack,

"Get in here quick. We've made a fire, so the bees won't dare sting you anymore!"

Scarface and Green Brow looked at each other, puzzled; far

from following us inside, they took a few steps back. Scarface gazed into the flaming fire; her coat stood up on end, and she cried in fear. Indeed, the whole pack looked terrified. I understand that all beasts fear fire, gold-back jackals included. Mountain hunters habitually build a fire if they encounter wild beasts such as jackals, wolves, tigers or leopards; their experience is that the beasts will dart away at the sight of the flames.

Just then, the wind dropped and shifted direction. The dark smoke cloud above their heads gradually drifted away. The bees wheeled in again to attack, this time stinging even more angrily, probably infuriated by the smoke. The jackals were forced closer to the fire and became enveloped in the smoke. The effect was instantaneous: the attack weakened. I believed that these smart jackals must have understood our reasons for building that fire—not to scare them off, but to help them out of their plight.

Even so, although I shouted myself hoarse, Scarface still refused to leap from beside the fire and through the dark smoke to get into the cave. Jackals have an inborn fear of fire. The flames were overwhelming to them. My only possible move was to dart forward in one big stride, nimbly grab Scarface around the middle and drag her inside. If I could pull her into the cave, the others jackals would be bound to follow. Scarface resisted for all she was worth, much stronger than I'd thought. I called on my every ounce of strength, but still couldn't budge her. It was like a tug-of-war between two well-matched sides, neither of them prevailing. Scarface did not howl at me nor did she snap. The indications were that she knew I meant well, but her insurmountable fear of fire prevented her approaching the uncontrollable flames.

Suddenly, I was struck by an idea from back in childhood. When wrestling with my friends and failing to throw them whatever I did, I would always use my secret weapon; tickling their armpits. As soon as the tickling made them laugh, their strength would immediately drop, making it easy for me to throw them. But are jackals ticklish? Never mind. I'd give it a go. While dragging her front legs, I tickled her "armpits" with two fingers. And what do you know, this childish method worked. Scarface twisted her neck, flexed her middle and wagged her tail. She looked tickled and her body became soft. Seizing my chance, I dragged her to the entrance of the cave. But just then, on the point of success, a stick of burning firewood suddenly exploded with a big "puff!" and shot out several orange flames. These landed on Scarface and me. *Hiss! Hiss!* Two holes appeared on my clothes. *Hiss! Hiss!* A piece of her back fur was scorched. She howled in fright, struggled free of me, and ran back to the other jackals. I stood, stupefied, under the dense smoke, without a clue what to do next.

Just then Moustache Boy and Autumn Water Girl, having no adult jackals guarding them, crawled out from where I'd put them inside the cave. Howling, they made their way to the entrance and stretched out their heads. Seeing her babies through the dark smoke, Green Brow started howling too. For every three steps forward, she took two steps back, restlessly pacing before the fire. Obviously, she wanted to rush to her babies, but lacked the courage to make her way through the smoke and fire.

Suddenly, I had a brainstorm! An excellent way of forcing her to bolt into the cave stuck me. Braving the smoke, I plunged back into the cave; then I raised my palms to slap the two pups, not too hard and not too soft either. You damned mongrels. I was forced to lick your faces just now. Gross! I all but vomited. Great, now I'm getting my own back. *Slap! Slap!* Not only did I slap their faces, but I also pinched their bottoms for good measure. The two pups yelped, crying for their family as if I'd put them into a pan of boiling oil. Green Brow and I were only ten paces apart. Even through the smoke, she could still see clearly. For a mother to witness her own kids being tortured is unbearable; as the saying goes, "when a child is struck, the mother feels the pain." Green Brow jumped up and down in front of the fire, howling fiercely, her eyes ablaze with malevolence and hatred. She looked eager to spring at me and tear me limb from limb. I knew that her fear of fire was stopping her jumping into the cave, even though she ached to do so for the sake of her two suffering pups. An intense conflict was going on within her. Her survival instinct and her fierce maternal feelings were at odds.

Okay, I'll help you make your mind up. I plucked a tuft of hair from Moustache Boy's back, like pulling out a radish. I did the same from Autumn Water Girl's neck, like picking off grapes. These hairs were enough to make a long writing brush. The pups rolled on the ground in pain, crying and howling with fear. Their mother stared at me ferociously, twitched her ears, bared her teeth, and pulled out her tongue; her expression changed dramatically. Then, with an uncanny howl, she sprang at me. Her need to save her babies helped her overcome her fear of fire. When their offspring are in danger, many female beasts caring for infant young demonstrate great maternal love, love for which they will risk mortal danger.

In fact, the risk that Green Brow took was not massive. Frightening as the great flames might look; there was a three-meter-wide gap between the fire and the sand cliff. It was a purposefully designed escape route for the jackals to get into the cave. Provided they kept close to the sand wall, they would not be burnt. At worst, their skin might feel a little hot or the smoke might choke them a little. There was definitely no risk to their lives. The important thing was to overcome their fear of fire. Green Brow plunged into the cave with a whoosh; not a single hair on her body was singed.

Without waiting for her to turn on me, I hurriedly stuffed the pups into her embrace. While she was busy kissing and pacifying her babies, I took my chance to run outside so she wouldn't bite me in an attempt to protect her cubs.

The cave was a safe spot: without the bees, the flames, and the smoke, it was probably the best refuge under these circumstances. Clever Green Brow soon understood this and howled gently at Scarface on the far side of the fire. I sensed that Green Bow was telling Scarface that to run away from the bees into the cave might after all be the smartest move after all. Then, I saw Scarface respond to Green Brow's howls by trying several times to approach the fire. Scarface was beginning to contemplate leading the pack into the cave.

Then, came another snag. Suffering from the unbearable pain from the bee stings, Crooked Mouth had tentatively approached the fire in hopes of saving herself. However, as she did so, some burning pieces of charcoal flew out of the fire and scattered over the sandy ground. In her weakness, she had stepped on one of the embers. She howled and dashed back, putting a large distance between herself and the other jackals and the smoke. How could the angry bees pass up such a prime opportunity? In overwhelming numbers, they dive-bombed her, and within seconds, her body suddenly became a mass of squirming bees; even her eyes were not spared. The bees swarmed her and enveloped her eyes until they looked like two immense, black eye-shades. She howled shrilly, blinded and disoriented.

As she jumped about blindly, her agitated movements only provoked even more attacks. Soon, the bees had swaddled her tight in a thick swarming blanket. The other jackals howled; Champa and I shouted, encouraging her to run towards the fire. That way, at least, there was some hope of saving her. But her ears too were full of bees, and she couldn't hear us. Madly, she ran on and on, trying to evade their stings. Sadly, she headed in the wrong direction. She ran to the steep river bank, missed her footing and fell into Nujiang River with a splash. In an instant, she and the bees smothering her body were swallowed up in the billows......

The other jackals looked at each and howled long, wretched howls. Scarface glanced up at the dark mass of bees and out at the raging Yangtze River, and then gave three brief howls. Then, like leaping a trench, she jumped through the dark smoke and fire and into the cave. In jackal society, the leader's example is the supreme authority. Without even being urged, the other jackals vied to jump into the cave. Old Bald Chest was the only one to get burned; jostled when crossing the fire, her tail touched the flames and was scorched as a result. The others all reached the cave unscathed.

Champa and I had dug quite a spacious cave; it could take seventy or eighty jackals at a push. Once they were all inside, Champa and I immediately built the fire higher and kept on adding fuel, producing roaring flames and dense rolling smoke and creating an impregnable line stretching from earth to sky. The bees were blocked outside the firewall. However, they refused to give up; they stayed and circled in the sky nearby. Whenever the fire died down, they flew over and tried to break through the firewall to sting the jackals sheltering in the cave. So Champa and I hurriedly threw dead branches and withered leaves onto the fire, sending the flames jumping hundreds of feet high into the air to burn their transparent wings. Like raindrops, their bodies fell into the sea of fire and crackled. The acrid smell of burning filled the air. By dusk, more than half the bees were dead; the remnant forces withdrew. They left the Nujiang River, their ambitions disappointed.

With this, the bitter war between the bees and the jackals came to an end.

17

CURE THE VENOM

After the bees flew off, Champa and I put out the fire and dismantled the firewall. The jackals crawled out of the cave. Every one of them of them had been bitten. Not one was unscathed. Some had swollen eyelids. Some had been stung on their legs. Some had swollen mouths and some had smoke inhalation. Still others were bleeding after being scratched by thorns. Most were unable to stand up, and uttered endless pitiful groans. They looked like a group of defeated generals with their beaten troops after a rout.

The two pups were hurt the worst. Although sheltered from the bees by Scarface and Green Brow, their tender skin and soft flesh made them the bees' favorite target. Moustache Boy's head had seven stings, like stars in the Big Dipper constellation, and Autumn Water Girl had a dozen red and swollen stings across her body. Scarface and Green Brow protected the pair, endlessly licking their swollen lumps. Saliva has the effect of reducing inflammation and relieving pain. It is a traditional healing method among jackals and has some efficacy, but saliva alone was clearly inadequate to deal with such serious apisin poisoning. After a while, far from being relieved, the two pups' toxic reaction got worse. Autumn Water Girl bit her own tail uncontrollably; she kept turning back on herself, spinning like a top. Moustache Boy twitched repeatedly; he would doze off for a while, wake in a panic, stretch out his soft neck and then bite repeatedly at the air. These were typical reactions to wasp stings and had to be treated immediately. Scarface's eyes looked woebegone. She looked at the fading sun and howled sadly. I too was hurt badly from the dozen or so stings to my face, hands, back, buttocks, and ankles.

Champa quickly dove and disappeared into the woods, and when he returned, he brought back a freshly plucked handful of pink meconopsis. Meconopsis is a flowering plant of the poppy family. It is also known as "silvery ginseng" and is widely used in traditional Tibetan medicine. It can be taken orally and applied topically and is effective in reducing inflammation, alleviating pain, stopping bleeding and treating mania. Champa intended to make a decoction from these rhizomes, and used a pebble to grind its flowers and leaves into a mushy paste.

The next task was to treat the jackals. Of course, we needed Scarface to set an example. That was our only chance of getting the others to agree to our help. Generally, veterinarians have a harder job than physicians do because animals lack a basic understanding. They refuse to take their bitter medicine or never actively cooperate. Therefore, when treating animals in a zoo, vets take unusual measures. They hog-tie the animal and force them to take medicine or an injection; otherwise, they shoot them with a tranquillizer dart and carry out their treatment plan once the animal is unconscious. There is no way in the world that the two of us could tie up these jackals individually; nor did we have a tranquilizer gun to shoot at them. We had no idea whether we could treat them without being harmed ourselves.

"If they don't cooperate, at least half of them won't live to see tomorrow," said Champa.

"How about applying the paste to their wounds? That seems a bit easier," I suggested.

Champa put a layer of paste on his palm and went over to Scarface. He tried to grab the nape of her neck and apply the paste. However, Scarface bounded off and howled. She gave him an angry stare, as if to warn him, "Don't think about touching me!"

"What do we do? How about using a trap net?" Champa asked.

"Hell, no! You'll just scare off the rest," I shook my head emphatically.

"So we watch them die of the stings?" Champa asked.

"You apply the paste on me first. Maybe if they see it works, they might change their minds." I said.

I lay on my stomach like them. I took off my pants and told Champa to apply the meconopsis paste to the bites on my backside in full view of the jackals. I observed that when Champa did so, Scarface remained still. She flared her nose trying to sniff the paste, showing great interest. I'd previously studied the body language of jackals and knew which particular posture expressed which emotion. Once the paste was applied, I turned onto my side and curled up in fetal position, neck, arms and legs all tucked in. Meanwhile, I rubbed the ground, and grunted softly, pretending jackal style that I was comforted by having the pain from the bites reduced by the paste.

Scarface watched, intrigued. Her eyes lifted at the corners, and her muzzle wrinkled. An envious look came across her face. Rough and ready as my performance might have been, but it did get my meaning across very well, I thought. I took some paste, crawled over to her on elbows and knees, and stuck out my tongue as if to lick. In jackal society, to fawn on the leader, ordinary jackals show their respect by voluntarily licking and cleaning the leader's coat. Of course, grooming has an element of pandering to others. By my action, I was asking Scarface's permission to lick and groom her fur.

Scarface took up a semi-lying-semi-squat position; her hind lay legs aslant, her front legs were bent and she laid her head between her front legs. This posture indicated her willingness. I slyly tricked her. Instead of licking her fur, I pushed her fur aside and spread the paste onto her swellings. Meconopsis treatment is highly effective. As soon as applied, it refreshes and relieves the swelling pain, producing a comfortable numbness. Scarface curled up and rubbed against the ground.

Then, those jackals in unendurable pain looked at me, eager for me to use the same method with them and so relieve their pain. Old Bald Chest was the quickest; he clung to me and wanted to be treated first.

Hmm, no hurry. There is enough paste for all of you. However, Moustache Boy and Autumn Water Girl are in the greatest need so they should be the first to get treated.

By nightfall, between the two of us, we had managed to apply the paste to all of them—nearly eighty jackals in total. But they were stung so badly that one application of paste was insufficient. To bring them safely through this crisis period, they also had to drink the thick Meconopsis brew.

By now, moon was high in the sky, round and bright as a silver dish, and illuminated the night. I spooned out some of the potion and tasted it. It was spicy and bitter and no more palatable than a potion of goldthread flower. It is really quite hard to swallow. However, I knew that good medicine does taste bitter. Humans have the power of reason and, in order to recover, they force themselves to bear hardships when they must. But jackals don't have this ability. Would they take such bitter medicine? It was impossible to reason with them. The only feasible method was to work on Scarface's understanding and support, and then, with her absolute authority, we could compel the others to drink the bitter medicine. I don't know why, but I was convinced that Scarface was different from the other jackals. There was an exceptional wisdom to this creature and she even seemed to exhibit some basic level of rational thinking.

I crawled toward her, carrying a bamboo bowl full of the medicinal soup. I placed this between us, our mouths on opposite sides of the rim. In jackal society, when one jackal brings food close to the mouth of another, it signals a willingness to share that food. My posture indicated that I was happy to share the soup with her. When Scarface gently touched the rim of the bowl with her lips, I guessed she'd accepted my invitation. I drank a large mouthful of it and swallowed it, grimacing. She put the tip of her tongue into the soup and rolled some into her mouth; right away, she screwed up her eyes and muzzle and her whole face puckered up as if she swallowed a lemon. She exhaled, shook her head and stared at me accusingly, as if to say, "Why are you asking me to drink such a bitter thing?" Then, she shook her tail and turned away.

Seeing that she was trying to leave, I was anxious and hurriedly grabbed the back of her neck. Ignoring the fact that she couldn't understand my words, I shouted at her, "I beg you, drink the soup. Yes, it's bitter and tastes terrible, but it can cure the poison from your bee stings. If you don't drink it, the rest of your pack will die!" As I said this, I seized her face to make her look at me. I then held up the bowl and took another large mouthful. Then I put the bowl to her mouth and tilted it slowly. Her mouth was tight shut, but she made no attempt to leave; she stood on the spot, thoughtfully studying the bowl in my hand.

I assume that up to a point that Scarface did understand my meaning. Otherwise, if she insisted on refusing, she would have overturned the bowl and bitten my wrist, or howled at me and run away. Since she didn't do any of these things, it was clear that she was considering whether to follow my lead and drink the bitter soup. I loosened my grip on her neck, showed her the swellings on the backs of my hands and pointed at contents of the bowl. Then I showed her the bumps on my face and pointed again at the potion. She looked at the bumps on my face and the bamboo bowl, connecting them visually ... and mentally too.

This time when I tried to feed her, I continued tilting the bowl, and the soup dribbled along the corners of her mouth. Suddenly, she opened her mouth, swept up the potion with her tongue and gulped it down. It tasted absolutely vile. Jackals have a gustatory sense every bit as developed as that of humans, and they can distinguish different tastes such as sour, sweet, salty, bitter, and spicy. She shuddered with every swallow. Having drunk less than half of the potion, she could take no more. Then, she took a step back, lay on her stomach and vomited up a pile of pasty, yellow filth. This continued for about a minute. Her stomach convulsed. When it was finally done, she raised her tearful eyes to look at me. She growled from the depths of her throat, as if cursing me, "You horrible being, are you trying to kill me?"

Under these circumstances, the bitter Meconopsis soup was my only way to help them. Every one of the jackals had been viciously stung. If they did not excrete the toxins quickly, they would all, as Champa predicted, be dead by morning. I did not have the ability to make the bitter medicine taste sweet nor did I have the strength and courage to force them into drinking it. If Scarface refused to drink it, then I would be unable to save these gold-back jackals.

As I crouched there, worrying, Scarface suddenly came up to me. She rubbed my shoulder with her soft neck and whispered gently. As I had studied jackal vocalizations before, I could identify changes to their feelings. She seemed to be telling me, "Though the soup tasted bitter, I don't blame you. I know you asked me to take it out of kindness." Then she walked up to the bowl and slurped up the soup. This was so unexpected. I'd never dreamed Scarface could have such strong reasoning ability; I thought that her capacity for reasonable judgment was on a par with that of a five- or six-year-old human child.

With every two mouthfuls, she raised her head, glanced at other jackals and emitted a commanding howl like a teacher giving a demonstration lesson. Soon, half of the soup was gone. She took a step back, stood by my side, and howled to the other jackals. They looked at each other, hesitating. Old Bald Chest volunteered first; like Scarface had done, he walked up to me and drank from the bowl. Then came Green Brow ...

All the adult jackals came and drank the medicinal soup, all except the young Purple Patch. Probably, thinking he hadn't been so badly stung and had no obvious symptoms of poisoning, he didn't want to drink that awful soup and so shrank to the back, intending to go back down the gully by the river and slip away. Nevertheless, Scarface saw him. She howled and jumped at him. She bit his tail, pulled him towards me and forced him to drink half a bowl of the potion.

At this point, any astute reader might well challenge me: would these jackals really cooperate by taking a medicinal soup or did the author simply make it up to suit the needs of the plot, just like the writers of fairy tales, who project human lives onto those of animals? Here, I can reliably inform readers that everything I have written are true stories that have happened in the forests without any fabrication on my part. Experts' observations of the lives of gold-back jackals in the wild reveal that they have a primitive knowledge of medical care, something passed down generation-to-generation, and elder jackals can identify several plants with medicinal uses. On the whole, jackals are only prone to two types of illness. One is gastric illness from eating decaying food. The other is illness due to trauma. As an example, when hunting, jackals can get hurt when their quarry fights back. So when a jackal falls ill, the elder jackals will take their fellow pack member into the forest to seek out these plants. When they find these medicinal plants, they instruct the jackal to chew their leaves or roots in order to cure their illness or relieve their pain. Indeed, gold-back jackals do have some rudimentary medical understanding.

Thanks to Scarface's example, Champa and I soon got the rest of the pack to cooperate. However, when we fed Moustache Boy and Autumn Water Girl, after just one taste, they refused to open their mouths again. Champa and I had to force their mouths open to feed them. However, they kept resisting and screeching as if we were torturing them, not understanding our intentions. Green Brow couldn't bear to hear her children crying, so she roared at us, and the others were ready to jump at us. Not daring to take any more risks, we hurriedly poured two spoons of soup into their mouths and let them go.

By now, it was late at night. The jackals were exhausted; Champa and I were half dead from fatigue so we huddled together with the jackals and slept in the cave.

18

TASTE OF HOME

I awoke the next morning to a mixture of howling and purring. I opened my eyes and saw the jackals were gathered at the shore outside the cave. Some were looking up at the watery-red glow of the distant sunrise. Still others were gathered in a circle, yelling anxiously, as if something was wrong. I quickly woke up Champa and then, crawled out to investigate.

Ah... the jackals were surrounding the pups. Pushing my way through the pack, I saw that the two pups were lying in Green Brow's embrace. Their eyes were half-shut and they looked listless. Moustache Boy's body was floppy and his thin, feeble neck seemed unable to support his drooping head. He appeared to be dozing. Autumn Water Girl seemed to be in a trance. The whites of her eyes were visible, and she was foaming at the mouth. These phenomena indicated delirium and that shock and death were imminent.

The two pups had a weak immunity. They had been stung the worst and their small bodies could not handle being stung en masse. The cumulative dose of venom was unbearably high and they were experiencing acute toxic reactions. They also had not drunk the Meconopsis soup. I observed the other jackals. Apart from Moustache Boy and Autumn Water Girl, their side effects had eased and their swellings had gone down considerably. They looked much better. Many of the clamoring pack were howling and were facing the woods. Scarface stood alongside Green Brow, one minute licking the pups, the next, eyeing the anxious jackals. The pack's emotions were clearly being pulled in two different directions.

Then I realized what was going on. Jackals are diurnal animals, lying low at night and active during the day. The goldback pack habitually went out to hunt in the early morning. That must have been the problem. At the first light of dawn, Scarface was leading the pack to find food in the woods, but they had hardly left the cave when their pups had collapsed. The jackals had not eaten for an entire day, and after fleeing the attack by the bees, they were exhausted and had little strength.. The apisin poison had also quelled their appetite, so when their wounds finally began to heal, hunger returned with a vengeance. They were famished, all skin and bones and eager to return to the woods and catch some quarry so they could finally fill their stomachs. Nevertheless, Scarface's love for the pups meant that she wouldn't abandon them; this reluctance bred discontent among the starving pack.

For jackals, the best time of day is the early morning; the golden time for hunting is when the first glimmer of dawn appears. It is a time when antelopes, yaks, river deer and wild rabbits emerge from the secrecy of the bushes, eyes foggy with sleep, to graze the green, dew-wet grass on the meadows. At this time of day, their visibility is poor. Their prey's vigilance is at its lowest and their reactions the most sluggish...all the easier for the jackals to find them and catch them. Once they are revived by eating their fill of dewy grass, they become more alert. Therefore, as the day lightens, their visibility improves, making hunting far more difficult.

"How about giving them the two red snow hares we brought along?" Champa suggested. They won't say no if we feed them now."

I gave the idea some thought before shaking my head. I

reckoned that the jackals were not yet at the end of their resources, so it wasn't the right moment to take out the hares. The red snow hares were our secret advantage, and needed to be saved until the very last.

However, a few of the jackals, desperate for food, ran to the damp sand beside the river and scavenged for rotten fish and shrimps. Unfortunately, with the river subsiding, even the stranded fish and shrimps had been carried away by the waves. They searched for a while, but couldn't find even a scrap to relieve their craving. They howled softly as if sighing.

Scarface kept on circling Moustache Boy and Autumn Water Girl, clearly uneasy and worried about what would become of them. Jackals have a strong collective spirit. It is always the leader that heads the pack when they go out to hunt. For Scarface, to give up the chance of hunting at the very best time of day meant that the whole pack would have to go hungry too.

I decided to relieve her worries. I lay face down, carefully pulled the pups away from Green Brow and cradled them myself. Imitating the jackals, I gently caressed their heads with my lower jaw and neck. This is a common behavior among jackals; females caress frightened pups this way in order to comfort them.. Female jackals usually do this in two particular situations. First is when they are going out to hunt. Pups are afraid of staying in the den alone and so they cling to the legs of their mothers. At this time, the female jackal will gently stroke their pup's heads with their lower jaw. The other time this behavior is seen is when a rainstorm is imminent. When dark clouds gather, lightning flashes and thunder rolls, young jackal pups often become frightened and thrust themselves into the embrace of their mothers. Then, the females will place their neck onto the pups' heads. Strangely enough, it is very effective: after rubbing their heads this way, the agitated pups soon calm down.

This action is much like the psychological effect that human mothers have when they hold their crying baby against their left breast and coax them into sleep. When a baby hears the rhythmic heartbeat of the mother, this makes the infant feel a heart-to-heart affinity, that of two hearts beating as one. Jackals show their affection in a similar way. As a jackal breathes, the trachea in the mother jackal's throat vibrates slightly due to the airflow, and when she places her neck onto the pup's head, the pup hears these rhythmic sounds, the sounds of love. By assuming this same posture, I was telling Scarface: Go hunt with your pack; don't miss the best time for hunting. I'll take good care of the pups with the same motherly love that you would have.

Scarface had considerable trust in me and soon understood my meaning. She gave a solemn howl to summon back the jackals beside the cove in the river. Then, in what was left of the early morning light, they ran off into the distant woods. Green Brow was the last to leave; she obviously had misgivings about leaving her pups with Champa and me. She stared at me with suspicious eyes for a full half-minute and emitted several short and sharp howls at my face, as if to warn me: Don't you dare to play any tricks on me. If I come back to find my babies gone, you'll have me to reckon with! I kept on rubbing the pups' heads. This body language, I knew, carried as much force as an oath written in blood. Only then did Green Brow leave to catch up with others. She did so reluctantly, turning to look back at every step. In jackal society, even females that have just given birth have to hunt together with the rest of the pack. The concept of maternity leave does not exist, nor does the concept of a free lunch.

Once the pack had left, I immediately asked Champa to prepare to operate on the pups. During our course of studying animals, we have to spend long periods working in the wilds, and so had to learn some medical skills in case we had to treat the animals or ourselves should it become necessary. The sores of Moustache Boy and Autumn-Water Girl were as swollen as rotten peaches. Their condition was very serious indeed: the only way to save them was to cut the sores open and squeeze out the poison. The pups would also need antibiotics against any further infection. I had some scalpels and antibacterial agents with me.

We wrapped them tight in a hunting net to restrain them, and forced them to take the pills. Then I took a small scalpel to cut open their swellings. There was no anaesthetic so it must have hurt badly. The little ones wailed like ghosts and howled like wolves; in fact, they screamed themselves hoarse. Fortunately, the jackals were far away by now; otherwise, Green Brow would surely have thought that that we were murdering her babies and would have attacked us with everything she had. No questions asked.

"This is far too dangerous," worried Champa, as he followed my instructions for squeezing out the pus and blood from their wounds. "What if the operation fails and the pups don't make it? How do we explain that to the jackals when they come back?"

"Don't worry. I know how we can save them." I reassured him. "Could you catch us a wild pigeon or the like and cook up some meat congee for them?" Champa went into the woods, and returned quickly with a turtle dove. By the time he had cooked an appetizing meat congee, I had successfully finished operating on the pups. Jackals are very resilient. Just half an hour after the operation, the pups could get to their feet and walk, albeit shakily. It was almost noon and the jackals had not returned so two humans and the two jackal pups shared a small pan of congee. The hungry pups gobbled up half of it.

That afternoon, the jackals still had not returned. The sky turned overcast and a cold wind blew across the river, making things feel chilly. Champa built a fire inside the cave and we sat on the ground beside it, trying to stay warm. Probably due to the cold or possibly to the after-effects of the operation, Moustache Boy and Autumn Water Girl gradually started to lean forward towards the fire. Fearful that the flames might burn their fur and unable to bear watching them shivering because of the cold wind, Champa simply picked them up, wrapped them in his Tibetan sheepskin robe and placed them against his heart. Tormented by bee stings all night long, the pups were sleep deprived, not to mention exhausted from the operation. Now, with their pain eased and with full stomachs, they snuggled up in Champa's warm embrace, yawned a couple of times and fell sound asleep. Champa and I were drowsy too. We propped ourselves up against the earthen wall and gradually entered the land of dreams.

Suddenly, I was woken up by the sound of fierce howls. I opened my eyes and saw Green Brow, Scarface and Bald Chest baring their teeth and howling at us. Oh, they're back! By the way they were looking at us, they were very angry! Because they couldn't find the pups, they were scolding us and demanding them back. The noise woke Champa up too. Seeing the tricky situation, he hurriedly untied his robe, lifted out the pups out and placed them on the ground.

After a good sleep inside the soft and cosy robe, Moustache Boy and Autumn Water Girl had recuperated and their energy was restored. They had recovered well. They yawned sweetly, rubbed their eyelids, widened their bright eyes, cried and threw themselves at their mother, Green Brow like spoiled clingy kids. They were so lively, so cute. When the adults had left that morning, the pups were at death's door following their ordeal. At dusk, they had returned to a complete transformation—to two pups brimming with energy. In my mind, this obvious improvement in their condition would convince every one of them that Champa and I had nothing, but good intentions.

Green Brow sobbed with excitement, and licked her babies' non-stop, from their ends of their ears to the tips of their tails. Such deep motherly love seemed about to melt the two little ones. Scarface lowered her tail and ended her hostile look. She bent her legs and lay down, howling at Champa and me in a soft and gentle manner. There was something of a sparkle in her eyes, perhaps even tears. I felt inexplicably moved by this. I saw

that in Scarface's posture, look and tone that she was expressing to Champa and me her feelings of guilt and shame; it was an act of apology and a plea for forgiveness and understanding.

Scarface gradually came closer to Champa, but still with her knees to the ground. She put out her long tongue and covered the sharp canine teeth on her lower jaw. Among all canines including jackals, this gesture means that they have no malicious intent or impulse to bite. But Champa was no ethologist versed in animal behavior, so Scarface's approach put him on guard. He had been sprawled against the sand wall, but now he suddenly sat up, one fist protecting his chest and the other reaching for the Tibetan knife that hung from his waist. He was poised to counter any attempt to attack him.

I was about to explain to him that Scarface did not mean him ill, but the words were barely out of my mouth before Scarface suddenly turned and lay aslant on the ground, twisting her neck to expose her carotid artery. We were both very familiar with this posture. Among jackals, it signifies that the weaker party is surrendering and it is placing itself at the mercy of the stronger party. Once this posture is assumed, the stronger party will quickly halt and resist the impulse to attack.

"What's going on? What's she up to?" Champa stared at me in astonishment.

"I think she's telling you she does not feel any malice towards you." With a little smile I explained, "She misunderstood you until just now. She thought that you'd killed the two pups, but discovered instead that you'd cradled them. She realizes that she blamed you wrongly, so she's apologizing to you."

"It's me who should be the one apologizing. Ah! I'm the one who despised them, and drove her pack out of Gamaer Grassland. It's me who should beg them for their forgiveness." Champa relaxed his grip on the knife handle and unclenched his powerful fist. Every one of his words was true. The feelings of this courageous and upright man had been moved. He stretched out a palm to stroke Scarface's head. Scarface did not avoid his; she even put out her tongue in welcome, licking his palm devoutly and rubbing her soft neck against his arm, just like a dog showing affection to its master. Green Brow and Bald Chest came up too and licked Champa's trouser legs and shoes.

"Hey, hey..." Champa smiled in pleasure. His face reddened, as if flushed with wine.

The gulf between humans and jackals, formed over generations, vanished like smoke. Hatred is solid ice, and love is like the sun. Under the warming effect of its rays, even the thickest ice will crack, melt and become flowing spring water.

Exactly at the same moment, from outside the cave, we

heard the screams of some jackals, telling us that something was wrong. Scarface pricked up her ears and bounded off. We followed. Many of the pack were gathered beside the Nujiang River, howling at the roaring waves. We dashed over there. There was young Purple Patch, struggling desperately in the rough white water, trying to swim back to the bank. The tide was receding though and because of the current, with every attempt he made to climb onto land, he was pushed back further by more incoming waves. He was clearly exhausted. Unless he had help, he'd soon be pushed further away and be swallowed up in its merciless whirlpools.

Champa took off his shoes, waded into the river, which came up no more than knee height, and pulled Purple Patch ashore, where he lay, coughing up mouthful after mouthful of turbid water. The watching jackals who looked on howled sadly, desolately.

Jackals are typical of most land predators in that they can swim, but not particularly well. Up to a point, they are somewhat afraid of water and cannot play in water like otters, water buffaloes, capybaras and hippos. It was easy to work out that Purple Patch had a good reason for plunging into the Nujiang. Eyeing the spectators, I noticed their bellies were flatter than when they had left that morning and their eyes were greener.

In other words, they were even hungrier than before. This must be why Purple Patch fell into the water. He must have seen a dead fish floating on the surface and thought to catch it, but the fish was bobbing on the waves from one spot to another. Purple Patch reached out for it unsuccessfully, time after time, before finally overreaching and then, slipped into the river. Alas! No fish. All he had gotten for his pains was a bellyful of river water.

Without a shadow of doubt, the pack had returned empty-handed from the hunt, with nothing to show for it. I wasn't surprised by their lack of success. Following the wasp attack, they had incurred serious injuries included swollen eyes, weak limbs, and twisted mouths. Our mecanopsis paste and medicinal soup had alleviated their apisin poisoning, but the toxic effects had not disappeared completely and this was a serious impediment to the full deployment of their hunting skills. Their swollen eyebrows affected their eyesight and made it more difficult for them to spot prey. And even if they did spot them, the jackals could not easily catch up with a fleeing quarry since many of them were lame and unable to move fast. The most troublesome thing was that, during the wasp attack, their instinctive attempts to bite their assailants had resulted in their muzzles being stung. Half of the pack was unable to close their mouths, so even if they did spot and catch up with prey, they could not inflict a lethal bite.

The jackals were scattered across the beach. Some clawed at the sand to uncover worms or voles. Some stared at the white-cap waves on the river in the hope that they might strand some fish on the beach. Some howled at the fiery sunset above the mountain on the far side, in the forlorn hope that perhaps, the sun would change into a giant pie and fall down before them so they could fill their stomachs. It was clear that these gold-back jackals were close to dying of hunger. If they did not eat by to-night, by morning, some of the old and weak members of the pack would be dead from starvation.

"I think it's time to feed them the hares," said Champa.

The moment seemed right to me too. As they say, get the timing right and things will fall into place. It was time to use our secret weapon, to arouse their homesickness and bring them back to the grassland. I nodded in agreement. "Let's feed them the red snow hares. Then, we can pack up our things and get ready to return."

Champa brought the two air-dried red snow hares from the cave and held them high. Just like two radiating diamonds, the red snow hares attracted the eyes of all jackals, which gave out a surprised and greedy light. The hares represented not only life-saving food, but also gifts from their homeland. Champa threw the red snow hares among the pack. They drooled in anticipation and were poised to jump and tear at them, but they seemed under orders not to move; they just stared at Scarface.

I knew that jackals have a good memory. They hadn't forgotten their leader, Scarface had stopped them two weeks earlier, when Champa and I threw them the hares, and were afraid she would forbid them to scrap over them this time as well. I shared this concern and watched for Scarface's reaction.

Whether accidentally or by design, Champa's throw landed alongside Scarface and she instinctively recoiled. However, immediately, like iron filings pulled to a magnet, her eyes were drawn to the hares. Clearly, they stirred a memory. The surprise and confusion in her eyes changed to a faraway look. Her expression was difficult to read. She seemed unsure how to handle the special gift we had presented. Only the sound of waves washing the beach was heard above the silence. Purple Patch whimpered, as if complaining that he was starving.

Scarface looked at the hares, turned to look at the slavering jackals, and then toward us, the two humans. Then, she howled as if in physical pain, and bounded away. It was an unmistakable signal. The pack could go ahead and eat the hares. Howling with delight, they fell upon the food. In less than three minutes, the two hares were torn apart. Green Brow grabbed a head and took it to share with her mother. Scarface sniffed and inhaled the scent. Finally, unable to bear her ravenous hunger or withstand the temptation for one moment longer, she started to take great bites of this treat.

Champa and I exchanged smiles. We both knew that among humans when one accepts hospitality or a gift from someone else. It establishes a certain obligation to that person. This rule of human society applies as well in the animal kingdom. Now that Scarface had eaten our red snow hares, she wouldn't refuse to go back with us to Gamaer Grassland.

Within five minutes, the hares were history; neither skin nor bones remained. Just a few bits of fur floated like dandelion fluff on the evening breeze. It was a case of "too many monks and too little gruel." Two paltry hares could not possibly satisfy seventy or eighty jackals. At best, these morsels could just hold starvation at bay. The jackals squatted on the beach, licking every last scrap of meat from the corners of their mouths. Then, one jackal howled and they all started, howling downstream in the direction of their beloved Riquka Peak. Their piercing howls echoed throughout the gorge. They were a memory of beautiful times gone by, and a deep-felt yearning for their return.

Champa had packed up his things. I brought my bag and he

carried the pups, Moustache Boy and Autumn Water Girl. We walked towards Gaoligong Mountains, followed by Scarface, with the pack at her heels. Life was unsustainable on this impoverished land where food was in short supply. Champa's action expressed to the jackals that the humans living on Gamaer Grassland had shed their fears and wanted to welcome them back to their home. So, without a backward glance, they set out to follow us back home. The days of bitter exile were gone forever. They sang exultantly all the way there.

BACK HOME

We crossed turbulent rivers, snow-capped mountains, and windswept wildernesses. Five days after leaving, Champa and I brought them safely back to Riquka Peak. After crossing the high col, the jackals rushed down to the foot of the mountain, down to Gamaer Grassland. They were like long-lost travellers, rushing to their mother's embrace, a mother who had never stopped missing them.

Just as I had expected, the moment that the gold-back jackals reappeared on Gamaer Grassland, the reign of the red snow hares effectively ended. The jackals did indeed prove to be their nemesis. On smelling a jackal's scent, seeing a jackal's figure or hearing a jackal's howl, the hares trembled with fear and swooned with fright; they became nervous wrecks. Many stopped mating, with an obvious impact on their reproduction rate. Even their labyrinthine, coral caves were of no help, since the gold-back jackals could follow them down into any crevice. There was no hiding place for them. The gold-back jackals particularly relished feasting on the newborn hares whose eyes had not yet opened and often entered the underground cave systems to take an entire nest of infants. This had the observable effect of damaging the hares' alarming reproduction rate. After only three months, the red snow hare population had fallen by two-thirds and the ecological balance of the grassland was restored.

Gamaer Grassland, a wasteland for more than a year, became green again. Late summer was at its height, and, with the coming of the rains, the land was revived by the rain and the dew. The grass sprouted and the wild flowers bloomed. Gamaer Grassland was like a beauty recovering from a life-threatening illness. When the grassland was in full bloom, it was even lovelier to behold. It was a spectacle of lush pastures and colorful flowers, vigorous and vital once more. The bony cattle and sheep gradually got plump and strong, and the Kaza villagers started once again to relax and smile.

Nevertheless, I was still uneasy about something: the fact that the villagers still considered gold-back jackals to be spirit beasts. On the first and fifteenth of every month, they would burn joss sticks and offer up sacrifices. They would solemnly pray to Riquka Peak to thank Heaven and the Sacred Mountain for sending these creatures to remove their bad fortune. When they met jackals on the grassland, they dared not shoot, but would give way to them, piously placing their palms together and chanting their prayers.

Once, Purple Patch and a few other daring males, probably wanting a change to their hare diet, attacked a straggling goat. The goat's owner saw the attack, but did not attempt to stop it. Instead, he believed that these spirit beasts were attacking his goat because they thought highly of him. After that incident, a foolish saying began to spread among the villagers: To those who sacrifice a goat to the spirit beasts, blessings come from Heaven and the God of Mountains.

Once this superstitious saying became widely accepted, some of the villagers started a new custom. On sacrifice days, some villagers would lead a goat to Gamaer Grassland and tie it to a tree stump so the jackals could come and rip it apart. Goatherds started tethering their dogs at home, lest they chase the jackals attacking the goats and thus displease the spirit beasts. With no dogs to guard them, the goats and sheep became vulnerable to the unchecked attacks from the wild beasts.

Power can go to the head in animals just as it does in humans. Purple Patch was a perfect example of this. Since he was worshipped like a god and nobody dared hurt him, his audacity grew beyond bounds; he even rushed into the flocks in broad afternoon sun to seize in his jaws some poor lambs. Despite feeling angry, all the sheepherder did was yell at Purple Patch a few times. Even then, Purple Patch snarled at him ferociously as if the owner was trespassing in a zone where humans were forbidden. He was savage, shameless and arrogant to the extreme.

I appreciated the fact that Scarface always behaved herself and never went after domestic livestock. When I hid in the dense bushes and observed her through my binoculars, I saw that not only did she not harm the herders' goats and yaks, but she also used her authority as the pack leader to prevent the misbehavior by the others. Once, the jackals happened to encounter a flock of sheep head-on. Several young jackals among them were itching to hunt them down, but with a few solemn howls, Scarface stopped them from running amok. Another time, while the jackals were lapping water from a stream, Purple Patch, together with several young ones, slipped away from the pack and ran to Gamaer Grassland. They broke into a herd of yaks and surrounded a little calf, which was about half a year old. The mother yak mooed angrily. As soon as Scarface heard this, she rushed there, but arrived too late. Purple Patch had jumped onto the calf's back, had clawed into its backside and had pulled out its guts. In an instant, the calf collapsed and was a carcass waiting to be butchered. Purple Patch howled cockily and ripped at the little yak, which was still wailing. Scarface jumped onto the assailant's back and bit him hard. Thanks to her actions, Scarface had chased Purple Patch and his young gang away from the calf's body.

However, this punishment had little effect on Purple Patch. In fact, it was quite the reverse. He became a maverick who went his own way. He formed a separate small group with seven or eight young jackals, and left Scarface's pack. Now, a self-appointed king, he attacked herders' cattle and sheep exclusively. The herders incurred increasingly heavy losses, but their awe for the God of Mountains prevented them from voicing their discontent.

I was despondent. The plague of hares had ended, but in order to win the support of the villagers to bring back the jackals, Champa and I had had to lie to the villagers and tell them that the gold-back jackals were sacred creatures. We just hadn't thought that there would be such grave consequences. It had been wrong to regard the jackals as unpardonable vermin, but it was equally absurd to worship them as magical creatures. I thought it was my responsibility to help the local herders discard this foolish notion, build a proper awareness of environmental protection, and treat the jackals in a rational manner.

It is always better when a culprit takes responsibility for his actions. Champa and I decided to capture Purple Patch first. After taking their leader, the gang of jackals would soon collapse. This would be a double-win move: it would help the herders understand the truth about the gold-back jackals and would disperse this small pack of renegades, which were up to all kinds of mischief. I believed that Scarface, if she knew our intention, would agree. She must have hated how Purple Patch had split up the pack and she did not want to see her fellow-jackals attack and harm the livestock raised by humans.

I borrowed a tranquilizer gun from the provincial Institute of Zoology and with Champa's help, drove a flock of sheep to Gamaer Grassland. This flock included some frisky lambs—perfect bait for Purple Patch. When the sun rose above the hills, Purple Patch came along exactly as expected with a few cocky, young jackals. They emerged from an underground cave to attack the lambs. When Purple Patch jumped onto the back of one lamb, Champa aimed the rifle at the jackal's backside and pulled the trigger. *Bang!* The syringe containing the anaesthetic pierced his body. Purple Patch fled, whining, but the drug kicked in before he was able to run ten meters. He staggered drunkenly for a few steps, before collapsing unconscious to the ground. His fellow gang members though were scared witless and they fled as fast as their legs would carry them, regretting that they possessed only four. I believed that the young jackals would learn from Purple Patch's lesson and would never again dare to attack domestic livestock. With their leader now taken, the small gang would eventually collapse. After hiding for several days, they would return to Scarface's large pack.

Champa and I put Purple Patch into a specially prepared metal cage and dragged the cage to display it on the threshing ground of Kaza Village. The villagers gathered around to see what the excitement was all about. Several elderly herders reproached us for treating the jackal this way, saying that the God of Mountains would punish us. By now, Purple Patch had revived consciousness and was jumping up and down inside the cage. Champa poked the animal's behind with a bamboo stick, so as to tarnish the sacred aura attached to the gold-back jackals. Purple Patch howled sadly and rolled about in the cage. Now, the godlike creature was no longer so godlike, not much different from a common Alsatian dog. One old woman, very religiously observant, kept on saying, "What a sin! What a sin!"

It was then that Champa stepped up onto the earthen platform and bravely confessed how he had misled them. He explained that his so-called dream in which the God of Mountains told him to treat jackals as spirit beasts was nothing, but a pack of lies; however he stressed that he'd lied for a good reason, namely to stop the disaster caused by the population explosion of the red snow hares. He then begged for their forgiveness. When Champa was finished, I stepped up as well to spread the message of environmental protection: that nature is an interdependent survival system; that gold-back jackals play an important role in maintaining ecological balance. I also told them that, in essence, protecting biodiversity is the same as protecting humanity. I explained the theory simply and the villagers listened with keen appreciation.

After this unique and powerful lesson, the Kaza's herders' awareness about the environment grew. They no longer prostrated themselves in worship to the gold-back jackals; nor did they return to indiscriminately killing them as harmful animals. With humans and nature living together in harmony, Gamaer Grassland became ever richer and more beautiful. And what happened to Purple Patch? I sent him to Kunming Zoo to be placed on public display as a rare animal. He would spend the rest of his life in a large iron cage at the zoo.

SHEN SHIXI

Shen Shixi, the celebrated writer of children's literature, is famous for his animal novels. He is known as China's "King of Animal fiction writing". Among his many recognitions include being a three time winner of the National Prize for Excellent Children's Literature by the Chinese Writers' Association. He has also won numerous times the China Book Award. His major works include *The Glorious Dream of the Mother Wolf* and *The Seventh Hunting Dog* among many others. *Scarface the Mother Jackal* won the 13th China Book Award. He lives in Shanghai, China.